Red Mountain Pass

A NOVEL Terry Cunningham

Cottonwood
enterprises inc

Cottonwood Enterprises, Inc.
3224 Hidden Springs Lane
Bozeman, MT 59715

ISBN: 978-0-578-63531-6

For Yi-Yi:
the miracle of my life

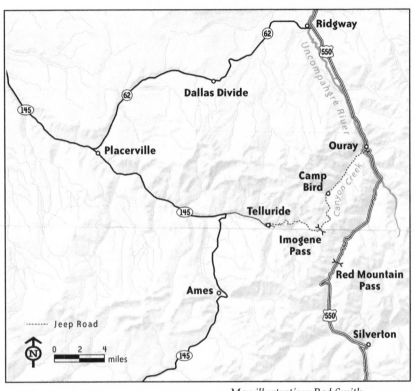

Map illustration: Rad Smith

Notes to the Reader:

This story is 20+ years old. It was written in the late-1990s when, for instance, a Vietnam veteran could be in his fifties. Since the story takes place in Southwestern Colorado in the late-90s, references to town population sizes, snow-removal equipment, mining activity and remediation efforts, etc. reflect that time period.

Why is this story 20+ years old? Beginning in 1997, I endeavored to write a novel that readers—and the publishing industry—would find interesting and compelling. I told myself that it would be a "one shot deal." If the literary community decided not to publish the novel, at least I would have given it my best effort. Red Mountain Pass is that story; my one shot.

I spent more than two years conducting research (around my day job), writing and refining the manuscript. My editor and my literary agent liked the Red Mountain Pass manuscript enough to recommend it to several leading publishers of action-adventure novels—and at one point we believed we had secured a two-book publishing deal. But publishing imprint consolidations and acquisitions intervened—and it was not to be.

For 20 years, the manuscript remained in the Archived Documents folder of a succession of personal computers. Shortly after turning 60, as I was looking for another document in that folder, I noticed the Red Mountain Pass file name and opened it for the first time in two decades. I still liked the story, so I published the novel through my marketing agency, shared it with my friends and offered it for sale online and at local bookstores. I hope you like it.

This is a work of fiction and—with the exception of references to Colorado Department of Transportation Red Mountain Pass Division employees who have lost their lives in avalanches on Highway 550 —all of the characters in the novel are fictional.

—Chapter 1 —

Low, gray clouds scudded across the mountain highway, obliterating the late-afternoon sunlight as Dr. James Philips eased his truck down the steep switchbacks that led from the summit of Red Mountain Pass. The storm had arrived two hours earlier than forecast and two inches of granular snow already covered the narrow, treacherous roadway. Dr. Philips had hoped that he would be able to rush through his meeting with Paul Brader, then drive the remaining twelve miles to Ouray, Colorado before the onset of the storm. Those hopes had been erased abruptly. And night was falling fast.

Pumping his brake pedal, Dr. Philips steered his Dodge Ram pickup into the snow-blanketed turnout that overlooked the abandoned Mineral King mining plant. Clouds had engulfed the bright orange slopes of the Red Mountains on the far side of the canyon, and Philips could see fresh snow clinging to the wooden signs announcing the extensive Superfund cleanup project at the old Mineral King mining operation.

Philips guessed that Brader selected this meeting place to make a point about responsible mining, and would cite the extensive revegitation and reclamation efforts as proof positive that mining in the San Juan mountains could be properly regulated. Still, Philips had no intention of selling his company to anyone associated with the mining industry.

He glanced at his wristwatch. It was 5:10pm. No other vehicle was in sight."I should've known he'd be late," he muttered to himself. "Might as well put the chains on."

Philips climbed down from the cab of his pickup and buttoned his overcoat. He pulled his lapels tight around his neck and tucked his head into his chest to shield his face from the wind-whipped snow. The sixty-eight-year-old physician knew he would need the help of tire chains to drive home. In winter, the twelve-mile ribbon of pavement from the summit of Red Mountain Pass to Ouray was arguably the most dangerous stretch of road in the American highway system.

As he reached into the enclosed truck bed, Philips noticed a flash of color to his left. Straightening up, he stared through a curtain of snow to see Paul Brader trotting from the woods on the far side of the turnout. Philips knew immediately that something was very wrong. Scanning the highway, Philips couldn't see Brader's vehicle. Where was it? Brader's attire was equally confounding. Philips's partner was wearing an ill-fitting yellow slicker and waterproof pants that were splattered with globs of dark mud. In his left hand, Brader was carrying a blue canvas gym bag.

"Hey, Jim," Brader called from twenty yards away. "Thanks for coming. Helluva storm we got brewing here, huh?"

"Where's your truck, Paul?" Philips asked warily. "What's going on here?"

Brader's tone was convivial as he walked briskly toward the elderly physician. "It's real simple, Jim. You've been giving me the bum's rush for the past two weeks. I figure it's high time I gave you a lesson about respect. Sooner or later, everyone gets their comeuppance, Doc. And this is yours."

Behind him, Dr. Philips heard the suddenly ominous crunch of footsteps on the snow-covered asphalt. He spun around to see another, much larger man walking into the turnout's opposite side. He wheeled back around to face Brader, now standing fifteen feet away with a self-satisfied smirk on his face. As Dr. Philips stood paralyzed by fear, Brader carefully scanned the highway to the south. Satisfied that no vehicles were approaching, he pulled the hood of the slicker over his head and tightened the drawstring.

Glancing over his shoulder again, the doctor saw the second man walking purposefully toward him. Although the snowstorm had shrouded the mountain pass in dull gray blanket, Dr. Philips could see that the hulking stranger wore a black ski mask over his head and face. In his gloved right hand he clutched what appeared to be several oversized white gauze pads.

Like a deer transfixed by headlights, Dr. Philips cursed himself for not having reacted more quickly to the two-pronged threat. He made a sudden break for his truck, veering wide of the man with the ski mask.

"Tackle his ass!" he heard Brader shout to his accomplice.

Still not believing what was happening, Philips bolted straight for the driver's side door of his pickup. His assailants momentarily flat-footed, he was able to yank open the door and climb into the driver's seat. As he fumbled to shove the key in the truck's ignition, he slammed the door closed. The man in the ski mask grabbed hold of the door and forced it back open. As he turned the key, Dr. Philips felt himself being dragged out of the truck by his leg. He desperately wrapped one arm through the steering wheel and with his free hand he grabbed his mobile phone, using his right thumb to dial 911.

"No you don't, slick!" the man in the black ski mask yelled.

With one vicious tug, Dr. Philips was pulled from the cab of the truck. The back of his head struck the pavement. In a daze, he saw Paul Brader picking up the gauze pads that had fallen beneath the truck. As the large man pinned his arms to the ground, the doctor watched helplessly as Brader shoved the sweet-smelling white pads over his nose and mouth.

— Chapter 2 —

Walter Hampton stood in the doorway of the Colorado Department of Transportation garage. Taking a long gulp of black coffee from a chipped ceramic mug, he soberly assessed the intensity of the late-February snowstorm. On the far side of the CDOT yard, a bank of overhead floodlights pierced the darkness of the raging storm, illuminating slanting sheets of thick, wind-driven snow. From the doorway, Hamp's line of sight extended to a black expanse of cloud-shrouded peaks to the south, some of which topped 14,000 feet.

One of his two "Colorado Special" snowplows was parked inside the State barn, its side-mounted diesel exhaust pipe coughing clouds of blue smoke toward the low ceiling. The force of the International 5000's engine rattled the door frame he was leaning against. One of the two white roll-up doors on the garage's far end had been opened to allow the noxious fumes to escape into the night air. As if in protest, the snowstorm sent swirling gusts of spindrift back through the open door.

Foreman of CDOT's Patrol 14, Hamp was responsible for a six-man crew whose endurance had been tested over the past several months by a seemingly endless succession of avalanches along their assigned section of the Colorado Highway system.

Under rows of fluorescent lights, one of Hamp's three full-timers was inspecting the hoses behind the steel plow blade, trying to isolate a malfunction in the huge snowplow's hydraulic system. Another CDOT employee sat in the cab of the Colorado Special, moving the levers that activated the front blade. The truck had been pulled out of service an hour ago after Phil Treacher had radioed his foreman that the plow mechanism had become sluggish and unresponsive during his last circuit through Red Mountain Pass.

"What's the word, Phil?" Hamp shouted over the thundering engine to Treacher, who was on his knees between the plow blade and the cab of the Colorado Special.

The lean, sharp-featured man stood up, wiped his hands on a blackened rag, and shook his head.

"Double whammy. Puncture in one line and a stripped coupling on another. The way it's leaking, it'll take another three or four hours before we can fix it. Looks like she took a real beating the last couple of days."

Treacher turned around and made a slicing motion with his hand across his throat and Arnie Watson shut down the snowplow's diesel engine. Its robust echo reverberated off the garage's metal walls.

Phil was right. On Sunday night, the Blue Point slide had dumped a fifteen-foot pile of densely packed snow, rocks, and timber onto US Highway 550, a typical late-season avalanche. The removal of the debris pile had taken its toll on both man and machinery. The rotary blower mounted to the patrol's Cat 950 tractor had thrown one shear pin after another as it churned through the tightly packed rock-strewn pile. The protracted cleanup had damaged both of Hamp's Colorado Specials, the best snow-removal truck ever made.

As Treacher was bringing the disabled snowplow limping into the yard, Arnie Watson was completing his repairs on the second truck's jammed rear-mounted spreading mechanism. Given the current storm's intensity, the prospect of having both of his International 5000's out of service was unthinkable.

"Helluva night to be hopping on one leg," Hamp muttered aloud.

What troubled him even more than the loss of equipment was the condition of his crew. Operating on little sleep, his entire crew working straight through from Sunday night until Monday morning, it had taken them sixteen hours to clear the Blue Point slide off the road. After they reopened the highway, Hamp had sent three of his men home to rest while he covered the 5pm to 5am shift with Treacher and Lyle Morrison.

It was now Tuesday night and the storm had already dumped nearly a foot of snow as it lumbered over Red Mountain Pass. Pulling a truck off the road had left US Highway 550 unplowed for the past hour, a situation that was unacceptable. Patrol 14's tradition, handed down from man to man through the years, was simple and straightforward: Once the first flake hits the ground, the second flake had better hit the plow blade.

Since the season's first major snowstorm blew through the San Juan Mountains in October, Patrol 14 had been operating twenty-four-hours-a-day in two twelve-hour shifts. Sending bone-weary men out into the night to plow one of the most treacherous roads in America was not a task that Walter Hampton relished, especially with avalanche season at its peak.

US Highway 550--also known as the "Million Dollar Highway"-- is a solitary stretch of road that winds through the craggy peaks to the south of Ouray, Colorado. Some claim that a million dollars' worth of gold-laden ore was unwittingly used in the construction of the road. Others argue that the road's nickname reflects the original cost of blasting the twisting roadway out of sheer mountain cliffs. Regardless, the Million Dollar Highway is renowned as the most scenic and deadly segment of the circuitous alpine highway network known as the San Juan Skyway.

Hamp considered the foreboding section of highway that led from the town of Ouray to the summit of Red Mountain Pass to be *his* road, just as every foreman before him had regarded the thirteen-mile stretch of pavement that they maintained to be their own. In 1992, the previous foreman of Patrol 14 lost his life on US Highway 550 at the East Riverside slide area. Hamp had lost a friend, mentor and boss when a sudden avalanche trapped Eddie Imel beneath a ten-foot pile of snow. Now it was Hamp's job to keep the most avalanche-prone highway in America open and passable even in the worst possible weather. It was a job he performed steadfastly, all the while knowing that one day, it might claim his life, too.

Treacher joined him in the doorway, still wiping hydraulic fluid from his hands. He nodded toward the mountains to the south.

"You need me to head back up with the other truck?"

Hamp ran a hand over his gray crewcut hair and downed the last of his coffee. He pointed to the second Colorado Special, which was being loaded with sand and pea gravel across the snow-covered yard.

"Nah, I called Lyle in early; he's almost ready to go. He'll work it for a while tonight and I'll spell him toward morning. You and Arnie head on home. We'll tackle the hydraulics problem tomorrow."

Phil Treacher looked at his watch. It was nearly eleven o'clock. He slapped Hamp on the shoulder before heading to the back of the garage to wash up. "Night, boss," he called over his shoulder.

Leaving the cover of the doorway, Hamp pulled the hood of his parka over his head and stepped into the yard. To his left was a tan-colored hangar-like structure that was shaped like an inverted U. Eighteen-feet tall and thirty-five-feet deep, the shed protected large stockpiles of sand and gravel from the elements. Hamp waited as Lyle Morrison used a front-end loader to deposit a final load of the sand mix into the back of the orange-painted Colorado Special. After pulling the tractor part-way through the shed's front door, he turned off the engine and climbed down from the machine.

Joining Hamp at the driver's side of the truck, Lyle handed over the keys to the front-end loader. A fresh dusting of snow covered the shoulders of Morrison's green nylon jacket and the hood of his grey sweatshirt. Hamp looked up at the big man who was half a head taller than the six-foot foreman.

"Thanks for coming in early."

Morrison's only response was a barely audible grunt.

"It's just you and me tonight," Hamp continued. "We're going to be running a bare bones operation until tomorrow morning, but don't think twice about asking for help. There's gonna be about eight inches or so on the road and Phil said it was real slick up there with all the melting and freezing."

Without saying a word, Lyle began a counter-clockwise circuit of the truck, inspecting the vehicle's tires, lights, and plow blades. Hamp followed him around the snowplow and continued his briefing.

"We haven't heard anything from the State Patrol or Silverton cee-dot about any new avalanche activity tonight, but Mother Cline and East Riverside are both past due for a major slide. This storm could trigger either one of them."

The major avalanche areas along the Million Dollar Highway were well known to the patrol. They knew them both by their historical nick-names and their exact milepost location. Slippery Jim crossed the high-way at milepost 87.55. Blue Willow at milepost 81.15. Each slide path had a distinct pattern and personality. During the winter, CDOT attempted to diminish the impact of unpredictable slides by firing howitzer cannons and gas-propelled shells into known avalanche areas.

Reaching the rear of the truck, Lyle ran his hands over the recent-ly repaired spreading mechanism that controlled the distribution of the gravel and sand mixture. Watching Lyle going through the visual check his co-workers had dubbed the "Lyle Morrison Pre-Flight Ritual," Hamp couldn't help comparing him to the truck that he was inspecting.

Although no longer in production, the Colorado Special was a mas-sive and reliable machine, perfectly suited for the type of heavy road-work the patrol routinely performed. With its massive steel front plow and side-mounted wing plow welded to its frame, the truck cut a sev-enteen-foot swath when its blades were fully extended. Its diesel engine generated enough horsepower to meet even the toughest demands of a Colorado mountain winter.

The fifty-one-year-old Morrison was somewhat of a throwback him-self, a quiet man who didn't seem to care what others thought of him. His thick barrel chest and club-like arms had earned him a measure of phys-ical respect in the six years since he arrived in Ouray, and he'd become something of a folk legend among the volunteers who served with him on Ouray County's search and rescue team, many of whom were half his age. His voice was disarmingly low and strong, as if it emanated from some deeper source. His words were few and measured, which made him the target of occasional jokes in the CDOT garage as well as a bit of an oddity among Ouray's residents.

Satisfied that the truck was in good working order, Lyle stopped beside the driver's side door and turned to face Hamp. Despite the crew's haphazard sleep patterns during the past week, the large man's eyes were clear and focused.

"Remember, all we need to do tonight is to keep a hole in the road." Hamp said. "It's not going to be pretty up there, so let's leave the fancy stuff for the morning. Lay down as much sand as you need and let me know what's happening up there on the radio."

Lyle scraped sand, snow, and gravel from the soles of his well-worn boots, and hoisted himself into the cab of the thirteen-foot-tall truck. When he pulled his hood back, a thick flow of gray hair fell down past his neck.

"Any profound words before you go?" Hamp asked as Lyle pulled the door shut and rolled down his window.

Morrison depressed the clutch and shifted the truck into gear. He had to shout to be heard over the rumble of the diesel engine.

"I still say it's a dumb place to put a road."

After leaving the CDOT yard, Lyle tested the truck's air brakes along the downhill stretch of County Road, 316, a graded dirt road that dead-ended at US Highway 550. He lowered the front plow blade using one of the levers protruding from the floorboard behind the truck's thirteen-gear stick shift. As he swung the truck onto the Million Dollar Highway, a sign with blinking amber lights announced to motorists in bright red letters:

Chains & Snow Tires Required.

"No kidding," he mumbled.

As Lyle expected, there were no vehicles on the road. Despite an increase in traffic through the mountain pass in recent years, Lyle knew he would encounter a deserted highway. It was difficult enough to drive on a well-lit, flat highway on a night like this, let alone on US Highway 550.

Starting out in the low hole in the shift pattern, Lyle worked his way through the gears. He angled the front plow blade to the right, then dropped the wing plow onto the snow-covered pavement. The front plow was designed to scrape the bulk of the wet snow from the roadway, pushing the heavy load to the right. Mounted against the right side of the truck, the wing plow caught the excess snow coming off the front blade and pushed it further to the right. The plow line that Lyle selected began five feet to the left of the center line and extended deep onto the highway's right shoulder.

The drive to the summit of Red Mountain Pass would cover a twelve-mile stretch of the highway. Reaching the summit, which served as the border between Ouray and San Juan counties, Lyle would turn the truck around and plow back down the twisting mountain road before continuing into Ouray. Given the amount of snow on the road, Lyle estimated that the round-trip would take almost ninety minutes.

Guiding the truck around a sweeping uphill curve, Lyle could feel a steady vibration through the floorboard as the plow blades scraped against the road. His hands and shoulders felt the throaty resonance of the diesel engine as it vibrated through the oversized steering wheel. The half-bucket vinyl seat absorbed the crunch and slap of the Colorado Special's thick tire chains. The truck's myriad vibrations made him feel connected to the vehicle as he piloted seven tons of machinery, sand and gravel along the slick mountain roadway.

Now in sixth gear, the truck was nearing the 20 m.p.h. plateau that Lyle used for night plowing. Even at this speed, the relentless fusillade of white flakes pelted his windshield. A column of slush began to build up on the windshield's left side almost immediately. Lyle knew that he would have to make several stops to scrape the windshield to keep the packed ice from obstructing his vision.

Blue and amber strobe lights flashed atop steel brackets on either side of the truck's cab, ensuring its visibility even in the midst of the furious storm. With the exception of a few stretches of level ground, the section of US Highway 550 from Ouray to the summit of Red Mountain Pass would be a steady uphill climb. Once he reached Bear Creek Falls, however, Lyle would be piloting the truck along a narrow corniche bordered by steep, ice-covered cliff walls, and an unprotected sheer drop of 200 feet or more into the Uncompahgre Gorge. Lyle tried to vanquish such thoughts. No sense worrying about it, he reasoned, until he had no choice about the matter.

As was his habit whenever he plowed at night, Lyle eased off the accelerator as he passed between the Amphitheater Campground and a scenic overlook. Through the passenger window, Morrison was treated to a spectacular view of Ouray, which spread out below him, cradled like a newborn in an oversized bassinet. The white-capped craggy peaks of the San Juan Mountain range seemed to encircle the quiet mountain town. Pinpoints of light from the streetlights below winked and danced behind wisps of low clouds and a thick veil of side-slanting snow. From the time the first settlers entered its amphitheater bowl, Ouray had been bestowed with fanciful nicknames such as, "The Jewel of the Rockies," and "The Switzerland of America." On nights such as this, with its nearly 700 citizens asleep and streets devoid of traffic, Lyle found such nicknames inadequate to describe the splendor of his hometown.

Lyle's view was soon interrupted by a stand of tall evergreens. He guided the snowplow around a sharp curve to the left and entered the Uncompahgre Gorge, a narrow box canyon created 10,000 years ago by a 3,000-foot glacier.

Among the newest and steepest mountain ranges in the world, the San Juans have not yet been blunted and eroded by the grinding forces of nature. With over twenty now-exposed layers of the Earth's crust visible, an incredible two billion years of geological history are laid bare in the San Juans. When violent avalanches send chunks of that history tumbling down sheer mountain slopes into the Uncompahgre Gorge, the only thing that stands in the way is US Highway 550: Carved into the face of cliff walls hundreds of feet above the canyon floor, the Million Dollar Highway hugs the gorge's east side.

Lyle leaned forward and turned the heater up a notch. A sharp wind sliced through the narrow canyon, buffeting the snowplow's windshield. He could see low dark storm clouds moving across his line of sight as they squeezed between the peaks flanking the gorge. With no streetlights to illuminate the roadway and sheets of wind-whipped snow now obscuring his view, Lyle relied on instinct.

The two-way radio bracketed to the floorboard suddenly crackled, and Hamp's voice came through the speakers as if he were sitting in the passenger seat.

"Three Mary fourteen to three Mary fourteen five. Radio check."

Lyle grabbed the microphone from a clip on the dashboard.

"Three Mary fourteen five. Loud and clear." *I hope you're not in a chatty mood tonight, boss,* he thought to himself.

"How's it look?" the foreman asked.

Lyle moved the lever to engage the spreader. In the side mirror he saw a thick spray of sand and gravel being flung to the pavement from the back of his truck.

"I'm approaching Rock Tunnel. So far, so good. There's about six inches on the road, but the blades are scraping pretty good. I'm going to spot sand from the tunnel up through the Engineer Road cutoff."

Lyle slowed the snowplow down a fraction as it passed through the natural rock tunnel at milepost 91. The Jackpot Slide, one of the area's smaller avalanche paths, ran across the top of the tunnel and into the canyon below the right shoulder of the road. Since it had slid only five days ago, Lyle was not expecting any trouble from Jackpot tonight.

Emerging from the tunnel, Lyle felt the truck's tire chains slip on an exposed patch of black ice. The rear of the truck slid suddenly to the left, forcing the front of the truck to the right. Lyle quickly steered into the skid, narrowly avoiding a plunge over the far end of the right shoulder. He straightened the truck out on the narrow highway and downshifted to fifth gear. Only then did he finally take a breath.

"How's the traction?" Hamp asked, as if on cue.

Lyle wiped his hand across his forehead and suppressed a grin. "Typical for this time of year," he answered flatly. "Everything that melted during the day is frozen solid tonight."

"I'm gonna make a fortune designing a truck with the spreader on the front instead of the back," Hamp said. "Damn thing doesn't do us a lick of good behind the tires."

Although some members of Patrol 14 appreciated an encouraging voice on the radio, Lyle preferred the solitude of plowing a deserted road. With the storm still raging, he didn't need the two-way radio's added distraction.

Keying the mike, Lyle said firmly, "That's it for now, Hamp. I'll check back in when I get to the snowshed."

Heading south at twenty miles per hour, the truck passed the dark and deserted Bear Creek turnout on the right side of the road. The roadside vista treated tourists to the sight of the 200-foot Bear Creek Falls cascading from the edge of the highway into Uncompahgre River at the bottom of the gorge. To Lyle, however, the view was merely a reminder of how far his truck would plummet if he were unlucky enough to slide off the slick, snow-choked highway. He wiped his palms on his jeans. The next few miles would be nerve-racking. With several hairpin turns and a narrow, crumbling shoulder, the stretch of road between Bear Creek Falls and the Riverside Slide area was a death trap.

Since the road ran along a narrow shelf that had been blasted into the side of steep mountain walls, the left-hand shoulder consisted of a few feet of gravel and a vertical wall of quartzite. To Lyle's right was a black abyss that seemed like a living, breathing beast. Glancing at the passenger-side mirror, Lyle could see that the wing plow was clearing a wide path into the right shoulder of the road. Along several stretches of the curving road, the wing plow would be left hanging over the rim of the canyon wall. At one time the right side of the road had been bordered by masonry blocks but they had long since been removed to aid in snowplowing. The absence of guardrails allowed the patrol's plows and blowers to disgorge their wintry payloads over the edge of the road. With guardrails in place, one heavy snowfall could easily turn US Highway 550 into a single-lane road flanked by towering snow piles.

In this exposed section of the Uncompahgre Gorge, visibility was poor and the shadows from the cliff walls could be deceiving. A mile south of Bear Creek, Lyle approached Engineer Pass road, a steep gravel jeep trail that was closed for the winter. This area was notoriously slick since the Uncompahgre River flowed down from the mountains and passed beneath the road. Lyle let the truck coast along the slippery highway without shifting or braking. The truck tires held a firm grip on the road as he coaxed the truck around a sharp bend that followed the contours of the cliff's sheer walls.

"Atta boy," Lyle said out loud as he patted the dashboard.

The truck was now less than a mile from the Riverside Slide area, which was past due for a major avalanche. All of the avalanche fatalities that had occurred on the Ouray-to-Silverton highway in the twentieth-century had taken place at Riverside Slide. Since avalanches in the area had been known to close the road from two to ten days, local residents knew to keep a warm blanket and food supplies in their cars and trucks when traveling through Red Mountain Pass. Each CDOT was equipped with avalanche bags containing ready to eat, military-style meals known as MRE's, as well as a blanket, flashlight and climbing rope.

As he approached a sharp left-hand turn just past the Mother Cline slide area, Lyle noticed that the windshield's left side was partially obscured by a vertical line of wet slush packed in place by the wiper blade. The right shoulder narrowed around the turn, so he glanced briefly at the side mirror to check how far his wing plow was hanging over the edge of the road. When he returned his attention to the road, the truck was halfway through the curve. To his horror, Lyle saw a dark shape directly in front of the plow.

"No!" he shouted, his deep voice filling the cab.

Barely fifteen feet in front of him, straddling the right shoulder of the road, was a dark pickup truck with a light-colored shell over its bed. The vehicle was parked at an odd angle, nearly broadside to the snowplow, with its front grille pointing toward the gorge. The bright red glow from the pickup's brake lights reflected against the left side of Lyle's windshield.

Knowing a crash was imminent, Lyle used the split-second before impact to minimize the force of the collision. Simultaneously, he stomped hard on the brake and clutch pedals and flung the steering wheel to the left. The air brakes squealed loudly as Lyle cursed.

"Stop, you son of a bitch!"

Any hope of stopping the seven-ton truck was erased when Lyle felt the sand and gravel mix shift forward, adding momentum to the plow's forward skid. Lyle hoped that the tire chains would find solid pavement to grind into, but no chance. The chains skidded atop a thick patch of ice on the surface of the highway as it bent around the sharp curve.

Lyle locked his left forearm across the steering wheel to keep from losing control at impact. His right hand shot to the plow levers, trying to raise the massive front blade and angle it to the left. The plow was just inches off the ground when the force of the collision lifted Lyle out of his seat and sent him crashing against the steering wheel. His right arm slammed against the dashboard and his head shot forward and down. Lyle craned his neck to see through the bottom of the windshield as the plow mechanism lurched up slightly, lifting the smaller truck off the ground. The sound of metal colliding with metal filled the cab and echoed off the canyon walls. Designed to move mountains of snow, the plow mechanism of the Colorado Special made quick work of the pickup, which flipped onto its side as it disappeared from sight and plunged into the dark chasm below.

Lyle fought to regain control of his truck. The back end slid to the right and the cab was pushed to the left as the snowplow skidded around the bend. As the road straightened out, Lyle saw that the skid was slowly spinning the truck in a sweeping counter-clockwise arc. The jagged rock wall bordering the left side of the road loomed large in his windshield as the rear wheels veered closer to the right edge of the road. The truck was now in a full skid, angling sideways down the road. Lyle knew that if the four rear wheels slid off the edge of the highway, the rest of the plow would surely follow.

"Stop, dammit!" he screamed.

Lyle steered into the skid and finally his rear wheels found a measure of desperately needed traction along the right shoulder. The tire chains ground the truck to a clamorous halt thirty yards from where the pickup left the roadway.

Lyle now faced the left shoulder of the highway, his heart pounding and his right arm throbbing. He ran his hands through his thick gray hair and unclenched his jaw. Gathering his senses, he shifted into the low hole, eased up on the clutch, and maneuvered the truck back in the direction he'd come.

It took just seconds to pilot the snowplow back to the hairpin turn where the accident had occurred, but the ride seemed maddeningly slow. Lyle brought the truck to a stop at the apex of the turn, the driver's side door three feet away from the edge of the shoulder. Reaching behind his seat, Lyle grabbed his avalanche bag and a flare canister, and jumped from the cab.

With the truck's strobe lights still flashing, Lyle could see glimpses of the sloping canyon walls directly below him. He pulled a large flashlight from the avalanche bag and scanned the gorge for any sign of the pickup. Just below the lip of the roadway, he could see a line of impact marks where the falling truck had scraped the snow from boulders that clung to the steep slope leading into the canyon's dark maw. For sixty feet, the ground sloped away from the shoulder at a steep angle, then it plunged almost vertically down the sheer face of rust-colored canyon walls. He trained the beam on the bottom of the canyon, where Red Mountain Creek flowed some 200 feet below the highway on its way to meet the Uncompahgre River. Standing on his toes to see the far side of the creek bed below, Lyle desperately scanned the bottom of the gorge for a dark shape against the snow-covered rocks.

Swinging the flashlight to the right, Lyle saw a muted reflection coming from a stand of spruce and fir trees fifty feet below. He shielded his eyes from the wind-blown snow as he scanned the clump of trees. His eyes adjusting to the scene, Lyle could see the undercarriage of the pickup. The truck had become wedged against the sturdy trunks of two tall trees, and was resting on its side, its driver's side door facing the sky. It appeared that the vehicle's weight was not centered between the two trees, indicating that it might topple from its precarious perch at any moment.

There was still a chance that the collision might not end tragically. Lyle knew he needed to act quickly to keep the truck's occupants from unbalancing the vehicle by clambering out of the ruined pickup.

He cupped his hands and shouted down into the canyon. "Stay where you are! Don't shift your weight! Help is on the way! Don't try to move!"

Lyle closed his eyes and listened for a response. The only sounds he could hear were the unrelenting whistle of the wind as it was channeled through the canyon walls and the sharp ping of snow pelting the cab of the snowplow.

Moving quickly, Lyle grabbed a flare and jogged down the road. His work boots slipped on the icy pavement as he rounded the sharp curve. He slid to a stop where the hairpin turn ended and the road straightened out. Averting his eyes, Lyle ignited a flare, which exploded in a brilliant burst of red light. He planted the flare in the middle of the road as a warning signal to any driver coming from Ouray.

Looking south, he concluded that anyone approaching from Silverton would see the truck's flashing lights. Satisfied that the area was secure, Lyle retraced his steps and leaned over the edge of the shoulder. He called down again.

"Please, stay where you are. Help is coming!"

Lyle's instincts were conflicted. As the captain of Ouray County's search and rescue unit, he advised team members never to attempt a rescue without adequate tools and additional manpower. On the other hand, twelve months of madness in the jungles of Southeast Asia had taught him the value of quick, decisive action; that waiting for orders from a remote command post could result in confusion and loss of life. He pounded his fist on the fender of the truck, angry for not having avoided the collision.

"Damn! Why didn't you see it?"

He climbed into the cab of the snowplow and switched the two-way radio to the emergency frequency which used a network of antennae called "repeaters" that were installed throughout Red Mountain Pass. Lyle keyed the microphone and forced himself to keep his voice level.

"3 Mary 14-5 is requesting assistance. Repeat, 3 Mary 14-5 is requesting assistance."

Lyle knew that his transmission would be picked up by a number of local dispatchers. He could envision Hamp back at the CDOT garage, itching to jump on the line. But since this was now a police matter, the foreman would know better than to interfere with the prescribed chain of command on the emergency frequency.

The dispatcher from the Montrose barracks of the Colorado State Police was the first to respond. "3 Mary 14-5, this is Montrose responding. Please describe your situation and location."

She would now take charge of the situation. Lyle didn't have to tell the dispatcher that he was on US Highway 550. He had identified himself as a member of CDOT Patrol 14, and the Million Dollar Highway was the only road assigned to the patrol.

"Montrose, a passenger vehicle is off the road. I am at milepost 90 just south of the Mother Cline slide. The vehicle is hung up against some trees about 50 feet off the shoulder."

"3 Mary 14-5, I copy. Any occupants in the vehicle?"

"Affirmative." Lyle caught himself and reconsidered. "I believe so. I haven't made contact as of yet."

"10-4. Stand by 3 Mary 14-5."

As he waited for a response, Lyle tapped his boot impatiently against the floorboard. He began second-guessing his decision to report the accident before going down to check on the pickup. He keyed the mike again to assist the dispatcher.

"Montrose, this is 3 Mary 14-5. Be advised that my location is accessible but slick from the Ouray side. Strongly advise not approaching from the south."

When it came to describing road conditions in the San Juan Mountains over the radio, understatement was key. A CDOT employee would never announce that the Million Dollar Highway was impassable. Even with a thirty-foot pile of debris on the highway and traffic halted in both directions, the road was never closed; it was merely being cleared. As a result, Lyle knew better than to announce that the tract of highway from his current position to the summit of Red Mountain Pass had at least eight inches of unplowed snow on it. He also knew it wasn't prudent to mention that a CDOT vehicle had been involved in the accident. Even at this late hour, too many ears were tuned to the emergency frequency.

"Understood, 3 Mary 14-5. We are rolling a wrecker and an EMT unit from Ouray. Ouray Sheriff's Department will be responding. Life Flight in Grand Junction is on standby. Do you require anything additional?"

"3 Mary 14-5. Not at this time, thank you. Over and out."

Lyle switched back to the truck's regular frequency. Walter Hampton wasted no time in getting on the air. His voice was urgent. "I'm headed to your location. Please don't take any action until I arrive. Do you copy that?"

"I copy. Hold short of the turn past Mother Cline. I'm parked in the roadway and there's a thick patch of ice underfoot."

Lyle lowered himself from the cab and called into the teeth of the storm. "Help is coming! Don't shift your weight!"

Walking between his truck and the edge of the highway, Lyle lost his footing. Steadying himself against the truck's fender, he saw that he had stepped into a deep groove in the ice that had obviously been cut by the pickup's tires. He saw a similar groove to his left, further down the roadway. Something about the position of the tire marks seemed odd to him, but he ignored his apprehension and got to work.

Pulling a fifty-foot length of coiled climbing rope out of the avalanche bag, Lyle hoped it would be long enough to reach the pickup. He tied one end of the rope to the steel frame that ran from the bottom of the plow mechanism to the undercarriage of the truck and leaned back to test the security of the knot. It held. He then reached behind the plow blade and removed a ten-foot length of chain that was draped on the blade's convex side.

Lyle threw the coil of climbing rope over the edge of the road toward the dark outline of the wrecked pickup truck. Standing on the shoulder, he shined his flashlight along the sloping canyon walls to select a path down to the pickup.

Realizing he would not be able to hold the flashlight and lower himself down the rope, Lyle shoved it in his right jacket pocket before looping the ten-foot section of chain and slipping the coil over his head, adjusting it like an ammo belt over his right shoulder and under his left arm. As he grabbed the rope with both hands and backed toward the edge of the shoulder, he could hear Hamp's voice trying to raise him on the radio.

"Sorry, boss," he said to himself.

Lyle straddled the rope, stepped backward off the edge of the road and began lowering himself down the embankment. He would have to make the descent without the aid of a harness, carabiners, figure eights, or any of the other climbing gear the Ouray Mountain Rescue Team used for this kind of rescue attempt. The most direct path to the stand of trees was over a large outcropping of rock that was covered with mounds of plowed snow.

With each step, Lyle leaned back on the rope, positioning himself perpendicular to the angle of the canyon wall. His head was hanging over the mouth of the gorge and his boots were trying to find footholds on the canyon wall. His arms strained with the effort of supporting his body. Fifteen feet below the road, he paused next to the rock outcropping to look down at the pickup.

Lyle tried to remember if the vehicle's headlights were on when the truck was plowed off the road. He distinctly remembered seeing the glow of its taillights. Actually, he thought, they were too bright to be just the taillights. They had to be the brake lights. Although the collision had happened in the blink of an eye, Lyle was certain that the taillights weren't blinking, as they would be if the emergency flashers had been engaged. The only logical explanation, he reasoned, was that someone had their foot on the brake pedal at the moment of impact. With even greater urgency, Lyle continued his descent.

Twenty-five feet below the road, both of Lyle's boots suddenly slipped, losing contact with the canyon wall. To prevent a free-fall, Lyle desperately clutched onto the rope above his head. The momentum of the fall sent him crashing into the rocky embankment, the truck chain digging deep into his chest. With his entire weight now suspended by his grasp on the nylon rope, Lyle pulled his legs up so he could regain footholds against the snow-covered slope. Looking down, he saw that he had slipped on a talus bed: a pile of fist-sized rocks that clung to the steep embankment. Even though the unanchored heap of rocks wasn't going to provide reliable footing, Lyle knew it was too late to change his path of descent.

He picked through the pile of snow-covered rocks, his boots giving way several times as he lowered himself ten more feet toward the evergreen stand. His arms ached from the strain of supporting his weight. His right forearm stung from its collision against the truck's dashboard and a keen-edged pain in his chest was making it impossible to draw in deep breaths. He realized that the impact of his chest against the truck chain might have broken a rib or two. The waves of pain made his senses more acute. He could hear the wind whistling below at the bottom of the gorge and the slow creaking of tree limbs behind him.

Now fifteen feet above the pickup, Lyle reached an aspen tree clinging stubbornly to the side of the sloping embankment. The gray skin of the aspen's trunk was caked with frozen snow. Lyle considered knotting the rope around the base of the tree, but decided that he was going to need every inch of the climbing rope to reach the truck. He grabbed onto the tree and shouted down to the pickup.

"I'm almost there!"

Again, there was no response.

Between Lyle and the undercarriage of the pickup was a nearly vertical cliff wall that flared out at the base of the evergreens. A thin rind of snow and ice was frozen to the steep canyon wall. Lowering himself toward the pickup, Lyle's breath came in gulps. When he exhaled, thick clouds of steam lingered in front of his face before being swept down the canyon. Wind-propelled snow peppered his frozen cheeks and stung his eyes like a barrage of darts. His gray hair was caked to his scalp and his hands were cramped from gripping the rope. As he descended, Lyle knew that the end of the rope was somewhere beneath him, but he had no idea how far. Each time he released a gloved hand to grasp a lower section of the rope, he half-expected to come up empty.

"Just a little further," he said out loud.

Suddenly, Lyle could hear a faint hiss coming from the radiator of the truck. He pushed off the canyon wall with his left leg, spinning his body counter-clockwise and bracing himself by pinning the soles of his boots against the wall behind him. Facing out into the canyon, he saw that he was eight feet above a small rock ledge protruding from the slanting canyon wall. The pickup, its dark underbelly just below him, had become wedged between the ledge and the trees behind it.

In the shadows, Lyle could see the end of the rope dangling a foot above the ledge. He quickly shimmied down the remaining eight feet, careful to avoid banging against the vehicle. His feet on the snowy ledge, he let go of the rope, shaking his arms to relieve their cramping.

"Hello! Can you hear me?" he called out.

There was no reply. Lyle felt a wave of nausea overcome him.

"Please be alive."

Knowing he had to stabilize the vehicle before climbing onto it, Lyle dropped to his knees on the ledge and lifted the coiled chain over his head. He found a gap between the ledge and the front right wheel well. Lying on his side and reaching his arm through the narrow opening, Lyle located the trunk of one of the supporting evergreens. He used both hands to snake the truck chain around the base of the trunk. He then looped the heavy chain around two sections of the truck's frame. Winding the links tightly around the frame, he pulled the ends together, securing them to one another with a s-hook.

Lyle took off his gloves and touched the pickup's muffler, finding it hot to the touch.

Carefully choosing his footholds on the pickup's exhaust system and undercarriage, he climbed up the upward-slanting belly of the truck. Nearing the top of the wrecked heap of metal, he leaned forward and grabbed the handle of the driver's side door.

He then heard the sound of vehicles arriving on the road above him. Looking up the slope, he saw that the gorge was awash in flashing strobes of blue, red and amber lights. A spotlight swept the area around him before coming to rest on the wrecked pickup. Lyle turned away to shield his eyes from the bright light.

By the light of the overhead beam, Lyle could now see the full length of the vehicle. It was a dark blue Dodge Ram pickup with a rectangular white shell that enclosed the truck's bed. His heart felt as if it was about to burst.

He turned toward the source of the light above and shouted. "It's Doctor Philips!"

The distinctive gravelly voice of Bill Withers, Ouray County Sheriff, carried down the canyon. "Is he okay?"

Oblivious to the risks, Lyle leaned forward and dove against the driver's side door, which was angled down into the gorge. He stopped himself from sliding off the truck by pinning his left arm against a thick branch. Reaching into his right pocket, he grabbed the flashlight and shined it through the driver's side window, which had remained intact during the fifty-foot plunge.

Through the window, Lyle saw that the glove compartment had sprung open, its contents strewn throughout the cab's interior. A black leather bag and cellular phone lay against the passenger-side window. Otherwise, the cab was empty.

Withers called again. "Do we need Life Flight?"

A sickening thought occurred to Lyle. Sliding forward against the tree, he trained his light into the black chasm 150 feet below.

— Chapter 3 —

Awaking from a nightmare, Casey Bailey bolted up in her bed, sweating and confused. In her dream, her weekly shipment of fresh flowers was stranded in Denver due to a fierce snowstorm that had closed all of the local airports. Just before she wakened, the diminutive twenty-six-year-old flower shop owner was announcing to her customers -including an irate mother of a bride - that she wouldn't be able to satisfy her weekly floral obligations. It was a recurring fear ever since she opened her shop in Telluride three years ago, and she could feel warm streaks of tears running down her cheeks. Before long the muffled ringing of the downstairs telephone chased away the lingering pangs of helplessness and she was wide awake.

She stared at the clock radio on the nightstand. Red digital numbers were blinking on and off. She surmised that there had been an interruption in electrical power due to the storm. That would explain why Dr. Philips's answering machine hadn't picked up the incoming call. One of the quirks of Jim Philips's phone system was that whenever the power went off, the outgoing message had to be re-recorded before the answering machine could be reactivated.

Casey peeled back the white down comforter and swung out of bed.

She stood up too fast and immediately felt light-headed and clumsy. She leaned down and held onto the mattress to steady herself. As the telephone continued to ring, Casey walked to the closed bedroom door, her bare feet slapping against the polished wood floor. She caught a glimpse of herself in the mirror on the back of the door and saw that her straight shoulder-length blonde hair was matted against the left side of her head.

Moving quickly now, she swung open the door that led to the upstairs hallway and ran down the hall stairs, careful not to trip on her long pink-and-white flannel nightshirt.

"I'm coming, I'm coming!" She shouted into the dark hallway.

Reaching the first floor, Casey saw that the master bedroom door was open. Her landlord wasn't home. She wondered where Dr. Philips could be at this late hour. Although it wasn't unusual for him to arrive home late, Dr. Philips was ordinarily quite diligent about leaving messages for her.

Crossing through the dark living room, Casey could see through the columns of floor-to-ceiling windows along the back of the house. The storm hadn't let up since she went to bed; the railings on the rear wooden deck were piled high with snow. She reached the kitchen at the far side of the house, flicked on the light switch and grabbed the portable phone from its base. She took a deep breath before answering. Calls in the middle of the night usually did not bring good news.

"Philips residence."

The voice on the phone sounded tinny and was accompanied by a hollow echo. "Casey, this is Sheriff Withers."

Casey snatched the phone from her shoulder and braced her hand against the doorframe. "Is something wrong?"

"We're not sure. Doc Philips's car was involved in a collision on the highway near Red Mountain Pass."

Casey walked quickly back into the living room and peered through the long vertical panes of insulated glass. "Oh my God!" she gasped, "Is he all right?"

"Jim's truck was pushed off the road, but so far, it doesn't look like he was in it. Do you know where he was headed tonight?"

Casey could make out the sound of a two-way radio in the background as she tried to collect her thoughts. "Pushed off the road?"

"It was hit by a snowplow rounding a tight turn up here in the pass. We just pulled the car out of the gorge with a wrecker and a winch. It looks like Jim got stuck in the storm and abandoned his truck. I take it you haven't heard from him tonight?"

"No." Casey replied. "He wasn't home when I went to bed at ten-thirty, but that's not unusual. I assumed that he was visiting a patient, or out with some friends."

The sheriff's voice was calm. "Listen Casey, I appreciate the info. Things are kind of a mess out here, but there were some tire tracks leading south from where Jim's pickup got stuck. We're guessing that he flagged somebody down, then got a lift to Silverton."

"Silverton? Why not Ouray?"

"We're still trying to figure that out. There's some confusion about which way the tracks were heading. If the driver was heading toward Silverton, then Jim might've just hitched a ride to the south. You know Doc Philips; he'd never inconvenience anybody. He might be bunking down with the Leonards or one of his other friends in Silverton for the night. Just to make sure, we're going to check the snowshed and all the turnouts along the highway."

"You'd think he would've called to let me know that he was okay," Casey protested.

"Maybe he didn't want to wake you," the sheriff suggested.

Casey walked back to the kitchen and checked the answering machine. The digital indicator for new messages read zero. "He may have called," she reasoned. "The answering machine isn't working. I think we lost power for a while."

"We lost the juice for an hour or so over at my place, too," he said. There were muffled voices in the background. "Okay Casey, try to get some sleep. We'll figure this out. I'm sure Jim's safe and sound and we'll be hearing from him in the morning. If he checks in, give me a call on my cellular. Do you have a pen handy?"

"Yes, but promise me you'll call back if you find out anything, okay?"

After copying down Sheriff Withers's number, Casey hung up the phone and returned to the living room windows. She put her face against the glass and looked toward Red Mountain Pass.

Dr. James Philips's house was located on the west side of Ouray, overlooking the town from a steep slope at the base of Twin Peaks Mountain. Supported by stilts, the modern timber-framed structure jutted out from the rocky slope, enjoying a panoramic view of the entire amphitheater-shaped bowl. The Uncompahgre River, after flowing through the gorge below the Million Dollar Highway, was joined by Canyon Creek as it entered the southwestern fringe of Ouray. The confluence of the two mountain-fed streams was a stone's throw to the right of the house, thirty yards down the slope.

Casey stared through the windows and above the branches of aspens and blue spruces that grew along the stony declivity beyond the deck. To the south, she could see the pale glow of overhead lights at the CDOT barn, perched on a hill above Ouray. She searched the darkness beyond the barn, straining to see if she could detect any vehicle lights on Highway 550 as it climbed toward Red Mountain Pass. She could not.

Casey felt a chill pass through her. She rubbed her arms and walked over to the fireplace on the south wall of the living room. She picked up a black glove from the top of the small woodpile. Mimi Philips had always used the glove to open the soot-covered flue. Casey slipped the glove on and pushed against the metal ring that opened the flue. She put two logs into the fireplace and lit a long wooden match. Turning a key at the bottom of the rock-faced chimney, she heard a brief hiss before the gas met the match and ignited in a blue flame. The dry logs began to crackle immediately, turning the tips of the flames to orange before they disappeared up the chimney. Staring into the fireplace, Casey couldn't shake the nagging sensation that she had overlooked some vital fact; something that would shed light on the situation involving Dr. Philips. Frustrated with herself, Casey shook her head.

A walnut grandfather clock near the front door chimed three o'clock. Her mind still racing, she sat cross-legged in an overstuffed leather reclining chair next to the fireplace. The worn recliner was Dr. Philips's favorite place in the house. Casey somehow felt closer to him as she settled against its cracked leather cushions. She reached down to the floor next to the chair for a neatly folded white afghan; one of several that Mimi had knit in the year before her death.

Draping the afghan over her shoulders, Casey suddenly grasped what had been eluding her. She pushed herself out of the deep recliner and raced to the kitchen.

"Of course!" she exclaimed triumphantly.

Affixed by a square magnet to the refrigerator door was a scrap of yellow paper containing Dr. Philips's pager number. Casey had used the number only twice since moving into the Philips residence three years ago. She picked up the phone and punched in the pager number. After two rings, Casey heard a series of rapid, high-pitched beeps on the line. She entered Dr. Philips's home phone number and hung up the phone. Returning to the living room, she paced back and forth in front of the fireplace.

As she waited in silence for the phone to ring, a hollow feeling began to spread through her chest. Gazing through the windows into the darkness, she whispered softly to no one in particular.

"Come on, come on, call."

— Chapter 4 —

The path to consciousness was an exhausting struggle to surface from thick depths. For what seemed like hours, he had fought to free himself from the muck, each time getting only marginally closer to extricating himself from the numbing grip of torpor. His body craved a deep breath he seemed incapable of drawing.

A bout of shivers shook the length of his body, inducing a gradual awakening of his senses. He focused on a biting cold that stung his hands, which felt as if they were being pricked by dozens of pins. His nose seemed swollen, and his tongue could taste the air as it moved inside his frozen cheeks. He couldn't open his eyes and wondered if they were frozen shut.

As he began to stir, his senses probed the darkness, recording information and feeding it back to his brain. His most immediate concern was that he couldn't see. Dr. Philips tried to lift his right hand toward his face, but it was heavy and difficult to move. Mustering more energy, he raised his hand again. Strangely, he felt his left hand rising as well, as if it was a marionette. His icy fingertips poked at his face. Though numb, his fingers could feel a cold ridged surface running laterally across his face, over the tops of his ears and around the back of his head. *Tape*, he thought to himself. Lifting both hands to reach the top of his head, he struck himself in the nose with something hard. The sudden, intense pain helped to clear his head, and the bizarre event on the highway flashed through his mind. Jim Philips made an instant connection between the attack and his present predicament. Now more alarmed than confused, his first impulse was to get to his feet. He tried to thrust both arms out to his sides in an attempt to lift himself off the cold ground. He was able to move his arms only a few inches before both of his wrists were pinched against the hard edges of ice-cold metal bands. He heard a chain rattle between his wrists. Pain shot up his arms and into his shoulders.

A blast of wind hit his cheeks. Now even more baffled about his surroundings, Dr. Philips became still, his heart beating wildly. He thought to himself. "What has that maniac done to me?"

Philips resolved to take his time and compose himself. He would take an inventory of his situation before acting again. He would not panic. If his kidnapper was watching, he wouldn't give him the satisfaction of seeing him flop around like a fish on dry land. The elderly man took a deep breath and began assembling clues.

He was sitting with his back propped against something solid. Pushing back with his shoulders, he noted that there was a slight bowing in the hard surface behind him. As he moved his torso from side to side, he could feel the fabric of his tweed jacket snagging against rough edges and splinters. His shoulder blades detected several unevenly spaced vertical grooves along what appeared to be a crudely constructed wooden wall.

The icy wind continued to blow fine ice pellets against his cheeks in intermittent gusts. He guessed that a door was open, exposing the interior of the building to blasts of subzero air and frozen spindrift. This seemed incongruous; if he were being held captive, why would a door have been left open? Was he being watched from the doorway? If he was correct in assuming that he was sequestered inside a wooden structure, why was he so terribly cold?

Dr. Philips used his right hand to explore his left arm. Two separate metal loops encircled his wrist. It was apparent that two sets of handcuffs had been clamped tight around his wrist, leaving little room for any kind of movement. Between his wrists, he located a ridged block of metal that was as cold as an ice cube—a padlock, its hasp threaded through a chain-link and locked around the center of the handcuffs. His fingers traced the length of chain as it ran down between his legs and under his left thigh. Shifting his body to the right, he stretched his hands to the left, where he located the chain as it emerged behind his left buttock.

Beneath the chain, he discovered that a tightly woven length of rough fabric had been placed under his rear end. He leaned forward, tracing the outside left edge of what appeared to be a blanket down toward his outstretched legs. With an abrupt jerk, the chain became taut digging between his legs and pinching his testicles. He let out a startled yelp that echoed off the walls to his left and right.

When the pain subsided, Dr. Philips began exploring the ground to the left of the blanket. His bare hands came to rest on a frozen, uneven surface of packed snow and ice. At the perimeter of his reach, the snow was piled in drifts as deep as six inches. Closer to his body, the snow had been trampled flat against the dirt floor.

Gathering the edges of the blanket around his frozen hands, Dr. Philips tried to make sense of the information he had gathered. How could he be both inside and outside at the same time? What kind of structure had walls but was open to the elements? He tried to determine the dimensions of the room by listening to the wind as it echoed off the interior walls. The sound was neither deep nor robust, indicating that the room wasn't particularly wide or tall. He sensed that the structure more likely the size of a tool shed.

Putting himself in his kidnapper's position, Dr. Philips concluded that the shed was probably in a secluded location where screams for help could not be heard. He briefly entertained the notion of calling out into the frozen darkness, but concluded that such an attempt would be futile. It was obviously not something his captor feared. Otherwise, he surmised, the thick tape that was wrapped around his forehead, eyes and nose would have covered his mouth as well. The mounting evidence that he had been spirited away to a remote location only served to amplify the gut-churning sensations of isolation and dread.

The physician licked his cold, cracked lips and mumbled, "Where the hell am I?"

His hands only marginally warmer after rubbing them against the blanket, Dr. Philips probed the layers of tape that had been wrapped around his head. He found a loose edge directly over his right ear. Peeling back the sticky material, he counted six different edges running in a horizontal circuit around his head. Dr. Philips knew that unwinding the tape was going to be far more painful than removing a bandage. The duct tape would yank every strand of hair from his scalp that was matted onto its thick adhesive backing.

As he began the slow, painful process of unwinding the tape with his shackled hands, he turned his thoughts to the person responsible for this madness. Madness, he reflected, was the only explanation. Dr. Philips recalled staring incredulously at Paul Brader, attempting to fathom how their relationship could have degenerated into such mayhem. As the ambush unfolded, he tried to comprehend why, to diagnose its root causes. Even in moments of panic, Dr. Philips couldn't help thinking like a clinician; after all, he had spent the better part of his adult life interpreting clues and organizing them into theories.

He knew that in a society governed by laws and accepted standards of conduct, there are those who live by their own rules, which they conveniently mold to accommodate their own self-interest. After a defeat in the court of debate and reason, they hone their hatred against a whetstone of pride and humiliation. They ache for a second battle, a battle heavily stacked in their favor and contested on a battlefield of their choosing. They choose to strike when their opponent is most vulnerable and attack in a manner that will ensure victory. Jim Philips had lost the second battle because he hadn't seen it coming.

He carefully unwound the first layer of duct tape. Because it was wrapped over other layers of tape, he was able to remove it without damaging his scalp. The combination of his arthritic, freezing fingers and the clumsiness of the handcuffs made the task maddeningly laborious. He balled the tape into a thick wad that dangled from his head. As he unwound the second layer, the hair above the collar of his jacket was pulled upward. He tugged on the tape quickly, feeling a patch of his hair being ripped out by its roots. The doctor let out a sharp grunt.

Pausing to steel himself for another painful unwinding of tape around his throbbing scalp, he was startled by the sudden beeping of his pager. Worried that Paul Brader might be nearby, he fumbled quickly to turn it off, tucked it into the breast pocket of his jacket, and listened for the sound of approaching footsteps, not daring to breathe.

As he waited, all he could hear was the low moan of a persistent wind and the sound of snow pellets striking the wooden wall behind him. With no response to the sound of the beeper, Dr. Philips was even more convinced that he had correctly guessed Brader's motives. By sequestering his adversary in a remote location, Brader could wage the battle anew, unimpaired by the norms and conventions of civilized conduct.

Knowing the underlying cause of his abduction as well as the complications that his disappearance would pose for his kidnapper, Dr. Philips was fairly certain he hadn't been left to freeze to death. He reasoned that if murder had been Paul Brader's intention, death would have been swift. Instead of shivering in an isolated shed, he would be searching the length and breadth of the Elysian Fields for Mimi Philips, his late wife. Dr. Philips knew that he had something this maniac needed. As a result, he was going to be tortured. Once drained of value to his kidnapper, his survival would be at the mercy of a merciless soul.

Now in a blind panic, Dr. Philips reached up to the back of his head and found the loose end of the tape once again. He took a deep breath and gritted his teeth. With a sharp tug, he ripped another patch of hair out of his scalp.

— Chapter 5 —

Having inventoried her supply of fresh flowers, Casey stepped out of the walk-in cooler at the back of her shop and pulled the sliding glass door shut behind her. Still shaken by her nightmare, Casey had already called various flower distributors and growers to track her recent orders. The five-foot, three-inch shop owner placed the inventory clipboard on a hook by the cash register and looked out The Petal Pusher's large plate-glass window.

Telluride's streets were alive this morning with both local residents and late-season vacationers on their way to the slopes or to the Air Garden snowboarding park. A parade of winter sports enthusiasts clad in bright ski attire passed in view along the sidewalks of Colorado Avenue, Telluride's main thoroughfare.

The monthly payments for her Colorado Avenue storefront were high, but Casey was convinced it was the only viable location for The Petal Pusher. Because her store relied on impulse purchases unrelated to the skiing or snowboarding trade, Casey had chosen its location based on optimal foot traffic. From her front window, Casey could conduct an instant audit of retail activity in the small resort town, which she measured in clusters of Gore-Tex-clad pedestrians.

Casey 's sole employee, Jason Zuckerman, passed in front of the window, took a quick glance over his shoulder at the ski slopes to the south, and shook his head. A cup of coffee in each hand, he elbowed the front door open and entered the flower shop.

"It's a beautiful day for retail, wouldn't you say?" Casey teased the twenty-six-year-old.

"With all this new snow on the double black diamond trails," he said, handing Casey one of the cups, "I can't think of anything I'd rather be doing than making up flower arrangements with you, boss."

"That's what I like to hear. I half-expected you to call in with a case of white flu this morning."

"Rumor has it, that particular illness can be terminal at The Petal Pusher, at least as far as employment goes. Until I brightened your doorstep two years ago, you went through part-time employees like green grass through a goose."

"It's amazing," Casey replied. "In Telluride, you're immediately branded a tyrant if you have the audacity to ask your employees to show up for work in the winter. And yet somehow I've managed to miss only one day's worth of work in the past two years."

Jason knew that she was referring to the day of Mimi Philips's funeral. He hung up his jacket and picked up a feather duster.

"Still no word, huh?"

"Sheriff Withers promised me he'd call if he heard anything. I taped a note to the front door for Dr. Philips, but he hasn't called either. Between not getting any sleep last night, and waiting for the phone to ring, I'm not going to be much use today."

"Why don't you head on home and let me look after the shop. After all, that's why you pay me such an inordinate amount of money, right?"

"Wish I could," Casey said with a sigh. "But it's Wednesday and we need to get our commercial orders out the door by tomorrow night."

Casey and Jason spent the next two hours creating dozens of arrangements to be delivered the next day to local resorts, lodges and condominium complexes. In late February and March, much of the town's skiing and lodging business was weekend-based, so Casey delivered only once a week to the majority of her commercial clients. The coming weekend was atypical in that she didn't have a single wedding on her schedule. Three of her celebrity clients were planning to arrive in Telluride on Friday, however, and they expected to find their foyers, great rooms and bedrooms bedecked with her fragrant floral masterpieces.

At 12:30 p.m., Casey was helping a customer choose an arrangement of dried flowers when the phone rang near the register. Jason walked over, whispered "Sheriff Withers" in her ear, and took charge of the customer as Casey hurried to the phone.

"Has he shown up?" Casey asked hopefully.

"I'm afraid not," Withers said in a weary tone. "Is it possible for you to take the rest of the afternoon off and meet me at my office?"

Casey swallowed hard. "What's going on?"

"I'm gonna need your help in reconstructing Jim's schedule for yesterday. We've taken a closer look at his truck and at the accident site, and things aren't adding up right."

"What do you mean? Not adding up how?"

"I'd rather show you in person, Casey. So, can you make it?"

"I'll be there in less than an hour."

Casey grabbed her jacket, found her key ring in a side pocket, and removed the key to the shop's front door. Guiding Jason away from the customer by the elbow, she dropped the key into his hand.

"He wants me to drive over to his office," Casey reported. "I hate to do this to you, but could you look after the place until closing time?"

"Don't worry," he said, urging Casey toward the door. "Just go. The place will still be standing in the morning."

• • •

Casey flipped the Jeep's sun visor to shield her eyes from the glare reflecting off the wet road and the snowscape that bordered the Ridgway-to-Ouray section of US Highway 550. Telluride and Ouray were only eighteen miles apart, but the most direct route connecting the two towns was over a rugged jeep trail that was closed up to ten months of the year. Casey's forty-seven-mile commute was nearly three times longer than the straight-line distance between her home and the store. But the road between Telluride and Ouray was generally wider and more gently graded than the most notorious sections of the San Juan Skyway.

In the three years that she had lived in the area, Casey had never second-guessed her decision to live in Ouray and commute to Telluride. She normally passed the hour-long ride by mapping out ways to increase The Petal Pusher's client base and listening to country-western music. The twangy ballads were the polar opposite of the progressive music she had preferred throughout her teens and her college years.

Today, however, the radio in Casey's jeep was silent. Her mind was focused on Dr. Philips's whereabouts and the sheriff's phone call. A growing sense of foreboding kept her stomach churning and her thoughts drifting. Each time Casey contemplated a worst-case scenario, a sudden shiver would course through her, as if she was trying to reject the disquieting notion altogether.

Approaching the town of Ouray, Casey could see the triangle-shaped Mount Abrams; one of a panoply of peaks that towered above the alpine town. As the town's signature mountain, Mt. Abrams provided a vast white backdrop for photographs that appeared in the Ouray visitor's guides and postcards. The striated cliff walls that encircled Ouray were crosscut by snow-covered ledges, giving the impression that the center of a multi-layered cake had been gouged in order to accommodate this small mountain town. The landscape was such a departure from the town of Darien, Connecticut where she grew up that Casey couldn't help comparing her current existence with the one she had left behind. Virtually since birth, her parents' most fervent wish had been for their oldest daughter to cultivate the social graces and connections necessary to attract a suitable spouse.

Rounding a sweeping curve that led into the north end of Ouray's box canyon, Casey passed the town's famous Hot Springs Pool on her right. Curls of white wispy steam rose from the surface of the 105° pool, beckoning tourists and residents alike to soak their cares away in its spring-fed mineral waters. US Highway 550 became Main Street as it passed through the center of town, bisecting Ouray's eight east-west avenues. Main Street was the only fully paved road in the town and, as such, served as Ouray's main retail and tourist strip.

Within seconds, Casey was driving through the center of the tiny town, passing turn-of-the-century brick and Victorian structures that lined both sides of Main Street. She steered her Jeep left onto Sixth Avenue, passing City Hall, a brick building topped by a white clock tower and golden dome. Crossing Fourth Street, Casey slowed down as she approached the Ouray County Courthouse and adjoining Sheriff's Department, and she parked across the street.

As she trudged across the slushy dirt road, Casey saw three white Jeep Cherokees bearing County Sheriff's emblems parked perpendicular to the red brick building. As usual this time of year, the vehicles' doors and rear quarter-panels were caked in mud. Casey saw that Dr. Philips's blue Dodge Ram truck was sitting ten feet away from the other vehicles. A lump formed in Casey's throat when she first saw the wrecked truck, with its crushed roof.

She stopped in her tracks, surveying the damage from the middle of Sixth Avenue. "Good God!"

Sheriff Withers stood on the near side of the truck. A stocky man in his early fifties with thinning salt-and-pepper hair, Withers was wearing a tan uniform he had outgrown a number of pounds ago and a dark green jacket with a gold badge prominent on its breast. His hands were shoved into his jacket pockets as he spoke with two uniformed deputies who Casey recognized as Jill Samsky and Mark Turlington. Samsky was as tall as the sheriff at five-foot, ten inches with wavy dark-blonde hair that fell just over her jacket collar. Although Casey had few close friends her own age in Ouray, Jill always seemed glad to see her around town, taking time to chat with Casey whenever they met. Mark Turlington was roughly the same age as Casey and was the most junior deputy on the force.

On the truck's far side, Casey saw a hulking figure whose hands were resting on top of the Dodge Ram's cab as he stared through the vehicle's driver-side window. She shuddered involuntarily at the sight of the brutish-looking man who she knew was named Lyle. She had never learned his last name. On those rare occasions when she would pass the peculiar, long-haired man on the street in Ouray, she noticed that Lyle would look at her with a somewhat pained expression. As a result, Casey made a point to steer clear of the six-foot-six stranger whenever she saw him. It now appeared as if she would no longer be able to avoid him.

Casey remained standing in the middle of the slush-filled street, preferring not to approach the wrecked pickup truck. She was gripped by a strange notion that if she got any closer to Dr. Philips's truck, the awful possibilities concerning her landlord's disappearance would somehow become a reality. Seeing the young woman frozen in place, Lyle rounded the truck, said a few words to the sheriff and nodded in Casey's direction. Bill Withers and Jill Samsky turned and walked toward her, taking note of her bewildered expression.

Withers extended a beefy hand to Casey. He attempted a smile and asked in his usual coarse voice, "Were you able to find someone to look after your shop, Casey?"

Casey shook his hand weakly and nodded a perfunctory greeting to Jill. "Yeah, it's all taken care of," she pointed toward the pickup truck. "I had no idea it was that bad. No one could've walked away from that."

"I know," Withers replied solemnly. "The good news is that we don't think Jim was anywhere near the truck when it was hit."

Casey changed topics abruptly, pointing at Lyle Morrison. "What's he doing here?"

"Lyle was driving the snowplow that was involved in the collision. Do you know him?"

"No," she answered quickly. "Was he hurt?"

"Not in the accident. He got pretty banged up rappelling down into the gorge trying to rescue Jim, though."

Withers took Casey by the elbow and led her over to Dr. Philips's damaged vehicle. Lyle looked up and rested his arms across his barrel chest. He was wearing a blue and green plaid shirt under a faded blue down vest. His Wrangler jeans were tucked into a pair of worn brown work boots. Up close, the man was even larger than Casey had remembered.

Deputy Turlington walked up to her, whipped off his hat and thrust out his hand. A big, toothy grin spread across his freckled face. He started to blush even before he spoke. "Hi, Casey, Mark Turlington. We've met a few times before, mostly around town," he said, enthusiastically.

"Hey, lover boy," Withers barked, obviously perturbed by the young deputy's behavior. "Why don't you make yourself useful and see if Nancy needs a hand making phone calls up in the office."

His face now an even darker shade of red, Mark Turlington bowed his head toward Casey before turning and shuffling his way to the front of the building.

Withers shook his head and addressed Casey. "First of all, I want to assure you that we're gonna get to the bottom of this. Jim's been a good friend of mine ever since he moved here twelve years ago. So, let's get started. We'll begin with what we know about the accident last night. Then, we'll go over some of the things that we still haven't made sense of. We're going to need your help in piecing things together, so it's best that you know everything that we know. No holds barred, understood?"

Casey nodded her head. "Understood."

As the sheriff walked to the right rear of the pickup truck, Casey surveyed the damage up close. A long gouge had been ripped along the full length of truck's right side, creasing the passenger side door and puncturing the sheet metal above the vehicle's rear tires. The passenger window was shattered and bowed inward. A web-like pattern of cracks made it difficult to see through the still intact piece of reinforced glass.

"This truck was sitting in the middle of a hairpin turn," the sheriff began. "It was parked sideways so that it was straddling the right shoulder, its front end facing the gorge. Since the headlights were turned off, Lyle couldn't see it until it was too late. There was just no way to stop the snowplow in time, especially with how icy it was around the curve."

Withers now made a sweeping motion with his arms toward the truck. "The plow blade hit the pickup broadside and pushed it off the road. As you can see, none of the windows are busted out, so there's no way that Jim could've been thrown out of the truck when it bounced into the gorge."

Casey nodded toward the driver's side. "What if Dr. Philips was crouched down on the far side of the truck, putting on tire chains or something?"

"The chains are still in the back of his truck. We've searched around the crash site, but there's no evidence that anyone or anything other than the truck was pushed over the edge. To be on the safe side, I've got Ouray Mountain Rescue on standby. If we don't hear anything from Jim today, I'll mobilize the search team in the morning," Withers explained.

Casey was about to ask a question, but Jill cut her off.

"Even if we get the rescue squad started right now, the gorge will be dark in a couple of hours. Sometimes, you have to operate on gut instinct, and we just don't think that Dr. Philips was at the scene when the collision occurred. Just to make sure, we have two deputies riding along with the cee-dot snowplows today, checking the sides of the road. From up in the cab of the truck, they should be able to see if there are any footprints along the shoulder of the road. Also, they'll be looking for any impact craters along the canyon walls. That's what we'd expect to see if either a person or a second vehicle slipped off the road last night. In addition, we have our dispatcher working the phones inside. She's calling down to Silverton and Durango to see if Dr. Philips might be working some kind of medical emergency. On top of that, we're in the process of contacting everyone who we know are either friends or patients of Jim's, but we're going to need your help in compiling a better list."

Casey nodded her head. "You mentioned that you've found some things that don't make sense, right?"

"We had an unusual situation in the pass last night," Withers replied. "Cee-dot pulled a malfunctioning truck off the road and it took a while to get a replacement truck back up there. Phil Treacher was the last driver through the gorge before the accident occurred, and he swears that Jim's pickup truck wasn't there at 9:45 p.m. From the way it was parked, there was no way Phil could've missed seeing it. Anyway, Lyle started up the road a little past 11 p.m. and the accident happened around 11:20. That means that this truck must've been abandoned within the ninety-minute gap between Treacher's last pass and when Lyle got there. We checked with Silverton cee-dot, and their drivers don't remember seeing anyone driving from the south side of Red Mountain Pass toward Ouray during that timeframe. Apparently, the snowplow drivers had the roads pretty much to themselves last night."

Jill now took over the briefing. "Lyle didn't see any fresh tire tracks in the road on his way up from Ouray, but he did see some tracks on the far side of the accident site, leading away from Mother Cline."

"Who's Mother Cline?" Casey asked.

Withers and Samsky exchanges bemused smiles. Casey looked over at Lyle, who did not change his expression. Jill composed herself before answering. "Mother Cline is the name of an avalanche path. It's named after the Mother Cline Lode; an old mine that's set into the slopes above the highway."

"Sorry, I didn't know," Casey said defensively.

"Anyway, after the accident, the highway still had to be cleared," Jill continued. "Since our hands were full trying to pull Dr. Philips's truck out of the gorge, the State Police asked Silverton cee-dot to come over the summit of Red Mountain Pass and plow the road up to the accident site. At the time, no one had any idea that the tire tracks on the south side of the crash site might be important, and the Silverton driver plowed all trace of them off the road. When he called him this morning, he couldn't recall whether the tracks led all the way back to Silverton or not."

Casey nodded, thinking aloud. "So, if Dr. Philips got stuck and then got a lift, it was from someone who was originally headed over the pass from Silverton toward Ouray. If the tire tracks are any indication, then whoever picked him up must've turned around and driven all the way back to Silverton, even though it was in the middle of a snowstorm and Dr. Philips lives in Ouray. That doesn't make sense."

"Exactly, unless Jim had a real powerful reason for getting back to Silverton and he was able to convince the driver to give him a lift back down there," Withers replied. "But you're right. It would've been a lot easier to drive to Ouray than to head back to Silverton. We're talking about a three-mile drive compared to a twenty-mile drive."

As Casey digested this information, Withers moved the group over to the driver's side of the Dodge Ram, which had two large impact dents on the door and quarter-panel. "Can you give me a hand with this door again?"

Lyle Morrison walked over and grabbed the door handle. As he pried the door open, there was an accompanying squeal of metal scraping against metal. Lyle stood beside the open door, wincing slightly and absently exploring his ribcage with his fingers.

"After we're through here, you're gonna get those ribs x-rayed," Withers commanded.

"When we were able to take a good look at the truck this morning, we noticed a couple of things. First of all, Dr. Philips's medical bag was still in the cab of the truck," Samsky said.

"No way," Casey interjected. "I can understand him abandoning his truck, but not his black bag; not on purpose anyway."

"That's what we figured, too." The sheriff nodded toward his office. "We've got the bag upstairs. It doesn't look like anything's missing, but we want you to check it out as well."

Samsky resumed the briefing. "Lyle came by as we were going through the truck. He had a few questions of his own about the accident. Why don't you pick it up from here, Lyle?"

Lyle turned to address Casey. As their eyes met, the female deputy noticed that they seemed to be sizing up one another. Finally, Morrison spoke in a soft but deep voice.

"Just before I hit the truck, I could tell that its brake lights were on," he noted succinctly. "This morning, Jill found that rock inside the truck." He pointed to a large rock that was propped against the truck's front tire. The snow-encrusted boulder was roughly twelve inches in diameter.

"She found it wedged under the driver's seat. If it had been sitting on top of the brake pedal before the accident, then that would explain why the brake lights were shining even though there was no one inside the truck," he said.

"A rock on the brake pedal?" Casey asked Jill.

"Last night, Lyle also saw two deep ruts in the road that must've been made by the pickup truck's rear tires. The shoulder where the accident occurred is banked slightly uphill, which explains why the rear tires were spinning on the icy road," Samsky replied. "What doesn't make sense is that from the angle of the ruts, it looks like somebody was trying their damnedest to send Dr. Philips's truck off the edge of the shoulder."

Casey was stunned. "You mean drive it into the gorge? That's suicide!"

Sensing Casey's panic, Withers jumped in. "That's where the rock comes into play. Lyle thinks it was being used to keep pressure on the gas pedal while someone was trying to pop the clutch. Show her what you mean, Lyle."

Lyle climbed into the truck and sat on the bench seat. "Let's say that I was trying to send this truck off the shoulder of an icy road. If it had an automatic transmission, it wouldn't be much of a problem, but as you can see, Jim's truck has a stick shift." He pointed through the windshield. "As close as the truck was to the edge of the road, once I popped the clutch and got it moving forward, I wouldn't be able to jump out the door fast enough. Sitting where I am now, the truck's probably going to go over with me in it."

Lyle slid off the bench seat and got out of the truck. "Even a contortionist couldn't operate both the clutch and gas pedal without being inside the truck." He grabbed the armrest on the driver's side door with his left hand, then extended his right leg into the cab of the truck. He leaned back, bracing himself against the ground with his left leg. With his right boot, Lyle depressed the truck's clutch pedal.

"If I needed to, I could shift the truck into gear and pop the clutch this way, provided I had two things. Number one, I need to find a way to keep steady pressure on the gas pedal."

Casey nodded. "The rock."

Lyle continued, brushing his long gray hair away from his face. "The second thing I need is luck. I have to hope that the truck finds some good traction with its rear wheels along the ice, and I have to hope that the pickup's rear end doesn't swing to the left and sweep me off the road along with the truck."

"That makes sense," Casey agreed.

"From the looks of it, they didn't have much luck," Lyle said. "The rock they used was way too big. It covered both the brake and gas pedal, which means that the truck was braking and accelerating at the same time. That explains why they couldn't get any traction on the road. Also, you need to be gentle on the gas when you pop the clutch in first gear, otherwise the truck will jerk all over the place. As deep as those tires cut into the ice, it looks like someone was at it for a while."

"Keep in mind that this is just one theory," Sheriff Withers cautioned. "Jill's the Department's lead investigator, and we've been running other ideas past her all morning. At first, we thought that the deep tire ruts meant that Jim might've gotten stuck sideways on the road and kept spinning his tires trying to straighten it out."

Jill shook her head. "If that was the case, all he needed to do was let the truck roll backward away from the banked shoulder, then straighten out the tires. Whoever made those grooves was trying to go forward toward the gorge, not backward toward safety."

A thought occurred to Casey. "If somebody was trying to ditch the truck, why didn't they pick an easier place to send it off the road? There are plenty of places in the pass where the shoulder's more level and there's more room to maneuver."

"That hairpin turn is the perfect place to stage an accident, provided you can do it right," Samsky said. "If Lyle had seen a set of tracks heading off the road, everyone would've chalked it up to a combination of icy roads and careless driving. More likely, given the snowstorm and the road conditions last night, he never would've even noticed the tracks. In that case, it would've been spring before anyone might've spotted Jim's truck in the gorge."

Casey was letting this new information sink in, trying to envision the accident site. Withers reached into his jacket pocket and removed a cellular telephone that Casey recognized as Dr. Philips's.

"This was inside the truck as well. This morning, Jill decided to press the phone's redial button to see who Dr. Philips's last call had been to."

Withers pressed the button, then held it toward Casey so she could see the LED display. Against a green background there appeared three black digital numbers: 911. Withers spoke into the phone. "Hello Montrose, this is Bill Withers over in Ouray. Please disregard."

Casey felt queasy. Her ears began to ring and her knees suddenly felt rubbery. Samsky placed a hand under the petite woman's arm to steady her. Withers did not seem to notice. "Local 911 calls don't come to our office, so we checked on the 911 logs from Montrose, Durango and Silverton," he said. "No one had a record of receiving a call from Dr. Philips, but the Montrose police reported that they had two 911 hang-ups last night."

"Standard procedure on hang-ups is for the 911 operator to immediately call back the number that shows up on their screen. Unfortunately, they can't trace 911 calls coming from cellular phones," Jill pointed out. "One of the 911 hang-ups was received at 5:10 p.m. and the second was at 9:18 p.m. Neither one could be traced. Since we know that Dr. Philips made one of those calls, that means he found himself in trouble a good deal earlier than when we estimate his truck was abandoned. We don't know which call was his, though."

Withers wrapped up the discussion. "Well, Casey, that's all we have right now. I'm going to go check out the accident site one more time while it's still light out. Jill, you go with Casey to see if there's anything at Jim's house that might tell us what he was up to yesterday. We need to get a fix on his medical appointments and anything else that he had on his calendar."

"Are you okay to drive?" Jill asked a still-shaken Casey.

Casey nodded.

Lyle's beeper sounded just as a female voice could be heard from above. The Ouray Sheriff's Department dispatcher called down to the street. "Lyle, it's Hamp. Blue Willow just slid. He needs you up at the barn *now!*"

— Chapter 6 —

The wad of duct tape lay on the ground next to Dr. Philips; thick clumps of hair still clinging to the loose ball of grey material. The tape's removal had ravaged his eyebrows and left his remaining hair matted and sticky.

With the makeshift blindfold removed, he was able, finally, to see his surroundings. He was being held in a crude wooden shed that was twelve feet long and eight feet wide. A two-foot-square section of roofing was missing on the shed's far side. To Dr. Philips's dismay, the sunlight that slanted through the hole in the roof did not reach his corner of the shed. Frigid winds blew through the opening, raising thick swirls of spindrift along the snow-covered floor. The slanting roof rose from the top of a five-foot high wall on the shed's left side to a height of seven feet where it met the wall to his right. From his vantage point, Philips could see a patch of cobalt blue sky through the splintered hole in the roof. There were no mountains or trees visible through the opening, indicating that the shed was either above the timberline or in a wide clearing. He also noticed that the air he was breathing seemed thin. After even the slightest exertion, the doctor had to rest for long stretches to catch his breath. He could not tell if his sluggish condition was attributable to the lingering effects of the sedative or if it was altitude-related.

Philips had been working feverishly to free himself since the early morning hours. The task was complicated by freezing temperatures and his captor's confounding ingenuity. The doctor no longer had the overcoat he was wearing when he was abducted. His boots had also been taken. He had been left with only a pair of woolen socks to protect his feet from the frozen snow packed on the earthen floor. One end of a steel chain -- secured by a padlock -- had been looped tightly around his right ankle. The chain had then been snaked under the wooden slats of the shed wall behind him, leading to the shed's exterior. With each movement of his leg, the ice-cold chain dug into his bare skin. A separate chain was attached to the center of his handcuffs. It was likewise threaded through the narrow gap between the base of the wall behind him and the frozen ground. His wrists were chafed and bleeding from attempting to wriggle free of his handcuffs and from pulling against the chain. The thin woolen blanket that Paul Brader had left for his prisoner provided little warmth, so Dr. Philips used it to rub against his feet and hands in an attempt to ward off frostbite.

For the past three hours, Dr. Philips had been trying to break through the shed wall, which was constructed of two-by-six planks of wood. Although the unfinished wood was rough, splintered, and heavily knotted, it was solid enough to withstand a barrage of kicks and shoulder thrusts. There was little slack in the chains that emerged from under the wall, limiting his range of movement inside the shed. With only three feet of exposed chain available, he was unable to mount a running charge against the wooden walls. Through the gaps and knots in the planks, he could see that a dark brown metal skin had been affixed to the outside of the shed.

By yanking the chain attached to his right ankle, Dr. Philips was able to force the steel links between the vertical planks of two-by-sixes. Two hours ago, he had found a gap in the planks that coincided with a seam between two sheets of the metal skin. He had been powering up the chain in short bursts, trying to ignore the pain. His wrists were rubbed raw and bloody against the handcuffs.

His efforts had paid off. Inch by inch, he forced the chain up the wall.

The steel links had peeled apart the rusted exterior sheets of metal. Each time the chain became wedged between the two wooden planks, Dr. Philips found the strength to tug the chain upward, splintering the edges of the wood and widening the gap. The chain had ripped a thin opening between the planks from the floor up to waist-level. When the doctor peered through the gap, he could see the bright glare of sunlight reflecting off an expanse of pure white snow.

Philips knew that it was getting late in the day. By exerting himself, he had managed to keep his body heat from being sapped by the freezing environs. There was little he could do for his feet, however. His toes were stinging from the cold and the soles of his feet were becoming numb. With his body clearly succumbing, he was desperate not to spend another freezing night in the isolated shed.

The physician plopped down into a sitting position on the blanket and tried to kick the planks on either side of the inch-wide gap he had created. The handcuffs prevented him from bracing his hands on the ground behind him, so he leaned back and held onto the chain between his wrists for leverage. Pain shot up his legs each time he slammed his heels against the wood. After several kicks, he realized that the plank on the right side of the opening was beginning to yield. He continued stomping against the left edge of the two-by-six. Slowly, the plank loosened, its nails gradually relinquishing their rusty grip. Dr. Philips stood up and wrestled with the plank, twisting it from side to side, yanking it from the wall. A final tug sent him sprawling backward, the plank in his hands. Simultaneously, the chain around his ankle and the chain around the handcuffs became taut and stopped his backward momentum with a sudden jerk. He pitched to his right and tumbled awkwardly to the ground.

Next was the plank to the left of the opening. Despite driving a two-inch splinter into his right heel, he managed to kick and pull the second plank free within fifteen minutes. Wheezing for air, Dr. Philips got to his knees and shoved against the corrugated metal skin with all the strength he could muster. After prying open a foot-wide hole, he realized that a thick pile of snow had drifted against the base of the shed's exterior wall. Each time he pushed against the metal sheets, his already frozen hands and wrists would tunnel deeper into the snowdrift.

With a hole barely wide enough to crawl through, Dr. Philips poked his legs into the snowdrift and snaked his lower body through the opening. As he twisted onto his side and burrowed out of the shack, his tweed jacket ripped against the sharp edges of the rusted metal sheets. With much effort, he was able to wriggle his torso through the narrow opening as well. His entire body now—finally—outside the shed, he stood up and brushed clumps of snow off his head and clothing.

Jim Philips was momentarily blinded as his eyes were assaulted by the white glare around him. He scrunched his eyes and looked away from the shed for something dark to focus on. Cupping his hands around his face, he could make out a faint dark outline looming beyond the brilliant white foreground. Gradually, he brought the shape into hazy focus. He moved his hands away from his face; in the distance and slightly below him, Dr. Philips could see the telltale orange slopes of the Red Mountains. He immediately recognized his location; he was being held prisoner at the summit of Imogene Pass. The building he was confined to was a crude mining-era shack that sat twenty feet north of the crest of the summit.

"Lord, no!"

Instinctively, he spun to his right and looked up, where he knew he would find the ruins of Fort Peabody. Towering nearly a hundred feet above him atop a steep, snow-covered conical incline, he could barely recognize the tiny outpost's stone cairn and crumbling wooden frame. The ancient fort looked like a handmade ornament atop a huge white Christmas tree.

Twisting to his left, he saw below him the barren, snow-choked bowl of Imogene Basin. Looking above the rim of the basin, his eyes swept over the top of the dull gray slopes of Chicago Peak. Further to his left, the 13,275-foot summit of Mendota Peak was visible in the distance, almost at eye-level. Making a full circle, he could see plainly the snow-capped summits of Telluride Peak and Trico Peak. Even though both of the peaks were over 13,000 feet tall, Dr. Philips did not have to shift his gaze upward to see the pinnacles of either mountain.

Dr. Philips's knees began to tremble. He fought to maintain his balance as a wave of vertigo swept through him. Standing in a frozen, wispy snowscape perched more than 13,000 feet above sea level, the doctor could not shake the bizarre notion that he was stranded on a cloud. Had he been able to walk twenty feet to the summit, he would have seen the distant rooftops of Telluride below, nestled in a box canyon to the southwest, nearly 5,000 feet below him.

Now painfully aware of both the depth of his isolation and the madness of his captor, his heart sank as he dropped to his knees in the snow. The daylong struggle to extricate himself from the shed had kindled his hopes of escape. Now, slumped on his knees atop Imogene Pass he knew that the odds were stacked overwhelmingly against him. Dr. Philips had no earthly idea how he could ever manage to descend -- or how anyone could possibly climb up and save him

Imogene Pass, the second highest vehicular pass in America, stands 13,114 feet above sea level. Even on dry summer days, the steep, forbidding jeep road that connects Ouray and Telluride presents a formidable test for off-road adventurers. While most other vehicular passes in the San Juan Mountains remain open to car and jeep traffic year-round, Imogene Pass is usually closed from late September until the following July. During seasons of particularly heavy snow and avalanche activity, Imogene Pass is inaccessible the entire year.

In the long San Juan winters, Imogene Pass is a desolate, lifeless place where temperatures plummet to twenty or thirty degrees lower than those experienced five-thousand feet below in Ouray and Telluride. While local heli-skiing operators have been known to fly thrill-seeking clients up to Imogene Basin, it is considered, at best, a risky proposition. Even the most extreme of the local extreme sports enthusiasts know that the sheer walls surrounding the basin are generally too steep and avalanche-prone for enjoyable backcountry bowl skiing or snowmobiling.

Dr. Philips rose slowly to his feet and faced the shed. In a state of shock and bewilderment, the physician did not notice that his feet and ankles had become dangerously numb as he stood in his stocking feet in the snow. To his left, two feet from the southeast corner of the shack, he spied an old gray mailbox made of tin. The loaf-shaped mailbox sat atop a brown steel pole. Dr. Philips saw that the far ends of both chains had been secured to the base of the mailbox's post with two separate pad-locks. He hunched down and thrust his shoulder against the pole. It did not budge. The elderly man then grabbed the ice-cold post between his hands. Leaning back, he attempted to shake the post loose from whatever was holding it in place beneath the snow-covered ground. He was unable to move the pole even a fraction of an inch.

Upon closer inspection, he saw that the tin mailbox rested atop a platform made of a foot-long slab of inch-thick steel. Looking under the mailbox, the doctor saw that the platform had been welded to the top of the pole, forming a t-joint. Since the chains had been fastened tightly around the base of the pole, he knew that it would be impossible to slide the chain up the pole and over the wide platform. Dr. Philips opened the tin door on the front side of the mailbox and looked inside. It was empty.

Leaning against the mailbox, Dr. Philips assessed his situation. His an-kle and his wrists were tethered to a steel post that was unmovable. His previous efforts to pick the handcuffs and padlocks with nails and screws had proved futile. Even if he were somehow able to unshackle himself, he still had to deal with the fact that his boots had been taken away. The long, steep climb down to Telluride or the highway at Red Mountain Pass would force him to wade through shoulder-deep snowdrifts. His body was being ravaged by prolonged exposure to the cold, and he hadn't eaten in over twenty-four hours.

As the sun began to slip behind the mountains to the west, Dr. Philips felt a bone-rattling shiver attack his body. To the east, the snow-laden peaks of the Red Mountains were still bathed in weak winter sunlight while the pumpkin-colored slopes below were cloaked in shadow. Dr. Philips pulled on his lapels to wrap his tweed jacket snug around his torso. A sudden blast of wind crested the summit of Imogene Pass, en-gulfing the physician in a cloud of spindrift. As the twilight faded, Dr. Philips walked toward the hole in the shed wall and lowered himself to his knees. With a sigh of resignation, he began crawling back into the shed.

— Chapter 7 —

Paul Brader had made several circuits of downtown Telluride in his black Chevy Suburban, but the aimless driving was serving a purpose. Driving somewhere, anywhere, was better than sitting in his office, ducking phone calls from his broker. Piloting the Suburban through the crowded streets also gave him a sense of forward movement: something that was lacking in the waiting game he was playing with Jim Philips.

Although his scheme required patience, ever since he set it in motion, Brader had felt like a caged animal. Driving past The Petal Pusher, Brader resisted the urge to find a parking space and see if Casey Bailey had anything to offer about the disappearance of her landlord. Rather than risk telegraphing his involvement in the matter, he decided to let things— including the investigation by Ouray law enforcement agencies—run their course.

He turned his attention back to something he could control: his upcoming encounter with Jim Philips. Soon he would be able to face down, on his own terms, the man who held the key to his financial solvency. As he began to mentally script their discussion, the ringing of his mobile phone interrupted his thoughts.

He snatched the phone from the truck's console. "Yes?"

"Paul, I'm calling on my cell phone from the lobby of my building," Al Vaughn informed him, "If Joe Deutch knew I was talking to you, he'd call me on the carpet. You haven't returned three days' worth of calls from him and he's in my office every hour, asking if I've heard from you. He's the firm's senior partner and he's not used to his having his clients duck him."

"Relax, Al," Brader replied to his New York based broker. "I'm not ducking him, I'm just waiting for a few things to happen on this end before I tell him how to handle the situation for me."

"*You're* going to tell *him* how to handle it? Paul have you seen the ticker today? This isn't a situation; it's a disaster! That short-sell play is eating up your portfolio like a flesh-eating virus. You're down from thirty million to less than five million. You could be wiped out by the time tomorrow's final bell sounds! It's getting awful close to margin call time, my friend."

"It's still my money, Al. I don't care what Deutch says; I'm not going to bail out yet. Like I said, I've got some other things working that'll make up for all this. I'm only going to cut my losses until I can afford to make a clean break, and that time is coming soon. Tell Deutch to stop calling me."

"He's pulled me off your account. I can't tell him anything! Paul, as a friend, I'm telling you; it's time to admit that you got burned on this one. You've got to get past the pride issue. Cut your losses before it's too late."

"I'm hanging up now, Al," Brader announced irritably, "But I want you to go into Joe Deutch's office and remind him that I've made your firm a ton of money in fees over the past ten years. If he places a margin call, I'm never going to trade with you guys again."

Brader terminated the call, cutting off Al Vaughn in mid-sentence. He knew that he couldn't stop the bomb from exploding. Joe Deutch was going to place a margin call in the next few days, and it didn't matter if he contacted his client or not. The firm had access to his portfolio and could liquidate his holdings on a moment's notice.

Brader hated to admit it, but Al Vaughn was right. He'd been burned by the same network of information peddlers who had supplied him with the choicest grist for his investment mill. He'd been fed a tantalizing tidbit of insider sweetmeat about a fledgling pharmaceutical company that was conducting clinical trials of a new blood pressure medicine. His tipster shared the news that there had been an alarming number of deaths among patients participating in the tests. The results of the study were going to be published during the last week of February, and Brader had decided to short-sell the stock in early February. Unable to finance the transaction with cash, he borrowed $5 million on margin from his brokerage firm, using a portion of his portfolio as collateral.

By betting that the disappointing clinical results would drive down the price of the company's stock, Brader stood to profit handsomely. When the pharmaceutical stock continued to climb in early February, he continued short-selling the stock, utilizing an even greater portion of his portfolio to finance the transaction with each up-tick in price. Despite daily warnings from Al Vaughn, Brader stubbornly held his position, unwilling to consider the humiliating prospect of having bet on the wrong side of the securities equation.

When nearly 60 percent of his portfolio was margined as collateral to cover his mounting losses, Brader decided to hedge his bets. He accelerated his discussions with Saratoga Mining about the purchase of Divining Rod Enterprises: the company he jointly owned with Jim Philips. Willing to accept any type of deal that would offset his short-sell losses, Brader was quickly able to negotiate the framework of the buyout of Divining Rod Enterprises by the multinational mining conglomerate. When Dr. Philips refused to consider the sale of Divining Rod to a prospective suitor, Brader became convinced that he had to force the issue at any cost. It was then that he began to formulate his plan to protect his financial future.

On Monday morning, Brader received a crushing bit of news from Al Vaughn. Select industry investment specialists had been given a preview of the pharmaceutical company's clinical test data, which was scheduled for general release on Friday. Not only had the drug been proven effective, there was speculation that the company would immediately attract the attention of larger, acquisition-minded drug companies. Researchers had explained away the relatively high number of patient deaths as a statistical anomaly; the pool of patients selected for the study had simply included a disproportionate number of high-risk candidates. There was no indication that the blood pressure medication had any effect on patient mortality rates.

Brader had known on Monday that he would be wiped out by Friday. It was now Wednesday and the stock price was climbing even faster than anticipated. The purchase price that he had negotiated for Divining Rod would result in a $12 million windfall, somewhat offsetting the $30 million loss that he was about to incur. The net effect was that he wouldn't have to alter his lifestyle in the least. He would simply have fewer dollars to invest in the market. It was vital, however, that a margin call not be placed prior to the Saratoga deal. If he were forced to immediately liquidate all of his assets, he would lose his current stake in Divining Rod Enterprises, which would ruin him.

— Chapter 8 —

Casey stood in Dr. Philips's kitchen, pouring boiling water from a cast-iron kettle into two glass mugs. She dipped a teabag in each mug and walked into the living room where Jill Samsky was leaning against the arm of an oversized couch that was upholstered in a Navajo-style print. The deputy was finishing a telephone conversation with Sheriff Withers.

The house's open floor plan yielded a large open area on its main floor which contained the living room, dining area and a pass-through to the kitchen. In the front of the house were the master bedroom and a second bedroom that had been converted into Dr. Philips's office and den. A mud room connected the two-car garage and the kitchen. With its floor-to-ceiling windows and comfortable, inviting furniture, the living room had always been a hub of activity.

Casey brought the two steaming cups into the living room and sat in an upholstered chair that faced the couch. She pushed a mug across a low, bleached-wood coffee table toward Jill, who had rolled the sleeves of her tight-fitting uniform shirt up to her elbows.

Behind Casey's chair, several manila file folders and a black leather-bound appointment book were arranged on the dining room table.

Jill's dark green uniform jacket and her holster were draped over the back of one of six dining room chairs.

"Bill wants to see what we've come up with, so he's heading over here now. Since we're striking out on all other fronts, he's given the rescue team the green light to start searching the Uncompahgre Gorge tomorrow morning around eight," Jill said.

"This whole thing seems so unreal," Casey said, sitting back in her chair. "I feel guilty about going through Dr. Philips's personal stuff. I keep thinking he's going to walk through the front door any second now."

"With any luck, he will and this will all be over," the deputy replied in a comforting tone. "Hey, I've been meaning to ask you something. Why do you always call him 'Doctor Philips' instead of 'Jim' or 'Doc'?"

"Mimi used to tease me about the same thing. I don't know. Somehow, it just doesn't sound right coming out of my mouth. I mean, it's not as if we're formal around each other; we get along great. Maybe it's on account of my Yankee upbringing."

Jill laughed and looked around the living room. "I haven't been here since Mimi's last Christmas party. How has Jim been handling life without her?"

"The fact that her death was expected may have helped some. They packed a lot of living into their last year together. This might sound awful, but toward the end, the cancer was mercifully quick," Casey said.

Jill nodded. "Still, it must've been tough for you to live here once Mimi found out her condition was hopeless."

"I offered to find a new place so they could have some privacy, but neither one of them would hear of it. They wanted to keep everything as normal as possible. On Sundays, my day off, Mimi would practically chase me out of the house, telling me that a young girl like me should be out enjoying herself, not wasting time gabbing with an old lady. She just didn't want anybody fussing over her. Can you imagine that? The woman who used to fuss over everyone she ever met didn't want any of the same in return. She would've made the perfect grandmother."

Jill shook her head. "Strange how things works out some times. People like Mimi and Jim wind up unable to have children while a lot of other couples don't seem to appreciate the ones they have."

"You can say that again," Casey nodded slowly and stared into her mug before continuing. "I was worried when I first moved in that Mimi was just looking for someone to mother. I couldn't figure out why a couple with such a great house, no money problems and no kids would want to take in a border."

"Well, why did they?"

"It was all Mimi's doing," Casey said. "When I first moved from Connecticut three years ago, I was renting a place month-to-month up in Ridgway. Over in Telluride, there's a waiting list a mile long for decent rental properties, so I took the first room that I could find in Ridgway. One Sunday three summers ago, I signed up for one of those guided jeep tours into Yankee Boy and Governor Basin and wound up getting assigned to the same jeep as Mimi and Dr. Philips. We all got to talking and the next thing I knew, Mimi was offering me their upstairs bedroom. It was too good a deal to pass up."

"Knowing Mimi, that doesn't surprise me at all," Jill replied. "But still, there must be times when you wish you had your own place. I mean, let's say you meet a guy. It's not like you can just invite him to spend the night after a date."

Casey blushed. "That isn't a problem I've had to deal with yet. Most of the guys I date live over in Telluride, so I just stick around after work, go out to dinner or whatever, then drive myself back to Ouray."

Jill eased forward on the couch, an impish grin spreading across her face. "But let's say one of those dates is going really well, if you know what I mean. It must be weird to have to call Dr. Philips to tell him you're not coming home that night, right?"

Casey's face and neck turned a bright shade of crimson. "I've never had to make that kind of phone call."

Jill was nearly off the couch. "*In three years*? What's wrong with you? I thought Telluride is where it is that beautiful people come from."

Casey snickered. "The beautiful people I've met are either married, ski bums or just in town for a long weekend. Then they get back on their private jets and fly back to wherever it is that beautiful people come from.

I prefer the down-to-earth type."

"What about Mark Turlington? He had those puppy dog eyes working overtime on you outside the Sheriff's Office today. Why not give him a shot? He might not be the kind of hard-charger that you're looking for, but he's a nice enough guy."

"Who says I'm looking for a hard-charger?" Casey asked with a slightly hurt look on her face. "Truth is, I'm not really looking for anyone right now. My life pretty much revolves around the flower shop."

Samsky threw up her hands. "Suit yourself, but you're not gettin' any younger."

Casey decided to turn the tables on the deputy. "What about you? You have your own place, but I never see you with a steady guy."

"In a town of less than seven hundred, there's only a handful of available guys to choose from, and a lot of them don't feel comfortable dating someone who has the power to arrest them," Jill answered. "And in my line of work, a lot of the guys I meet on the job are not exactly the cream of the crop in Ouray County. So, I usually spend date night up in Montrose where the pool of talent is a lot bigger. Nothing serious yet, but as we say in the investigation business, I'm working on a couple of leads."

The doorbell rang. Casey walked down the hallway to the front door, then led the sheriff back to the living room. Bill Withers placed his hat on the arm of the sofa and pulled up a chair near the stacks of papers that were spread out on the dining room table. Casey and Jill joined him.

Withers placed his elbows on the table and said to Casey, "Here's where we are." He counted out the items on his fingers as he spoke. "We're going to continue calling Jim's pager number every hour. Debbie, our dispatcher, is taking care of that."

Casey interrupted. "Does that mean I should stop? I've tried his pager about a dozen times so far."

"It's up to you. Don't feel like you have to, though; we've got it covered," he continued. "We're having Jim's cell phone and the inside of his truck dusted for prints by the State Police Forensics Unit. Unfortunately, we pawed everything over pretty good before we realized we might have a crime on our hands, so I don't know if the Staties are going to find anything. Just the same, I may need to send someone over here in case we need to get a set of Jim's fingerprints."

Casey nodded. "I won't run the dishwasher. There are a couple of drinking glasses in there that he used yesterday morning."

"Good idea." The sheriff shifted his weight in the chair. "Word back from Red Mountain Pass is that they can't find any footprints along the road on either side of the accident site, and there's no sign that another car might have slid off the highway. Tomorrow morning, we're going to send Ouray Mountain Rescue down into the gorge."

"I want to be there. Tell me where and when."

The sheriff mulled it over before responding. "That's probably not such a good idea, Casey. The people on the rescue team are trained for this type of work. Things could get pretty hairy down in the gorge. If one of those huge icicles falls down from Ruby Walls or if Riverside Slide decides to let loose, it's good night, Irene."

Casey looked him squarely in the eye. "I mean no disrespect, Sheriff, but I *need* to be involved in that search. Please don't tell me I can't."

Withers shrugged. "Suit yourself. We're meeting in the turnout just above the snowshed at eight in the morning. You can show up, but the final decision's not up to me. Lyle Morrison is the captain of the squad and it's strictly his call."

"The snowplow guy? In the past three years I've only seen the guy a handful of times, but ever since the accident, it seems like he's involved in everything."

"Not really," Withers replied calmly. "On my side of the world, I run into Lyle all the time. I think the two of you just run in different circles. Anyway, when it comes to search and rescue, Lyle's the best man in the San Juans."

Jill nodded in agreement.

The sheriff hesitated before continuing, "Lyle wouldn't want me to spread this around, but he also happens to be a bona-fide war hero. I should know. I spent eight months in the jungle with him and there's no one I'd rather have on my side; and I don't just mean as a soldier."

Jill appeared confused by her boss's comment. "I never knew that you and Lyle knew each other before he moved out here."

"And I'd appreciate it if you would keep that to yourself. For a lot of guys, including Lyle, the past is the past. He wanted to come out here to start from scratch. Let's just leave it at that. The guy feels guilty as hell about the accident and I don't want Casey to get the wrong idea about him."

Casey proceeded cautiously. "What kind of past is he trying to leave behind?"

Withers took a deep breath and shook his head. "I knew I shouldn't have said anything. Lyle Morrison's just a guy who needed a quiet place to put some pieces back together. And that's all I'm going to say."

He terminated the line of discussion by pointing to the files stacked on the table. "What do we have here?"

Picking up a black leather appointment book, Jill began the briefing. "There are three handwritten notations on Dr. Philips's calendar for yesterday. The first is just a name: Meg Gleason. She's down for one o'clock in the afternoon."

"We know about that one," Withers announced. "Meg is a patient of Jim's. She lives down in Silverton and is seven months pregnant. Apparently, Jim called her on Monday, saying that he was going to be in Silverton on Tuesday, so he scheduled her for a house call. He showed up at one o'clock and spent about thirty minutes with her. She recalls Jim telling her that he was planning to be in town for most of the afternoon."

"Then at two-thirty there's the name Sara Moultrie," Jill continued.

"Also lives in Silverton," Withers said, "Her brother Sam's a helicopter pilot for a charter outfit out of the Montrose Airport. He earned his wings in the Army, but got booted out for getting drunk and taking a swing at an officer. I've had some dealings with him over the years, but Sara seems nice enough. We'll give her a call. Jim may have said something to her about what he planned to do after he left Silverton."

"The third notation seems to be at five o'clock and it's just two words: Mineral King," Jill said.

"Isn't Mineral King the company that's managing the Superfund cleanup project up in Red Mountain Pass?" Casey asked.

"That's part of it," the sheriff agreed. "The Mineral King Mining Company has two idle surface plants; one in Red Mountain and one over in Pandora. The cleanup project is pretty much done. There are only a couple of people working part-time at both of the surface plants. They monitor the dumpsites and try to keep the surface plants from falling apart in case the company ever decides to get things cranked up again. It all has to do with ore prices. Anyway, they've pretty much shut the place down, so I doubt that Jim had an appointment with the company. Maybe that notation is just to remind him about a phone call he wanted to make around five o'clock. I'll have Mark Turlington do some poking around tomorrow at the Red Mountain surface plant. I'll also try to raise one of the part-timers on the telephone and see if they know anything about Dr. Philips."

"In terms of the timeline," Jill explained, "we know that Dr. Philips spent yesterday morning in Ouray. We now know that he drove to Silverton to keep his one o'clock appointment with Meg Gleason, then probably saw Sara Moultrie at two-thirty. In calling around today, our dispatcher also found out that he visited with his friends Earl and Elisabeth Truman in Silverton 'til around four o'clock, which is right around the time the snowstorm started. The timing makes sense if he wanted to keep a five o'clock appointment or phone call that had something to do with Mineral King. We can assume that he took Highway 550 through Red Mountain Pass since it's the only way to get from Silverton and Ouray in the winter. He was expected at the Ouray Elk's Club meeting last night at seven o'clock. He never made it."

Casey pointed to the appointment book. "I'd like to know more about that Mineral King thing."

Jill lifted one of the manila folders and flipped through it. "That brings us to these. Casey and I found over a dozen folders in Jim's study that have to do with mining claims and mining patents. The documents look pretty complicated. There are at least five different corporations involved and there's a slew of corporate filings and agreements: all related to mining claims and mineral rights. We haven't gone through the files with a fine tooth comb, but Casey recognized one of the names that appears in several of the documents. It's a guy named Paul Brader, who's one of Casey's big clients over in Telluride."

"The Master of the Market," Casey said. When Bill Withers looked at her curiously, she explained. "He's one of those Horatio Alger-types who was born with nothing and got filthy rich by playing the stock market. He gives investment seminars once a month in Telluride but I've never gone to one. My take on the whole thing is that he's doing it to stroke his own ego and to meet girls."

Jill laughed. "Do you mistrust everybody or it is just men?"

Withers took the folders and arranged them in a stack in front of him. "I doubt that these files have anything to do with our investigation. If I think we need to look at them, I'll meet with Jim's lawyer up in Montrose."

"From what I saw, those documents could have a *lot* to do with the investigation. I'll admit that I didn't understand half of what I was looking at, but it sure seems like it involved a lot of money. And what's strange is that Dr. Philips never mentioned anything to me about owning any mining claims," Casey said as she pointed to the folders. "I'd like to spend some more time with those files."

Withers placed them on the rug next to his feet. "If Jim wants to share these files with you, he can do so when he gets back. Until then, I'm keeping them with me."

Casey set her jaw and glared at Bill Withers. The man's tone reminded her of her late father, who was often stern and heavy-handed while rearing Casey and her younger sister. Since her mid-teens, Casey had made her own decisions, free of the strong opinions and bombastic edicts of Samuel Bailey. In subsequent years, she made it a point never to be bullied by anyone who used bluster and puissance instead of reason to settle differences of opinion.

Jill tried to ease the obvious tension in the room. "I'm sure that Bill's just protecting the doctor's privacy. Besides, he's got a badge and a gun, so I wouldn't argue about what he can and can't do."

Casey let out a long sigh and slumped in her chair. "I'm sorry, Sheriff. I know you want to figure this whole thing out as much as I do. It's so damn frustrating! I'm ready to leap at anything that holds even the slightest bit of promise. I just want Doctor Philips back home, that's all."

"I know, Casey," Withers replied, "I promise you that no stone will go unturned. But you have to give me some leeway on what I think needs to be investigated and what needs to remain confidential."

Casey nodded. "That pretty much wraps things up here," Jill said. "As I said on the phone, Casey and I only did a top-line search of Jim's office. We didn't go through his phone records, bank statements, that kind of stuff. We concentrated on retracing his steps on Tuesday."

Withers stood up, the stack of folders under his arm. "I'd like Jill to stay here with you tonight," he said to Casey. "I'm not trying to scare you; I just think it might be best to have someone else in the house until we can get a handle on what's happened to Jim."

Casey smiled at Jill. "She's been great company, but I'll be fine. I didn't get much sleep last night and I doubt I'm going to sleep any better tonight. If I change my mind, I've got Jill's number."

Despite the sheriff's protestations, Casey saw them to the door. As she waved goodbye and closed the door, the house suddenly seemed empty, quiet and cold. She tossed two logs into the fireplace and lit the gas flame. Realizing that she had not checked in with Jason Zuckerman, she called him at his apartment in Telluride. He picked up on the first ring. He explained that he was on his way out to do some after-hours snowboarding with a group of friends.

"Sorry to bug you at home, Jason. How'd things go today?"

"A record day for sales! The new buy-one, get-five-free policy that I instituted is turning out to be a real barn-burner. I tell you, I'm a regular P. T. Barnum."

Casey laughed in spite of her dark mood. "You'll run me out of business in no time. Any problems or messages?"

"No problems, just messages. I have them written down on a pad in the shop, but I think I can remember the biggies. Let's see, your mom called. She didn't *exactly* ask me when you were gonna give up this pipe dream and come back to Connecticut where you belong, but I think that was the underlying message."

"Great," Casey said. "What else?"

"We got a cancellation for the Catalano wedding. Nothing against us, the lovebirds just decided to postpone. They'll let us know if the nuptials get rescheduled."

"We'll have to eat that one. The ceremony was supposed to be a week from Saturday and I've already placed the order. I'll take the centerpieces over to the Visitor's Center and we'll spread the rest of the flowers around to our restaurant accounts. Anything else?"

"Sissy Brader called wanting to know if you could be a *dear* and drop by her house sometime tomorrow. They're hosting a party on Sunday night and the house would look absolutely naked without some of your inspired designs. Those are her words, not mine."

"I figured that out. Speaking of tomorrow, I'm not going to be at the shop until sometime in the afternoon. I feel awful asking you to look after the store by yourself again, but there's a search going on tomorrow and I want to be part of."

Jason's tone turned serious. "I understand. Still no word, huh?"

"No."

"Do you want to talk about it?"

"No, besides, those miscreants that you call friends are waiting on you. I'll fill you in tomorrow. Just don't break anything important tonight. I need you in one piece."

"Number one: I'm going to look up the word miscreant, and I might have a word or two for you when I see you tomorrow. Number two: I can assure you that all of my floral-related appendages will still be intact in the morning. Goodnight, Casey, and try to get some sleep."

Casey hung up the phone and sat down heavily in Dr. Philips's chair near the fireplace. A loud rumbling in her stomach reminded her that she hadn't eaten all day. She briefly considered making herself a sandwich, but decided that she had neither the appetite nor the inclination. She picked up the phone, murmured a short, wistful prayer, then dialed the pager number that she now knew by heart.

— Chapter 9 —

The Blue Willow slide path crossed the Million Dollar Highway roughly 400 feet north of the Blue Point slide, which Hamp and his men had cleared just three days earlier. The crew had been gouging away at the massive debris pile for the better part of the day. Although at 9:00 p.m. it was pitch dark in the pass, the highway was flooded with light from four orange-painted CDOT vehicles. Every member of Patrol 14 was at the scene, as was as a sergeant from the Colorado State Patrol barracks in Montrose. The snow mass had been whittled to a fraction of its original size but remained, in sections, as tall as the trucks and tractors that were working to remove it.

Since 101 known avalanche paths cross US Highway 550, this type of operation was all too familiar to CDOT Patrol 14. Hamp did not need to provide direction; each man knew his assignment. They were working the north side of the slide pile, trying to punch a hole in the right flank of the towering heap of snow, rocks and timber. Once the wall of snow was breached, they would be able to work both sides of the snow mass.

Five passenger vehicles were parked on the south side of the avalanche pile, waiting until a path wide enough to accommodate safe passage could be established. Since the Blue Point slide was less than a tenth of a mile behind them, the motorists had been advised to park their vehicles at the midpoint between the two avalanche crossings. For those travelling to Ouray, Ridgway, Montrose and destinations further north, there was no easy alternative to waiting patiently for the road to be cleared. Those unwilling to wait were advised to turn their vehicle around, drive south on US Highway 550 over the 11,075-foot summit of Red Mountain Pass to Silverton, then continue south over two other mountain passes to Durango, then west on Route 160 toward Cortez, then northeast on Route 145 over Lizard Head Pass toward Telluride, then west through Placerville, then east on Route 62 to Ridgway. This 236-mile loop, known as the San Juan Skyway, would deposit them a mere 20 miles north of their current position on US Highway 550.

A cluster of motorists were leaning against their vehicles, passing the time swapping tales about near-misses with the unpredictable avalanche paths along Red Mountain Pass. Frequent travelers on US Highway 550 also knew from personal experience the monotony of being stuck for days between avalanche slides.

Hamp made sure the stranded motorists were kept apprised of his crew's progress. When a member of his patrol took a break, they would often climb over the top of the debris pile with thermos in hand to dispense updates and hot coffee. Common courtesy was not uncommon in this section of the country. In the San Juan Mountains, the harsh climate, rugged terrain and uncertain transportation routes necessitated a heightened level of interdependence among residents, which in turn fostered a strong sense of community.

Lyle Morrison had been operating the 950 Cat for the past three hours. With a high-pitched whirl, the rotary blower mounted in front of the tall tractor churned through the base of the thick debris pile. The circular blades of the blower gouged into the packed snow, dislodging it from the debris pile and shooting it at high speed through a chute that protruded from the blower's right side. Lyle sat in the cab, urging the rotary blower forward and sending a thick, thirty-foot tall spray of white powder into the upper branches of the firs, spruces and aspens on the right side of the road.

After hours of powering steadily through the base of the pile with the blower, Lyle saw the top of the mass begin to crumble. He backed the Cat 950 away from the debris pile just as the entire right side of the structure collapsed on itself. Lyle waved to Arnie Watson, who was operating the 14-foot bull plow. Arnie entered the area vacated by the rotary blower and lowered the bulldozer's massive plow blade to the asphalt. He sounded the horn to alert anyone who might be loitering on the far side of the slide, then sent the tractor lurching forward. Powering through a three-foot-deep, fifteen-foot-long pile of loosened snow, the bull plow emerged on the far side of the slide path to the cheers of the motorists. The first goal of the operation had been accomplished; Patrol 14 had punched a hole in the beast.

As Watson worked to widen the hole, passenger vehicles cranked to life in anticipation of impending departure north. Lyle climbed down from the tractor and stretched his legs. He walked fifty yards up the highway and swiveled his head from side to side in an effort to loosen his tight neck muscles. Away from the noise and the flashing lights, he gazed up between the rows of tall spruce trees that lined both sides of the highway. He exhaled and watched as his frozen breath wafted up into the night sky.

In the thin, clear air of the cloudless alpine sky, the stars above glistened like pure white gems strung on invisible necklaces, haphazardly tossed into the heavens. Having lived in Denver for most of his life, where smog and streetlights in the sprawling metropolis allowed only the most prominent constellations to be seen in the night sky, Lyle found delight in the simple interplay of light and darkness. Rather than appearing flat and opaque, the sky above Ouray County seemed vast and multi-faceted as it spilled over the horizon.

As he stared into the sky, he reflected on the day's events. Despite all that had occurred within the past twenty-four hours, the one image that immediately sprang to mind was that of Casey Bailey standing beside Dr. Philips's wrecked pickup. The sight of the thin-boned, blonde-haired woman always evoked powerful emotions in him, but speaking with her today for the first time was nearly too much for him to bear.

He had listened to Casey's speech patterns, studied her eyes and body type, and noted the young woman's habit of tucking her hair behind her right ear with her index finger. He was unsure whether he had noticed genuine similarities between the twenty-six-year-old florist and his thirty-one-year-old daughter, or if he was merely trying to mentally bridge the gap between the two women. Maybe he was attributing to Emily Morrison those traits he noticed in Casey Bailey, or perhaps it was vice-versa. After all, it had been twenty-five years since he last saw Emily. As he recalled his last encounter with his daughter, Lyle dropped his gaze to the pavement and felt his heart being seared anew.

Emily Morrison, dressed in a sky-blue snowsuit, struck a defiant pose in the middle of her bedroom. Behind her, three suitcases were stacked atop a bed that had been stripped of its linens. With his wife Anne standing impatiently behind him, Lyle pleaded with the five-year-old girl not to leave. The tow-headed child placed her mittens on her hips. With all the anger the child could muster, Emily laid bare the facts to her hulking father.

"Mommy and I are going somewhere you can't find us. One day we'll find a daddy who wants us and loves us. We're leaving and you can't stop us."

It had been over two decades since his wife Anne had informed him that she was leaving and taking their daughter, Emily, with her. Lyle had implored her to give him the time he needed to straighten himself out. He tried to make her understand that only six months earlier he had been fighting for his life in a world turned upside-down; a world where a faceless enemy hid behind the eyes of women and children; a world where the very soil itself could erupt in chaos as black-clad warriors emerged from a network of earthen tunnels to ambush the American interlopers.

Anne would not listen. She informed him that he was not the same man who she had packed off to war two years earlier. The man who emerged from the jungle was distant, cold and frightening. Lyle's violent nightmares, incapacitating flashbacks and lack of intimacy were the least of her worries, she explained. She feared for Emily. A father who retreated into long periods of isolation and refused to embrace his only child would shatter Emily's self-image permanently.

Why, Anne asked him, had he refused to seek comfort and solace in her arms? Why couldn't he explain in detail what had happened to him in Vietnam and Cambodia? Why wouldn't he share with her the stories of heroism that were reflected in an array of medals and commendations tucked away in the bottom of his army-issue duffel bag?

Lyle could not enunciate his reasons for keeping such memories buried until he could face them; that they were too fresh and too gruesome to share. On being discharged, Lyle knew that returning immediately to his family was a mistake, but he also knew that the alternative would have been equally as damaging. Two of the remaining members of his platoon had planned to gradually immerse themselves back into "the world" by spending six months on a remote Greek Island. Unlike Lyle, however, they did not have a wife and five-year-old waiting for them at home.

Six months later, Lyle was clinging desperately to Anne and Emily, hoping that he could change their mind by hugging them closer. Emily screamed and Anne pushed him away. Downstairs, Lyle could hear their front door opening and the authoritative voice of Anne's brother Tom, an off-duty state police officer, asking if everything was okay. Lyle sat on his daughter's bed and watched his wife and child walk out of his life. Through the upstairs window he could see Anne's Chevy Nova receiving an escort away from their home.

"Hey, Lyle! You with us?" Hamp called from twenty yards away.

Lyle turned to face the man who was striding up the highway toward him. He shrugged and nodded toward the sky. "Just admiring the scenery."

As both men looked up, they heard the distinctive sound of a helicopter hovering above the mountains to their west. The lights of the craft were barely visible through the upper boughs of the trees in the foreground.

"That's strange," Hamp declared. "Who'd be crazy enough to be flying up there at this time of night? He's taking a helluva chance."

Having been battle-trained to identify helicopters by the distinctive sound of their rotating blades slapping against the air, Lyle tried to isolate the sound of the copter from the noise of the heavy machinery on the highway. At that moment, a column of vehicles poured through the hole in the avalanche pile, their occupants waving and honking their horns in appreciation.

— Chapter 10 —

From the moment he heard the distant slap of the helicopter blades, Dr. Philips began shoving against the shed's loosened corrugated metal sheets. His hands were numb and his fingers frozen as he desperately clawed at the rusting metal's sharp edges.

Altitude sickness, hunger and caffeine deprivation all conspired to increase the throbbing in his head. He knew that the cold was sapping his strength. Still, he was able to wriggle his torso through the opening as the helicopter drew nearer. Lying on his stomach and watching the copter spiral down toward the barren summit of the pass, he hoped that his rescuers had arrived. The doctor had been encouraged that his beeper had sounded almost hourly since he emerged from a drug-induced slumber; he knew he had not been given up for dead by his friends Casey Bailey and Bill Withers.

As Philips scrambled to his feet, he frantically waved his manacled arms skyward. He ran toward a bright circle of white illuminated by the helicopter fifty feet east of the shed. But just six feet from the shack, the chain around his right leg tautened, pitching his body forward. Unable to brace his fall, he crashed face-first into a two-foot bank of snow.

● ● ●

Paul Brader and Sam Moultrie watched this bizarre sight unfold as the single jet-engine Bell 206L-4 Long Ranger hovered twenty-five feet off the ground.

"Poor bastard's gone nuts!" Moultrie yelled to his passenger over the sound of the rotors.

"Just put her down!" Brader barked impatiently.

"It's not going to be easy," the pilot cautioned. "The winds are a bitch up here. I'm catching currents from Red Mountain, Canyon Creek and San Miguel Pass. And I'm getting blinded by the landing light reflecting off the snow."

"Then shut the light off," Brader ordered.

Moultrie nudged the collective gently, easing the helicopter toward the ground. As it touched down, a cloud of wind-whipped snow engulfed the craft's front windscreen.

Brader leaned toward the pilot. "Shut it off! I can't see a thing out there."

Moultrie, a tall, solidly built man in his late thirties with a large, bent nose and an unkempt goatee, shook his head. "If I can't get it cranked up again, we could be up here 'til summer."

"I'm not going to get blown off this damn mountain or sliced to pieces by those blades," Brader protested. "Besides, I can't talk to that old fool with all this racket."

Moultrie sneered at Brader and reluctantly complied. As the rotors slowed, the landscape around the copter once again came into view. Moultrie busied himself shutting down the helicopter's flight systems as Brader zipped up his thick black ski jacket. Fifty feet in front of the helicopter, Dr. Philips was on his feet and wiping snow from his face.

The cab was now quiet. "I may need some help, here, Sam," Brader said in an even tone. "He was able to get out of the shack somehow, and he might have something else up his sleeve."

Moultrie seethed. "Look, Brader, let's get something straight. I'm not getting paid enough to let old man Philips get a good look at me. I still have to live around here when this is all over. This is strictly your deal."

Brader's dark eyes bored into those of his accomplice as he slowly reached his right hand into the pocket of his jacket and withdrew a stainless steel pistol with a black handgrip. He clicked off the safety with his thumb and inspected the weapon as he turned it over in his hand. Looking back up at Moultrie, he saw a flicker of fear cross the man's face. Brader smiled, his lips stretching across a row of white capped teeth.

"Let me say it again," he replied as he opened the passenger-side door and braced himself against the cold. "If I get any trouble from him, I expect to see you climbing out of this copter in a big hurry."

Moultrie nodded at the pistol. "I got news for you, tough guy. I've got one of those too. Now, you just do what you gotta do and get back here right quick. I'm not waiting all night for you."

Brader grabbed a large duffel bag and flashlight from between his feet. He hopped out the passenger door, then crossed in front of the helicopter. On the wind-swept pinnacle of Imogene Pass, the undulating snowdrifts were waist-deep. The steady wind curled over the summit, sending swirls of loose powder skipping over the surface of the snowpack toward the cavernous basin to the north. The flowing spindrift disappeared over the southern rim of the basin like a ground-fog being blown into the ocean. Slowly picking his way between the drifts, Brader cut a path toward the weathered shack that sat on the summit's north side.

Even without his eyeglasses, Dr. Philips recognized Brader's rigid posture and gel-slicked black hair before the moonlight revealed his features clearly. His heart sank as his frozen body was wracked with unrelenting shudders. Knowing that this conversation would likely determine his fate, Dr. Philips tried to control his nerves and summon a modicum of composure. If he appeared too eager to please, Brader would sense his insincerity. If he appeared too hostile and intractable, he would be executed. While Dr. Philips was not afraid of death, the prospect of not being laid to rest next to his beloved Mimi was unbearable.

The beam from a high-intensity flashlight bounced along the top of the moonlit drifts before Brader trained it on his quarry from twenty feet away. Dr. Philips shielded his eyes with his hands as he heard Brader shout to him. "Walk as far as you can toward the light."

The doctor complied, moving two steps forward until the chain around his right leg halted his progress. Philips knew his adversary was testing the limit of his range of movement. He lifted his right leg, pulling the chain off the ground. Brader shined the beam along the full length of the chain, which ended at the base of the mailbox. Still keeping his distance, Brader used the flashlight to explore the hole that the doctor had pried open in the shack's east-facing wall.

"Glad to see you made it through the night. I was worried about you."

The physician's voice was hoarse and brittle. "Would you turn that thing off? I can't see a thing."

Brader turned off the flashlight and approached his prisoner. Philips slowly raised his arms, the blanched moonlight reflecting off the chrome handcuffs. "Paul, what have you done? What could you possibly be thinking?"

Brader pointed to the ground, where the doctor's thin wool socks had sunk beneath the surface of the snow. "Your feet must be freezing, Jim. Let's have a seat."

"Freezing? I'm lucky to be alive! The temperature's already below zero and the sun only went down a few hours ago," Philips shot back, as her lowered himself awkwardly to his knees then tumbled onto his buttocks. "Couldn't you have left me with my boots?"

Not saying a word, Brader leaned to his left and let the straps of the black duffel bag slide off his left shoulder. The bag landed at his feet and Brader took a seat on top of it, perched a foot above the doctor. With a deliberate motion, he placed the pistol on top of the nylon duffel bag next to his right hip, making sure the doctor saw that he was armed.

"I wish I could have handled this differently, Jim. I honestly do. I just couldn't see any other way out." He lifted his hands in resignation. "I still can't."

Dr. Philips nodded, even though his teeth chattered uncontrollably as he tried to reply. "Paul, surely you can see how asinine this is."

Brader's face clouded for an instant, and he sighed heavily before continuing. "I'm in a jam, doc. A deeper jam than you could ever imagine," he said. "I need this Saratoga Mining deal to go through and I need you out of the way until it does. I've got a meeting on Sunday night; the management team from Saratoga is ready to move and I can't risk your interference. I can't turn back now."

The explanation sent a fresh jolt of terror through Philips's frayed nervous system. "Are you telling me you're going to keep me chained up in this shack until Monday?" He pled, his voice cracking. "That's crazy, Paul. As a physician, I can assure you that I'll be dead long before then. I'm already showing signs of frostbite and hypothermia. You're not going to be able to keep me alive up here."

Brader tried to interrupt, but Dr. Philips would not be silenced. "As for your pipe dream about selling my company to Saratoga Mining, that's equally ludicrous. You don't have the authority to make a deal with Saratoga or anyone else for that matter; you're a minority shareholder, Paul. Saratoga's lawyers aren't going to deal with you, especially once they find out that I'm missing. For crying out loud, they're a publicly traded company. They can't risk being involved in this kind of criminal activity."

"As far as keeping you alive is concerned, I've brought enough warm clothes, blankets and food to make your stay far more pleasant than it's been in the past twenty-four hours," Brader said evenly. "As long as you're willing to cooperate with me, your survival won't be a problem."

Dr. Philips eyed the duffel bag as Brader continued. "Now that we have that issue behind us, let's discuss the matter of our relative ownership positions in Divining Rod Enterprises. It's a little less cut and dried than you think."

Brader's capped white teeth shone in the moonlight.

"It's more than just cut and dried, Paul," Dr. Philips said, leaning forward to make his point. "It's clearly spelled out in a contract. It comes down to simple math. I've invested over sixty percent of the capital in Divining Rod; I'm the majority shareholder. What about that isn't clear to you?"

Brader chuckled. "I'm not going to debate the issue with you, Jim. Suffice it to say that when our contract was drafted, I made sure there was a loophole that could be taken advantage of when the time was right."

"You've been planning this for eighteen months?" Philips asked, incredulous.

"I hate to say this, Jim," Brader patronizingly explained, "but you used a two-bit, small town lawyer to negotiate the terms of our deal. The lesson to be learned here is never let the other guy draft the contract, particularly when he's got a better lawyer."

Philips paused to gather air into his overworked lungs. "I don't care how experienced your high-priced firm is; fraud is fraud and kidnapping is kidnapping. All the legal hocus-pocus in the world can't turn you into the majority investor. Besides, I made it clear the first time I met you that I had no intention of selling a single one of those mining claims to a company like Saratoga unless I got some serious concessions on their part." He shook his head in disbelief. "What happened to all that talk about the two of us leaving a legacy to the community?"

Brader brushed a few windblown flakes from his face. "I'm not going to lie to you, Jim. Two years ago, when I first looked into who owned the mining rights in these basins, it was just a fishing trip from an investment perspective. Once I realized what you were up to, I knew my only hope of buying my way into Divining Rod Enterprises was to pass myself off as a kindred spirit."

"Which, of course, you're not." Dr. Philips replied flatly.

"Give yourself some credit, Jim," Brader said encouragingly. "The main reason I saw dollar signs is the work that you did for five years before I entered the picture. It took a lot of patience to accumulate those claims and patents as quickly and quietly as you did. If anybody found out how extensive your portfolio of holdings was becoming, it would have set off a whole new ripple of speculation in the area. You kept it from becoming a feeding frenzy. Hell, I had to pay my attorneys dearly just to unravel the web you created."

Brader had to duck his chin into his chest to avoid a wind-whipped gust of snow. He tried to see if his words were having an effect on the man who was shivering on the ground in front of him.

"What I don't think you realize," he continued. "Is how valuable the claims you've cobbled together are to any mining outfit that has the patience to wait out the marketplace until prices rebound – especially now that the claims, shafts, mines and tunnels we own can all be connected via one underground network."

"Of course I realize it, Paul!" Philips fumed. "And *you* ought to realize that what you're asking me to do in selling out to Saratoga is exactly what I have been trying to prevent. I'm never going to allow another huge mining operation to come in here and devastate these basins."

Brader tried to mask his frustration. Somehow he had to bring Brader around. "All I'm asking you to do is to listen to me. After all, I've got over $4 million invested in Divining Rod Enterprises, and let's not forget that my investment also allowed you to take $2 million out of the company to buy the land for your hospice project."

A chained man on the verge of freezing to death, Dr. Philips knew that he needed to at least appear willing to cooperate. "Paul, I do appreciate what you've done as a partner. Until yesterday, I thought we made a pretty good team. But negotiating with Saratoga behind my back after I told you how I felt about their offer? How am I supposed to react to that?"

"You're right," Brader admitted frankly. "Like I told you, I'm in a bind."

"What kind of bind?" Dr. Philips asked as a sharp gust of wind flung a volley of ice pellets into his face.

"The financial kind," Brader said as he looked down at his insulated boots. When he looked back up at the doctor, his expression was pained. "I need to liquidate my holdings in Divining Rod Enterprises by Monday at the latest."

"You need $4 million by Monday? What have you gotten yourself into?"

"It's too complicated to get into now. Let's just say that where the stock market is concerned, there's no such thing as a sure thing."

A small hope flickered in Philips's chest. "Why didn't you tell me? We can work this out. I'll buy out your interest in Divining Rod and get you over half of the money first thing in the morning. $4 million is a stretch, but I can sign a promissory note or something. That should buy you some time."

But Brader was shaking his head grimly.

"I give you my word as a gentleman." Philips went on, fighting the desperation in his voice. "All you have to do is fly me out of here tonight. We'll figure out some story about where I've been." His mind was racing. "I'll claim I got stuck on the highway, got disoriented in the snowstorm, and wandered off the road into the woods. With all the frostbite I've got, no one is going to question that. You can even hide me somewhere until my bank opens tomorrow morning. You'll get cash and a promissory note to cover your $4 million obligation. Problem solved."

Brader ignored the fact that his business partner was now wheezing for air and shivering violently. He shook his head. "$4 million isn't going to cut it, Jim. I need over $12 million and I need it all on Monday. Tuesday at the absolute latest."

"Twelve million dollars? My God, Paul. What on earth have you done?"

"That's not important," he said with a dismissive wave. "What *is* important is getting the Saratoga deal signed on Sunday. Not only will the proceeds of the deal make you a very rich man, they'll also get me out of the jam I'm in."

"I'm sorry, Paul." Dr. Philips replied. "You know I won't approve the sale. Forget Saratoga. Let's figure another way to get you out of the mess you're in. Would it help if I talked to your creditors?"

His pride wounded and his frustration rising, Brader angrily pushed himself off of the duffel bag and got to his feet, pocketing the pistol in the process. "I can't believe I have to sit here and beg you to let me make you filthy rich!" he shouted. "Something's very wrong with this picture. Why can't you listen to reason?"

"What Saratoga is offering is a sucker's bet, Paul," Dr. Philips said as he flexed his numb, icy fingers. "The last time you mentioned the deal, you said that they were offering $30 million for all of the claims. That might be triple our original investment, but it's still a steal. Any geologist worth his salt will tell you that there's hundreds of millions of dollars in gold, silver and other ores still left to be discovered in our claims."

Brader now began to pace back and forth in front of Dr. Philips, his patience at a breaking point. "Then why hasn't anybody been working those claims lately, you moron? The last of the big-time mining operations around here called it quits in 1978. For the last twenty years, the only things getting mined around here are investors and speculators."

"If that's so, then why did you invest? Why is Saratoga willing to spend $30 million for our claims? First you tell me I've amassed a desirable portfolio of claims, now you're trying to tell me it's worthless. You're arguing out of both sides of your mouth."

"Why did I invest? Because all it takes is an up-tick in the precious metals market to make companies like Saratoga crawl out of the woodwork. These people aren't fools. They know that the market is going to rebound eventually, it always has." He stopped pacing to make a crucial point. "And as for your worries about ruining the environment, the engineers at Saratoga tell me you won't even be able to tell that they're working the mines. All the work can be done underground and all the ore will be taken out through one huge portal. Tourists can still drive their jeeps up through here and they'll never even know that the mountains are being mined. When push comes to shove, isn't that what you're really concerned about?"

"Saratoga's engineers are feeding you a lot of rubbish, Paul," Jim Philips croaked, knowing that arguing was getting him nowhere. "Of course they're going to be doing the bulk of their work underground: that's where the ore is! When they pull a thousand tons of ore per day out of the mountain, the dump piles and tailings will cover hundreds of acres. Where are they going to put all of that waste? Who's going to stop the chemicals in their tailings from getting into the streams and rivers? That's the problem."

Dr. Philips's throat began to spasm, producing an intense coughing fit.

"You're fighting something as inevitable as the tide, you idiot!" Brader ranted. "This is one of the most highly mineralized places on Earth. Are you actually naïve enough to think that you can single-handedly put an end to mining in the entire Western Slope of Colorado when the market comes around?"

"Not the entire Western Slope, Paul, just in three basins." Dr. Philips counted them on his fingers. "The Imogene, Yankee Boy and Governor Basins. There are over fifty miles of tunnels under those three basins and I, for one, think that's enough."

Brader squeezed his own head with both hands in exasperation. "I can't believe I'm hearing this. These claims are in the middle of national forest land. If the federal government isn't worried about them, then why are you getting so worked up? It makes no sense!"

Brader fought for composure. "Listen, Jim, why don't you use the money you get from the Saratoga sale and do something positive for the world rather than try to protect something that nobody else cares about protecting. You'll be able to help a shitload of people that way. Think about it!"

The desperate eagerness in Brader's tone finally brought Philips up short. He had to put an end to this. Gulping for air and licking his cracked lips, he appealed to his captor. "Calm down and sit back down, Paul. Let's see if we can work this out."

As Brader moved to resume his seat on the duffel bag, Moultrie's voice carried to the top of the pass from the helicopter parked fifty feet away. "We're off schedule. Let's go, already! I need to get this bird back!"

"Hold your horses," Brader called back. "I'll be there in a minute."

Realizing that his kidnapper was about to leave him, Dr. Philips's tone became more urgent.

"Let's put our cards on the table, Paul. You need something from me; otherwise you would've already done away with me. If your goal in imprisoning me up here was to get my attention, I can assure you that I'm all ears. What do you want?"

Brader was encouraged by the doctor's frankness, and chose his words carefully. "What I want is simple. A document was delivered to your lawyer on Tuesday afternoon by courier. I kept your copy knowing you wouldn't be around to take delivery of it."

"And you've got it with you?"

Brader smiled and patted the duffel bag. "It's right here. All I need is for you to sign your name to the document, saying that you accept its terms and conditions. I have access to a Notary Public who's willing to verify that the document was executed on Tuesday."

"What is it?"

"The paper I want you to sign is merely an acknowledgment that I have the right to exercise an option under the terms of our original contract. By exercising that option, I become the majority shareholder of Divining Rod Enterprises, which allows me to negotiate on the company's behalf with Saratoga Mining."

Dr. Philips shook his head. "For argument's sake, let's say you've actually found a loophole to take control of my company. If this document is merely an announcement of some sort of corporate restructuring, then why do you need me to sign it? If by exercising this option, you suddenly become the top dog, then you don't need my permission for anything, right?"

"Technically, that's correct. The problem with not having your signature on the document is more of an issue of perception than a legality," Brader lied. "I'm sure my attorneys would prevail against any challenge, but I don't want any loose ends. If you or your lawyer got word to Saratoga that there was a dispute regarding ownership of Divining Rod, their management team might balk. It's a small risk, but one I don't want to take."

Dr. Philips bit his tongue. He needed to know the rest of Brader's plan. "Okay, let's say I sign the restructuring deal. What happens next?"

Brader could not spit the words out fast enough. "I've got a cell phone with me. All you need to do is call your lawyer's office and leave a message on his answering machine telling him you've accepted the terms of the restructuring document. It's important that you tell him that you sent me a signed copy of it and that we never had a face-to-face meeting. And especially don't mention anything about the meeting we had scheduled near the Mineral King on Tuesday."

"How do I explain to my lawyer that I've dropped out of sight?"

"On your message to him, just say you had to respond to a medical situation last night and wound up spending the night in Durango. Tell him that you'll be out of town until Monday visiting friends. That's all I need, but I need it *now.*"

"Why not call my attorney at home? Wouldn't that make more sense?"

"I don't want you talking to him. I can't risk your getting cute on the phone."

"Fair enough. Then what?"

Brader patted the duffel bag. "Then you get all the supplies you'll need to stay up here until Monday without a problem. Once the guys from Saratoga leave town, I come back up here in the copter and fly you to the Durango airport. Between the two of us, we can work out a story that will satisfy anyone's curiosity about where you've been. Then, within forty-eight hours, you'll have your portion of the proceeds. Not only will you have doubled your investment in Divining Rod Enterprises; you won't have to deal with me anymore. I'm going to take my money and relocate someplace warm."

Dr. Philips nodded as he calculated his options. "Okay, so what guarantee do I have once I make that phone call and sign your document that everything will happen as you say?"

Brader's eyes narrowed. "What do you mean by guarantee?"

"Just what I said, Paul. Once I sign the paper and make the call, what's to keep you from putting a bullet in my head, then dumping my body someplace where it won't be found for months? After you've done the deal with Saratoga, you'd probably just as soon not have me around."

Brader could sense his salvation seeping through his fingers like melting snow. It was all he could do not to scream in frustration. "If I wanted to put a bullet in your head, Jim, I would've done it already. We have to trust each other on some level here; otherwise there's no use in continuing this discussion."

Dr. Philips held his manacled wrists out toward Brader. "No offense, Paul, but you haven't exactly earned my trust. In case you haven't noticed, I'm sitting here chained up like a dog. Once I sign that document and make that phone call, are you ready to take these chains off as a show of good faith? I'm not asking you to let me go, I'm just going to need more freedom of movement so I can keep my body temperature up."

Brader shrugged. "No problem. You do what I've asked and the chains come off in a heartbeat."

Dr. Philips knew then that Brader was lying. Without chains to tether him and with a fresh supply of warm clothes to protect him, he would have a fighting chance of making it to either Telluride or to US Highway 550, some five-thousand vertical feet below him. Even with the prospect of avalanches and snowdrifts as high as the treetops, Dr. Philips knew that he would gamble his life on even a slim chance of survival. He also knew that Brader would never allow him that chance.

"I've got a better plan, Paul. You fly me to Durango or Montrose right now. Once I'm on the ground and in a public place where I feel safe, I promise I'll do exactly what you've asked me to do. Understand that I'm not questioning your sincerity; I'm just trying to buy a little peace of mind."

Brader shook his head emphatically. "Absolutely not. Who's to say you won't stroll right to the cops and have me brought up on kidnapping charges?"

"Who's to say I won't do the exact same thing once you let me go on Monday?" As soon as the words were out of his mouth, Dr. Philips knew he had made a grave mistake.

Brader sprang up from the duffel bag and coldly drew the pistol on Philips. "Listen to me, you son of a bitch. This isn't a goddamned negotiation! I've laid out my terms and that's the only option on the table." His excitement then turned derisive. "You have five minutes to make your decision." He tapped the stainless steel pistol against the face of his Rolex watch. "If I leave here tonight without that signed piece of paper, I won't be back. If things start heating up and the cops start asking questions, I'm not going to risk flying up here again to save your ass. If you think last night was cold, you should hear what they're predicting for the rest of the week!"

Dr. Philips felt his stomach turn. "Paul, use your head. You know that document you want me to sign isn't worth the paper it's written on. You have no chance of pulling off a deal with Saratoga without my consent. Do you honestly think Saratoga's lawyers won't check out our corporate documents and our management contract? Do you think they won't put two and two together? The primary shareholder has mysteriously disappeared and the minority shareholder is selling the company out from under him? What you're doing is sheer lunacy."

Brader looked at his watch again. "You're wasting a lot of time, doc."

"The offer I made earlier still stands. I gave you my word that I'll buy out your stake in Divining Rod. It may not cover all of your obligations, but $4 million would be a start. I can also give you my word that if I'm flown out of here tonight, I will never breathe a word about this to anyone. And that," Philips concluded with all the courage he could feign, "is my final offer."

Brader's response was swift and brutal. He kicked the elderly doctor in the chest with his right boot, toppling him over backward. The sound of air being violently expelled from Dr. Philips's chest was quickly followed by a dull thud as his head struck the ice-covered snowpack behind him. Brader then reached down, snatched Philips back into a sitting position by yanking on the handcuffs, and held the gun to the physician's temple.

"That's my retort to your offer. Do you have any other ultimatums for me? Speak up!"

Dr. Philips was stunned from Brader's blow. The pain spreading through his chest was now accompanied by a wracking cough as his lungs fought for oxygen in the thin air. When he swallowed, he tasted blood in his throat.

As the doctor fought to control a fit of coughing, Brader knelt beside the bulky black duffel bag and unzipped it. Behind him, the helicopter's blades began to rotate as the single jet engine whined to life. "One last chance, doc," he intoned as one by one he removed articles from the bag. "Down parka," he said flatly, holding the hooded garment tantalizingly in Philips's face. He laid it in the snow just out of the doctor's reach and then held up a tightly folded foil-textured blanket. "Survival blanket." Next came thick ski gloves and a pair of insulated slipper-boots.

Dr. Philips was finally able to draw a breath without coughing, but he was forced to turn his head to avoid the ice pellets that were being whipped toward his face from the rotor blades.

Now holding two large plastic bags, Brader had to shout to be heard. "Protein bars, beef jerky and apple juice. Look yummy, don't they?"

The doctor realized that he had not eaten or ingested any liquids in over twenty-four hours. His throat was raw and parched, and the thought of apple juice made his thirst an unbearable pain.

"So!" Brader yelled at him as he held a cellular phone in one hand and a green file folder in the other. "One last chance. Remember, this is your choice, not mine!"

He held the phone out toward the doctor and repeated. "One last chance, *damn it!*"

Having witnessed Brader's barbarism, Philips knew his partner could never be trusted. He looked over his shoulder toward the dark, crumbling shed, then turned back to face Paul Brader. Either choice, he reckoned, was a death sentence. He decided that he would rather risk his life in the frozen Colorado night than rely on a duplicitous bully for survival.

Dr. Philips grabbed one of the chains and pulled himself to a standing position. His words came out raspy, but strong. "God help you, Paul Brader." He turned away and began to trample slowly toward the shed.

Brader tore open the plastic bags and grabbed a quart container of apple juice and two sticks of beef jerky. He threw one of the beef sticks at the doctor, hitting him in the back. Philips stopped, but did not turn around. Brader dropped the apple juice and the other beef stick in the snow where the elderly physician had been sitting.

He shouted over the torrent of wind and the noise of the jet engine. "Remember, this is on your head, not mine!" He noticed that the old man did not stop to pick up the food that he had thrown at him. "Crazy bastard," he mumbled to himself as he repacked the supplies into the duffel bag. He pocketed the pistol, shouldered the duffel and snatched the flashlight from the ground. He shielded his face with his arm and ran toward the helicopter, bending forward to avoid the spinning blades.

Moultrie was seething when his accomplice climbed aboard. "I saw the whole thing. You didn't get him to sign squat, did you? I can't believe I put my butt on the line to fly you all the way up here and you turn around and let him off the hook! What kind of candy-ass are you?"

"He just needs some more softening up, that's all," Brader responded defensively. "I'm gonna give him tonight and all of tomorrow to think about it while he's freezing to death. When we come back tomorrow night, he'll be begging me to sign that document."

"You never said anything about flying back up here tomorrow night. There's no guarantee I'll be able to get this bird three nights in a row. I'm not the only charter pilot my company's got and you're not the only customer they've got. This copter might be booked already."

"I don't care how you do it, Sam. We're gonna need this helicopter again tomorrow night. Tell your boss that your customer is willing to top any offer he gets."

"I still don't see the problem," Moultrie complained. "Go back out there and get this deal done. Hell, give me a crack at old man Philips. I'll get him to sign that thing in two seconds flat!"

Brader was in no mood to argue. Still, he needed to keep his accomplice in check. "We're gonna do things my way. Believe me, this is far from being over. We'll get everything straightened out tomorrow night."

"Fine by me. I'm not the one who needs that paper signed, you are. As far as the flying goes, it's like I've told you all along: my services are strictly cash-and-carry. You give me enough cash and I'll carry you wherever you want. But I'm already up to my neck in this thing. I'm not gonna let you screw this up and get me put behind bars again. If you don't have the nerve to bring this mess to a close, I do."

Brader had no choice but to stomach the pilot's bravado. "I'll keep that in mind. In the meantime, let's get the hell out of here. It's freezing."

— Chapter 11 —

Casey sat frozen in the darkness, her head cocked to one side. For the second night in a row, she had been jolted awake by an unexpected sound. She was certain that the loud scraping sound she heard was not part of a dream. Anxiety about Dr. Philips had kept her shifting beneath the sheets in her second floor bedroom until midnight, when fatigue finally overpowered her jittery nerves. Now, with her ears trained toward the open bedroom door, she strained to hear over the thumping of her heart. She tried to pinpoint the source of the noise and concluded that it was the sound of wood scraping against wood.

She felt a chill breeze that seemed to be drifting through the bedroom door. The light blonde hairs on her forearms were standing up straight. She had secured all of the doors and windows before heading up to bed, and now felt foolish for having rejected Jill Samsky's offer to spend the night. Still, Casey resisted the impulse to reach for the telephone atop her nightstand, and got out of bed slowly, trying not to make a sound. Moonlight poured through her bedroom window, silhouetting the swaying boughs of the evergreen trees bordering the house. Tiptoeing to the window, Casey saw that a strong wind was swirling through the southwest corner of the Ouray box canyon. As she watched the tops of spruce and fir trees bend in the breeze, Casey suspected that a dead branch had snapped in the wind and fallen onto the deck, accounting for the scraping noise that had awakened her. With enough force, the impact of the falling branch could have jarred the sliding glass door leading to the back deck off its track, producing the draft.

Casey knew that she'd never be able to fall back asleep until she could confirm her suspicions. She walked slowly toward the bedroom door, using her toes to temper the sound of her footsteps on the hardwood floor. As she stood in the doorway, Casey paused and listened intently. She could hear the sound of the furnace blowing warm air through the baseboard vents, the low hum of the downstairs refrigerator and the muffled timbre of wind blowing through the Ouray bowl.

Casey dried her palms on her flannel nightshirt and started down the staircase, aware of every creak and groan that her feet were making on the wooden steps. When she reached the landing, she looked across the dark living room and saw that the glass doors to the deck were resting securely in their tracks. More confused than ever, Casey walked into the living room, determined to search the back deck.

Suddenly, she felt a cold rush of air against the back of her neck. She wheeled around and looked down the narrow hallway to the front of the house. The front door that she had double-locked two hours earlier was now wide open, swinging against the foyer wall. A frigid wind blew into the house, coating the foyer floor with a thin layer of frozen snow and pine straw. As she stared at the open door, a gold-colored aspen leaf tumbled down the hallway toward her.

Casey let out a muted yelp and spun around in a tight circle. She scanned the shadows in the living room for signs of an intruder. Standing in her nightshirt in the dark house, Casey felt cold and vulnerable. She frantically searched for something to defend herself with. The fireplace poker was on the far side of a leather recliner that was large enough to conceal someone crouching behind it. The portable phone was in the kitchen on the other side of the house. As she tried to decide what to do, Casey was startled by a noise behind her.

Instinctively, she jumped back and whirled toward the front hallway.

Casey recognized the sound immediately, having heard it almost every day for the past three years. It was the scraping of a warped wooden drawer being pulled out of an antique bureau in Dr. Philips's bedroom. Each morning, the physician struggled with the temperamental piece of furniture as he retrieved his clothes from the dresser.

Clinging to the hope that her landlord had arrived home and was now getting dressed for bed, Casey crept slowly down the hallway. Standing fifteen feet from the master bedroom, she saw that the door to Dr. Philips's room was open. The light was not on. Her eyes were drawn to the vertical column of square windowpanes next to the front door. One of the windows had been broken from the outside, the glass pane now reduced to a jumble of shards that littered the foyer floor. How, she wondered, could she have slept through the sound of breaking glass?

Her impulse was to flee through the open front door, but her escape route led past the master bedroom, and she didn't want to risk a confrontation. Instead, she retreated quickly down the hall toward the living room. Her plan was to grab the portable phone in the kitchen and run out of the house through the mud room and garage door. She would then sprint through the snow to a neighbor's house while calling 911 on the cordless phone.

Hearing heavy footsteps behind her, Casey broke into a run. Looking over her shoulder, she saw a dark figure lumbering toward her. The intruder was a tall, well-built man dressed in black with a dark ski mask pulled over his face.

Now in a dead run through the living room, Casey could hear her pursuer's boots striking the hardwood floor directly behind her, his long strides quickly closing the gap between them. She knew that her only chance was to reach the telephone and dial 911 before the phone could be wrested from her. Five feet from the kitchen, Casey could sense that the man was lunging toward her.

"Help meeeeee!" she screamed.

A thick arm wrapped around her neck, choking off her screams. Tackled from behind, Casey collapsed under the weight of her attacker. Her knees hit the floor first, then her chest. The collision sent her sliding forward, her forehead striking the baseboard near the kitchen door. Pinned to the floor, Casey twisted her head to the right and tried to look up. She felt a strong, gloved hand press against her right ear, holding her head in place against the floor. She saw a flash of black above her as the intruder raised his right fist.

"Bitch!" The man grunted as he prepared to pound his fist into her skull. Casey was able to shift her head only fractionally as the blow crashed against the side of her face. Striking her directly above her right cheekbone, the impact bounced her head against the hardwood floor. A shower of sparks burst before Casey's eyes, followed by a high-pitched ringing in her ears. The pain was instantaneous and excruciating.

Through the pain and disorientation, Casey saw the man scramble to his feet, enter the kitchen and rip the telephone cord out of the wall. When the intruder tried to step over her on his way back into the living room, Casey lifted her leg and swept it against his ankles, sending him tumbling face-first to the floor. She managed to get to her feet and pounce onto his back, reaching forward to grab the ski mask. With one arm clamping the mask over his face, he reached back, hooked an arm around Casey's back and threw her to the floor beside him. In a flash, the attacker grabbed her under her arms, snatched her off the ground and hurled her over the sofa and into the living room.

Pulling herself unsteadily to her feet, she was assaulted by waves of dizziness and nausea. Barely able to keep her balance, Casey pursued the fleeing man down the dark hallway to the open front door. Shards of broken glass in the foyer sliced the soles of her feet, sending her hopping down the short flight of stairs from the porch onto the snow-covered front walkway. She saw the dark figure sprint across the lawn and through the trees before disappearing over a ridge and onto Queen Street. Standing in calf-deep snow with her feet cut and bleeding, Casey felt tears of anger and frustration welling in her eyes.

— Chapter 12 —

Weak early-morning sunlight illuminated the mountains looming above the west side of Uncompahgre Gorge as Casey's jeep approached the East Riverside snowshed. The steel-reinforced concrete structure had been constructed over US Highway 550 in 1985 to spare the road and its travelers from the ravages of the massive East Riverside avalanche path. The snowshed, which resembled a steep ski-jump hill, provided a channel for avalanches to slide over the highway and into the canyon on the right side of the road.

All of the avalanche fatalities on US Highway 550 in the 20th century had taken place at the Riverside slide area, and Casey pressed down on the jeep's accelerator as she neared the snowshed. She did not ease off the gas pedal until she had passed beneath it and was well clear of the slide path. Five hundred yards further up the highway, she saw the Riverside turnoff.

Casey felt miserable. She was operating on two hours' sleep. Both sides of her jaw were visibly swollen and discolored. A red knot the size of a golf ball sprouted from the center of her forehead. No amount of aspirin had been able to quell the throbbing in her head. Unable to chew, Casey's breakfast had consisted of three cups of black coffee, which only served to further jangle her unsettled nerves.

Bill Withers, Jill Samsky and another Ouray County deputy had arrived at Dr. Philips's house within five minutes of her call for help. After hearing Casey's account of the attack, Withers mounted a search of the area. A trail of footprints led from Dr. Philips's house to the corner, where a fresh set of tire tracks was discovered. The vehicle was either a pickup truck or a sports utility vehicle. Unfortunately, attempts to follow the tire tracks down into the heart of Ouray proved fruitless. Strong winds had blown loose snow into the frozen tire ruts that ran along Third Avenue, rendering one indistinguishable from another.

Withers and his deputies were convinced that the break-in had been a burglary attempt. The intruder had confined his activities to the master bedroom, where he had emptied dresser drawers, searched through cabinets and overturned jewelry cases. Casey was able to confirm that many of Mimi Philips's most valuable brooches, pins and necklaces had been stolen. A true accounting of the theft would have to wait until Dr. Philips was able to take an inventory.

Although she had arrived early for the search of Uncompahgre Gorge, Casey saw that several trucks were already parked in the turnout. Two white Jeep Cherokees from Sheriff's Department and a white Ouray Mountain Rescue truck were among the assembled vehicles. Casey turned her jeep into the nearest open space, directly in front of two monuments commemorating victims of the Riverside Slide.

As was the case with many passing motorists drawn to the curious roadside memorials, she considered them both intriguing and disturbing. Casey was studying the marker closest to her jeep when she was startled by the sound of Jill Samsky rapping her knuckles against the window. Casey took a moment to compose herself, then climbed out of her jeep.

"You okay?" the deputy asked.

"Yeah," Casey smiled. "Those monuments always get to me."

"I mean are you okay *physically*? There's a good chance you suffered a concussion. You really shouldn't be out here; you should be getting checked out up in Montrose."

"I'll be fine," Casey sighed. "Thanks for staying with me last night. You probably got less sleep than I did."

"Just doin' my job, ma'am," Jill joked before changing the subject. "By the way, Bill and I both think that the break-in last night was probably related to Doc Philips's disappearance. It's no secret that Jim is missing. Ouray's a small town and word travels fast around here. We're guessing that some opportunistic low-life was looking to make a quick score, knowing Dr. Philips wasn't home."

"Whoever did it obviously wasn't worried about me being there. Smashing your fist through a window isn't the most subtle way to break into a house."

"He probably didn't know that you live there too," Samsky replied. "That leads us to believe that it's someone who's not real familiar with Ouray."

Jill took Casey by the elbow and guided her toward the center of the turnout. "Anyway, we can't let what happened last night distract us from finding Dr. Philips. With any luck, we'll get this all cleared up today. The search of the gorge is only part of it; we're going to keep burning up the phone lines all over Southwestern Colorado today. I know it seems like it's been forever, but Jim's only been missing for a day and a half. Hopefully, we'll get it all sorted out today, then we can all head over to The Prospector for a big steak dinner, and Doc Philips can tell us about his great adventure."

Casey nodded, wishing that she could share the female deputy's optimism. Sheriff Withers approached from the far end of the parking area. There were heavy bags under his eyes. He stopped in front of Casey and addressed her without preamble. "Looks like we've got good weather for the search. Sun's out, and the wind's died down since last night. We've got a good crew here today, Casey." He gestured over his shoulder in the direction of the rescue volunteers who were in the process of extracting clothing and climbing gear from the Ouray Mountain Rescue truck and their personal vehicles.

"You should recognize most of these people from town. We had so many volunteers, we had to turn some folks away. And every person assembled here knows Jim Philips personally. If there's anything to be found, they'll find it."

"Ouray Mountain Rescue is the best crew I've ever worked with," Jill agreed. "Your best bet is to stay with me up here on the highway and let them do their thing down in the gorge."

The sheriff nodded. "As soon as things get started here, I'll head back to the office. We need to start expanding the search. We're going to be calling every hospital and law enforcement agency within a three-hundred-mile radius. I talked to Jim's lawyer this morning, and he's headed down to my office from Montrose. This is getting ridiculous already. People just don't disappear like this."

"So you don't expect to find anything here?" Casey asked.

Withers looked at Jill, then at Casey. "I hope not." He chose his words carefully before continuing. "Normally, we would've mobilized the hasty search team as soon as Dr. Philips's truck went off the road. Hasty is smaller group within the rescue squad. They're experts in quick-response operations. I decided not to call them out on Tuesday night because we were convinced that Jim wasn't at the crash site when his truck was pushed into the gorge. But now that he's been missing for over thirty-six hours, I've gotta cover all the bases."

Sounds from the highway interrupted their conversation. They turned to see two CDOT vehicles heading up the steep hill from the direction of the snowshed. A Colorado Special led the way, followed by a Caterpillar 950 tractor, its rotary blower raised above the pavement. The vehicles passed the turnout and pulled onto the right shoulder of the road fifty yards to the north, where US Highway 550 snaked through a series of steep switchbacks.

A green 1990 Ford pickup that had been trailing the other vehicles pulled into the parking area. The truck's wheel wells were caked with mud and its well-worn plow blade bobbed up and down as the vehicle came to a stop. After lowering the blade to the pavement, Lyle Morrison stepped out of the pickup and began retrieving gear from the truck's bed. A cream-colored Labrador retriever leaped down from the truck bed and sat on its haunches looking up at Lyle.

Withers pointed to the two CDOT vehicles and explained to Casey. "I asked them to skip over the stretch of road that we're going to be searching this morning."

As if on cue, the rotary blower fired into action, gouging into a five-foot pile of ice-encrusted snow that had been plowed against the right shoulder of the road. The blower shot the snow thirty feet into the air.

"It wouldn't be much fun at the bottom of this gorge with that thing spitting snow down on you," Jill remarked.

"Not only that, but it would dump a new layer of snow down into the search area. The last thing we need is to be covering up potential clues. Believe me, they're going to have enough problems down there as it is."

Withers turned to Casey. "I know that you want to be involved in this search, but you don't have the training that these people do. I'd rather you stick close to Jill up here on the road. I sat in on Lyle's briefing at the rescue barn this morning and his plan calls for a good deal of the work to be done from the highway, so you won't be missing much."

"Sheriff?" A deep voice beckoned from behind. Casey turned around to find Lyle Morrison standing behind her with a thick red nylon jacket and a yellow helmet in his hands. He offered them to Casey, who noticed that the jacket bore the insignia of the Ouray Mountain Rescue Team. "We've got a lot of ground to cover, so if Casey wants to help, I can put her to work. I could really use an extra set of eyes down there in the canyon."

As Withers shook his head, Lyle continued. "We're going to be breaking the team into pairs, so Casey can be my partner. I'm going to be spending a lot of my time coordinating things on the radio, so I can use Casey's help in searching my grid assignments. She'll be right by my side and I won't ask her to do anything she's not trained for."

The sheriff glared at Lyle for several seconds before responding. "You're in charge of the search team, so I'll defer to you on this one. I can promise you one thing, though; if anything happens to Casey, there's gonna be hell to pay."

Lyle nodded his head. "Got it."

Casey removed her coat and pulled the oversized red jacket on over her sweater. The Ouray Mountain Rescue jacket came down to her knees, and she had to roll up the sleeves in order to expose her hands. After inspecting the helmet, she looked inquisitively at Lyle.

"Everyone's going to be wearing helmets, not just you," the team leader assured her. "I've also got a figure eight, carabiners, gloves and binoculars that I need to outfit you with before we get started. We'll start our final briefing in a few minutes."

Clearly irritated, Withers turned his attention to Jill. "Come with me. We need to talk about traffic control. With this many people on the road, we're gonna need to keep things safe around here." They walked toward the sheriff's Jeep, leaving Lyle and Casey standing at the edge of the turn-out.

Uncomfortable alone with Lyle Morrison, Casey twirled the helmet in her hands, pretending not to notice the fact that he was staring at her battered face. After a long silence, Lyle finally addressed her.

"I heard about what happened last night. From the looks of you, you might have a concussion. Do you feel nauseous?"

"Not a bit."

"Light-headed?"

"Nope."

"Any problem with blurred vision?"

Casey pointed to the monument next to her jeep. "I can read every word on that marker. Wanna see?"

"I'll take your word for it."

Casey's tone softened. "Did you know any of those guys personally?"

Lyle turned to his left and studied the gray marble marker that resembled a gravestone. A detailed rendering of a Colorado Special snowplow had been etched in the center of the smooth slab. Below the snowplow, the names of three CDOT employees had been engraved, along with their dates of birth and untimely deaths. Above the snowplow an inscription read:

**This monument is dedicated to those who
have given the supreme sacrifice in the**

maintenance of Red Mountain Pass.
The lonely vigil of the night is known
only to these men of courage.

"They were all before my time, but I've heard the stories from the other guys at the shop," Lyle replied. "We've got a few minutes before I have to give my final briefing, so I can tell you what I've heard. If we cross over the highway, we can see down to the avalanche path."

Casey nodded. She followed Lyle as he crossed the narrow highway. Their boots crunching against the packed snow underfoot, the mismatched pair walked twenty yards down the steep grade before Lyle stopped on the left shoulder of the road. He nodded to the steep slopes above the concrete snowshed to the northeast. Casey saw that this section of mountainside was largely denuded of the evergreen trees that dotted the surrounding slopes. The mountainside was blanketed in white, except where rust-colored cliffs poked through the snow.

Lyle gazed up at the slopes as he explained to Casey, "The starting zone for the Riverside Slide is actually about 3,200 feet above the road. Since you can only see the last few hundred yards of the slide path from down here on the highway, you can't tell if an avalanche is coming until it's too late. By the time the slide hits the road, it can be going over 100 miles an hour. The slide path crosses one of the last flat stretches of highway before the road starts climbing up toward the summit of Red Mountain Pass. As a result, it's a logical place for drivers to stop and put on tire chains before heading further south. If you get caught standing in the road when an avalanche hits, your chances of survival are only slightly better than nil."

"I can imagine," Casey replied.

"The first guy listed on the CDOT monument is Robert Miller. He was only thirty-six-years old when he died in 1970, long before the snowshed was built. He was using a tractor to clear an avalanche pile from the road down there when a second avalanche hit. He never had a chance," Lyle explained with a distant look in his eyes.

"Almost the exact same thing happened eight years later to Terry

Kishbaugh, except he was driving a rotary plow at the time. Clearing avalanche number one when avalanche number two came down on top of him. Terry was only 29."

"Both so young," Casey remarked. "What about the last name on the marker? That happened in 1992, right?"

"Yeah. Eddie Imel. He was the foreman of our patrol before Hamp. Most of the guys in the shop today were good friends of Eddie."

"Did he die the same way as the other two?"

"No, this one was different," he explained somberly. "It was after midnight in the middle of a storm that wound up dumping over four feet of snow in Red Mountain Pass. Eddie Imel and one of his crew had stopped about 200 feet short of the snowshed, trying to replace a chain that had slipped off their snowplow. They didn't hear the avalanche until it was practically on top of them. Both of them were buried alive. Danny Haramio managed to scratch, claw and tunnel his way through the snow for twelve straight hours before he bumped into Eddie, who was breathing, but in real bad shape. After six more hours, Danny finally broke through to the top of the pile and saw the lights from the snowshed. Danny then dug back through the pile to try and rescue his boss, but he was too late. They brought Eddie's body back to town the next day."

Lyle pointed to the second marker in the turnout area. The older of the two monuments consisted of a bronze plaque and three wooden crosses atop a flagstone and concrete pedestal.

"That is for Reverend Hudson and his family. He was on his way to preach in Silverton in March of 1963 with his daughters Amelia and Pauline. They had also stopped to put on tire chains when an avalanche hit. It took searchers a week to find the Reverend's body. A week after that, they found Amelia's body and Rev. Hudson's car. It was down in the gorge, more than 500 feet north of where the slide hit."

"What about the second daughter?"

"They found Pauline almost three months later when the Spring thaw arrived."

"What a horrible way to go." Casey shook her head. "When was the last time this slide ran?"

"It's been a while. They're planning to blast it down with explosives on Monday if it doesn't slide over the weekend. Unfortunately, we're going to be working under the slide path for a while today, but this is the best place to climb down into the gorge." He pointed to a creek that ran along the highway, fifteen feet below the left shoulder of the road.

"We'll follow Red Mountain Creek down into the canyon. The creek is fairly level through here, but it takes a sharp drop down into the gorge after it passes the snowshed. It'll take us four or five hours to cover the area between here and Mother Cline, where the accident happened." Lyle turned to face Casey. "Are you sure you're okay with this? No one in the world would blame you if you backed out now."

Casey nodded her head. "I'm sure."

"One more thing," Lyle cautioned. "I think it's only fair to let you know that we don't expect to find Dr. Philips today."

"I know. Sheriff Withers already told me that this is just to cover all of the bases."

"Just the same, we're not treating this like a cursory walk-through. We're going to search every inch of ground between the highway and the bottom of the gorge. If Jim's body is down there, we're going to find it."

Seeing Casey cringe at his last statement, Lyle explained in a gentle tone, "I didn't mean that to sound so insensitive. Please understand that when we conduct an operation like this, it might seem to an outsider as if we're looking for an object rather than a person. Today, you're going to hear us refer to Dr. Philips as either the subject, the target, or the body. But don't let that color your judgment about the people conducting the search. Every person on this team has been touched by Dr. Philips in some way."

Casey looked down at her boots and nodded slowly. "I understand. Thank you for that."

Lyle turned and walked back up the highway toward the turnout area. Casey fell into step, walking rapidly to match the tall man's stride. As they skirted the waist-high bank of plowed snow along the shoulder of the road, Casey saw that the CDOT crew was still clearing the south-bound shoulder above the Riverside turnout.

"What do you guys do in the summer when there's no snow to plow?" Casey asked.

"Well, the full-timers spend most of their time patching and resurfacing the highway or clearing the ditches and culverts alongside the road. This stretch of highway gets pretty beat up during the winter."

"Are you a full-timer?"

"It sure seems like it in the winter, but no; I work as a carpenter in the spring and summer. With all of the new homes going up around here, there's always plenty of work to be found." Lyle glanced at Casey. "As a matter of fact, I helped build Dr. Philips's house six years ago. It was my first job after I moved out here."

"No kidding?" Casey replied.

As they stood on the shoulder waiting for a southbound car to pass, Casey asked. "I hope you don't take this the wrong way, but why did you choose this line of work?"

Lyle grinned. "Do you mean working for cee-dot, working search and rescue, or working construction?"

"All three, I guess."

Lyle considered the question before responding with a shrug. "This might seem overly simplistic, but at the end of the day, I like being able to point to something and say 'I did that.' Whether it's a plowed road, a rescued hiker or a new house, I feel like I've accomplished something. I never seemed to find that kind of satisfaction in any of my previous jobs. Maybe it's a guy thing."

Lyle and Casey walked across the highway to the turnout, where the members of the search team were assembled with their gear. Lyle walked to the front of the group. The rattling of climbing gear grew silent as the team gathered in a tight cluster. Lyle's yellow Labrador bounded forward with a length of coiled climbing rope dangling from her mouth. Lyle accepted the rope from his dog and patted her on the head. Casey bent down and stroked the dog's head, earning an appreciative lick on her cheek.

"For those of you who don't know her already, this is Casey Bailey," Lyle began. "Dr. Philips is Casey's landlord. She's going to be working alongside me today."

Still bent down next to the lab, Casey looked up and nodded to the group.

Having settled the issue, Lyle continued with his briefing. "I know we covered most of this back in town, but a couple of issues bear repeating. First of all, the accident occurred three hours before the end of the snow-storm, so the target of our search could be buried beneath the surface. Any lump, bump or impact crater needs to be investigated to your satis-faction before you move on. Also, there's no good reason for anyone to be hiking through the gorge this time of year, so any footprints that you see need to be reported, no matter how faint they appear. You all know which grids you've been assigned and who your partner is, so let's keep it slow, meticulous and safe. I'd rather take twice the time to search half the area than have any doubts that we may have missed something."

There were nods of agreement from the team of men and women. Lyle turned to a younger man with a slight frame and dark beard who was wearing a climbing harness and holding a length of nylon webbing. Casey recognized him as Tim Vanderwall: one of the area's premier ice climbing guides.

"Tim will be coordinating the two crews that will be working up here on the road. If something is spotted along the canyon wall, he'll decide whether we should climb down from the road or climb up from the gorge to investigate it. Before anyone rappels down from the road, Tim needs to personally sign off on your tie-off and your path of descent. If you can't find a boulder or a tree to anchor the ropes, you can tie off from the rescue truck. What'd I miss, Tim?"

"Even if we think we've found something concrete, everyone needs to hold their position until we can confirm it," Vanderwall added. "Other-wise, we'll wind up trampling through each other's grids and sectors."

Lyle nodded in agreement. "We're breaking down into four main squads. I'll be down in the gorge working south to north with my group. Laura, you'll put in just north of Mother Cline and work the gorge north-to-south with your squad. Tim, your team will be working the road south to north, keeping pace with my team. Doug's crew will be working the road, keeping pace with Laura's team. All teams have chosen a spotter. That person should have binoculars and sunglasses, right?"

Four hands were raised, holding binoculars aloft.

"Tim and Doug: you each need to assign someone on your team to keep an eye on the avalanche paths when we're working near Riverside and Mother Cline. Whoever you designate as your slide spotter will also need binoculars and a radio. We won't have much time to react, so it's going to be a mad scramble. Look for your team leader and do whatever they do. Let's not get separated from one another."

Casey noted that Lyle had elected to place himself in the area of greatest risk. If the Riverside avalanche were to run, the bottom of the canyon would be buried in untold tons of densely packed snow, rocks and timber. She was sure that this fact was not lost on Lyle's fellow team members. As she scratched under the yellow lab's chin, Casey could not help glancing down the road toward the slide area.

"For those of you on the road teams, don't lose sight of your counterparts down in the canyon," Lyle continued. "It's a lot easier to make time on the road than it is in the gorge, so you're going to need to be patient, especially with me. I'm not getting any younger."

"Just let us know if you need to stop for a nap, gramps," Tim replied with a smirk.

Lyle took the jab in good humor as he pulled his helmet over his long gray hair. "Keep an eye on your partner and don't ever be afraid to ask for help. Let's get through this and live to fight another day."

The team broke down into smaller groups. The two teams assigned to the Mother Cline area climbed into the back of two pickup trucks and headed north along US Highway 550. Vanderwall pulled the Ouray Mountain Rescue truck onto the left shoulder of the road and assembled his climbing team for equipment checks.

Once their gear was apportioned, six members of the rescue squad followed Casey and Lyle as they crossed to the west side of the Million Dollar Highway and climbed fifteen feet down the far embankment to the edge of Red Mountain Creek. Lyle stopped to let the rest of his team pass. As the group moved north along the winding creek, Lyle's dog loitered behind, taking a long drink from the creek. Lyle called back to her. "Come on, Sandy." The Labrador broke into a trot, passed Lyle and fell into step with Casey.

Casey called over her shoulder. "Is Sandy a trained avalanche rescue dog?"

"Well, that was the plan when I adopted her from the pound. In rescue training school, she could find a doggie treat buried under five feet of snow, but she was no good at following a human scent. Unfortunately, we don't get many calls to rescue lost doggie treats."

"That's okay, girl," Casey said as she patted the dog on her head. "You just stick with me."

Following the creek, the rescue team passed below and to the left of the concrete snowshed, which sloped down the embankment from the highway above. A massive debris pile from previous avalanches spread over and around the creek bed, blocking their way. The point man led them up the slope of the fifteen-foot high, forty-foot long snow mass. Casey placed her boots in the footprints of the other team members until she reached the far end of the frozen pile, where Red Mountain Creek reappeared from beneath the debris pile and plunged down the canyon wall into the gorge below. The slope that led into the Uncompahgre Gorge was not severe enough to require technical climbing apparatus, but the descent would require a blend of skill and extreme caution. On either side of the creek bed that they followed, there were large boulders and thick piles of snow deposited by a full season of avalanches and snow-removal activity.

The descent into the gorge below was a slow, slippery undertaking. Unstable snow banks and loose talus piles were identified and avoided. Where necessary, lengths of rope were strung between trees to serve as safety lines. As the last person in line, Lyle was responsible for untying the safety lines once the rest of the team had reached a secure area.

As she carefully followed the path of the team member in front of her, Casey noticed that they were rapidly losing sight of the road above them. On either side of the down-sloping creek bed, the icicle-laden, rust-colored canyon walls were nearly vertical, pitched severely toward the foot of the gorge.

Two hundred feet below the road, Red Mountain Creek rushed through the narrow, rock-strewn floor of the v-shaped canyon. Casey felt her pulse begin to quicken as she approached the base of the canyon, which was barely wider than the creek bed. She felt as if the icy walls of the gorge were closing in on her. Prone to claustrophobia since childhood, Casey kept her eyes trained on the person in front of her and took deep gulps of air to keep her fear in check.

When they reached the bottom of the gorge, the rest of the group waited for Lyle to descend the last few feet of the slope. Over the sound of the wind being channeled through the narrow canyon walls, Casey heard a low rumbling noise from above. All heads turned as one toward the sound, and an urgent shout came from Lyle's radio.

"Slide!"

Lyle jumped down to the creek bed and pointed to the far side of the canyon. "Over and up, now!"

Casey felt herself being lifted off the ground as Lyle scooped her up on the run. Splashing water erupted from the knee-deep stream as the team trudged across the ten-foot-wide creek. Lyle avoided the ice-covered boulders protruding from the creek, preferring to power his way through the swift current.

"Climb as high as you can!" he screamed when they reached the near-vertical wall on the far side of creek bed.

Handholds were furiously sought along the icy wall as a thick shower of snow began falling from above. Holding Casey in his right arm, Lyle reached up with his left hand and grabbed hold of a horizontal ledge in the rock wall. He hoisted himself two feet off the ground then tried to find footholds to boost them even further from the canyon floor. As his hand slipped off the ledge and a torrent of snow spilled over him, Lyle pinned Casey against the wall and curled his body around hers.

The cascade of snow quickly tapered off into a thin spray then stopped completely. When Lyle turned around and looked up toward the road, Casey could see that six inches of new snow had been deposited on the canyon floor.

After making sure that the rest of his team was safe, Lyle called up to the roadside spotter on his radio.

"What's going on?"

"The bottom hundred feet of the slide path let loose," was the out-of-breath response. "For a second, I thought the whole thing was going, but it looks like it's holding, at least for now."

"Anybody hurt up there?" Lyle asked.

"Nah, everyone cleared out in time. It dumped about a foot of snow on the road, though."

Lyle clipped his radio onto his belt and addressed his shaken crew. "We caught a break this time, but let's not push our luck. We'll break down into pairs, search our grids and get the hell out of this deathtrap."

— Chapter 13 —

Deputy Mark Turlington scanned the white landscape below the road with high-powered binoculars, looking for footprints or any other irregularities in the surface of the snow. His task was made difficult by the late-morning sun, which reflected off the snow like a brilliant white spotlight. To complicate matters further, the red-roofed buildings at the Mineral King Mining Company's Red Mountain surface plant cast shadows across his search area. Convinced that the turnout overlooking the surface plant didn't provide a sufficient vantage point, Turlington pulled the white Jeep Cherokee out of the parking area.

Sheriff Withers had been explicit in his early morning meeting with his deputy. Turlington's assignment was to search along both sides of US Highway 550 between Ouray and Durango for any sign of Dr. Philips. Withers had made it clear that he expected a thorough search of the entire 80-mile stretch of highway, even if it took the twenty-eight-year-old deputy the entire day. As the youngest and least experienced deputy, Turlington knew that he had been given the most mundane assignment of the expanding search for Dr. Philips. He also knew that locating any sign of the missing physician would improve his standing with his boss immeasurably.

Turlington found the break in the tree line that he was looking for along the side of the highway and eased the Sheriff's Department vehicle onto the steep, snow-covered access road that led down to the surface plant. He tapped the brakes to keep the truck from sliding down the un-plowed road and crashing into the locked gates thirty yards below the highway. He didn't have time to contact an employee of the Mineral King Mining Company to unlock the gates, so he pulled the Jeep Cherokee to within inches of the gates, climbed onto the hood and boosted himself up and over the chain-link fencing.

Walking away from his vehicle, Turlington considered radioing his lo-cation to the Sheriff's Office dispatcher, but he suspected that Bill Withers didn't want to hear from him unless he had something to report. A glance down the unused access road convinced him that his search of the area would prove fruitless, but his boss had instructed him to pay particular attention to the area near the Mineral King surface plant at Red Mountain Pass. The thin, fair-skinned deputy let out a resigned sigh, ran his hand through his wiry blonde hair and began to trudge through the deep snow along the access road. Before long, his uniform pants were caked in snow to his knees.

Fifty yards from the truck, Turlington noticed an unusual pattern along the surface of the snow atop the access road. It appeared as if the snow had been leveled out and smoothed over in two parallel strips that extended beyond the first of several abandoned storage buildings. Look-ing behind him, the confused deputy saw that the same marks extended back to within fifteen yards of the gate. The pattern reminded him of the smooth, shallow marks left behind by a child pulling a circular snow disc. But there were no footprints.

As he continued walking further into the plant, it dawned on Turl-ington that the two identical strips were evenly spaced down the entire length of the winding tree-lined road, as if someone had attempted to erase a set of tire tracks. He had seen no evidence of the peculiar marks from the highway, and he suspected that all trace of the unusual pattern would be obliterated in a matter of hours.

Turlington unclipped the two-way radio from his belt, following the path of the shallow grooves between two small metal sheds. He saw a sudden movement to his right.

"Put that damn radio down!" A deep voice commanded.

The deputy pivoted to face the man who stepped out from behind a gray metal storage shed. At first, the only thing that Turlington saw was the pistol.

"Reach for your gun and I'll blow a hole in you."

Even though the tall, pistol-wielding assailant was wearing a dark knit cap low on his forehead, Turlington recognized the man's large, bent nose and bushy goatee. The frightened deputy felt his stomach turn as Sam Moultrie quickly moved in, grabbed the radio out of his hand, pocketed it, then yanked the handgun from the lawman's holster. Moultrie stepped back a few paces, scowled at the stunned deputy and spit on the ground.

"What the hell are you doing, Sam?" Turlington asked in a higher octave than he had intended.

A wicked smirk broke across Moultrie's face as he trained both pistols on his captive. "Start walking toward that big building." he ordered, using the guns to point deeper into the complex.

Turlington knew he was in trouble. He cursed himself for not reacting faster. In a matter of seconds, he had been stripped of his radio and handgun; he had lost his primary means of communication and self-protection. He suspected that he could outrun the burly ex-con, but the deep snow ruled out any chance of making a quick getaway.

"Walk in a straight line, kid," Moultrie shouted from behind, "Thanks to you, I've gotta do this whole road over again."

"I know we've had our disagreements in the past, Sam," Turlington called over his shoulder as he shuffled toward the open yard of the Mineral King plant complex, "but this is uncalled for. You're way out of line here."

"Disagreements? Is that what you call it? I call it harassment. You guys bust my balls every chance you get! I can't even have a little fun in that sorry-ass little town of yours without you punks giving me a hard time."

"Getting all liquored up and sucker-punching a defenseless tourist might be fun for you."

"Defenseless my ass!" Moultrie interrupted as he continued to march his prisoner through the wide, vacant yard, "If they can't stand toe-to-toe with another man, then they've got no business in a bar. If Withers and his goon squad would let me knock a few of those high and mighty business types on their butts, we'd have less of those candy-asses coming around here in their Range Rovers, rubbing our noses in all their money."

"And without those tourists, the town would dry up in about ten seconds flat. Good plan, Sam. Now why don't we stop all this nonsense before it gets out of hand? You've made your point. If you want, I can talk to the sheriff about how you think you're being treated."

"Those precious tourists you're trying to protect could buy and sell every one of you guys ten times over," Moultrie continued as if he hadn't heard Turlington. "You think they give a rip about guys like us?"

Turlington stopped twenty yards short of the large Quonset-hut style building that Sam Moultrie was directing him toward. He turned around to face Moultrie. "You just said 'guys like us,' so it sounds like I'm not the real enemy here, Sam. Don't take this out on me. I'm just trying to earn a living."

"Don't give me that mealy-mouth crap, sonny. You get your rocks off bossing me around just like the rest of them. You've never shown me one ounce of respect even though you're still wet behind the ears. You think that just because you've got a badge and a gun I'm supposed to be impressed by you? Well, you still got your badge, but you ain't got no gun. Can you see how impressed I am with you now?"

With the situation getting bleaker by the moment, Turlington knew that he had to make a stand. His hands balled into fists and he glared at the bigger man. "Is that what you're looking for? A fair fight, just you and me? If that's what this is all about, then why don't you throw down those guns and we'll see what's what."

"I ought to just whip your ass just for the fun of it, but I got enough work to do around here as it is."

Seeing the confused look on Turlington's face, Moultrie burst forth with a throaty laugh. "You know what the funny thing is?" he asked, leveling the deputy's own gun at him, "You have absolutely no idea why I'm going to kill you!"

Moultrie lunged forward and pinned the muzzle of the pistol against Turlington's chest to muffle the gun's report. The deputy had just managed to clasp his hands around the gun when Moultrie pulled the trigger.

— Chapter 14 —

Paul Brader swirled his bloody Mary with a celery stalk, lost in thought as he gazed into the large stone fireplace near his corner table. He hadn't touched his sandwich, and his basket of french fries had gone cold. The AlpenHaus in Telluride Mountain Village was his favorite après-ski haunt, but Brader was not enjoying himself today. His bright blue and yellow ski outfit belied the dark mood that was etched on his face.

His regular waiter, Hardy—who Brader knew only by his first name—stepped between him and the fireplace.

"Everything okay, Mister B?"

Brader excused the lanky waiter's informality, just as he excused his open-toed sandals and dreadlocks. After all, the young man had been both respectful and attentive in the two years that they had been acquainted. Not only was he a frequent attendee of Brader's investment seminars, he had also become somewhat of a confidant.

"Yeah, Hardy. Things are fine. Just a little tired, that's all."

"No luck on the slopes this morning?" Hardy asked in a hushed tone, "Looks like there's a fine crop of ladies in town this week. I thought for sure you'd find some young thing on the bunny slopes who'd enjoy a free lesson and a romantic lunch with a dashing gent."

Brader leaned toward the waiter, adding with a smile. "While her husband or boyfriend is trying to out-macho his buddies on the black diamond trails. Works every time. At least that's the impression I get whenever I see you in here having cocktails with one of your new students."

"Not every time," Brader corrected modestly, "I treat each one like one of my investments; I keep expectations to a minimum, so I'm never disappointed. Over a couple drinks, I make it obvious that I'm interested and available, but I always leave it up to them to make the first move. The worst that can happen is I wind up sipping cognac in a ski lodge with an attractive woman. Sure beats working."

"Is Mrs. B still making noise about learning to ski? That could put a kibosh on your side trips over here to Mountain Village."

Brader laughed out loud. "Every time she gets hot on the idea, I come home with a gruesome story about some poor soul breaking their neck on the beginner slopes."

Hardy slapped him on the back. "Good plan. Hey, have you checked the markets today, or are they all on hold until the 'Master of the Market' gets back to his office?"

"You're working hard for your tip today." Brader joked before doling out a pearl of wisdom to the young man. "Nah, time, tide and the financial markets wait for no man. The key is to come up with a bold plan and stick to it. And, as I tell all my buddies back in New York, when divine investment inspiration spills from the heavens, I'm always the first to catch it, out here at an altitude of over 8,000 feet. That's why I always get a jump on them."

Hardy rocked back and forth on his heels, pretending to be amused by the multi-millionaire.

"Speaking of the office, I'd better get back there," Brader said as he reached into his wallet and tossed a fifty-dollar-bill onto the table.

Grabbing his skis and poles from the restaurant's checkroom, Brader walked outside into the sunshine. The early afternoon sky was cloudless and blue. His ski boots crunched against the packed snow that blanketed the pathway leading to the Telluride Mountain Village gondola station. Passing a stream of skiers heading in the opposite direction, Brader reflected on his uplifting conversation with Hardy.

He calculated that the young waiter was roughly the same age as he had been when he graduated from New York City's CUNY system with a business degree. As he often chronicled at his monthly investment seminars, his decision to accept a job at a major Wall Street brokerage firm was the springboard to the financial stratosphere. His timing and career choice could not have been better suited to a young man with lofty ambitions. During the early 1980's, as the stock market began its furious climb, a broad spectrum of private investors, mutual fund managers and pension fund managers solicited the advice of, and demanded the attention of professionals in the flourishing brokerage industry. As a result, stockbrokers were in high demand.

Brader had developed a reputation in the hallways of the brokerage house as a proficient churner. Constantly advising his clients to reshape their portfolios based on his own hunches and on new research data, Brader generated an unusually high number of trades per client, netting substantial fees for his firm.

Despite several raises and year-end bonuses, Brader remained frustrated with his personal financial situation. With the intoxicating aroma of money all around him, he became vexed that he was not accumulating personal wealth at a brisker pace. After all, he reasoned, it was his portfolio management skills that were enriching both his clients and his employer.

Brader's first break came after four years. His 1984 year-end bonus check was more than a million dollars; a sum comparable to those earned by other senior Wall Street brokers. Instead of investing his windfall in the type of portfolio he recommended to his clients, he waited patiently for a chance to make a bold move in the market. He began paying particular attention to the "whisper market," a network of fellow brokers who operated in the margins of the marketplace. In an industry where information was the key to personal profit, a hot tip could come from a copy room clerk, a caterer, a corporate pilot or a masseuse.

After six months of keeping his ear cocked to the murmurs emanating from the market's bottom-feeders, Brader gambled his entire bonus check on a relatively obscure American-based oil exploration company that had negotiated a long-term land lease in the West African country of Namibia. A company executive had leaked the findings of a geological survey to his brother-in-law, who happened to be a stockbroker. When the survey was released by the company, Brader realized a five-fold return on his investment.

His ability to unearth such juicy nuggets of insider information allowed him to accumulate a vast stock portfolio as well as a string of vacation houses in Hilton Head, Santa Fe, Telluride, and Maui. As his personal fortunes kept improving in the late 1980's, his interest in the firm's clients began to wane. Bored with the stock markets, Brader began to experiment in overseas markets, commodity futures and arbitrage markets for his clients. He became frustrated that he could not coax or cajole his customers into allowing him to speculate in such markets on their behalf.

In 1991, having accumulated over $20 million in assets by playing his hunches in the market's dark underbelly, Brader decided to resign from the firm and manage his personal portfolio on a full-time basis. He sold his home in New York's Westchester County and moved to Telluride, where he assumed the role of a big fish in a small but chic pond. In the insulated community of full-time Telluride residents, Brader could lay claim to the moniker of "Master of the Market." On Wall Street, such a proclamation from a man of Brader's means would elicit snickers, jeers or dismissive yawns.

When Paul Brader reached the Mountain Village Gondola station, there were only a handful of skiers lined up to climb aboard the glass-enclosed cars that arrived within seconds of one another via an overhead tramway. Brader stepped into an empty car and leaned his skis and poles against the left side of the gondola. As the car was whisked out of the station and up the tram line, Brader remained standing. He did not want to miss the view. The 13-minute ride from Telluride Mountain Village to the historic town of Telluride was exhilarating, scenic, convenient and free. Through the window, he saw the pure white ribbons of powder-packed trails that creased the tree-lined, rugged slopes of Palmyra Peak and Gold Hill. Looking up, he could spot individual skiers trying their luck on Telluride's most notorious double black-diamond trails, which bore such nicknames as The Mine Shaft, North Chute, Power Line and Kant-Max-M.

The shrill ring of his cellular phone broke the spell of the splendid view. He reached inside his ski jacket and fished a small phone out of a deep pocket. "Yeah," he snapped impatiently. Brader immediately suspected that Al Vaughn had given his private number to Joe Deutch. But since he hadn't yet received a confirmation from Sam Moultrie about the availability of the charter helicopter, he decided he had no choice but to answer the call. It was Moultrie.

"Sam, I'm glad you called," he began, trying to conduct the sensitive portion of the discussion before the gondola reached the station. "I'm sorry I had to send you back over to the Mineral King, but we left there in an awful hurry Tuesday night. We covered our tracks near the highway, but we left footprints and tire tracks all over the rest of the place. It's only a matter of time before they give that place a thorough search."

"Too late," Moultrie replied grimly. "I ran into a little problem while I was there, but I took care of it."

Brader's throat went dry. "What kind of problem?"

"I'm not gonna get into the details 'cause I don't want you using them against me if this Dr. Philips thing blows up," Moultrie seethed. "All I'm gonna say is that your whole plan was about to go up in smoke and I bailed you out."

"Oh, no!" Brader exclaimed as the gondola doors sprung open, surprising him. He had to grab his equipment with both hands and drag it out of the car before putting the phone back up to his ear. "Sorry, Sam. I'm gonna be walking down a crowded street to my office now, so I need you to do the talking here. Tell me exactly what went on at the Mineral King."

"No way. I learned a long time ago not to go flapping my gums about this kind of stuff. The less you know about this, the better I feel. All you need to know is that I put my butt on the line for you today, and it wasn't part of our deal."

"Sam, what are you trying to tell me here?" Brader pleaded as he walked down a set of stairs to San Juan Avenue, bumping fellow skiers with an armful of crisscrossed skis and poles.

"I'm telling you I'm going to need more money, man, if you want me to keep playing!" Moultrie thundered through the receiver. "And after tonight, we're through."

"Just tell me what you did, Sam." Brader said in as calm a tone as he could muster. "I need to know. I promise I won't use it against you."

"Not a chance. Besides, I've taken care of everything. By the time anyone figures out what happened, we'll both be long gone."

Paul Brader reached the parking lot behind the Monte Vista Condominium building on Pacific Avenue. He dropped his ski equipment in a heap next to his black Chevy Suburban and leaned against his car, not believing what he was hearing.

"That's not acceptable, Sam. I can't have any loose ends coming back to haunt me after this is all over. You can just drop out of sight so no one can find you, but I don't have that option; I'm too visible."

"And you've got a pot of gold waiting for you over this rainbow," Moultrie muttered. "Me, I'm just the guy who's been bailing you out left and right so you can get your payoff. Well you'd better show up tonight with a check for twenty grand or I'm not flying you anywhere."

"Twenty grand! This is extortion! I didn't ask you to…" Brader looked around the parking lot to make sure no one was listening. "Look, Sam, we can discuss all of this tonight."

"Just be sure to bring your checkbook. Are we going to meet at the place we talked about? I still don't know why I can't just fly to Telluride Airport and pick you up."

"Because we can't be seen together. Are you sure you know the pick-up point?"

"Positive. Just be ready to move as soon as I touch down. It's a strange place for a copter to be landing, so I can't stay on the ground long," Moultrie warned, before changing topics. "Oh, by the way, I've got a bone to pick with you."

"*You've* got a bone to pick with *me*? What is it now?"

"How come you didn't tell me that Doc Philips has some chick living with him?"

"What are you talking about? How do you know there's someone living with him?"

Moultrie became evasive. "Hey, don't get all bent out of shape. I stopped by the dude's house on my way home from the Montrose Airport last night to see if there was anything lying around. You know, easy pickings."

"You did *what*?" Brader thundered, not believing his ears. "Are you telling me that you were actually stupid enough to risk everything for a two-bit break-in? Did anybody see you?"

"No," the pilot lied, uncharacteristically on the defensive. "I saw the girl through the window when I drove by, so I just kept on going."

"Thank God." Brader slumped against his vehicle. "Sam, you're absolutely killing me here. You're causing more trouble than you're worth."

"More trouble than I'm worth?" Moultrie hissed. "You got no idea what trouble I can be! You talk to me like that again and I'll beat the tar out of you. And if you don't show up with a check for twenty large tonight, I'll toss you out of the helicopter!"

The phone clicked in Brader's ear. He stared at the receiver, trying to make sense of the conversation. He couldn't believe Moultrie was willing to jeopardize their undertaking by committing petty larceny. And what was the veiled reference to an incident at the Mineral King surface plant?

Brader picked up his gear, tossed it into the back of his Suburban, and changed into a pair of hiking boots. He then walked across the parking lot, entered the Monte Vista condominium building, and walked up two flights of stairs to his office.

Two blocks from the Oak Street ski lift and the Telluride Station gondola stop, the Monte Vista was an ideal office location for an avid skier. Although his house on the northeast side of Telluride contained ample room for an office, Brader had renovated a condo on the southwest side of town to use as a daytime retreat. Not only did the office provide him with the necessary privacy for his business dealings, but it also saved him from the prospect of being trapped at home with Sissy, his wife of eighteen years.

Walking down the hallway, Brader heard two female voices from behind his office door. He could tell that his wife was chatting with Kimberly Cousins, his receptionist. Hearing Sissy's thick Brooklyn accent, Brader shook his head. In his metamorphosis from an unremarkable college student to the "Master of the Market," Paul Brader had refined himself both economically and socially. Over the years, he had managed to shed most traces of his humble origins. The only connection between the man he had been and the man he had become was his wife. As he frequently told Sissy, she was the personification of the Brooklyn Bridge and a Coney Island hot dog. She, of course, took such comments as compliments.

Brader opened the office door and stepped into the small reception area. Kimberly, a plump, plain-featured woman in her mid forties, sat up straight in her chair and reached toward a pile of pink message slips.

"Joe Deutch has already left several messages. He says it's urgent."

"What could possibly be more urgent than lounging around over there in Mountain Village?" Sissy teased. "Straighten Kimberly out, Paul. Nothin' is more important to my hubby than unsupervised play time."

"What brings you here, dear?" Paul Brader asked with mock cheer in his voice.

Sissy Brader took the three-quarter length mink coat that was folded over her arm and draped it over a nearby chair. She crossed her thin arms across her chest and faced her husband. "I need to talk to you about the menu for our dinner party on Sunday night. It will just take a minute. You've got a minute, don't you, Paul?" Sissy said with some sarcasm. "I thought we'd start with crab cake appetizers, then serve a rack of lamb. For dessert, the caterer is recommending a warm pear tart…"

"Please, Sissy, I don't have time for this. I've got a bunch of calls to return."

"You don't have time?" his wife replied dismissively. "I'm up to my ears in caterers, cleaners and florists. You think I can just pull a dinner party out of my butt? And whose party is this anyway?"

"Are you going to be using Casey Bailey for the flowers?" Brader asked abruptly.

"I am. She's stopping by the house today at four-thirty to go over the arrangements."

"I'll come home a little early. I want to be there when you two meet."

"What's the sudden interest in flowers, Paul? You thinking of changing careers?"

"Very funny, dear. It just so happens that I'm concerned about Jim Philips. I haven't heard from him since Tuesday."

"We're not expecting him on Sunday, are we? If so, you'd better tell me now."

"Not to worry, honey. Jim Philips is letting me handle the Saratoga side of this transaction," Brader assured her as he walked out of the reception area. As he opened the door to his private office, he called over his shoulder. "I'll be home around four."

Closing the door behind him, Paul Brader let out a deep sigh. To compensate for what he considered his wife's tasteless decoration of their home, Brader had furnished his office like an exclusive gentleman's club. The walls were painted hunter green. Brass accent pieces including umbrella stands, ashtrays and humidors dotted his office. A bronze Frederic Remington sculpture stood on a polished wooden pedestal beneath an Ansel Adams print. Two burgundy leather chairs faced his uncluttered mahogany desk. He sat down heavily in his custom orthopedic chair and contemplated how to handle Casey Bailey.

Her visit would provide him with an update regarding the investigation of Jim Philips's disappearance. He needed something from an informed source and was glad he no longer needed to concoct a reason for visiting Casey at her shop. He had invented reasons to see her before, but this time his motives were much different.

From the time the Petal Pusher opened its doors, Brader had taken notice of Casey Bailey's perfect smile and fresh-scrubbed appearance. She had a blend of confidence and vulnerability that was extremely sexy to the 42-year-old multimillionaire. Over the past three years, Casey had politely rebuffed his offer of expert counsel regarding the financial aspects of her business. She likewise artfully spurned Brader's many requests to accompany him for dinner, hiking, skiing and snowmobiling.

Kimberly's voice sounded over his telephone's intercom. "It's Mister

Deutch calling again."

"Tell him I'll be out on business all day," he barked. "If he calls again, I don't want to know about it."

Brader pulled at the collar of his black turtleneck. His personal finances were like unseen tentacles choking the life out of him. He felt so impotent. He had compounded one errant roll of the dice in the stock market by risking another wild gamble with Jim Philips and Saratoga Mining. Now, Sam Moultrie was jeopardizing his only hope of deliverance by taking foolish risks.

In an effort to shake himself out of it, Brader angrily slapped his palm against the top of his desk. He got up from his chair and began pacing back and forth between his desk and the office window. The plan he had developed two weeks ago was still the best, and only, option available to him. With Jim Philips's signature on the Divining Rod Enterprises document, he would have the authority to close the deal with Saratoga Mining on Sunday. That money, in turn, would allow him to weather the impending loss from his short-sell stock play.

He had to change tactics with Dr. Philips. The elderly man needed to be shown the futility of resisting a stronger man's will. Tonight's encounter was a make-or-break situation, and he intended to make Philips break.

When he first conceived the kidnapping, Brader had hoped that Philips would attribute his rash act to the desperate situation that precipitated it. Once he was returned to Ouray, Brader had theorized, the physician would show his gratitude by remaining silent about his abduction. The level of trust and friendship they had built over the past eighteen months had to account for something, right? In the light of day, however, the plan seemed like a product of wishful thinking. It was clear that Jim Philips could not be trusted to keep silent. Brader decided that he had no choice but to prepare for the alternative. He had already given the matter a great deal of thought.

Brader fully expected that he would be questioned about the doctor's disappearance, particularly given the timing of the Saratoga deal. He doubted that the local law enforcement agencies would shift their focus to him until after the deal closed on Sunday night. He was counting on it.

If he was somehow identified as a suspect, Brader knew that the police could not build a case solely on motive. Without a body, there would be no evidence, and Brader did not intend to serve up a body. In the rugged terrain of the San Juan Mountains, there were countless places to dispose of a corpse. And with hundreds of miles of mine shafts and tunnels to choose from, his secret could lie buried for centuries. Besides, his alibi for Tuesday night was virtually foolproof.

Finding himself standing at the window, Brader pressed his face against the cool windowpane. His view did not allow him to see the peaks that flanked Imogene Pass. Although the doctor had clearly been in dire straits when he last saw him, Brader assumed that Jim Philips had lived through the night. In a few short hours, he would see.

Distracted, Brader was startled by Kimberly's voice on the intercom. "Do you want to speak with a Sheriff Bill Withers from Ouray County? He says it's urgent."

— Chapter 15 —

The pacing was becoming maddeningly monotonous, but Dr. Philips knew that it was vital to keep moving. He was becoming hypothermic and his extremities were numb from the cold. He had stretched the thin blanket over a square patch of trampled snow four feet from the wall of the shack. He paced back and forth over the folded blanket, stomping his feet to keep blood circulating. The throbbing pain in his head increased with each passing hour. He was being attacked by intense coughing fits every few minutes.

He found that he could no longer wiggle his toes. The ice pellets that clung to his wool socks had frozen the fabric against his skin during the night. His attempts to warm his feet by rubbing them between his bare hands had proven futile. Realizing that he had already lost his first battle against frostbite, Dr. Philips decided to concentrate his efforts elsewhere. As he paced, he continually flexed his icy fingers and blew on his hands. But there was little he could do, however, to protect his nose and ears from the cold. Pulling the collar of his jacket over his head did not help. The gale blowing over the exposed mountain pass sliced through the threads of his tweed jacket.

The midday sun was more intense at the 13,000-foot altitude, but the thin slanting rays seemed to be doing more damage than good. His eyes were being seared by the blinding white snow around him. He knew that his face would become more sensitive to the cold if he became sunburned.

Dr. Philips couldn't decide whether to seek refuge from the wind and crawl back into the shack where he had spent a shivering, sleepless night in sub-zero temperatures. Despite the brutal conditions, he resolved to remain outside until nightfall. If a search effort had been mounted, he would need to be visible from the air. No rescue party would attempt to search Imogene Pass on foot unless they had a firm fix on his location. The doctor suspected that his only hope of rescue would be a search helicopter conducting a random sweep of the area. Any pilot willing to battle the thin air and swirling winds of the San Juans would not be hovering in one spot very long. Dr. Philips needed to be in plain sight in the event a search helicopter suddenly appeared.

A deadly mix of exposure, cold and hunger was slowly eroding Philips's strength. He had spent the morning trying to break free of his restraints, but no matter how he twisted or tugged at the handcuffs, he could not slip them over his wrists. And the chain around his right ankle had been padlocked too tight to be forced off his foot. Sawing the chains against the sharp metal of the shack's outer skin proved fruitless. So did attempts to pick the locks of his handcuffs with the ballpoint pen he found in his jacket pocket. His voice was hoarse from screaming for help every ten minutes.

The mailbox post still would not budge. Located at the southeast corner of the weather-beaten brown shack, the mailbox was the epicenter of his accessible universe. The chains ensured that he could not walk more than eight feet in any direction from the sturdy iron post. Since he had trampled the snow within the eight-foot radius, his attempts to scrape the letters "SOS" in the snow down to the dark rock underneath proved to be a waste of time and energy. A layer of white ice clung to the uneven surface of the rocky ground beneath.

He had saved the wrappers from the beef jerky Brader had flung at him the previous night, hoping to use them to increase his chances of being spotted from the air. But no aircraft had flown close enough for him to signal with the clear cellophane wrapper. He had eaten one of the two sticks of dry, processed meat. The other remained in his pants pocket. The carton of apple juice had frozen overnight, and he had been licking it like a snow cone during the day, savoring the sweet juice on his frozen tongue.

Philips knew that his body's natural defenses were being compromised with each passing hour. His lungs burned with each intake of frigid air. His teeth chattered with each wave of shivers that convulsed him. Even his bones seemed frozen. What surprised him was the gradual failure of his mind's ability to concentrate. Several times, he had found himself staring into the white, gauzy distance for long stretches, unable to recall when the bout of confusion and lethargy had started or why it had ended.

After the latest episode, Dr. Philips stopped pacing and sat down on the blanket. He folded his legs painfully and tucked his feet underneath him for warmth. In order to keep his mind occupied, he turned his attention to the barren wintry landscape. He reasoned that if he could contain his thoughts to his immediate surroundings, his mind could not drift very far.

Below the summit ledge on which the shack was perched, the deep bowl of Imogene Basin spread out before him. Bordered by sheer, battleship-gray rock walls, the vast basin cradled shifting snowdrifts that were dozens of feet deep. The doctor shaded his eyes from the glare and tried to make out the path of the meandering jeep trail that lay buried beneath the frozen snow. He could not recall a summer when the snow had completely disappeared from the slopes surrounding Imogene Basin. Treacherous even for experienced 4-wheel adventurers, the slow drive along the primitive jeep road tested the limits of any 4-wheel drive vehicle. For Dr. Philips, though, the effort it took to reach the mountain basins between Ouray and Telluride was always worth the reward.

Once the snowpack melted, Imogene Basin was awash in a vibrant spray of colors. Rich fragrances clung to pure mountain breezes as brittle wildflowers burst to life in a brief yet glorious display of alpine splendor. Blue and white columbines shared the stage with white osha, purple monkshood, red paintbrush, blue larkspurs and yellow sneezeweed. The resilient wildflowers sprang from a thin crust of alpine tundra that had required decades to form within the windswept glacial cavity. Closing his eyes, the doctor could picture the landscape beneath him in full bloom, tiny runnels of snow-fed water braiding their way through the basin floor. It was no wonder, he thought with a melancholy pang, that Imogene Basin had been one of Mimi's favorite places on earth. Several times each summer, Mimi would pack a picnic lunch to share with her husband in a field of wildflowers amid the majestic backdrop of the San Juan Mountains.

In addition to the natural splendor of the alpine basins, tourists were attracted to the area by the relics of old mining camps that could be explored by jeep roads and hiking trails. Constructed in the 1880s and 1890s at the height of Colorado's great silver mining rush, the camps that had not been obliterated by the ravages of time and weather had been reduced to desolate ghost towns. The crumbling ruins of old stamp mills, mining cabins, bunkhouses and assay houses still dotted the landscape, affording tourists a glimpse of the area's hard-rock mining heritage. As they picked among the few wooden structures that remained, most visitors had no idea that entire towns had been erected in this inhospitable mountain terrain to support year-round mining operations that yielded tons of precious gold and silver.

From his vantage point near the summit of Imogene Pass, Dr. Philips could see rows of ridge-like, snow-covered mounds that stretched hundreds of feet along the basin floor. The piles were vast mine dumps consisting of pulverized ore from the upper workings of the Camp Bird Mine. At an altitude of over 11,500 feet, the upper level of Camp Bird Mine was worked on year-round basis during the 1890s. Avalanches had long since demolished the three-story boarding house that accommodated up to 400 miners. Dr. Philips knew that he was now experiencing firsthand what life during the long winters was like for the hardy miners a century ago. He wondered why any rational human being would choose to subject themselves to such cold, bleak conditions above ground in order to earn a living in the cramped, dark, acid-filled shafts and tunnels beneath Imogene Basin.

Everything Dr. Philips was able to see was somehow related to the history of hard-rock mining in the basin. He felt a sharp sting of irony, as if it was being carried on the icy winds swirling around him. After all, it was his attempts to ensure that large-scale mining operations could never again sully these pristine mountain basins that had resulted in his being deposited in this place, surrounded by relics of past mining booms.

On his first jeep tour of Imogene Pass with Mimi, their driver had informed them of the historical significance of the engineer's hut that was now his prison. Constructed of wood planks and corrugated metal sheets nearly a hundred years ago, the shack was built during the height of the Colorado silver rush. The Telluride Power Company had run electrical power lines over the summit of Imogene Pass to provide power to the mining camps on the Ouray side of the pass. In an effort to provide uninterrupted service, the power company stationed a maintenance man in the hut to inspect and repair the lines leading to the mining complexes below. As an incentive to keep the alternating current flowing, and to keep themselves from freezing to death, the servicemen were provided with electric heaters. One of the stories that Dr. Philips had heard was that the servicemen would hike up to the shack before the first snowfall and climb back down once the spring thaw arrived. Staring at the shack, Dr. Philips promised himself that, if he ever made it back to civilization alive, he would find out if this tale was true. He could not conceive how anyone could possibly endure six to eight months of isolation in these conditions.

He was equally curious about the mailbox that he was chained to. He had first assumed that a bored maintenance worker might have erected the mailbox on a lark. Having tested the sturdiness of the mailbox, however, Dr. Philips now concluded that it had been intended as a permanent fixture. While the U.S. Postal Service credo promised the delivery of mail through rain, snow and the gloom of night, whoever coined the phrase surely never contemplated travails such as those required to deliver mail to the summit of Imogene Pass. Dr. Philips theorized that the mailbox had once been serviced during the spring and summer months by the mail carrier assigned to the town of Tomboy, a ghost town situated along the Jeep trail that wound down from Imogene Pass toward Telluride.

Shifting his position on the blanket so that he was facing to the southeast, Philips craned his neck to locate the ruins of Fort Peabody. Framed against the clear cyan sky, he saw the dark outline of the outpost, perched atop a steep 100-foot hill. He pulled his jacket over his head to shield his nose and cheeks from the wind now blowing directly into his face, and resisted a strong impulse to lay down on the blanket with his jacket over him. His body seemed to be urging him to seek the comfort of sleep. He knew he had to fight to remain alert. With a great deal of mental effort, he tried to recall everything he knew about Fort Peabody.

The tiny sentry post was not an official U.S. Army fort. It was a tiny state militia outpost built in the early 1900s in response to labor troubles in Telluride. After several armed conflicts between union and non-union workers, Colorado's Governor Peabody declared martial law, threw the pro-union agitators out of town and posted armed sentinels at the summit of Imogene Pass to make sure they didn't sneak back.

From his position near the foot of the steep incline, Dr. Philips could see the crumbling fragments of Fort Peabody's rock walls as well as the skeletal remains of its steep-pitched wooden roof. He had heard that when the Jeep road was cleared to provide tourists with access to Imogene Pass in the late 1960s, workers were amazed to find a flag still flying from the top of Fort Peabody's flagpole, nearly sixty years after it had been abandoned.

The mines on the Ouray side of Imogene Pass had been spared labor troubles due largely to the generosity of the area's mine owners. Tom Walsh, the owner of Camp Bird Mine, never skimped when it came to his workers' comfort. In addition to steam-heated boarding houses and recreation facilities, he provided lavish meals and telephone service for his employees. One of Ouray's great benefactors, Walsh became one of the richest men in Colorado as his Camp Bird Mine continued to churn out huge deposits of gold-laden ore. Walsh's daughter Evalyn became a fixture in society and went on to marry the publisher of *The Washing-*

ton Post. Evalyn and her husband purchased the famed Hope Diamond, eventually selling the "jinxed" gem after a series of misfortunes. Walsh eventually sold the mine for $5 million, a princely sum in the early 1900s.

As the current owner of Camp Bird Mine and its network of nearly 100 mining claims, Dr. Philips had a great deal of respect for Walsh, who he admired as a compassionate employer and a generous town benefactor. Just as the Hope Diamond was now a national treasure on display at the Smithsonian, Dr. Philips hoped that the Camp Bird Mine would serve as a living historic treasure. Unencumbered by the claims of profiteers, the ore-laden basins surrounding Ouray would finally be allowed to rest peacefully. Instead of being measured by their per-ton yield of gold and silver, the value of Imogene, Governor and Yankee Boy basins would now be measured in terms of their sublime beauty and the delight they provided for their intrepid visitors.

Dr. Philips continued to scan his immediate surroundings, and turned his eyes east to the peaks of the Red Mountains.

"You started this whole mess," he muttered in the direction of the mountains.

The perceived ore content of the orange-tinted slopes of the Red Mountains had first attracted the interest of prospectors in the early 1870s. The distinctive hue of the mountains was due to the presence of pyrite and hematite that had bled through to the soil. Early prospecting of the chimneys, fissures, pipes and veins in the Red Mountains revealed that the copper and lead ore bodies contained rich concentrations of silver. It was not long before word leaked out and the "rush" was on. The Red Mountain Mining District exploded almost overnight. Until the collapse of the silver market in 1893, the most daunting problem facing mine operators was how to transport the ore to smelting plants as quickly as it was being mined.

As he accumulated his portfolio of mining rights, Dr. Philips never attempted to purchase any of the claims in the Red Mountain District, or in the Savage Basin on the Telluride side of Imogene Pass. The Mineral King Mining Company held those claims. In an effort to provide sufficient access to their network of over 90 miles of subterranean tunnels, drifts and shafts, Mineral King engineers had blasted a huge main portal to connect the mines in the Red Mountain District to those in Savage Basin. The tunnel ran beneath Imogene Pass, but did not intersect any of the claims now owned by Divining Rod Enterprises. The Mineral King Mining Company had worked the two mining districts extensively from the 1930s through the 1970s, out-producing nearly every other mining operation in mineral-rich Colorado.

Chemicals were used in the milling process to separate the desired metals from their host ore bodies. After a century of mining in the San Juan Mountains, huge dump piles of chemically-treated, pulverized rock stretched for acres around major milling sites, creating both an eyesore and an environmental time bomb. As environmental concerns mounted in the 1960s and 1970s, sins of the past were visited upon the present-day owners of the mining claims. The Mineral King Mining Company, which had played such a crucial role in the mid-century economic survival of towns such as Ouray and Telluride, spent the 1980s and 1990s re-vegetating, reclaiming and generally mopping up the end product of 100 years of San Juan mining activity.

Dr. Philips rubbed his hands together and flexed his stiff, waxy-looking fingers. The sun was beginning its rapid late-afternoon descent; its flat rays no longer providing even a modicum of warmth. He now wondered how he would cope with the inky darkness of the engineer's shack for another night.

As he rose from the blanket and resumed pacing, a disquieting notion took hold. Dr. Philips had the distinct impression his every movement was being observed. He spun around slowly in an attempt to locate the source of his unease. It appeared to be coming from the mountain peaks around him and from the very ground upon which he was standing.

Alone at the summit of Imogene Pass, surrounded by the ghosts and relics of days long past, Dr. Philips felt as if he were being judged. Still semi-lucid, Dr. Philips tried to establish a connection with the spirits and souls that he imagined were swirling around him. Were they mocking him for having financed an undertaking rooted in naiveté and folly? Were they praising him for staking a claim that elevated the status of the land itself above the status of its overlords? He didn't know. What was becoming increasingly apparent to him, however, was that he was paying dearly for his convictions. His body was already beginning to sacrifice itself to the elements. For the first time, he began to acknowledge the fact that he was dying.

— Chapter 16 —

As she rang up one of her regular customers, Casey glanced at the thermostat mounted on the wall near the register, and blew on her hands.

"Are you feeling a cold coming on, honey?"

"I hope not, Mrs. Humboldt. I was outside most of the day and I can't seem to shake the chill," Casey replied. As she waited to receive an authorization code for the woman's credit card, she could feel the woman's gaze alight on her battered face. It was clear to Casey that Gloria Humboldt belonged to a generation where bruises and abrasions like Casey's were not commented on.

"They say it's going to get even colder tonight. Did you get weather like this in Connecticut?"

Casey smiled as she placed two jars of locally made raspberry jam and an arrangement of dried flowers into a white paper bag bearing the yellow and green Petal Pusher logo. After three years of presiding over her retail shop, Casey was considered a Telluride veteran by some. To Mrs. Humboldt, however, the twenty-six year old blonde was still a newcomer.

"Every time I think I'm finally getting used to it, Mother Nature throws a new surprise at me. I'll bet you've seen her whole bag of tricks, though."

Mrs. Humboldt beamed. "You can say that again. Stick with me and we'll get through it together, okay?"

As the woman exited the shop, Casey looked at her watch and opened the door to the walk-in cooler.

"I've gotta run up to Sissy Brader's for a four-thirty appointment," she called to Jason Zuckerman over the sound of the refrigeration equipment. "If I'm not back by closing time, just lock up when you leave, okay? I've got another meeting at six-thirty with the Sheriff over in Ouray. I may wind up going straight there from the Braders' house."

Jason smiled and his light green eyes twinkled mischievously. "Even Houdini couldn't escape the clutches of Sissy Brader in less than an hour. Don't worry about coming back; I'll take care of things."

"I've been leaning on you a lot the last couple of days," Casey said. "Why don't you take tomorrow afternoon off? I'll pay you for a full day."

Jason dropped the clipboard in a mock display of shock. He swept both sides of his long, jet-black hair behind his ears and put his hands on his head. "Do you mean to tell me you're actually going to pay me for not showing up? You'd better be careful or you'll ruin your reputation."

"I can always change my mind," Casey retorted. "All you're going to do anyway is mope around with a bunch of powder-hound slackers whose idea of fun is sitting around watching Hardy Bennett pull insects out of his dreadlocks."

Casey pulled on her multi-layered nylon winter jacket and pocketed her keys. She pulled her hair into a short ponytail and threaded it through the adjustable strap at the back of a New York Mets baseball cap. She walked two blocks to her Jeep, parked on a snow-lined side street. Navigating the Jeep through unpaved streets glazed with packed snow and frozen slush, she turned left onto Colorado Avenue. Driving east, Casey followed the path of the San Miguel River as it wound past the Town Park. During the summer, the park hosted the town's popular bluegrass and jazz festivals. In the winter months, the park featured an ice rink, Nordic ski trails and rolling hills for sledding and inner-tubing.

Making a left onto Columbine Street, she downshifted into second to climb the steep hill, then turned left onto Primrose Avenue. The Braders' house resembled a Scandinavian ski chalet with dark wood and large panes of glass. Built into the craggy slopes on the north side of Telluride, the home overlooked the historic downtown district. Glancing through the windows of the ground-floor garage, she saw Paul Brader's black Chevy Suburban and Sissy Brader's red Ford Explorer.

Casey climbed a steep flagstone staircase that led to the front door. Lights blazed through the tall strips of glass windows, and she could hear faint strains of music. Casey rang the doorbell, removed her cap, and stomped her boots on the welcome mat, removing the caked snow. She finger-combed her dishwater-blonde hair and swept it away from her face.

Sissy Brader opened the door. She wore a shiny pink warm-up suit and white cross-training shoes. Her thick dark hair was pulled back into a ponytail, held in place by an elastic loop of pink terrycloth. She smiled broadly at Casey.

"There she is, always right on time!" She clasped Casey's hand and led her into a foyer that had a tall vaulted ceiling. An elaborate crystal chandelier hung ten feet above their heads. "You're a dear for stopping by. Can I get you something to drink?"

"No, thanks, Mrs. Brader. I just had a cup of coffee at the shop."

"How many times do I have to tell you? Call me Sissy."

Stepping into the Braders' living room, Casey was once again struck by the seeming incongruity between the exterior and the interior of the home. Sissy waved her toward a large sectional couch with pink and white orchid print upholstery. The couch formed a u-shape around white wicker-framed coffee table with a glass top. On top of the table were two large conch shells that sat astride a deep white porcelain bowl filed with green and pink marbles. Casey unzipped her jacket and girded herself for the requisite twenty minutes of small talk that preceded any substantive conversation with Sissy.

"I love your perfume," Casey lied as she inhaled the strong musky scent.

"Oh, that. I'm surprised it hasn't worn off, what with all the runnin' around I've been doing. This dinner party that Paul and I are throwin' on Sunday is drivin' me nuts."

"In that case, why don't we get right down to business so you can check this off your list." Casey rubbed her hands together and looked around the home. "As far as the foyer is concerned, I just got a shipment of long-stemmed white tulips that I can blend with budding willow branches in a tall tapered glass vase. That might do the trick."

The conversation was interrupted by the sound of approaching footsteps. Paul Brader was wearing a black cashmere turtleneck, soft grey flannel slacks and a pair of handmade Italian loafers. His sculptured, gel-slicked black hair was as stiff as ever.

Brader appeared both surprised and delighted to find Casey sitting on the couch. "If it isn't Telluride's favorite petal pusher. How've you been, Casey?"

Casey rose and extended her hand.

"What *happened* to you?" Paul Brader asked, placing a finger under Casey's chin and inspecting the welts and bruises on her face.

"There was a break-in at Dr. Philips's house last night," she answered matter-of-factly. "It looks worse than it feels. I'll be fine."

"Oh, for heaven's sake!" Sissy Brader exclaimed. "What kind of host am I? You walk in here with your face all swollen up and I don't even notice?"

"Like I said, it's really nothing."

"Did they catch the person who did this to you?" Paul Brader asked in genuine shock.

"Nah, he got away, and I never got a good look at him."

"Well that's a shame," he replied, trying not to sound relieved.

Unnerved by the attention she was receiving, Casey tried to change the subject. "You're home early, Mr. Brader."

"Here we go with that Mr. Brader nonsense again," he teased, sitting down on the couch. "I'm actually heading out for a meeting in Montrose later this evening. That's the price I had to pay for having a go at the fresh powder on the slopes today. Sissy thinks I've got my priorities all messed up, but then again, she's not exactly a fan of the sport."

"A while ago, you said you were considering taking up skiing. Did you ever get around to it?" Casey asked, turning toward Sissy.

Paul Brader answered for his wife. "I've practically begged her to take some lessons from me, but for some reason, she seems to think it's too dangerous."

"I don't need to be pushing my luck on slopes packed with a bunch of reckless kids." Sissy declared. "Paul, on the other hand, likes to throw caution to the wind. Hopefully, that won't land him in trouble one day."

Paul Brader ignored his wife's comment. He leaned forward on the couch seat and addressed Casey solemnly. "I got a phone call today from a Sheriff Withers over in Ouray. He tells me that Jim Philips has been missing since Tuesday night. Naturally I wanted to learn more about what's happening, but to be honest, the sheriff wasn't very forthcoming. Do you know what this is all about?"

Casey felt relieved to be able to discuss the situation with someone who shared her concern about Dr. Philips.

"His pickup was knocked off Highway 550 by a snowplow late Tuesday night," she began. "Ouray Mountain Rescue spent the better part of the day today searching the area north of Red Mountain Pass. We came up empty, which I'm told is good news."

Sissy spoke up. "You mean you were out there looking too?"

Casey replied, "Everyone who's ever met Dr. Philips has been trying to help. The entire Sheriff's department is working on it, but Bill Withers keeps things pretty close to the vest. I arranged a meeting with him tonight so I can find out where things stand. He wasn't thrilled about me elbowing my way into his investigation but after all, I've lived with Dr. Philips for the past three years."

Brader nodded sympathetically. "Has this Withers character even developed a theory about Jim's disappearance?"

Casey shook her head. "That's what's so frustrating. *No one* has a good theory yet. It's as if everyone expects Dr. Philips to breeze back into Ouray at any minute. I wish I could be optimistic, but I'm the one who waits up at night for him to come home. I wish I could figure out something else I can do to help. It might seem silly, but I've been dialing his pager number every hour for two days straight."

Brader leaned forward. "That's a good idea. Do they know for sure that he has his pager with him?"

"It wasn't in his truck when they pulled it out of the gorge."

He nodded slowly. "I see. Jim and I have been friends and business associates for over a year now, and I'd like to help however I can."

"You know what's funny?" Casey asked. "I had no idea that you and Dr. Philips even knew each other until yesterday when I saw your name on some documents in his den. You never mentioned him and he never mentioned you. Don't you think that's kind of odd?"

"How can I put this without betraying Jim's confidence?" Brader replied tentatively. "Let's just say that our business involves a certain amount of speculation. If word got around, it would drive our acquisition costs through the roof."

"I guess that explains why Sheriff Withers is being so protective about those files. He must know that Dr. Philips wants them to remain a secret. To be honest with you, I know those papers have something to do with mining claims, but the sheriff took them out of the house before I had a chance to study them. Anyway, you don't have to worry about me blabbing about what you've got going on with Dr. Philips," she assured Paul Brader.

Alarmed, Brader fixed Casey with a stare and asked as casually as he could. "Are you telling me that Sheriff Withers actually confiscated business correspondence from Dr. Philips's house without a search warrant or a subpoena?"

"I don't know if he had a search warrant or not," Casey replied hesitantly. "I probably shouldn't have said anything."

"I don't want to put you in the middle of this, Casey, but who does he think he is? Just because he's the sheriff in a Podunk town doesn't mean he can waltz into somebody's home and cart away confidential documents."

"Do you want me to say something when I see him tonight?" Casey offered.

For the first time since Casey had met Paul Brader, she saw him run his hands through his meticulously styled hair. He forced a smile. "No, that won't be necessary. I think it's time to get my lawyer involved here."

"It sounds like I stirred up a hornet's nest. I'm not telling you what to do, but why don't you arrange a meeting with the sheriff and the two of you can get this straightened out? I'm a big believer in dealing with problems head-on and face-to-face. Besides, he's really not such a bad guy."

Sissy Brader seemed concerned. "Is any of this stuff you're talking about going to affect the dinner party? It's too late to back out of all the commitments I've made."

Brader stood up and shook his head. "This has nothing to do with our dinner party, dear."

"But I thought that the guys from Saratoga Mining…"

"Sissy!" Brader cut her off.

"What?" she asked defensively.

Ignoring his wife, Brader smiled at Casey and said. "Sometimes, it's even tough to keep a secret within your own home."

He turned on his heels, marched out of the living room and headed for the stairs. The two women were left staring at one another in embarrassed silence.

Finally, Casey spoke in a deadpan voice. "Did I happen to mention that I have some great looking white tulips for your foyer?"

— Chapter 17 —

Lyle Morrison stood near his open garage door, waiting patiently for Sandy to emerge from the nearby woods. The overnight temperature was expected to drop into the teens, and Lyle had ferried a stack of split wood into the house.

To ensure that his guests could navigate his steep driveway, Lyle had plowed the sixty-foot stretch of hard-packed gravel leading from County Road 361. Two miles from downtown Ouray, Lyle's house was nestled among aspen and spruce trees on a flat shelf twenty feet above the secluded backcountry road. The split-level ranch house was nondescript compared to the more opulent Victorian homes in the center of Ouray, but over the past six years Lyle found that it adequately suited his needs.

Morrison could not remember the last time he had more than one guest in his house. Aside from occasional visits from Bill Withers, Jim Philips or one of his co-workers, Lyle lived a relatively solitary life. At home, he often spent his spare time in the garage, where he kept a Nautilus machine, a treadmill and an array of hard-rock mining tools. He had converted part of the two-car garage into a woodworking shop. With a table saw, band saw, lathe and an assortment of woodworking tools, here he could indulge his hobby of creating custom furniture, cabinets and ornamental wooden carvings and sculptures.

Hearing the whine of a vehicle travelling in low gear, Lyle peered through a tangle of low-hanging branches to see Casey's Jeep Wrangler climbing his driveway. Casey pulled up next to Lyle's green Ford pickup and flicked off her headlights. As she climbed out of her vehicle, Sandy darted out of the woods, making a beeline for the new arrival. Casey bent over and hugged the enthusiastic yellow lab, rocking her from side to side.

"Hey, girl, did you miss me?"

Sandy placed her paws on Casey's jacket and tried to lick the young woman's face.

"Sandy, get down," Lyle called. "She doesn't want you slobbering all over her."

"Don't listen to him, he's just jealous," Casey teased. "By the way, thanks for offering your house for this meeting."

"No problem. Withers called to say he was running late, but he also said they think they're onto something."

Casey's face brightened. "Really?"

"I guess we'll find out soon. Come on inside."

Lyle led the way into the garage. Casey looked around, noticing several woodworking projects in various stages of completion scattered around a large workbench. Her attention was drawn to an unstained rocking chair that sat on a drop cloth. She ran her hands over the smooth wood, admiring the gentle curves of the chair's arms and back rails.

"You made this?"

"Yep. I still need to do some fine sanding on it; then it has to be stained."

"Are you going to use it in your house?"

"No, I've already got one inside."

"Are you going to sell it?" Casey asked.

Lyle looked at the rocker and replied in a soft voice. "Actually, I made it with my daughter in mind. She's at the age now where she might be raising a family."

Casey was confused. "Might be?"

The fifty-one-year-old man let out a long sigh and looked Casey squarely in the eye. "I haven't laid eyes on her since she was five years old. She's thirty-one now. After her mother and I split up, I haven't heard a word from either one of them."

"I'm sorry, I didn't know. This obviously isn't something you want to talk about."

"Casey, I'll make you a deal. If our paths are going to continue to cross, it would be nice if we could be up-front with each other. If you've got a question, I promise I'll answer it as best I can. Straight questions deserve honest answers, okay?"

Lyle led the way into a white-tiled mud room that housed a washer and dryer. They removed their boots, left them in the mud room and walked into the kitchen. Large squares of salmon-colored Spanish tiles covered the floor and countertops. The kitchen cabinets were painted white with black cast-iron handles and hinges. On a counter, Lyle had filled bowls of pretzels, dips, chips and salsa for his guests. Unopened bottles of soft drinks, beer and liquor were arranged around a full ice bucket.

"What can I get you?" Lyle asked.

She angled her head toward a coffee maker with a fresh pot. "I'm still freezing from the search this morning."

As Lyle poured her a cup, Casey left the kitchen and called over her shoulder. "Mind if I take the nickel tour?"

"Not much to see, but be my guest. I'll be right in."

Three stairs led from the kitchen hallway to a sunken living room. Casey spotted a rocking chair that matched the one in the garage. She assumed that the knotted pine dining room table and matching chairs were also hand-made. Three of the dining room chairs had been arranged in a semi-circle opposite a brown leather sofa. The room had a polished hardwood floor and stone fireplace. Casey had expected that the bachelor's house would be decorated haphazardly, but she noted a clean symmetry among the furniture, rugs and decorative pieces. She called to the kitchen.

"Did you build this house yourself?"

"Six years ago. I had some help from the construction guys I work with in the summer. We did most of the work after hours, sometimes in the dark, but it turned out okay, I guess. Nothing important has collapsed yet."

Casey crossed to a tall maple bookshelf that dominated the far wall. Scanning the volumes, she noted a mix of bestsellers and geology reference books.

"Are you some kind of amateur geologist?"

Lyle walked into the living room and placed Casey's coffee mug on a low coffee table in front of the sofa. He sat in the rocking chair, setting a glass of ginger ale on a nearby lamp table.

"I used to make a living at it. Two years after I got out of the army, I used the GI Bill and got a degree in geophysics at the Colorado School of Mines in Golden. Then I got a job working for a big oil and mining company in Denver. I was a geophysicist in their exploration department, which basically means that I traipsed around the country finding stuff that the company could come and dig out of the ground. In addition to oil, coal and natural gas, the company was mining everything from cobalt to carnotite."

"Ah, good old carnotite."

"Sorry. You extract uranium from it," Lyle laughed. "Anyway, I worked there for fifteen years."

"Then what?"

"I took a job with the Department of the Interior, still based in Denver. I spent most of my time settling land use disputes and bird-dogging mining companies to comply with environmental and hazardous waste laws."

Casey nodded. "So you've seen both sides of the coin, so to speak."

"Unfortunately, the more involved I became in the politics of the mining industry, the more I lost my appetite for it. I found myself missing the times when I would head out to the hills of South Dakota looking for some rare mineral like pollux. It was like going on a treasure hunt."

Casey was examining three photographs on the mantel above the fireplace. Her eyes were drawn to a faded color photograph of a dozen young men in green tee shirts and fatigue pants standing in front of a thatched hut. Casey immediately recognized a much younger-looking Lyle Morrison in the back row, towering over the other soldiers. His dark hair was closely cropped, a dog tag hung from his thick neck, and his large arms were crossed over his chest.

"Do you recognize anyone else in that picture?" Lyle asked from the rocking chair.

Casey scanned the faces. Finally, her eyes settled on one of the soldiers in the front row. Her eyes grew wide. "Sheriff Withers!"

Lyle nodded. "I'll bet two dozen different people have seen that picture in the past six years and no one has ever noticed him before."

"If you hadn't said something, I never would've guessed. My God, look how young he looks with all that curly hair! I'll bet that was fifty pounds ago."

"He was quite the dashing young doughboy," Lyle agreed.

"He's standing there with his hands on his hips like he's the boss."

"Actually, this was a special recon group; we were all Sergeants. Generally, whoever had been in the field the longest was considered the leader. When that picture was taken, Bill and I had seniority," Lyle explained. "I first met him at Ranger Training School. We wound up on the same rotation through stateside bases before we were shipped out."

"And you've stayed in touch all these years?"

"On and off," Lyle replied. "Seven years ago, I gave him a call. I was looking for a change. I'd done okay for myself and since I didn't have the expenses that go along with raising a family, I could sort of pick and choose what I wanted to do next. Bill invited me to Ouray and after one week out here, I was hooked."

"What about the other guys in this picture?"

"Three of them were killed two weeks after that picture was taken. We were setting up an ambush near the Cambodian border along an enemy supply line. All of a sudden, the Vietcong were popping up out of the ground all around us. They had tunnels all over the place and they were just lying in wait for us. We were trying to ambush them but they beat us to the punch," Lyle recounted soberly.

"Anyway, when I came home, I wanted to leave the war behind me; I didn't make any effort to stay in touch. The only reason Bill was able to keep track of me was that I kept the same address and phone number for almost twenty years."

Casey put down the picture and picked up the one next to it. A young girl with blonde curls, a red dress and a shiny pair of Mary Janes smiled for the camera.

"Is this your girl?"

"That's Emily," Lyle nodded. "She's the reason I stuck around in Denver as long as I did. I knew that my wife wasn't going to try and contact me. Hell, she didn't even bother filing for divorce. She just took Emily and drove out of my life. I tried every way I could to contact her over the years, but she just dropped out of sight. Even her relatives wouldn't help me locate her."

"I'm sorry," Casey said quietly.

"I hoped that one day, Emily would want to see her father again. As the years rolled by, I tried to picture what she might be doing. I imagined her going off to college when she was eighteen. I envisioned her getting married when she was in her twenties. She'll be thirty-two in April, so by now, who knows? I might even be a grandfather."

Still staring at Emily Morrison's picture, Casey could not turn around. Hearing the man describe his yearning for his daughter, her eyes welled with tears that threatened to spill over.

"Finally, I realized that I was doing myself more damage than good by staying in that house in Denver," Lyle continued. "I needed to stop reliving the past and decide what I wanted to do with the rest of my life."

Casey smiled. "So you moved out here and became a part-time snow-plow driver?"

"Exactly!"

Their conversation was halted by the sound of the mud room door opening. Sheriff Withers led the way, followed by Jill Samsky and an older man Casey did not recognize.

Withers shouted in his cracked, husky voice. "You're being invaded,

Morrison. Hope you have enough chairs."

Lyle rose to greet them. Withers introduced the man who accompanied him as Douglas Shultz, Jim Philips's attorney. After Lyle served them beverages and placed the snack bowls on the coffee table, the group assembled in the living room. Withers and the lawyer sat on the sofa. Lyle returned to his rocking chair, and Casey and Jill sat next to one another on dining room chairs.

"It looks like our missing person case has taken an interesting turn." Withers began. "I know you called this meeting, Casey, but before we begin, you need to know that this is strictly confidential." He waited for her to nod her consent.

"Jill, why don't you start from square one so we can bring Lyle and Casey up to speed?" he asked his deputy. "Just hit the important points; I don't want to make this an all-night event. We've got a lot of work to do once we finish up here, and I'm shorthanded. Deputy Turlington hasn't checked in yet and he's got one of my trucks with him."

Samsky addressed Casey and Lyle. "After coming up empty on today's search, we have to assume that Dr. Philips ran into some serious trouble on Tuesday night, and I'm not talking about just car trouble. If it was that simple, he would've called by now."

"That's what I've been saying all along," Casey said impatiently.

"Given what we found inside Jim's truck and at the accident site, it certainly looks like there was some sort of foul play involved. As a result, we're investigating this as a possible robbery, kidnapping or, God forbid, a homicide. In that case, the first thing we need to figure out is whether this was some sort of random, opportunistic crime, or if it was premeditated."

Casey interrupted. "I find it hard to believe that some thug just happened by in the middle of a snowstorm, robbed Jim of whatever cash he was carrying, then felt the need to do something drastic to cover up the crime. Have you checked around to see if there were other reports of robberies or suspicious characters hanging around in Montrose or Silverton or Durango?"

"We've checked all over the Western Slope and we've come up empty, except for the break-in at Dr. Philips's house last night." Withers addressed Casey. "And let's leave that out of this for the moment."

"That leaves us with the possibility of a premeditated crime," the deputy said. "Meaning that someone either had a grudge against Dr. Philips or was operating from some sort of greed motive. We've checked with the area clinics and with Jim's lawyer," Withers said as he nodded toward Douglas Shultz. "As far as we can tell, none of Jim's patients had a beef with him. Has he said anything to you about that subject, Casey?"

"Not at all. Dr. Philips should be retired, but he makes house calls all over Ouray County and San Juan County. He only charges what his patients can afford and he knows all of them by their first names. Who would hold a grudge against someone like that?"

"That's where we netted out as well," Jill replied. "Then we started taking a hard look at the greed angle. Mr. Shultz is familiar with his financial affairs -- his investments, his will, his insurance policies and his side businesses. He was kind enough to spend the day with us today, trying to help us with the investigation."

"You're thinking that someone did this for insurance money or an inheritance?" Casey asked.

Jill Samsky looked at Withers, who in turn looked at Shultz, who responded by shaking his head. Withers replied, "Let's just say that in terms of money, the person who would benefit the most from Jim Philips's death is not...yet...considered a suspect."

Casey was confused. "Why not? It seems to me that'd be the first person I'd want to haul in for questioning."

"Is that right?" Withers replied with a smirk. "I'll take that under advisement."

Lyle shifted in his chair. Casey noticed that he had chosen to remain in the background. Still, he too seemed to be bothered by the conversation's cryptic nature. Casey locked her eyes on Lyle's and appealed silently for his help. Finally, Lyle spoke up.

"I think the problem here is that Mr. Shultz doesn't want Jim's private affairs discussed openly until the case is resolved one way or another. Having said that, I would also assume that there's another reason why everyone's being so evasive. I'd venture a guess that *you're* that the primary financial beneficiary of Dr. Philips's estate."

Casey's face went white. "That's absurd! Why would you say that?"

Sheriff Withers shot Lyle a warning glance. "End of speculation! As Lyle says, this is privileged information between Jim and his attorney. Jill, steer us out of this mess, would you? And get to the point already."

Samsky could not suppress a wide grin. She cleared her throat, then said, "Although you wouldn't suspect it from the way he conducts himself, Jim is a very wealthy man."

Unprompted, Shultz chimed in. "The original source of Dr. Philips's wealth was tobacco company stock. His grandfather was a tobacco farmer in North Carolina, and, over the years, the family accumulated a sizable amount of stock in the company that bought their tobacco. With stock splits, dividend reinvestments and the overall company growth, the value of the stock was already a few million dollars when Jim inherited it in the late 1960s. Despite his personal distaste for the cigarette industry, he held onto the stock until six years ago, when he finally cashed out. Since he and Mimi are childless, they didn't have the option to pass the wealth along to the next Philips generation, so they decided to do something worthwhile with the money."

"Let's cut to the chase here, shall we, Douglas?" Withers pleaded.

"Five years ago, there was a rumor that the Camp Bird Mine was being shopped around to prospective buyers. The company that owned the complex had all but stopped production on account of falling mineral prices. When Dr. Philips found out that another mining syndicate had expressed an interest in Camp Bird, he instructed me to make a competing bid."

"Why didn't he do it himself?" Casey asked.

"He wanted to keep it under wraps. His plan was to buy the patents, seal the mineshafts and tunnels, and pay the necessary holding fees on the claims each year. In effect, he was retiring the mining claims at his own expense." The lawyer sipped his coffee before continuing. "He and Mimi had a real fondness for the back-country basins around Camp Bird. Anyway, I set up a corporation for Jim and made a bid on Camp Bird."

Casey's eyes narrowed. She tilted her head in the direction of the Camp Bird complex three miles up the road. "Are you saying that Dr. Philips owns Camp Bird? He and I have driven past it a dozen times and he's never said a word to me about it."

The attorney nodded. "As I said, it was important to Jim that this be done very quietly. In fact, we set up five different corporations to handle various purchases so that it wouldn't look as if one company was making a run on the mining claims in the basins."

Casey shook her head in disbelief. "So he bought other mines beside Camp Bird?"

"That's where Lyle comes into the picture," Withers interjected.

Casey turned to face Lyle. "You mean, you're in on this too?" She threw up her hands. "I live under Dr. Philips's roof and apparently I know less about him than anyone in this room!"

"If it makes you feel any better, I didn't know squat until about three hours ago," Jill Samsky offered.

"A few years ago, Dr. Philips stopped by and asked if I'd be interested in doing some part-time research for him on the mining patents in the Imogene, Yankee Boy and Governor basins," Lyle said. "Apparently, Bill had mentioned to him that I had a background as a geologist. Jim wanted to know which claims would be the most appealing to an acquisition-minded mining company.

"You mentioned both mining claims and mining patents. What's the difference?" Casey asked.

"Let's say you're a prospector and you head up into the mountains in search of gold. Chances are, the area you're prospecting in is either U.S. Forest Service or Bureau of Land Management land, which makes it public property. If you find a promising vein that isn't already claimed by someone else, you can file a claim as well as a document called a Notices and Plan of Operations with the county. You pay a hundred-dollar application fee and you're granted the sole right to develop that claim. In order to maintain your rights to the claim, you have to prove that you are actively working it. The BLM requires that you perform a minimum of $500 worth of documented assessment work."

"Okay, so that's a claim," Casey asked. "Now, what's the deal with a patent?"

"To turn a claim into a patent, all you have to do is fill out the paperwork, pay an application fee of $250 and an annual holding fee of $100," Lyle said. "Once a hard-rock mining claim is patented, it's withdrawn from the public domain, meaning that it is now private land: your land. With a patent, you can hold the claim indefinitely without ever having to begin mineral exploration or production. You can sell the patent rights to a third party or charge them a royalty for mining on your property, and you don't ever have to pay a single penny of royalties to the government. As long as you continue to pay the $100 holding fee, the land and all of the mineral content in it is yours."

"On federal land? You're kidding me," Casey exclaimed. "So let's get back to Dr. Philips. He was interested in patents rather than claims. Otherwise, he'd have to prove that he was actively working the claims, right?"

"Exactly," Lyle answered. "But, after a century of mining around here, the most valuable claims have been located and patented. Since a patent is a matter of public record, it was relatively easy to find out who owned the claims that Jim was most interested in. I spent a lot of time at the local BLM office and the county courthouse. Of course, nothing beats getting your hands dirty and doing your own unofficial survey."

Douglas Shultz continued. "Through the years, Jim was able to purchase most of the mining patents that Lyle had recommended to him. With the recent state of the precious metals market, it wasn't hard to find good bargains. Lyle's research also turned up the fact that many of those claims were abandoned, so all we had to pay were the back taxes on the annual holding fees. I handled all of the negotiations to ensure that Jim's name wasn't attached to the deals."

Withers leaned forward on the couch and rubbed his hands together, still impatient with the pace of the discussion. "Are you familiar with a man named Paul Brader?" he asked Casey pointedly.

Casey was taken aback. "He's one of my biggest clients. As a matter of fact, I was at his house earlier, helping his wife plan a party."

The sheriff appeared relieved. "I'm glad you mentioned that. You see, I have a deputy over in Telluride keeping an eye on his house."

Casey was stunned. "You mean you're staking him out?"

Withers nodded. "He's now our prime suspect."

Casey was still reeling from the sheriff's comment when Shultz resumed speaking. "Paul Brader first contacted me two years ago. You see, my office is listed as the mailing address for all of the corporations that Jim used to buy the various patents. Apparently, Brader had been doing some research of his own into the local mining claims. He asked if he could meet with me to discuss a possible investment in the main holding company: Divining Rod Enterprises. I reported the inquiry to Jim, but he wasn't interested."

"Knowing Brader, that must have really piqued his interest," Casey said. "He's probably not used to being given the cold shoulder."

"You're right," the lawyer said. "A week later, he stopped by my office in Montrose and again asked for a meeting. Jim happened to be in my office at the time, so he agreed to speak with the man rather than turn him away."

"Mistake number one," Withers chimed in.

"Looking back on the meeting, Brader was very shrewd," Shultz recounted. "He asked Jim what the ultimate goal of his investment was. I thought Brader would be floored when my client told him that he had no intention of selling the claims and that he had tied up nearly $10 million to protect the three basins from future exploitation. Surprisingly, Brader didn't seem to find Jim's stance either peculiar or irrational. The only warning sign came when Brader asked if Jim could envision a scenario in which he would consider selling out to a mining company."

"What did Dr. Philips say to that?" Casey asked.

"His answer surprised even me," the lawyer admitted. "He said that he would consider a sale only if it meant a better standard of living for Ouray's residents. Not only would the acquiring company have to agree to strict waste disposal guidelines, they would be required to hire their labor force from the local area and agree to pay a royalty on the minerals they extracted to a list of Ouray-based charities."

"How did the meeting end?" Casey asked.

Shultz finished his coffee with a gulp. "Brader said that he'd be interested in acquiring a minority stake in Divining Rod Enterprises. He told
Jim it was a shame to have to shoulder the entire burden of protecting
those claims, particularly when others were willing to help. Brader went
on and on about how much he enjoyed hiking and trail riding in the back
basins and how committed he was to their preservation. He was very
convincing. Jim took the man at face value."

"Mistake number two," Withers mumbled. "I'm surprised Jim didn't
see right through Brader's charade."

"Jim had invested more than $10 million purchasing and paying the
holding fees on the patents that Lyle had recommended," the attorney
argued. "So, you can understand why Jim was receptive to the prospect
of being able to take $4 million out of Divining Rod Enterprises to use
for other worthwhile pursuits. What Brader had to offer, for a minority
interest, was very compelling. I recommended that Jim try to formalize
an agreement with him."

The sheriff sat back and folded his arms across his chest. "And that
may have sealed his fate."

"So, that explains how Brader became Dr. Philips's partner in this Divining Rod business," Casey mused. "But how does that make him your
primary suspect?"

"I think we're finally getting to that. Is that right, Douglas?" Sheriff
Withers asked the older man.

"At first, their business dealings went along swimmingly. In fact,
Brader even found a few key mining patents that were missing in the
Divining Rod Enterprises portfolio. Together, they put up the funds to
buy thirty additional claims in Governor Basin."

Casey asked Lyle, "If those claims were important, why didn't you
recommend them to Dr. Philips from the start?"

Lyle's head was resting against the top rail of the rocking chair. His
eyes were closed and he seemed to be in deep thought. "Originally, I
didn't consider those patents valuable in terms of provable mineral reserves. When Jim asked me about them, I explained that the only thing

that makes them attractive is their location. They lie between the Mountain Top Mine and the Virginius Mine: two very substantial patents. If a mining company wanted to dig a main tunnel in order to connect all of the claims in Governor basin, they'd need to buy up those missing claims or they'd be infringing on someone else's patents."

He then opened his eyes and addressed the attorney. "Since I had no idea that Dr. Philips's claims might ever be sold, I was a little surprised that they went to the trouble of buying those claims. I'll bet you that Brader was trying to fill in the holes in Divining Rod's network of claims so he could make the whole package more attractive to a potential buyer. Is that where all this is heading? Did Brader have a prospective buyer in mind all along?"

"That's exactly right," Shultz agreed. "Four months ago, Brader approached Jim with an offer from a company called Saratoga Mining."

Lyle gripped the arms of the rocking chair and leaned forward. "Saratoga! I had plenty of run-ins with those clowns when I was with the government. They are as sleazy as it gets when it comes to weaseling out of cleaning up their dump sites. As soon as they sense any regulatory or oversight trouble from the Interior Department, they unload their holdings for pennies on the dollar, leaving someone else holding the bag. Now this is all starting to make sense. I'll even bet that Saratoga was working behind the scenes, coaching Brader about those missing claims."

"Well, Jim rejected the offer outright," Shultz continued. "He told Brader there wasn't a single good reason to sell. From his perspective, it looked like Saratoga was just fishing for a bargain in a depressed market. All they wanted to do was buy up the patents and wait out the market until it became profitable to begin operations. Even if Jim wanted to liquidate his holdings, which he doesn't, this is absolutely the wrong time to sell.

"To top it off, Saratoga wasn't willing to consider any of the conditions that Jim had originally mentioned to Brader. Things started getting testy, so Jim demanded that Brader cease and desist his discussions with Saratoga."

"That must not have gone over well," Casey intoned.

"No, it didn't. Then, two weeks ago, Brader really started putting on a full-court press. Finally, Jim told him that it was a dead issue and told him to stop calling my office. We didn't hear from him for a few days until I received this document at my office on Tuesday." The lawyer removed a thick sheaf of papers from his briefcase and waved them in the air.

"What is that?" Lyle asked.

"This," the attorney sneered, "is the biggest collection of horse-hockey that I've seen in thirty-five years of practicing law. Brader's law firm is trying to take advantage of an ambiguous clause in the shareholders' agreement they drew up eighteen months ago. This document announces that Brader is exercising his right under the original agreement to reallocate his ownership position among the five corporations that fall under the Divining Rod Enterprises umbrella. Instead of having a 40 percent stake in each of the five companies, Brader is asserting that he has the right to take a 67 percent stake in three of the five companies, which would, in effect, give him control of the holding company."

"Surely your original agreement doesn't allow him to do that," Casey stated.

"When we got the first draft of the agreement from Brader's law firm, I objected to some of the vague language in it, but Jim overruled me. His feeling was that as long as he was the majority shareholder, all the ambiguous language in the world didn't bother him. Anyway, as I recall, the original agreement states that Brader can allocate his shares among -- and I quote -- 'each, any or all' of the five corporations which actually own the patents. It's buried among three paragraphs of legal gibberish that pertain to Brader's rights as a minority investor. To be honest with you, I didn't read a great deal of significance into it when I originally reviewed the contract. There were other issues I was more concerned about."

"I'm still confused about what the issue is," Jill Samsky interjected. "How does that reallocation thing make Brader the top banana?"

"It doesn't!" Shultz replied adamantly.

Lyle explained the situation to Jill. "Let's say that I have a pitcher with six ounces of water in it and you have a pitcher with four ounces of water in it. If we wanted to spread our water among five different glasses, we would each pour a proportionate amount of water from our pitchers into each glass, right? That would leave all five glasses with more of my water than your water. In the case of Divining Rod Enterprises, that would mean that I own the majority of each of those glasses of water, right?"

Jill nodded. "Okay."

"On the other hand, let's say that after I poured my water equally into the five glasses, you had the option of pouring your water into 'each, any or all' of the glasses that you chose to," Lyle continued. "Well, you might choose to pour your four ounces of water into only three of the glasses, ignoring the other two. In that case, I'd wind up with complete ownership of two glasses, but you would have majority ownership of the remaining three."

"Lyle is right on the mark," Shultz said. "As a holding company, Divining Rod Enterprises derives its corporate mandate from the five companies that comprise it. Theoretically, whoever controls the majority of the constituent companies controls the holding company. It is a flimsy argument, but a clever one. I'm confident that I can prove that Brader's interpretation is contrary to the spirit of the original contract, but that would involve a pitched battle against Brader and his attorneys. And without Dr. Philips around, I don't have a client to fight for."

Casey snapped her fingers. "That's where I heard that name before!"

"What name?" Samsky asked.

"Saratoga Mining." Casey swiveled toward Sheriff Withers. "When I was at the Braders' house, Paul's wife told me that their dinner party on Sunday night is for some executives at Saratoga Mining. Come to think of it, Paul wasn't exactly thrilled that she volunteered that piece of information."

Sheriff Withers asked Shultz, "Do you think Brader's actually planning to go forward with the sale of Jim's company to Saratoga this weekend?"

"I can't see how." He gestured to the paperwork sitting in his lap. "This is still an open issue. Until it's resolved by the courts, there's no way that anyone from Divining Rod can engage in any substantive discussion that requires the consent of its owners. The company's in limbo."

"Unless Jim has already agreed to the terms of that new document," Lyle corrected.

Shultz shook his head emphatically no. "There's no way he would do that."

"I hate to bring this up, but what does the original contract say about the death of the majority owner? In that case, does Brader take control of the company?" Jill Samsky asked.

"No," The lawyer declared. "His stake in the company would immediately revert to his designated beneficiary. It would be up to that person to deal with Paul Brader and Saratoga Mining."

All eyes in the room shifted toward Casey.

— Chapter 18 —

D espite the fact that it was an off-season Wednesday night, there were few empty tables at the Prospector Saloon. Located on Main Street in Ouray, the Prospector occupied the ground floor of a brick building erected in 1904. Through the years, the structure had housed a succession of retail establishments including several saloons, a gambling emporium, a bawdy house, a feed and supply store, an assay office and a blacksmith's shop.

True to its roots, the Prospector Saloon's décor evoked images of Ouray's past as a frontier outpost. Turn-of-the century photographic prints hung on the saloon wall, and depicted Ouray streets clogged with miners, prospectors and ranchers. Dark paneled walls were adorned with elk antlers, primitive mining tools and framed copies of outdated mining claims.

As Casey sipped a glass of ice water, Jill took a long pull on a long-necked bottle of Coors. The deputy studied the petite woman with a bemused expression. "After what you've been through in the past two days, I would've thought you'd be ready for a couple of beers."

"Actually, a couple of scotches would do the trick, but with what's going on with Dr. Philips, I'd feel guilty sitting here getting a buzz on."

Their heads turned when Lyle Morrison pulled open the front door and walked through a pair of swinging saloon doors.

"Here comes the original mountain man himself," Jill whispered to Casey.

As Lyle shed his jacket and approached the table, Casey could not help noticing the older man's physique. He had neither the lean, angular muscle tone of a distance runner nor the sculpted features of a bodybuilder. Nonetheless, he was an imposing figure who emanated raw strength. His meaty arms hung down as if they were a burden to his shoulders. His neck seemed as thick and sturdy as a fire hydrant. With his long mane wet and plastered to his scalp, his grey hair appeared darker, making him look ten years younger.

"You didn't have to shower for us," Jill joked. "This isn't like a date or something."

"With all the overtime I've been putting in lately, I haven't been able to spend much time with Sandy. She likes rough-housing in the snow, so I did battle with her for a while." Lyle replied sheepishly, "I figured you two might not appreciate it if I showed up covered in sweat and doggy drool."

"You've probably got a few broken ribs, tough guy. You shouldn't be wrestling around in the snow, even if it is with your dog," Jill chastised him.

Liz Mahew, a thin woman in her forties with shoulder-length auburn hair, approached the table. "Any news on Doc Philips?" the owner of the Prospector Saloon asked.

Samsky rocked back in her chair and sighed heavily. "Not yet. We've got the whole department working on it, though. And we've got another missing person on our hands. Mark Turlington was supposed to head down to Durango today, but no one's seen hide nor hair of him since he left town this morning. If he doesn't show up in the next hour or so, I gotta go retrace his steps. This is starting to get ridiculous."

"Well, we've all got our fingers crossed. Something to drink, Lyle?"

"An iced tea would be great, Liz."

"The ladies have already ordered. You want your usual?"

"Sounds good."

As Liz retreated to the kitchen, Casey shook her head. "This business with Paul Brader is outrageous. We need to put the pressure on him. After what I heard tonight, there's no question that he's our man."

"Let's see what the sheriff can come up with. He's on the phone with the State Police right now. Believe me, this has got his blood boiling, too. Bill's got some old-time frontier justice running through his veins and this has gotten personal," Jill said. "Now, if you'll excuse me, I've got to hit the little girl's room."

As Jill got up from her seat, Casey peeked over at Lyle to see if he was watching. Since she was old enough to notice, Casey had made a habit of watching men watch women. Her father's propensity for ogling attractive women had turned Casey's stomach as a youngster. As Jill walked away in her form-fitting uniform pants, Casey was certain that Lyle would be tempted to stare at the shapely deputy's figure. Instead, Casey saw that Lyle was looking at the deep purple bruise on her forehead.

Liz arrived carrying three plates. She placed a club sandwich with a side order of french fries at Samsky's place setting. "No stealing the deputy's fries, now."

She placed a large bowl of chili con carne topped with shredded cheese and diced onions in front of Casey. "I know your jaw hurts, so I asked the chef to chop up your beef extra fine."

"Thanks, Liz."

"And for our favorite snow removal expert, one extra large baked potato loaded with creamed spinach and grilled chicken strips. Can I get you anything else?"

Lyle smiled. "I think we're all set."

The woman patted Casey on the shoulder. "We don't see enough of you in town, Casey. You need to stop in more often. We can swap stories about trying to eke out a living in a man's world."

"Thanks, I'll do that."

As Jill Samsky returned, Liz Mahew excused herself to check on her other patrons.

"I'm supposed to be on stake-out duty tomorrow afternoon in Telluride," the deputy informed Casey as she took a bite of her sandwich. "Do you mind if I stop by your shop first? I've never seen it."

"No problem. I guess I'm supposed to operate on a business-as-usual basis for now. I'll tell you, though, I don't know if I'm going to be able to control myself around Paul and Sissy Brader."

"Bill may need to use your connection with them to our advantage," Jill cautioned. "You're going to have to find a way to keep your cool."

"That's the problem; everyone's playing this too cool," Lyle said. "Up 'til now, Paul Brader's been calling all the shots. I say it's time to take the offensive."

Casey noted that Lyle was much more animated in select company than he was in a large group. "I'm with you, Lyle."

"That's exactly what we're planning on doing tomorrow," Jill assured Lyle. "Bill and I are going to talk strategy later tonight. We're going to put the squeeze on Brader and maybe he'll make a mistake. We might need you to deliver a message to him, Casey."

"At least I'll be doing something. This waiting game is killing me."

"Well, Brader's putting up a brick wall. He's refusing to answer any of Bill's questions about Divining Rod Enterprises, Saratoga Mining or anything else for that matter," Jill explained. "But he was more than happy to rattle off a list of people who he said would confirm that he never left Telluride on Tuesday. We started checking out his story today and we'll keep working on it tomorrow. These days, it seems like we've got more Ouray deputies over in Telluride than we do on this side of the mountains."

"What about jurisdiction?" Lyle asked. "Do you need their permission to conduct an investigation over there?"

"Bill's brought the San Miguel County Sheriff up to speed on what's going on. They're old friends, so I don't think we're going to have a territorial pissing match," Jill said. "The real problem in manpower. And now that Mark Turlington's decided to turn a five hour assignment into an all-day adventure, we're stretched even further."

A sudden yelp came from the next table. One of the young boys was pointing toward the front of the saloon. "Look, a deer! No, a whole mess of deer!"

All heads turned toward the front window. Beneath the amber glow of an overhead streetlight, a herd of five deer were trotting in single file along the snow-covered curb on the east side of Main Street. Headed for the open pastureland just north of Ouray's cliff-ringed bowl, the herd was oblivious to the curious onlookers. Within seconds, they had disappeared from view.

"Just another herd of tourists traveling the San Juan Skyway," Jill joked.

The deputy's comment gave Lyle pause. He turned to face Samsky. "Speaking of the Skyway, tell me again about Brader's alibi. Exactly where and when was he spotted on Tuesday?"

"Are you trying to figure out if Brader ever had enough time on Tuesday to drive back and forth between Telluride and Red Mountain Pass?" Jill asked.

"I drive that route every day," Casey chimed in. "At least the part between Ouray and Telluride. The whole thing would take him around an hour each way, plus he needed time to do whatever he did to Dr. Philips. So, that makes a round-trip of close to two-and-a-half hours."

"Bill and I have done the math, but you're forgetting something," Jill said. "We figure that there were two separate incidents. The first occurred sometime around five o'clock. That's when Dr. Philips disappeared on his way from Silverton to Ouray. The second incident happened between nine forty-five and eleven-thirty. That's when someone tried to ditch Jim's truck near the Mother Cline Slide."

"So, if Brader's our guy, that means he either had to make two separate trips or he had to have left Telluride around three-thirty and returned around midnight," Casey reasoned.

"The all-night scenario is impossible," Jill counseled. "Based on what we've turned up already, we can place him at a number of different locations in Telluride on Tuesday afternoon and Tuesday night. He was seen ice climbing at Bridal Veil Falls 'til around 4 p.m. He bought a gift for his wife at a jewelry store at around five forty-five. He had dinner with

Sissy at a place called Montrachet's from seven to eight-thirty. Around ten o'clock, he spoke with a bartender at Garfinkel's. He's forbidding us from interviewing Sissy, but supposedly she can verify that he came home before midnight."

"What about the possibility of two trips?" Casey asked. "It sounds as if there are still two gaps in his alibi, and they match up with the timing of the two incidents you mentioned."

"He claims he was at his office between four-fifteen and five-thirty, but Tuesday was his secretary's day off, so he doesn't have anyone who can back up his story," Jill said. "If we had a better case, we could subpoena his phone records to see if he made any calls from his office. Still, he would've had to make exceptional time to make the round-trip to Red Mountain Pass and back in less than ninety minutes."

"And since the snowstorm started around four-o'clock, it makes it near impossible," Lyle stated dejectedly.

Jill continued, "As for the gap between ten o'clock and midnight, he claims he was at Garfinkel's having a few drinks with some tourists from St. Louis that he met on the ski slopes the day before."

"Can the bartender verify that?" Casey asked.

"He definitely remembers seeing Brader walking into the bar around ten o'clock," the deputy said. "After that, he said it's anyone's guess. Apparently, the place was packed for a Tuesday night."

Lyle let out a sigh. "If the bartender saw him at ten o'clock, we have a big problem. From nine-thirty until eleven-thirty, not a single car went into Red Mountain Pass from the Ouray side, otherwise would've seen the tire tracks."

"What if he went the other way around the Skyway loop and came up from Durango?" Casey asked.

Lyle shook his head no. "It's a round trip of nearly 350 miles. As bad as the roads were on Tuesday night, he couldn't have driven the circuit in less than eight hours."

"Like I said, Bill and I have studied this from every angle. It comes down to a matter of physics. Brader just didn't have enough time to do what we suspect he did," Samsky concluded. "So, we either have some bad eyewitnesses or Brader's got an accomplice. And Telluride's too small a town to keep a secret for very long, so if Brader found someone to do his dirty work, it's bound to leak out soon."

Casey scrunched her eyebrows. "This whole thing is so unbelievable. Paul Brader may have an ego the size of Colorado, but it's hard to believe that he could be involved in something like this. I mean, he doesn't even look like a criminal."

"This might sound jaded," Jill replied. "But if I walked you into any jail in America and lined up the last ten people arrested for burglary, drug dealing or assault, they'd look exactly as you'd expect. But on the other hand, if I walked you into a federal prison and lined up the last ten people arrested for stock fraud, money laundering or murdering a relative for their insurance money, do you know what they'd look like? They'd look like the guy next door. They'd look like Paul Brader."

— Chapter 19 —

Paul Brader eased off the accelerator of his black Chevy Suburban as he approached the intersection of Highway 62. The fifteen-minute drive along Highway 145 leading out of Telluride had been fast and uneventful. The road was clear, dry and devoid of traffic. He was on pace to arrive ten minutes early for his nine o'clock rendezvous with Sam Moultrie.

Throughout the drive, he had kept a wary eye on his rear-view mirror. His phone conversation with the Ouray County Sheriff, coupled with Casey Bailey's revelation about the Divining Rod Enterprises documents, had raised his already heightened sense of apprehension. The surprising pace of the investigation had caught him off-guard. As a result, Brader resolved that caution and vigilance would be the watchwords for tonight's enterprise.

Rather than turning onto Highway 62 immediately, Brader pulled his Suburban onto the shoulder on the road and waited. With his radio off, he could hear the bubbling flow of Leopard Creek as it passed beneath the highway to join the San Miguel River. Within seconds, a pair of headlights appeared over the crest of a hill on the roadway behind him. As the vehicle drew near, Brader turned on his hazard lights. In the side mirror, he watched as a black Toyota pickup truck slowed to a stop alongside him. His heart began to race.

The other driver flicked on his overhead map light, illuminating the interior of the pickup. A wiry man in his late thirties, he leaned over and rolled down his passenger-side window. The bill of the man's cap cast his face in shadows, revealing only a thick black mustache. Brader wavered for a moment before deciding to lower his own window.

"You okay, buddy?" the man called to Brader.

From his elevated position in the Suburban, Brader scanned the interior of the Toyota for a police radio or scanner. Seeing none, he replied with a forced grin. "Yeah. I'm waiting on a friend of mine to catch up to me. Thanks for checking, though."

"No problem. Good night."

Brader watched as the driver rolled up his window, drove forward to the stop sign and turned left, following Highway 145 toward Norwood. Brader let out a sigh of relief as the pickup's taillights disappeared around a sweeping curve. Checking his rearview mirror again, Brader swung the Suburban back onto the road, gunned it through the stop sign and turned right on Highway 62 toward Ridgway. As the road began a steady ascent through a dense forest of aspen trees, Brader glanced at the clock on his dashboard. He was still on schedule. After driving less than a mile, a high-pitched ring came from the cellular phone mounted in the truck's center console. He stared at the phone with trepidation. "Damn it, Sam, not another problem."

He jerked the phone out of the console. "Who's this?"

Despite the tinny background echo, Brader recognized the caller's voice at once. "That's some greeting, Paul. It's Joe Deutch."

Brader felt his stomach muscles tighten. "Geez, Joe, it's almost eleven o'clock New York time. How'd you get this number?"

"I called your house and Sissy gave it to me. She said you were driving to Montrose for a business meeting. You've been so hard to get a hold of for the past two days, I figured this would be the perfect opportunity to talk."

"I'm sorry, Joe, but I'm really rushed right now and I don't know how long I'll be able to hang onto this signal," Brader told the broker. "I know why you're calling and I promise I'll give you a ring first thing in the morning."

"Nobody likes a margin call, Paul, but ducking me isn't going to make your problems disappear. My partners and I aren't the enemies. After all, it's not the house's money you're playing with: it's yours. As it stands now, your portfolio has barely enough marginable reserves and hard assets to cover your exposure on this pharmaceutical stock. If that stock jumps another point or two tomorrow, you're sunk."

"I can't tell you how relieved I am that you and your firm aren't at risk," Brader replied sarcastically. "The only reason I use you guys is because you give me liberal margin terms. Your firm has made tons of money in commissions off me, and I've never asked for a single piece of advice. Now that one trade has gone bad, you're all over me."

"We're not all over you, Paul, and you know it. You've been in this business long enough to know that there's nothing personal about a margin call. Besides, we've stuck our neck way out for you on this trade. There's not another brokerage house in the country that would extend you as much credit as we have. You know the rules about what percent of your securities we're allowed to let you borrow against. Not only did we let you borrow against the full value of your portfolio, we even let you pledge your real estate holdings as collateral."

"Don't pretend like that was some sort of magnanimous gesture on your part. I told you from day one, Joe; that's the price of doing business with me. You want my account, you gotta play ball with me," Brader said. "It may not be normal, and it might not even be legal, but those were the terms. Hey, I didn't exactly hold a gun to your head."

"Okay Paul, let's stop the posturing. You've been hoping for some kind of miracle on that drug company stock, but the time for miracles is past. Two weeks ago, you said you were working on something to offset your losses on the short-sale. You begged us not to place a margin call until you had the cash in hand from this other scheme of yours. Well, we haven't seen any wire transfers into your account, and it's time to cash in your chips. I need to know exactly what's going on."

"What's going on is that I'm about an hour away from clearing this whole mess up. I'm taking care of it right now. If you make that margin call now, I'll lose everything! I just need you to hang on until Tuesday of next week. Now, if you'd get off this damn phone and let me get to my meeting, I'll be able to explain it all to you in the morning."

But Deutch was adamant. "I'm afraid that's not good enough, Paul. I need to hear some convincing answers now. I've got a breakfast meeting with the partners tomorrow to discuss this matter. At nine o'clock, we're going to begin liquidating your portfolio and taking title to your real estate."

The broker's message hit Brader like a fist to the teeth. He screamed into the phone. "No, no no! You can't do that!"

Brader stomped on the brake pedal and brought his truck to a screeching halt on the highway. "Hang on, hang on!" He shifted into reverse and backed the Suburban fifty yards down the road, pulling the truck into a turnout near the Dallas Divide. It was now 8:41 p.m.; it would take him ten minutes to reach the rendezvous point. He had nine minutes.

He tried to compose himself before pleading his case. "Listen, I've pulled the truck over so I don't have any other distractions. I'm in the middle of frigging nowhere and I'm afraid I'm going to lose the phone signal. I literally have less than ten minutes to give you; my life depends on making this appointment. So you can be assured that you have my undivided attention."

"Good," Deutch replied. "I hate to do this to you, Paul, but you need to come clean with me about this mysterious deal you're working on. Unless you can convince me that it's real and that it's definitely going to close in the next day or two, I'll never be able to sell it to my partners."

Brader nodded his head eagerly. In his frantic state, he failed to notice the black Toyota pickup that crept slowly past the turnout.

— Chapter 20 —

The call came in to the Sheriff's Department dispatcher at 8:15 p.m. Deputy Perry Yancey reported from his stakeout post that Brader was leaving Telluride at a high rate of speed. Sheriff Withers wasted no time in responding. By 8:20 p.m., he was speeding north on US Highway 550 toward Ridgway in his patrol vehicle, trailed by Deputy Steve Mapes in his blue Ford Bronco.

After receiving an update from Yancey, Withers was relieved that he had asked Mapes to follow in an unmarked vehicle. Concerned that either Paul Brader or an accomplice might be leading the deputy on a wild goose chase, Withers had instructed Yancey to verify the driver's identity. Unfortunately, Yancey's roadside encounter with Brader complicated the task of keeping the Suburban under covert surveillance. If Brader continued driving toward Ridgway, Withers was confident that Mapes could pick up the tail.

As the sheriff approached the junction of US Highway 550 and Highway 62 on the outskirts of Ridgway, he pulled his Jeep Cherokee into a well-lit gas station. He gestured for Mapes to pull up alongside him.

"Pull up over there," the sheriff said, pointing to the north end of the gas station. "Brader's bound to see my truck when he comes to the intersection; I don't want your truck parked next to mine."

"You got it," the deputy nodded. "Any idea which way he's gonna turn?"

Withers looked toward the intersection. Highway 62 came in from the west and dead-ended at the traffic light. Making a right on US 550 would lead Brader south toward Ouray. A left would lead north toward Montrose. "I don't have a clue. Park your truck so you can head in either direction."

Perry Yancey's voice sounded on both of their radios. "I just passed our target. He's parked in the turnout near Dallas Divide. It's real wide open out here and there's no place to find cover. I'm gonna keep heading your way."

"Did he see you?' Withers asked.

"He's facing away from the road, but he couldn't have missed me. I'm the only other truck on the road. I think I'm burned."

Withers closed his eyes and pictured the area around the scenic overlook. He knew the highway was bordered on both sides by treeless, snow-covered pastureland.

He keyed the microphone. "You're right. That's the second time he's pulled over, so he must be getting paranoid. I can't risk him seeing you a third time."

"That's a Roger," the deputy replied.

"Drive this way 'til you get to 550, then pull behind the Conoco station. I'm heading over to Dallas Divide; I'll pass you on the way." Withers shifted the Jeep Cherokee into park.

Mapes shouted from the vehicle beside him. "Are you sure that's a good idea?"

"There's no choice," Withers answered. "The man's not going to sit by the side of the road all night. He might be planning to double back on us and head back past Telluride. Or maybe this little joyride was his way of flushing us out. In any case, if he's loitering in a turnout after dark, it gives me an excuse to finally meet this guy face-to-face. And I'm looking forward to that."

Withers pulled out of the gas station and made a left onto Highway 62. Heading west, the road passed over the Uncompahgre River and through the tiny town of Ridgway. Withers considered his options as he pressed the gas pedal to the floor and began the long uphill climb out of the Uncompahgre Valley.

With Turlington and one of his patrol vehicles still unaccounted for, Withers was understaffed and under-equipped. He decided to place his remaining deputies on stand-by. As the sheriff reached for the clip-mounted microphone to alert his dispatcher, he heard a noise that seemed out of place.

Poking his head out the window, he spotted a helicopter hovering over the road a half-mile ahead of him. The pilot appeared to be searching for a place to land near the apex of the steep grade that Withers's truck was climbing. As he stared through his windshield, the helicopter disappeared from view over the crest of the ridgeline to the left of Highway 62.

"Yancey! Do you see that?" Withers shouted into the microphone.

"See it? I thought it was gonna land on my head!" the deputy replied.

"Where'd he put down?"

"Behind the cemetery. I'm parked at the front gates right now. I can't see it from the road, but I hear blades turning. What's going on?"

"I don't know, but something's going down for sure. Turn off your lights, pull through the gates and stash your truck so it can't be seen from the road. I don't want to spook either one of them." The sheriff's mind was racing. "Proceed on foot and get as close as you can to that copter. I want those registration numbers."

As he drove toward the cemetery, Withers knew he was in a quandary. He assumed that Brader was heading in his direction, but he couldn't confirm his suspicions without driving past the cemetery. His first instinct was to pull up short of the graveyard and wait to see what developed. If Brader was meeting the helicopter for some sort of incriminating pick-up or drop-off, they might be able to surprise him. On the other hand, if Brader's intention was to fly to some remote location, Withers could not let him board the helicopter. Without assistance from the air, he had little hope of tracking his suspect. He grabbed the microphone, ignoring standard radio protocol in favor of expediency.

"Mapes. I need you up here, now! Keep coming this way until I can get a visual on our suspect." Then to his dispatcher: "Mary, get me a helicopter in the air however you can. Call the State Police in Montrose first. If they can't get a bird up on the double, then call down to Durango. If that doesn't work, get in touch with one of the heli-ski guys in Telluride."

As acknowledgments were radioed back to him, Withers arrived at the cemetery. He slowed his jeep and looked to his left. He could not see Yancey's Toyota through the iron posts of the graveyard gates. The deputy had taken cover as requested. Peering into the darkness, Withers scanned above the rows of headstones. The steady slapping noise of rotor blades was the only indication that a helicopter was sitting in the shallow swale behind the secluded cemetery.

"Damn good pick-up spot," he muttered to himself as he continued driving west toward Dallas Divide.

• • •

Speeding down the eastbound lane of Highway 62, Brader took his eyes off the road long enough to see that his clock read 9:03 p.m. He was late. Deutch had grilled him for fifteen minutes on the details of the Saratoga Mining deal. Brader was unsure whether his hasty explanation of the complicated affair had earned him a reprieve, but he had given it his best shot. He had described the prospective acquisition by Saratoga Mining as a smooth and amicable transaction that would be finalized at dinner on Sunday. Finally, he had no choice but to terminate the conversation.

"Hang on Sam, I'm coming!" he pleaded aloud, as he raced along the moonlit highway.

A mile from the cemetery, Brader scanned the horizon for the helicopter, but the headlights of a vehicle approaching in the westbound lane were impeding his search. As he raced past the vehicle, he spotted a row of roof-mounted police lights. "Damn it, not now!"

Brader lifted his boot off the accelerator. His attention riveted to the rear-view mirror, he murmured through clenched teeth, "Keep going, keep going."

To his horror, he watched the vehicle swerve onto the shoulder and execute a U-turn in the middle of the highway. Within seconds, the Jeep Cherokee was gaining ground on the Suburban. Brader slowed down to fifty-five miles an hour, hoping against hope that the lawman wouldn't pull him over. A row of sweat broke out on his upper lip and his ears began to ring. As he approached the cemetery, he maintained his speed, heartened by the fact that his pursuer hadn't engaged his lights or siren. Passing within yards of the cemetery gates, he could hear the helicopter's blades whirring in the shadows to his right.

• • •

"He's going past the cemetery," Withers radioed to his deputies. "I'm pulling him over."

The sheriff flipped a toggle switch, activating the Jeep's overhead lights and strobes. "Yancey, draw your weapon and move in on that copter. I want that pilot detained. Mapes, I need you up here *now!*"

Although he was being tailgated by a law enforcement vehicle with lights flashing, Brader was not stopping. Withers sounded his siren and aimed his door-mounted searchlight at the Chevy Suburban's rearview mirror. Brader decelerated in gradual increments as he descended into the Uncompahgre Valley. Finally, he steered onto the right-hand shoulder, slowing his vehicle to fifteen miles per hour.

"I know what you're up to, wise-guy," Withers said aloud as the Suburban crawled to a stop a half-mile beyond the cemetery. "Trying to move me out of earshot of that copter."

Deputy Steve Mapes crossed from the westbound lane and pulled his Ford Bronco in front of Brader's SUV. Withers got out of his Jeep with his hand on the butt of his pistol. Mapes positioned himself five feet from the Suburban's right front bumper and drew his weapon. As Withers walked cautiously toward the driver's door, an urgent voice came over the police frequency in both the Jeep and the Bronco.

"He's taking off!" Yancey yelled over a clamorous bed of background noise. "He must've seen your lights and got spooked. I couldn't even get close to him."

Withers raced back to his Jeep and grabbed the microphone. "Get those n-numbers! At least we can track the registration."

The sheriff saw the helicopter rise over the crest of the slope, duck its snout, and make a beeline to the west. "He's disappeared over the ridge-line. I can see him."

Yancey's voice crackled over the radio. "It just turned north. He's setting a course for either Montrose or Grand Junction."

"Keep your eye on it for as long as you can."

A nearby sound drew the sheriff's attention. Brader, dressed all in black, climbed out of his Suburban. He took three steps toward Withers with a befuddled expression on his face. "What's all the commotion about?"

Withers drew his pistol and assumed a shooter's crouch. "Freeze or I'll drop you where you stand, Mister!" he shouted. "Hands up, turn around and face your vehicle."

As Brader complied, Mapes holstered his weapon and walked briskly around the truck. With a vigorous stiff-arm, he pinned the man's chest against the side of the Suburban. While the deputy frisked Brader, Withers sized up the multimillionaire.

"Do you have any weapons in your vehicle, sir? I intend to search it, so you'd better be straight with me."

"There's a registered pistol in the glove box," Brader replied, his voice quivering. "But I haven't done anything to warrant this kind of treatment."

Mapes spun Brader around so he faced the sheriff. "Nothing else on him," he said. "I'll secure his weapon."

Sheriff Withers returned his gun to its holster and squinted at the driver as if puzzled. "I believe I recognize your face, young man." He stroked his chin. "You live over in Telluride, don't you? What's the name again?"

Brader eyed him warily. "Actually, I don't believe we've met. My name is Paul Brader."

Sheriff Withers smiled broadly. "Well how about this for a small world? I spoke to you on the phone earlier today. I'm Bill Withers and I'm the Sheriff of Ouray County. What are the chances of us crossing paths here tonight? Quite a coincidence, wouldn't you say, son?"

Brader felt a sudden wave of nausea rise in his throat.

— Chapter 21 —

The hymn had been one of his wife's favorites. In her final weeks, Mimi Philips could often be heard quietly humming the paean as she leafed through her scrapbooks and photo albums. Visitors to the Philips household were surprised that Mimi appeared to be accepting her fate in such good spirits and with a song in her heart. Only her husband knew that the song was a plea for strength as she girded herself for death.

As Jim Philips sat engulfed in darkness with his back against the frigid walls of the lineman's hut, the hymn "You Are Mine" echoed from the recesses of his brain.

I will come to you in the silence.
I will lift you from all your fear.
You will hear my voice, I claim you as my choice.
Be still and know I am here.
Do not be afraid, I am with you.
I have called you each by name.
Come and follow me.
I will bring you home.
I love you and you are mine.

He could barely summon the strength to loll his head from side to side in time with the hymn. With the onset of hypothermia, the physician was suffering extended bouts of confusion and delirium. He was no longer able to recognize and treat the effects of the cold as it stealthily ravaged his body.

During the two nights of his captivity, the moon's faint rays had peeked through the hole in the roof, adding a pale glow to the hut's interior walls. Tonight, the engineer's shack was black as storm clouds rolled overhead. Earlier that night, Jim Philips had draped the stiff, frozen blanket over himself to block the wind that streamed through the opening in the roof. The smell of wet wool filled his nostrils as he stared into the darkness beneath the blanket.

Images unexpectedly appeared to him in bright flashes, as if emanating from an unsteady film projector housed in his subconscious. Brief snippets of light and sound danced before his eyes. At first, they arrived as snapshots, selected haphazardly from an archive that spanned the seven decades of his life. Helpless to stop the flashes and the images, Jim Philips tried to make sense of the bizarre slide show.

Soon, the photographs arrived in three dimensions. Sound and motion replaced the maddening, intermittent flashes. Words became sentences and grainy photos became people. As the night enveloped him, he felt as if his mind had slipped from its moorings; he was now helpless and adrift.

The first continuous image that floated through his mind was of his grandfather's tobacco farm in rural North Carolina. He could feel the broad green leaves brushing against his legs as he saw himself playing hide-and-seek with his older brother among endless rows of tobacco plants. Although his own feet were becoming black and lifeless, Dr. Philips could feel the warm mud from the irrigated field squishing between his bare toes as he scampered among the tobacco plants, trying to outrun his brother.

As the picture froze and faded to black, it was replaced by a bright, sun-soaked image of the Duke University campus on a spring morning in 1950. It was the final week of the semester and students were rushing between classroom buildings and dormitories. For Jim Philips, the bustling campus seemed deserted except for one person: the red-haired girl with the sparkling eyes who was walking between her parents on the sidewalk. She seemed to glow as she soaked in the university's sights and sounds. Impulsively, the normally reticent pre-med student walked up to Mr. Grover Barnes and thrust out his hand.

"Sir, I couldn't help but notice that you appear to be taking a tour of our university. My name is James Philips and I'd be honored to escort you around campus."

A stern-faced man with a handlebar mustache, Mr. Barnes pointed to the stack of textbooks Jim Philips was balancing in the crook of his arm. "It looks like you have somewhere else to be right now. Don't let us slow you down, son."

It was Mrs. Barnes who came to the aid of the nervous young man and changed his life forever. "We'd be delighted to accept your kind offer," she interrupted. "Our daughter Mimi here is planning to attend Duke this fall."

Jim Philips hesitated before extending his free hand to greet the smiling young lady in the yellow sundress. Staring into her light green eyes, he feared that he would never be able to let go.

Beneath the dank, icy blanket, Dr. Philips broke into a grin, cracking his chapped, frozen lips. But when he recognized the image that followed, his smile retreated and his shoulders began to tremble.

Dr. James Philips's wing-tip shoes slapped the linoleum floor as he dashed down the hushed corridors of the municipal hospital in Winston-Salem. The young resident had rushed home from Atlanta, where he had been interviewing for a staff position at Emory University Hospital.

Unable to reach Mimi at their home after his first round of interviews, Jim Philips felt a nagging premonition of dread. It was Mimi's mother who broke the news to her son-in-law. Standing in a public phone booth in Atlanta, he learned that his pregnant wife had been rushed to the hospital in the early morning hours with severe cramping and bleeding. Without bothering to cancel his next interview, he hailed a taxi to the airport and bullied his way onto the first flight to North Carolina.

Jim Philips nearly slid past Mimi's hospital room as he ran through the hallways searching for her. As he entered his wife's room, he was shocked to see how pallid and frail she'd become. His wife of three years lay in a hospital bed, hooked up to bottled oxygen and a bag of intravenous fluids.

Mimi had been carrying a girl. The desperate attempt to save both mother and child had failed. Not only had the Philips's lost the child three months short of full-term but Mimi had to undergo an emergency hysterectomy.

When she awoke, Mimi looked plaintively at her husband.

"I'm sorry, honey," she whispered softly. "I tried my best to keep her."

Shaken by the flashback, Dr. Philips felt warm rivulets leaking down the sides of his face, tears flooding the deep creases in his cheeks, soothing his wind-burned face.

Without warning, the scene changed. Mimi was now at the wheel of their 1988 BMW, her loose gray hair buffeted by an alpine breeze. She had lowered the windows to let in the fragrant mountain air as they cruised north on US Highway 550. On their annual late-summer vacation, they had chosen a route that led them west to Albuquerque, then north through Santa Fe and Taos, and over the Colorado border into Durango.

They were scouting a place to retire. The Winston-Salem area had seen decades of steady growth, and Jim Philips's twenty-five years in private medical practice had been both fulfilling and prosperous. Now, they both longed for a smaller town and a less hectic existence.

Originally, Ouray, Colorado was a dot on the map between two of their intended destinations. Having spent the previous day touring the Anasazi cliff dwellings in Mesa Verde National Park, they were headed north from Durango to visit the Black Canyon of the Gunnison.

Driving along the Million Dollar Highway, the Philipses were stunned by the view of the Uncompahgre Gorge and the sun-dappled streams that flowed through it. As they began the serpentine descent into Ouray's glacier-carved bowl, Mimi pulled the BMW into an overlook on the left side of the highway.

"Will you look at that?" She pointed to the tiny town that was spread out beneath them, nestled between the broad shoulders of steep San Juan Mountain peaks.

Jim Philips looked at the unfolded map in his lap. "How do you think they pronounce it: 'ooh-ray' or 'you-ray'?"

The doctor recognized the twinkle in his wife's jade-colored eyes as she pulled back onto the highway. "I don't know, but let's find out," she said.

They proceeded to explore the town with the enthusiastic vigor of the area's original prospectors. Mimi toured the Ouray County Historical Society Museum while her husband visited the local medical clinic. They rummaged through tourist shops on Main Street and chatted with local residents at a crowded coffee shop, where they learned of the popular Wiesbaden Inn. To their delight, the Inn featured a subterranean vapor cave. Jim and Mimi donned their bathing suits and spent an hour in the sauna-like cave where a natural hot spring trickled through fissure cracks in the cave's walls and collected in a shallow rock pool. They giggled like teenagers as the steam from the hot springs thickened the air and clung to their sweaty bodies.

The next day, the Philipses extended their unplanned sojourn and went on a guided jeep tour of the historic backcountry basins. As they returned to town that afternoon, their driver eased the jeep through a steep descent along County Road 361: the Camp Bird Mine Road. Rounding a sharp bend in the dirt road, the dusk-veiled town came into view. The sun was slipping behind the upper rim of Ouray's box canyon. In the back seat of the open-topped jeep, Mimi Philips reached for her husband's hand.

"Do you know what this feels like, Jim?"

"It feels like home," he replied.

In an instant, the pleasant memory was gone, supplanted by an image of the recent, terrifying incident at the turnout above the Mineral King surface plant. In the engineer's hut, Dr. Philips jerked his head violently to avoid the chloroform-laced pads that appeared in the flashback. He threw off the blanket and took deep gulps of the sub-zero night air, bringing on an intense coughing fit. When his eyes were finally able to focus amid the darkness, he saw snow was falling into the far end of the shack. Looking through the jagged-edged opening in the roof, he saw thick storm clouds passing just inches above the top of the hut.

— Chapter 22 —

"Hold my calls. I don't want to speak to anyone." Brader shouted, entering his office as he stomped clumps of dirty snow from his boots and brushed snowflakes from his winter jacket.

Kimberly Cousins waved a pink message slip in the air. "This extremely rude man has been calling every ten minutes since I got here this morning. He says he's waiting at a phone booth and you'd better not ignore his call."

Brader snatched the phone message from her hand. The word "Sam" and a phone number with the local 970 prefix was scribbled on it.

"I've been trying to reach him all morning," Brader muttered as he strode into his office, swung his door shut, reached for the phone, and punched in the number. Moultrie answered on the first ring, his voice raised above the din of traffic sounds in the background.

"How come you didn't answer your cell phone?" Moultrie yelled.

"I'm trying to duck a call from my broker. Now that everything's gone to hell in a hand basket, I don't know what to tell him."

"What happened last night?" Moultrie demanded. "All of a sudden there were cop lights all over the place, then some dude came running toward me from the graveyard with a gun in his hand!"

"Things got screwed up," Brader said.

"No shit! They almost nabbed my ass at the Montrose Airport. Three State cops came tearing into the parking lot just as I was leaving."

"Calm down a second, Sam. Let me explain what's going on here."

"I know exactly what's going on," the pilot interrupted angrily. "They're on to us! The staties called my boss around midnight, asking him who was logged into the copter I was flying last night."

Brader was shocked. "How'd they know it was from your charter service?"

"The damn n-numbers! They're painted on big as life. Now they know that I was piloting that bird."

"I'm sorry, Sam," Brader massaged his temples with his free hand. "I was running late and they caught me speeding. Things just snowballed from there."

"You bet your ass it snowballed! As soon as my boss got off the phone with the cops, he called to chew my ass out. I put up with ten minutes of his bullshit before I realized that the staties were probably on their way down to Silverton to haul me in."

Brader held his breath. "What'd you tell them?"

"Do you think I'm stupid? I wasn't going to wait for them to show up. As far as I knew, they had the whole thing figured out. I told my sister to say that I hadn't been home all night. Then I grabbed some things and high-tailed it down here to Durango. I spent the night sleeping in my truck."

"You should have stayed home, Sam. You could've told them you had to put down in the cemetery because of engine problems or something. Skipping town makes things look a lot worse."

"This isn't the first time I've had to bolt in the middle of the night," Moultrie announced. "What did you tell the cops when they stopped you?"

"I told them I was on my way to Montrose for a late-night meeting."

"And they let you go just like that? They didn't say anything about the copter?"

"Oh, they tried to make a big deal about it," Brader said. "Matter of fact, the guy who stopped me is the Ouray County Sheriff -- the same guy who's been asking questions about Dr. Philips."

"We're sunk!" Moultrie exclaimed.

"We're nowhere near sunk. Not yet, anyway. They may have some of the pieces, but there's no way they can solve the puzzle. That hot-headed sheriff tried to play it rough with me, but I called my local lawyer and he threw some cold water on him."

"Well, that's fine and dandy for you, but it doesn't help me a lick," Sam said. "Thanks to you, I'm up to my ass in alligators. Looks like I've gonna have to blow town."

"What for? Landing by the side of the road isn't a crime."

"Yeah, but shooting a deputy is."

"*What?*" Brader asked, incredulous. "Sam, please don't tell me that's what happened at the Mineral King yesterday."

"Don't act like this is my fault! The guy had me dead to rights. I had no choice. In fact, I saved your freaking ass." Moultrie shouted. "Then last night you showed up with a frigging police escort. Great move, Pauly boy. Now I've got the cops looking for *me*. What the hell am I supposed to do now?"

Brader was stunned by Sam Moultrie's confession. "I'm sorry, Sam. I going to need time to sort all of this out."

"I'll sort it all out *right now*. Skipping town with the law on my heels wasn't part of the bargain when I signed on. It's time to pay up, Brader. I want fifty grand in my hands *today* or I swear I'll rat you out to that sheriff friend of yours. And don't think I won't."

"I can't just walk into my bank and get that kind of money over the counter!"

"Spare me," Moultrie countered. "I'm going to try to make my way up to Telluride without anyone spotting me. At three-o'clock, I'll be on the Last Dollar Road, four miles up from Sawpit. You'll see my truck near an old cabin fifty yards off the road. Bring fifty grand, or don't bother showing up. And I'm serious about going to the sheriff. They'll be more than happy to let me cop a plea if I hand them you."

The phone went dead. Brader numbly replaced the handset, Sam Moultrie's words about shooting a lawman still echoing in his ears. He leaned forward and kneaded his forehead to relieve the throbbing headache that hadn't subsided in twelve hours. He had been less than candid with Moultrie about his encounter with Sheriff Withers the previous night. The gruff lawman was proving to be a much tougher customer than Brader anticipated. Withers had grilled him both at the roadside and at the Ouray County Sheriff's Office. Brader's only means of defense had been a staunch refusal to answer any of the sheriff's questions. After what seemed like hours, his local attorney finally managed to extricate him from the Withers's grasp.

Brader had spent a tortured night on his living room couch, knowing his plan was unraveling. He had concluded that the botched rendezvous with Moultrie had ruined his entire scheme. Without access to a helicopter, he would be unable to produce an agreement signed by Jim Philips. Without an agreement, he was powerless to negotiate with Saratoga Mining. Even if he somehow managed to reach Imogene Pass without Moultrie's help, there was no guarantee that the doctor would be alive.

Brader had conceded that the game was over. He resolved that he would call his contact at Saratoga Mining in the morning to cancel Sunday's meeting. He would then call Joe Deutch, advising him to proceed with the liquidation of his assets. The most difficult conversation would be with Sissy. He would be forced tell his wife that they no longer owned their home. They would move back to New York, where Paul Brader would have to look for a job.

The revelation came to him in the shower the next morning. Brader cursed himself for not thinking of it sooner. In his haste to pursue a blockbuster deal with Saratoga, he had ignored the fact that there was a simpler deal to be made. Maybe there was a way to salvage his financial future after all.

Unsure about what to do with Sam Moultrie, Brader decided that the best use of his time would be to implement the alternate scheme. He picked up the telephone and dialed his New York attorney.

When Carl Trudeau answered the call, his voice was upbeat. "I understand it's snowing out there in God's country."

"That's right, Carl," Brader responded. "The bunny slopes await, you old daredevil."

"With a little bit of luck and a decent flight connection in Denver, I should be landing at that postage stamp that you call an airport around one o'clock tomorrow. That means we're going to have to hustle to get in some runs before the lifts close. After that, we can concentrate on the humdrum details of Sunday's meeting."

"Not a problem," Paul Brader assured him. "But speaking of hustling, I'm going to need some quick work from you today."

"Problems with Saratoga?" Trudeau asked. "I told you they're a squirrelly bunch."

"No, the problem's on my side of the equation. At first, I thought it might queer the whole deal, but I think I've finally come up with a back-up plan."

"You must be getting some pushback from Philips on the corporate realignment we sprung on him Tuesday. I knew he wouldn't be thrilled with that play."

"Actually, he was a pretty good sport about it," Brader lied. "I suspect he's secretly relieved that I'll be taking over the day-to-day management of Divining Rod. At his age, running a corporation can be a real grind."

"No kidding? You must be a better salesman than I give you credit for. So, what's the problem?"

"The problem is he's missing. Everyone on the western slope of Colorado is out looking for him. He got stranded on the highway in the middle of a storm late Tuesday and his truck was plowed into a ravine. They managed to salvage his truck, but they can't find him. The local sheriff seems to think he may have become disoriented and wandered off into the woods."

Trudeau whistled in disbelief. "Talk about bad timing. Did he sign the documents before the accident?"

Brader decided to preserve his options. "The last time we spoke, he said he would have it notarized and drop it in the mail, but as of yesterday, it hasn't shown up. I've been in close touch with the sheriff over in

Ouray County and he tells me they didn't find it in his truck."

"What about Philips's lawyer? What does he say?"

"I've decided not to involve him at this point," Brader replied cautiously. "Jim made his own decisions. Besides, I don't want to raise a red flag with Douglas Shultz. The last thing I need is for him to start raising hell before Sunday's meeting."

"Don't you think it would be wise to cover our bases, though?" Trudeau said. "I can place the call if you want."

Brader suddenly became agitated. "In case you forgot, I get to call the shots."

"Calm down, Paul. I'm aware of the pressure you're under, but you have to be realistic. Without that document, our hands are tied. There's no reason to meet with Saratoga."

"That's why I'm calling, Carl. I need to salvage that meeting, even if it means leaving a couple million dollars on the table."

"I'm not following you," the attorney responded.

"This whole thing becomes moot if that document shows up in the mail today, but I need to prepare for the worst. I want you to draft an alternate proposal where Saratoga Mining buys my forty-percent stake in Divining Rod Enterprises for $10 million until we can get this whole matter with Dr. Philips straightened out," Brader continued. "Since Saratoga's willing to spend $30 million for the entire corporation, that makes my position worth $12 million. I'm willing to discount my share of the purchase price by $2 million in order to get this part of the deal done on Sunday night. It's like a fire sale; they should jump all over it."

The attorney sounded skeptical. "I don't know if it will work, Paul."

"Don't you see the beauty of it?" Brader asked excitedly. "I get to take $10 million out of the company so I don't get completely wiped out on my margin call, and Saratoga gets to save $2 million on the interim transaction."

Trudeau contemplated the issue aloud. "I agree with your logic. According to your original shareholders' agreement with Dr. Philips, you can sell your shares to whoever you want. But you need to keep in mind that Saratoga Mining isn't interested in just a portion of the company:

they want the whole thing. Forty percent doesn't represent a controlling interest and believe me, Saratoga is a very control-minded."

"Saratoga's a long-term player, Carl. This isn't a get-rich-quick scheme for them. They've got plenty of patience and they know a bargain when they see one."

"Let's say you're right about that," the lawyer conceded. "What guarantee can we give them on Sunday that they'll eventually be able to buy the rest of the company from Dr. Philips? The purpose of the corporate realignment was to allow you to negotiate on the company's behalf. If you cash out on them, they're going to be stuck having to deal with a man they've never met before."

Brader tried to sound downcast. "I hate to say this, Carl, but the man's been missing for almost three days now. He got plowed into a gorge that's notorious for swallowing up bodies until the snowpack melts."

"What a way to go," Trudeau said. "So, it looks like Saratoga's going to wind up dealing with Dr. Philips's beneficiaries."

"And I have no idea who they are because Philips wasn't required to identify his beneficiaries in our contract. I can tell you one thing, though. They aren't going to think twice about selling out for a cool $18 million, especially when they realize they have to pay annual holding fees on thousands of claims in order to keep them current."

"You got that right," Trudeau chuckled. "There's a chance that Saratoga might actually be swayed by that reasoning. Let me get to work on a proposal. I hate to see you giving up $2 million, but you're right, Saratoga should see this as a gesture of good will. Hopefully, that'll soften the blow that we don't have the whole thing wrapped up."

"Who knows?" Brader added. "Maybe we'll catch a break and that signed document will arrive before the meeting."

"I don't mean to put you on the defensive, Paul, but is there anything else I should know before I arrive tomorrow? Anything you haven't told me about what's going on out there?"

Brader smiled as he sat back in his chair. "The only thing you need to know is that it's snowing to beat the band. By the time you get here, there'll be enough powder on the slopes to keep even you from busting your ass. See you tomorrow."

As he hung up the phone, Brader was startled by a sharp rapping on his door. He could hear Kimberly Cousins's voice rise in protest as the sound of knuckles striking wood echoed through his office.

"Open the door!" a booming voice commanded from the other side.

Brader assumed that he was about to be arrested. His first impulse was to flee, but his only means of escape was the third-floor window. He felt his nose beginning to twitch wildly; a lifelong tic that appeared only in moments of panic. A band of perspiration sprouted along his forehead. He took several deep breaths to compose himself, then slowly opened the door.

Seeing a hulking figure staring down at him, Brader took a step backward. The man seemed to take up the entire doorway. Growing up on the streets of Brooklyn, Brader had learned to recognize trouble when he saw it; trouble had just arrived.

Brader swallowed hard. "How can I help you?"

"I need to speak with you outside."

The intruder's voice betrayed not a hint of emotion. Brader searched the man's steel-blue eyes for some inkling of his intentions, but could find none. The man was dressed in blue jeans, scuffed work-boots, a blue fleece vest and a checkerboard flannel shirt. His slate-colored hair was longer than any law enforcement agency would tolerate.

"This is a private business concern located on private property. In case you didn't see the sign on the door in the lobby, soliciting is prohibited. If you'd like to make an appointment, you can speak to Miss Cousins."

Lyle Morrison ducked his head under the top of the doorframe and took two steps into the well-appointed office. He locked his eyes on Brader's and spoke slowly, without a trace of malice.

"I'd prefer to have a private discussion in the parking lot. If you don't come down in five minutes, I'll drag you down the steps by your neck. Do you understand?"

Without waiting for a reply, Morrison turned on his heels and walked out of Brader's office.

Kimberly rushed to Brader's side, wringing her hands and blinking nervously. "What on earth was *that* all about?"

Without replying, Brader crossed to his office window. He saw the massive gray-haired man emerge from the building's ground floor and tramp through the snow-covered parking lot toward the black Suburban. Morrison leaned his back against the grille of Brader's truck, a boot heel resting on the Chevy's front bumper. He draped his arms across his chest and stared up at the window at Brader.

Backing away from the window, Brader contemplated his options. He could telephone the San Miguel County Sheriff's Office, but given his recent brush with the law, he decided not to draw any more attention to himself. He could barricade himself in his office until the stranger left, but Brader doubted that the steel deadbolt on his outer door would keep the man out. He appeared capable of kicking a hole in the office wall large enough to walk through. Brader considered phoning his local attorney, but doubted that the threat of legal action would impress the man who was reclining against his truck.

Finally, Brader concluded he had no choice but to face the man in the parking lot. If he tried to turn the encounter into a physical altercation, Brader would be prepared. While the older man had a physical advantage, Brader had something that would tip the scales in his favor.

Sliding open a drawer at the bottom of his mahogany desk, Brader ran his hand beneath a row of green hanging file folders and located a semi-automatic Beretta 92 series pistol. He held the loaded weapon at arm's length and with a satisfied smirk, placed it in the pocket of his ski jacket.

— Chapter 23 —

As he crossed the parking lot, a thick white curtain of wind-driven snow obscured Brader's view of his truck. Dense clouds lumbered across the face of the slopes towering over the parking lot. Brader could hear the spirited clamor of skiers as they congregated at the base of the Oak Street Lift and Telluride Gondola Station two blocks to the south.

Brader pulled the hood of his ski jacket over his head and ducked his chin into his chest. His right hand was clasped around the handle of the Beretta. As he approached the stranger, Brader saw that the man had made no attempt to cover his head or brush the snow off of his face and hair. When he closed to within six feet of his Suburban, Brader stopped and stood his ground. Even at this distance, Brader did not feel comfortable. He pivoted slightly to his left so that the gun in his right pocket was aimed at the man's chest.

Morrison slowly pushed himself off of the front bumper of the Suburban. Without speaking, he reached his left hand into the back pocket of his jeans and removed a three-by-five white index card. He offered it to Brader, who cautiously accepted it from man's large callused hands. He glanced at the words printed across the face of the card. "What's this?"

When Lyle spoke, his voice was slow and measured.

"My name is Lyle Morrison. I work for the Colorado Department of Transportation over in Ouray. I've also written down my home address and phone number." He jerked his thumb toward a green Ford pickup that was parked next to Brader's truck. "I drive that truck right there."

"And why do I need to know all of this?"

"I've made it my business to find out where you live, where you work and what you drive," Lyle explained. "I think it's only fair that you have the same information about me."

Brader stuffed the index card into his left jacket pocket. "I'll be passing this along to my attorney. I'm sure he'll be contacting you, especially if you make any future attempts to trespass in my office or threaten me."

"Then you'll definitely want to give that to him," Lyle replied soberly. "Speaking of threats, I saw that you used your left hand to take that card. Is there something wrong with your right hand?"

Instinctively, Brader tightened the grip on the Beretta in his right pocket. "Nothing wrong with it at all. I plan to keep it exactly where it is."

"I've had some experience with firearms, so you might say I'm a little touchy about the subject," Lyle Morrison explained, nodding at Brader's pocket. "For instance, I assume that when a man points a gun at me, he intends to kill me. Do you intend to kill me, Mr. Brader?"

Brader saw a flash of intensity in Morrison's eyes. His right hand suddenly felt clammy around the steel handle of the gun. He swallowed hard, knowing the weapon was his only source of leverage.

"Let me make myself plain," Lyle Morrison continued, inching toward Brader. "Take that hand out of your pocket or I'll take it out for you."

Brader felt lightheaded, as if he had stood up too quickly and had to struggle to retain his balance. The sound of the massive man's boots crunching into the snow reverberated in his ears as Morrison began circling to Brader's left, away from the weapon.

"Okay, okay!" Brader conceded as he slipped his right hand out of his pocket. Lyle continued circling until he had backed the younger man against the front of the Suburban.

Morrison leaned forward and stared directly into Brader's eyes. When he spoke, his breath froze into steamy puffs that lingered around Brader's face. "I'm going to ask you a question, but first, I want you to understand something. I'm not a cop, so I don't give a damn about your rights. This is a personal matter between you and me. Is that clear to you, Mr. Brader?"

Brader fought hard to control his trembling and his tic. Snowflakes fell onto his face as he looked up at the gray-haired man whose tone was becoming lower and angrier.

"I choose my friends carefully and Dr. Philips is a friend of mine," Lyle continued. "Even though you seem to have an alibi for Tuesday night, I know that you're behind whatever happened to him in Red Mountain Pass."

As Brader shook his head, it dawned on him that Jim Philips had once mentioned Morrison's name in connection with Divining Rod Enterprises. He could not recall the context of the discussion, or the relationship between the physician and Morrison.

"I'm going to be square with you," Lyle explained. "I haven't figured out the details yet. I don't know if you did this by yourself or if you had some help, but that doesn't matter to me. What *does* matter is Jim Philips, and I intend to find out where he is."

"I wish I could help you, but I have no idea what's happened to him," Brader pleaded, his palms facing the stormy sky. "If you ask me, Sheriff Withers needs to do a better job searching that gorge and he needs to start asking some serious questions of the snowplow driver who knocked Jim's truck off the road."

"That snowplow driver is standing right in front of you!" he thundered, pinning Brader against the grille of his truck. "Exactly what *serious questions* do you want to ask me? I'm also in charge of the two dozen volunteers who risked their lives trying to find Dr. Philips down in that gorge. Do you have any tactical improvements to suggest regarding our search and rescue procedures?"

The blood drained from Brader's face. He shook his head violently. "I didn't know."

"What have you done with Jim Philips?" Lyle demanded.

"I swear to God I don't know where he is!" Brader pleaded.

Lyle reached under Brader's nylon hood and grabbed his neck with both hands. Extending his thumbs under the jawbone, he lifted Brader off the ground until he was at eye level. "Do I have your attention, Mr. Brader?"

Brader tried to nod, but his head was locked in a vise-like grip. A gurgle came from his throat.

"Good," Lyle remarked. "You have twenty-four hours to produce Dr. Philips. If he doesn't show up safe and sound by this time tomorrow, I'm going to pay you another visit. I don't care how many lawyers you have or how much police protection you get. I'll track you down and I promise it won't be nearly as pleasant as today's chat."

Brader's face was growing redder by the second. He attempted to reduce the strain on his neck by grasping his assailant's forearms, but Lyle squeezed his neck even tighter.

"Take a good look at my face," Lyle commanded. "If anything has happened to Dr. Philips, I promise you that this face will be the last sight that you see before you die. Do you understand?"

Brader's eyes went wide and he tried to shake his head. Lyle bent at the knees and in one explosive movement, he threw Brader over the hood of the Suburban. The multimillionaire bounced once on the snow-covered roof and went sprawling onto the ground behind the vehicle's rear bumper.

Lyle walked through a wind-propelled snow squall toward the parking lot's east exit. As he turned left on Aspen Street, he saw a familiar vehicle parked at the curb. Ouray County Deputy Steve Mapes was sitting in the driver's seat of his blue Ford Bronco with a pair of binoculars dangling from his neck. Mapes climbed out of the truck and followed Lyle along Aspen Street until he was certain that Brader could not see them.

"That was not a good idea, Lyle," the deputy said as he fell in step. "I'm on surveillance duty, so I had to radio Withers about what just happened. Needless to say, he's not a happy man. He wants you to call him."

"I'd rather deal with him face to face. Bill's butt-chewings lose a lot in translation over the phone," Lyle replied. "Tell him I'll stop by his office on my way to work."

"He probably won't be there. He's making a sweep through Highway 550 with Yancey, trying to see if he can find what the hell happened to Turlington."

"Still no word?"

"Nope. Mark's not the kind guy who'd just blow off an assignment and go cruising around in a county jeep all night. Withers thinks this might have something to do with Dr. Philips."

Lyle cast a glance back toward Brader's condo. "We've got to keep squeezing this guy. Next time you talk to Bill, ask him if he wants me to get the hasty team ready."

"Where are you headed?" the deputy asked. "Your truck's back at the parking lot."

"I'm going stick my head into Casey Bailey's flower shop for a second. In the meantime, you'd better keep an eye on our boy back there. Something tells me he might be ready to make a move."

Mapes smiled and lowered his voice. "Just between you and me, I wish I could've been on the other side of the truck when you heaved him over. We could've played catch with him until he confessed."

— Chapter 24 —

T hrough the plate glass window of The Petal Pusher, Casey Bailey watched familiar faces as Telluride's year-round residents walked purposefully toward the post office, the bank or their favorite lunchtime haunt. Meanwhile, newly arrived weekend tourists wandered the sidewalks at a more leisurely pace, soaking in the town's sights and rustic flavor. While the locals were oblivious to the falling snow, the vacationers took delight in the fresh coat of white frosting that the storm was slathering onto every level surface in the quaint mountain hamlet.

"You looking for anyone in particular?" Jill Samsky asked as Jason Zuckerman escorted a customer to the front door.

Casey turned from the window and faced Jill, who was dressed in black denim jeans, a white cable-knit sweater and a dark gray ski jacket. "Steve Mapes said over your radio that Lyle was on his way up here. I just wanna make sure he doesn't get into any more trouble on the way."

Jason chimed in. "Is that bad-ass coming here to trash the place? If so, I'd like my paycheck a few days early."

"Keep it up and you can forget about getting the afternoon off," Casey taunted her employee. "The tile grout in the cooler could use a vigorous scrubbing."

Jason pointed to a clock on the wall behind the register. "According to Mr. Clock over there, I've only got one hour 'til quitting time. A deal's a deal, boss-lady."

"A deal is a deal," Casey agreed. "I'll tell you what, why don't we ignore Mr. Clock and let you take off early. It's snowing, so I'm sure your cohorts are already jostling for position over at the Coonskin lift."

Jason snatched his jacket from a wooden coat rack and headed for the door. "See you in the morning." He patted Casey on the shoulder, then turned to face Jill Samsky. "By the way, ma'am, if I ever get in trouble in Ouray, I sure hope that you're the one who nails me. If you don't mind me saying so, you certainly are one *arresting* officer."

Before Jill could respond, the young man bolted out the door.

"He's some piece of work," Jill commented before changing the subject. "Well, the store's finally empty, and we know that Brader's gone back up to his office. I think it's time for you to place that call."

Casey took a deep breath and reached for the telephone beside the register. As she dialed, Lyle Morrison opened the front door and entered the shop. Before he could speak, Jill put her fingers to her lips.

"Hello Kimberly, it's Casey over at The Petal Pusher. I need to speak with Mr. Brader if he has a minute."

Casey nodded in response to the receptionist's reply. "I'm sure he is busy, but could you please tell him that I'm on the line?"

Casey noticed the curious look on Lyle's face. After a brief pause, she resumed speaking. "Thanks for taking my call, Paul. Kimberly says you're busy, but you asked me to keep you in the loop about the search for Dr. Philips."

Lyle shot a questioning glance at Jill, who was nodding encouragement to Casey.

"It sounds as if they've had a breakthrough. I don't know if this is supposed to be confidential, but Sheriff Withers didn't say anything about keeping it a secret." Casey closed her eyes, concentrating on her message. "Apparently, the state police have flown in two technicians from some high-tech telecommunications company in Denver. A lot of what Withers was saying was over my head, but I remember he said they're planning to use something called reverse telemetry."

Casey listened for a few seconds before responding. "Like I said, it was a lot of gibberish to me, but it has something to do with low-frequency emissions from Dr. Philips's beeper and his pacemaker. The technicians are going to use this new receiver to home in on the signals and pinpoint their location. I gather it's a pretty new technique."

With her free hand, Casey began twirling a strand of her blonde hair into a tight loop around her index finger. Realizing that Casey was growing uneasy with the conversation, Lyle quickly grabbed a note pad and a pen, and started jotting notes for her to use. As Brader continued to fire questions at Casey, she looked down at the note pad. Lyle had written the phrases 'helicopter sweep,' 'manufacturer's serial numbers' and 'unique electronic footprint'.

"Well, I do recall Withers saying that they're going to make a helicopter sweep of the area with their electronic gear. Apparently they've gotten the serial numbers from the manufacturer of Dr. Philips's beeper as well as his pacemaker. They're convinced they'll able to track them because both devices emit a unique electronic footprint. They'll start the sweeps as soon as the weather clears tomorrow morning."

Lyle could hear Brader's voice through the receiver. He made a motion with his hand across his throat, mouthing the words "that's enough" to Casey.

"I'm sorry I don't have any more details, Paul, but I've got to get off the line. I have a store full of customers. I'll let you know if I hear anything more."

Casey hung up and exhaled. She wiped her palms against her soft burgundy sweater. "Talk about a bad poker player. You could hear the panic in his voice."

Lyle shook his head. "You played it perfectly, Casey. Whose idea was this?"

"Bill and I cooked it up last night after Brader's lawyer came by to collect him," Jill explained. "We figured he must've been rattled after the incident at the cemetery, so we decided to push as many buttons as we could. We enlisted Earl Dobbs as our technical consultant in coming up with the story."

"Earl Dobbs?" Lyle asked.

Jill grinned. "He manages the Radio Shack up in Montrose."

"I never knew that Jim has a pacemaker," Lyle informed the deputy.

"That's because he doesn't," Jill explained. "We invented the pacemaker because we didn't want to rely solely on the pager. Just because we didn't find it in his truck doesn't mean that it's still with him. On the other hand, a pacemaker would still be with him, no matter what."

"Good idea," Lyle said. "I'm glad Bill's finally getting aggressive with that creep."

"Not as aggressive as you just got with him. Bill's awful pissed about that stunt." Jill zipped up her jacket and pulled on a pair of black leather gloves. "Well, I've got to relieve Mapes at noon. I'm on stakeout until eight o'clock tonight. Do you want a police escort back to your truck or are you gonna stick around here and pick out a bouquet for the sheriff?"

Lyle smiled and looked around Casey's store. "I'm going to kill a few minutes here before I drive back to Ouray. I imagine that Hamp is going to be calling for reinforcements soon; looks like this storm is going to be sticking around awhile. Also, if Mark Turlington doesn't show up today, the hasty team's going to need to be ready."

As Jill left, Lyle began browsing through the aisles. "I had a completely different picture of what your shop would look like."

Casey seemed disappointed. "How so?"

"For one thing, there's a much wider variety of products. Scented candles, preserves, dried flowers, wreaths, potted plants, gift baskets, pottery, soaps, bath salts, cactus. How do you decide what to stock?"

"Mostly through trial and error," Casey explained eagerly. "Each year, I add a few new items to see what the response will be."

Lyle then looked through the glass door of the walk-in cooler. Rows of white shelves held glass vases filled to overflowing with a seemingly endless variety of flowers.

"Where do you buy your flowers from?"

"I try to deal directly with the growers instead of going through distributors," Casey replied. "You should see my phone bill. In an average month, I'll call growers in New York, California, Hawaii, Holland, France, Israel, Ecuador."

"Ecuador?"

Casey laughed. "They're a big player in roses."

Lyle was clearly impressed. "How'd you learn all of this?"

"It seems like I've worked in florist shops my whole life. When I was in high school and college, I worked after school and on weekends."

"What made you decide on Telluride?" Lyle asked.

"I came out here on vacation when I was a junior in college," Casey explained. "I majored in business administration because I wanted to open a florist shop of my own one day. I loved Telluride, but with only fifteen hundred year-round residents, I figured it was too small to support even one florist. Before giving up on the idea, I decided to spend my vacation trying to get a feel for the business climate out here. To be honest, I spent most of my time people-watching."

"And apparently you found the people to your liking," Lyle surmised.

"Well, this town sure had an interesting mix of people, from celebrities to small business owners, tourists to trust fund kids."

"You don't have to answer this, but I'm curious about how you arranged your financing. This had to require a decent chunk of start-up capital."

Casey brushed a strand of blonde hair away from her face. "It did. Some of the money came from my father's estate. He died of a heart attack when I was sixteen."

"I'm sorry to hear that, Casey," Lyle said.

"It's okay, Lyle," the petite twenty-six year old replied. "I'm just trying to answer your question."

Lyle was taken aback by the impassive tone of her response.

Casey continued without missing a beat, "He was a Wall Street banker; his estate affords my mother a fairly comfortable lifestyle. My younger sister and I were the beneficiaries of one of his life insurance policies. I used my share to cover my college tuition, and when I graduated, there was enough left over to help me finance this shop."

"I'm sure your dad would be proud of what you've accomplished," Lyle said.

"I don't know what he'd think," Casey replied. "The insurance money helped me with the initial capital, but that was only the tip of the iceberg. The real work was in developing a business plan that would convince the bank and the landlord that I was a good risk. Colorado Avenue retail space is a tough swallow for most start-ups, but I was determined to get the best storefront I could. It was tough, but I was finally able to secure the financing I needed."

"What about your suppliers?" Lyle asked. "How'd you establish credit with them?"

"At first, I ordered the bare minimum from my growers, but I paid my bills in full and on time. After three years of being a thirty-day payer, I have all the credit I need."

Lyle was buoyed by Casey's obvious zeal for her business, but he found her earlier comments troubling. "Would you be offended by a personal observation from someone you only met a few days ago?"

"Feel free to offend at will."

"You're pretty quick to downplay the importance of your father's insurance money in the success of your store. It almost seems like you're trying to distance yourself—and the success of the store—from him. It makes me wonder what type of relationship you had with your dad."

Casey's eyes narrowed.

Sensing that his question had struck a sensitive chord, Lyle added, "I'm not trying to put you on the spot, Casey. It's just that father-daughter relationships are something I'm always curious about. Let's drop the subject."

Looking into Lyle's blue-gray eyes, Casey sensed a deep sadness, and she decided to explain herself. "My father was a real man's man. As a kid, I got the impression he would've gladly traded in his two daughters for one son. He commuted back and forth between Connecticut and New York City, so he usually didn't get home 'til late. On the weekends, he spent most of his time golfing with his buddies and entertaining clients."

"Sounds like it was hard to get his attention," Lyle observed.

"On top of that, he was impossible to please," Casey said. "Whenever I brought home a good report card, he'd pick it apart 'til I felt like a failure. If I'd played well in a soccer game, he'd want to know why a girl was wasting her time playing sports."

Lyle shook his head slowly. "They say that the children of demanding parents spend the rest of their lives trying to live up to their expectations."

"Who says that?" Casey challenged him. "I'm not doing this for him; I'm doing this in spite of him."

The young woman's face was a mix of anger and despair. Lyle saw that her cheeks were flushed and her eyes glistening.

Lyle asked softly, "Are you mad at him, Casey?"

Casey looked down at her boots. "What's to be mad about? It's not his fault that he died."

"It's okay to be mad, Casey. It's even okay to resent him for dying before you could show him what kind of person you could become. And it's okay to wish that he could walk through that front door and see what you've accomplished."

As she looked up at Lyle, a steady stream of tears rolled down Casey's cheeks. Lyle noticed that she did not sniffle, sob or break down in any way. She tried to control her emotions by biting her bottom lip.

"You know that rocking chair that you made for your daughter?" Casey began. "That reminded me of one of the best memories I have of growing up. I was four years old and my mother was eight months pregnant with my sister. She was tired all the time, so for two weeks, my father would read me a book before bedtime. I can still remember everything about it. We'd sit in a rocking chair in the corner of my room with me in his lap. My Winnie the Pooh lamp gave off a little circle of light and it felt like my dad and I were the only two people in the world. I don't remember even one of the books he read me; all I remember is the feeling of his whiskers against my face and the sound of his voice. It was like he was sharing these wonderful little secrets with me as we rocked back and forth. Anyway, that's the last time I can remember spending any one-on-one time with my father."

Lyle knew that it would be too painful for Casey to delve further into the subject of her relationship with her father. He changed the subject.

"So, what's next? What's your end game?"

"End game?"

"You know, what're your plans? I mean, for most people, working is just a means to an end. What are your goals apart from the store? Do you want to buy a house, get married, have kids?"

"Sure, all of that, I suppose. It's just that I don't have time for those things right now. I guess they're just not as important to me as they are to other people."

They were interrupted by the sound of the front door opening. In one quick move, Lyle wiped the tears from Casey's cheeks with his large fingers. The shopkeeper walked toward the register, trying to compose herself.

As Casey greeted her customer, Lyle looked out the front window onto Colorado Avenue. A snowplow came into view. The driver guided the plow slowly along the busy street, mindful of the thick pedestrian traffic. As the customer inspected a display of hand-blown glass figurines, Casey joined Lyle at the window.

"I'd better get back to Ouray before Hamp starts wondering where I am." Lyle announced.

"I thought you worked last night. Surely Hamp doesn't expect you to go back to work without any sleep."

"It wouldn't be the first time," Lyle commented. "If I'm lucky, I might be able to catch a few hours this afternoon. My shift begins at midnight, but if this storm doesn't let up, I'll probably get a call around six o'clock."

"Well, be careful on the roads," Casey said. "I don't care if you are a grizzled snowplow driver; you haven't slept in over twenty-four hours and you've got a fifty-mile drive ahead of you."

Lyle smiled and pointed east. "It'd make life a lot simpler for all of us if they'd build a road from Telluride to Red Mountain Pass. It's only about eight miles as the crow flies."

"I'll bring it up at the next Chamber of Commerce meeting," Casey joked. "Take it easy and stay out of trouble."

Lyle opened the front door and stepped onto the snow-dusted side-walk. He drew in a deep gulp of the crisp mountain air and pulled on his gloves. Snow squalls whipped down Colorado Avenue. He turned to his left, tracking the gusting wind as it blew through Telluride's box canyon toward Telluride Peak and Trico Peak to the east of town. Lyle heard the sudden sound of the door being yanked open behind him. He turned to see Casey rushing through the door, calling over her shoulder to the customer.

"I'll be back in a second."

"What is it?" he asked, seeing the intense look on Casey's face.

"Red Mountain Pass is only eight miles away as the crow flies," she repeated, guiding him down Colorado Avenue to the east. "Brader's alibi hinges on the fact that it takes two hours to make the round trip from here to there and back. But what if he didn't take the highway?"

They followed Colorado Avenue east for two blocks until it intersect-ed Willow Street. Storm clouds and slanting gusts of snow obstructed their view of the far end of the canyon.

"You're right," Lyle agreed. "We must be overlooking something."

Pedestrians were gawking at the tall, long-haired man and the sweat-er-clad young woman who were standing in the middle of the busy side-walk, scanning the eastern horizon.

"Is there a shortcut over the mountains between here and the pass?" Casey asked.

"Not during the winter," Lyle replied. "The terrain is really brutal back there. We're talking steep cliffs, frozen creek beds and thick forests. It would take a lot longer, either by snowshoes or snowmobile, than sim-ply driving the Skyway. No way he could've done the round trip in less than two hours."

"Are you sure there's no other way?"

With the storm clouding his view, Lyle closed his eyes and tried to pic-ture the significant landmarks between the far end of Telluride's box can-yon and Red Mountain Pass on the other side of the mountains. On the outskirts of Telluride, Bear Creek Road led past the Pandora Mill com-plex that now sat idle behind barbed wire fencing. Further up the steep, winding road, a refurbished hydroelectric plant was perched atop a sheer vertical cliff three hundred feet above the valley floor. Directly below the power plant, the frozen flow of Bridal Veil Falls would be shimmering like a giant blue-tinted icicle down the full length of the cliffs.

Suddenly, his thoughts shifted back to Pandora Mill. The realization hit him like an electric shock.

"Where was the last place Paul Brader was seen before Dr. Philips disappeared?" he asked excitedly.

Casey's mind raced. "Ice climbing at Bridal Veil Falls."

Lyle's eyes were wild. "I think I know how he did it."

"Tell me!" Casey demanded as Lyle began walking quickly back toward The Petal Pusher.

"I'll do better than that, I'll show you," he said, breaking into a run. "First, I need a favor. Close up your shop, then find Jill down near Brader's office. Tell her to radio Withers and have him meet us in an hour at the portal to the Treasury Tunnel."

"Where's that?"

"Bill will know," Lyle replied. "I'm going to hit the hardware store across the street and I'll meet you back here in five minutes. We'll take your Jeep."

— Chapter 25 —

The Jeep's deep-grooved tires chewed through the snow and gravel as Casey downshifted into third gear. The route they had taken was a straight shot down Colorado Avenue, past Lone Tree Cemetery and into the historic mining town of Pandora to the east of Telluride. The graded dirt and gravel road that climbed to the Pandora Mill surface plant had not been plowed since the storm began.

"It's ahead on the left," Lyle urged her. "Pull in front of the gates."

At the road's crest, Casey saw a large odd-shaped building to her left. A chain-link fence topped with strings of barbed wire paralleled the road. Casey steered off the road, sliding to a halt in front of the fenced gates. Posted signs warned that the mill was private property and that trespassers would be prosecuted. As they climbed out of the jeep, Casey saw that the gates were secured by a thick chain and sturdy padlock. "They're pretty serious about security."

"Very serious," Lyle agreed. "Here, hold this for me."

From a plastic bag that contained his hardware store purchases, Lyle handed Casey a large metal tool with long handles and a curved pair of sharpened pincers.

"What's this?"

"Bolt cutters," Lyle answered.

He removed the bag's three remaining items, placing two flashlights with yellow rubber handgrips and a hand-held air horn on the hood of the jeep.

Casey surveyed the items as Lyle checked the flashlight batteries. "You still haven't told me what we're doing here."

Lyle pointed in the direction of the tall building at the base of a steep cliff that stood fifty feet inside the gates. "We're headed in there."

"Into that building?"

"Into that mountain," Lyle corrected.

He retrieved the bolt cutters from Casey and placed the tool's small thick blades around the hasp of the padlock. "This lock looks brand new."

"They must've changed it recently."

"Somebody did, but I'm not sure it was the part-timers who work here."

Lyle grunted as he jerked the bolt cutter's handles together, snapping the steel hasp. He dropped the tool to the ground and unwound the chain securing the gates.

"We'll leave your Jeep here," Lyle announced. "If Brader comes by, he's going to see the busted lock anyway, so there's no need to be cute about things."

Lyle led Casey through the gates. "So you think Dr. Philips is in here somewhere?"

"I hope not," Lyle replied grimly. "But I think we're getting closer to figuring this whole thing out."

As they approached the main mill building, Lyle inspected the wide lot. The snow was six inches deep in the flat expanse of yard. Beneath the fresh layer of snow, he could make out several sets of tire grooves that wound between various outbuildings and the front gate. From the relative width of the two distinctly different sets of tracks, Lyle surmised that a large vehicle towing a small trailer had made several trips through the lot. The faded tracks disappeared behind a low metal garage building, fifteen feet to the right of the main structure of Pandora Mill.

"Do you think those tracks are from Brader's truck?" Casey asked.

"This mill is owned by Mineral King Mining. They still have a few people on the payroll to keep the water pumps running and to make sure the operation stays in environmental compliance. It's possible that those tire tracks were made by Mineral King's own employees."

Casey finished Lyle's thought. "But you doubt it."

"Have you ever seen Paul Brader towing a trailer?"

"All the time," Casey replied. "In the winter, he tows his snowmobile to the local trailheads. He's invited me to go riding with him, but I've always turned him down."

Lyle nodded. "What else have you seen him tow?"

"In the summer, he tows this funky-looking all-terrain vehicle up into the mountains. He once told me that he likes to go artifact hunting around Tomboy and some of the other ghost towns."

Lyle began following the tire tracks. Casey looked up through the wind-driven snow at the tall mill building to her left. The six-story structure was constructed of dark unpainted wood. The building's most prominent feature was a steep-pitched metal roof that accentuated its truncated A-frame design. From its peak, the near side of the roof extended down one hundred feet until it met a vertical wall thirty feet from the ground. The roof's far side extended only twenty feet until it met a vertical wall over a hundred feet from the ground.

"That's one weird-shaped building," Casey noted. "It looks like a giant lean-to."

"Most of the mills around here look like that; even the ones from the nineteenth century. In its heyday, this mill processed over 800 tons of ore a day. In order to move that amount of rock, you need to let gravity do the work for you. The raw ore is fed into the top tier of the building from the rear, then dropped to the lower levels so it can be crushed and milled."

As they reached the far end of the garage, Lyle and Casey followed several sets of tire tracks between the mill's vacant administrative office on the right and a fenced-in electrical substation on the left. Beyond the substation, the tire tracks converged, then bisected two small freestanding buildings to their left.

"What goes on back here?" Casey asked.

Lyle pointed to the structure on the right. "That's the scale house. The one on the left is the assay house."

"Assay house?"

"Let's keep moving and I'll give you a quick version of Mining 101," Lyle told her. "We're actually seeing the mining process in reverse. Milling is the final stage; it's the process of extracting various metals from the ore that's been hauled out of the mine."

The wind intensified as they walked between the two buildings. Casey pulled the bill of her baseball cap lower on her forehead. Lyle nodded to the right.

"The scales are the last stop before the refined ore is shipped out. Since metals like gold, silver, zinc, copper and lead are valued according to weight, it's important to keep track of how much you're shipping." Lyle then gestured to the left. "The assay house is where they determine the value of the metals that have been extracted from the ore. In the case of the Pandora Mill, the last fifty years of operation were spent extracting base metals like copper, zinc and lead instead of precious metals like gold and silver."

"Why is that? You'd think that precious metals would be more valuable, right?"

"In the San Juans, the richest deposits of gold and silver tend to be near the surface. The deeper you dig, the weaker the vein becomes. After a while, you run out of significant deposits of gold and silver. So, if you want to maximize the value of your claims, you have to switch over to base metals at some point."

Lyle continued to follow the faint tire tracks. Once they passed the far end of the assay house, the tracks again veered to the left. Casey noticed that the wind's intensity diminished considerably once they rounded the far corner of the massive mill building. Directly ahead, she saw a network of large metal chutes that resembled oversized air-conditioning ducts. One chute led from the back of the mill building down to a tall metal structure that looked like a grain silo. Another chute led from a short, squat ground-floor building to the top of the main mill building.

"Like I said, gravity is used throughout the process," Lyle explained. "Large chunks of ore are dropped from train tracks leading out of the mine down a chute that feeds into that silo-like building in front of us. That's called a coarse ore bin. The coarse ore bin feeds the raw ore into that small flat building, which houses a jaw crusher. The crushing plant smashes the raw ore into smaller stones. From there, a conveyor system brings the crushed ore up that other chute to the fine ore bin on top of the building. From the fine ore bin, the stores are dropped into the main building where a cone crusher breaks them into pebbles. After that, the pebbles are fed into a series of ball mills until the ore is the size and consistency of sand."

Casey shook her head. "I still don't see how they get gold and silver out of the rocks."

Lyle pointed to the main mill building. "It happens in there. When the raw rock comes in from the mines, the metals are still embedded in the ore. All the crushing in the world can't separate out the metals because they're chemically bonded to the host ore. The first step is called amalgamation. The crushed ore is coated with mercury and then run over an electrically charged copper plate. Mercury attracts gold -- and the biggest pieces of gold will stick to the copper plate. Once the larger pieces of gold are collected, the rest of the ore goes through a process called flotation. They wash the pulverized ore with a chemical mix called reagents. The reagents break down the chemical bond and the metals literally float away from the host ore. The metals are scooped out of the chemical mix and separated out for further refining."

"What happens to the waste that's left over after the good stuff is taken out?"

"That's the million-dollar question," Lyle answered. "The end product of the milling process is a mix of pulverized rock and chemically treated sand. Usually, it's dumped near the mill into holding areas called tailing piles or tailing ponds. When you consider that this mill alone processed 800 tons of ore a day for decades, you can see the magnitude of the problem. When a major mining operation runs out of dump space near their mill, they need to find someplace else to unload their waste. And since a lot of mines are located in public forests, guess where it all gets dumped?"

Casey nodded. "No wonder Dr. Philips didn't want big-time mining to make a comeback around here."

Lyle stopped walking and pointed to a series of tire tracks at the rear of the coarse ore bin. "It looks like this was used as some sort of turnaround and staging area."

In the flat open area behind the bin, the tire tracks looped in a wide circle. The area inside the circle was dotted by dozens of faint footprints. Lyle bent down and scooped the fresh snow from several of the shallow indentations.

"At least two different people," he concluded.

"Paul Brader and that pilot guy?"

Lyle stood up and looked to his left. He noticed a single set of tire grooves that led away from the circle. The tracks followed directly beneath the rear-most overhead chute, which slanted up a steep slope along the back of the main building. The width of the tracks that led up the hill indicated that the vehicle had a relatively short wheelbase.

"Looks like an ATV," Casey observed. "You couldn't drive up there in a truck."

The rock-strewn hill beneath the coarse ore chute was covered in snow. Only the largest rocks and tallest brush peeked through the blanket of white.

"Are you up for a little climbing?" Lyle asked.

"I still don't know what you're hoping to find," Casey replied. "You said we might be able to blow a hole in Brader's alibi but all I see so far is a bunch of tire tracks."

"I'm not sure Brader has the know-how to do what I think he did. The only way to find out is to follow those tracks."

"Then let's go."

Casey led the way up the snowy incline. The tire tracks led through a tangle of brush and rock outcroppings. Unsure footing beneath the snow made the sixty-yard climb slick and tedious. Finally cresting the hill, Casey stood in snow up to her knees. She wiped perspiration from her top lip and looked around. She had emerged in an abandoned parking area directly behind the central mill building; to her right was a freestanding garage. The chute she had followed up from the coarse ore bin was now just barely over her head. Lyle came up behind her, found the tire tracks and nodded to the far end of the parking lot.

"Looks like they lead toward the shop," he observed.

Casey followed him as he tracked the faded prints that paralleled the elevated chute. She was forced to jog to keep pace with Lyle's long, urgent strides. As they rushed through the upward-slanting parking lot, the supporting legs of the chute to their left became shorter. After twenty yards, the peaked chute dropped to ground level, losing its bottom sheet of metal where it came into contact with the ground. The narrow structure now appeared to be a long shed rather than a chute. Ten yards farther, the shed joined a wide metal-skinned building. The building's roof flared upward at a severe angle until it butted against a sheer gray cliff wall.

"That's a snowshed," Lyle explained. "It protects the portal of the main tunnel from avalanches coming down the mountain."

"How do we get in there?"

"If Brader found a way in, so can we."

The ATV tracks turned left toward the building that was covered by the snowshed. The narrow tire grooves ended at a wide garage door in the center of the building. Lyle brushed snow away from the handle at the base of the garage door and tugged upward. The door wouldn't budge.

Casey checked out a wooden door to the right of the garage door. A steel fastener connected the side of the door to its metal doorframe, secured by a rusted padlock. She noticed that the screws securing the hardware to the wooden door were protruding from the fastening device. She pulled on the hasp and the three long screws pulled free of their holes in the door.

"They must've pried it open with a crowbar," Lyle said.

Casey opened the door and stepped into the pitch-black building. Lyle followed behind her and ran his hand along the wall to the left of the door. He pushed a button and the garage door began to rise, which illuminated the interior of the building.

"If they've abandoned this mine, why do they keep the power on in here?" she asked.

"They still need to check their pumps and measure the toxicity level of the water that flows through the mine."

Casey looked around. Two sets of narrow train tracks ran from left to right, disappearing from view beyond the margin of light coming from the open garage door.

Lyle took the two yellow-handled flashlights from his pocket. He turned both of them on and handed one to Casey. Lyle scanned the wet floor of the building for tire tracks, but could find none. Moving the light slowly around the long, narrow building, the beam reflected off of the shed's metal walls and illuminated patches of ice on the gravel floor. There was no trace of the ATV.

"Looks like Mineral King moved all of their ore cars and man-trips out of here. This place is more deserted than I thought," Lyle said. "They probably shipped most of their equipment to their other mining operations."

Casey shined her flashlight beam along the train tracks to the right, in the direction of the mine. The prospect of entering the deserted subterranean complex sent a shiver up her spine. "Have you ever been in here before?"

"Rick Quinn was the chief geologist here until Mineral King shut things down in 1978," Lyle said, referring to a year-round Ouray resident. "He's shown me schematic drawings of this complex, but now I wish I'd paid more attention."

Lyle led Casey away from the garage door, following the nearest set of narrow-gauge train tracks to the right. Ten yards into the widening metal shed, he shined his flashlight towards the ceiling. The snowshed's roof was pitched at a sharp angle until, at some unseen point, it abutted the upper lip of the massive hole in the cliff wall. As they walked toward the far end of the metal structure, the two sets of tracks converged at a railroad switch. From that point, a single set of tracks continued into the darkness.

To the right of the train tracks, a wood-paneled wall jutted out from the right side of the shed. In the center of the wall was an unlocked wooden door. Lyle opened it and entered a long, narrow room with an eight-foot ceiling. He flipped a switch and the room was bathed in stark fluorescent light. Two rows of tall gray lockers lined the walls on both sides of the long rectangular room.

"This is the dry room," he explained, walking between the rows of lockers. "It's where the miners change from street clothes into work clothes."

Lyle began opening several locker doors on the right side of the room, finding each empty. Casey checked the lockers to her left with the same result. When they reached the far end of the room, Lyle opened the last locker in the row. Hanging from hooks were a pair of bright yellow waterproof pants and a matching jacket. On a shelf above the hooks, he found a pair of plastic-coated orange work gloves and a flashlight. A pair of knee-high rubber bog boots sat on the floor of the locker. Lyle opened the locker directly to the right, finding a matching set of work clothes.

"I was hoping we'd find a couple of masks and oxygen tanks. They must keep them in the administration building."

He grabbed the two yellow jackets and handed one to Casey. "It can get pretty wet in the mine."

Lyle opened a door to their left that led out of the dry room. They emerged into a wide rock tunnel. Casey looked to her left and saw that the shed walls had ended where the dry room had begun. They turned right and continued following the tracks. Ten yards beyond the dry room, they came upon a short, squat wood-paneled enclosure with a large glass window. Lyle tried to open a door to the room, but it was locked. He shined his light through the window and saw racks of wood shelving lining the far wall.

"This is called the light room," he explained, "It's where miners pick up their helmets before boarding man-trips that take them into the mine."

"The kind of helmet with a light on it?"

"Yeah, but it looks like we'll have to make do with our flashlights."

Beyond the light room the tunnel had narrowed significantly from where they had entered the mine. The rock-framed passageway was now ten feet wide and nine feet tall. A single set of narrow-gauge train tracks ran through the center of the tunnel floor. Casey aimed her flashlight into the tunnel ahead of her. The tracks continued in straight lines and disappeared from view beyond the far reaches of the flashlight's beam. Dark, wet walls of solid rock lined the deserted tunnel. The air around her felt dank and heavy. She detected the faint odor of rotten eggs.

"I take it we're in the guts of the mine now."

Lyle turned to face her. Casey aimed her flashlight at his midsection so she could see the older man's face without blinding him.

"What's the matter?" she asked.

"We've got some decisions to make and we're gonna have to make them together."

"What kind of decisions?"

"This mine complex has over ninety miles of tunnels, drifts and shafts that veer off in all directions," Lyle began. "It's a maze like nothing you've ever seen before. There's only one series of paths that'll take us where we need to go and the only thing I have to go by is a schematic drawing I last saw more than six months ago. If we take one wrong turn, there's a good chance we'll wander around in here 'til we suffocate."

"Suffocate?"

"The ventilation system's been shut down and we don't have supplemental oxygen. There's some natural ventilation in here, but not much. Some of the vertical shafts go all the way up to the surface, but most of those have been sealed or blocked by snow."

"How far do we need to go?"

"Six and a half miles. And I have no idea if the hoists are still hooked up to the main power source. If not, we're going to have to climb two different ladder systems, each of which is nearly a thousand feet—straight up. With that kind of exertion, we're gonna be burning a lot of oxygen."

"What are our options?" Casey asked.

"I don't have a radio, but we can head back down to Telluride, call Withers and get the search team mobilized. With any luck, he might be able to get a hold of someone from Mineral King so we can get an experienced guide down here."

"That could take the rest of the day," Casey noted. "Besides, you're in charge of the search and rescue team, so you're the one the sheriff would turn to anyway."

"True, but I could get an experienced team down here with some oxygen tanks. I wouldn't be operating alone."

"Operating alone?" Casey asked incredulously as she pointed down the long, black passageway. "Are you saying that I'm going to be a non-factor in there? Or, do you think I won't be able to keep up with you?"

"You asked me what our options were," Lyle replied defensively. Seeing the crestfallen look on Casey's face, he explained further. "I'd hoped we'd be able to find the ATV by now. The way I figure it, Brader had to make four separate trips through here on Tuesday night. Given the timeframe he was operating under, there's no way he could've done it on foot. At a pace of four miles an hour, it would've taken him over three hours to make each 13-mile round trip."

Casey completed Lyle's thought. "And if we can't find the ATV, we might run out of oxygen before we get wherever it is we're going."

"Right, and oxygen deprivation is tough to gauge. By the time we start feeling the effects, we could be past the point of no return. Even if we manage to find the right route, it's going to take us nearly two hours to hike through here."

"But you think this'll help us find out what happened to Dr. Philips, right?"

"It's the first solid break we've gotten so far. I think we owe it to Jim to follow every lead. But if we don't find the ATV soon, we're going to have to rethink this."

"I'm with you. Let's get moving."

Lyle reached into his pocket and passed the hand-held air horn that he had purchased at the hardware store to Casey. "If we get separated and you start feeling light-headed, give me a long blast on the horn. With any luck, I'll be able to get you out of here before any permanent damage sets in."

"What if something happens to you?" Casey asked. "I'm not exactly going to be able to throw you over my shoulder and carry you to daylight."

"You're right. If it comes to that, you need to get out of here as fast as you can."

"And leave you to die?"

"Like I said, we've got some tough choices to make. The bottom line is that Brader may have already killed Dr. Philips and possibly Mark Turlington too. The last thing we need is to start adding to the body count. If it comes down to it, you need to get the hell out of here and tell Withers what we've found."

Lyle turned and shined his flashlight into the ten-by-nine tunnel. The beam glinted against the steel train tracks, glazing them with a pale yellow sheen. To Casey, the tracks looked like two long phosphorescent fingers, beckoning them into the mine's dark expanse.

— Chapter 26 —

B rader left his office and hurried across the parking lot, convinced his every move was being observed. Climbing into his Suburban, he noticed that Lyle Morrison's truck was still parked next to his, two inches of snow coating its front windshield. Only when he was safely inside his vehicle did he steal a glance through the side window of the battered pickup. Morrison was nowhere in sight. As he eased out of the parking lot at the corner of Aspen and Pacific, Brader took note of the vehicles parked nearby.

Rather than drive directly to his destination, Brader made a right turn onto Aspen Street. Where Aspen dead-ended at the base of the ski slopes, he turned left onto San Juan Avenue. He drove slowly along the snow-slickened road, keeping an eye on his rearview mirror. At the next intersection he turned left and proceeded north at a leisurely pace. Since the ski patrol enforced a four-o'clock curfew on the mountain, the sidewalks were becoming crowded with skiers lugging their gear back into town. Brader made another left turn on Pacific Avenue and followed it to the intersection of Aspen Street. Having made a four-corner circuit of the block, Brader was now facing the parking lot behind his condo.

Stopping his truck in the middle of the intersection and scanning the area near the parking lot, Brader recalled that a tan Toyota 4Runner had been parked in a now-vacant space along the far curb. In his rearview mirror, he spotted the tan vehicle slowly emerging from the side street onto Pacific Avenue.

"Damn it!" he cursed, thumping his fist against the steering wheel.

Having confirmed he was being followed, Brader made a quick left onto Aspen Street, cutting off a car heading in the same direction. He saw that the 4Runner had to wait for several cars to pass before picking up the covert pursuit. At the intersection of San Juan Avenue, a car pulled away from the curb, leaving a vacant parking space that Brader swerved in to. He walked quickly to the back of his truck, popped the rear hatch and retrieved his skis and poles. He didn't bother pulling out his boots and bindings. Ducking his head into the blowing snow, he half-walked, half-jogged up the pedestrian walkway toward the Telluride gondola station, resisting the temptation to look back. He checked his watch. It was 2:45.

• • •

"He's got his skis with him and he's getting into a gondola, heading toward Mountain Village," Jill Samsky radioed to her boss. "I'm still in my truck. You want me to grab a gondola and see what he's up to?"

"Nah, if you hightail it over there in your truck, you might be able to beat him," came the reply.

"On my way. Where are you now?"

"Well, Yancey and I *were* twenty miles south of Silverton when you called with Lyle's message. Now we're about five miles south of Red Mountain Pass. I had to cut short our search for Turlington, so this had better be worth it."

• • •

Jason Zuckerman leaned with his back against the AlpenHaus's wooden bar. He wore baggy tan cargo pants, a black Polartec pullover and a black flap hat that extended down over his ears. His snowboard was propped at a similar angle against the base of the bar. As Hardy Bennett walked by with a tray of steaming Irish coffees in his hand, Jason grabbed his elbow. The tall, stoop-shouldered waiter had to swing the tray in a wide arc to keep the drinks from spilling.

"Woa, dog. Don't be doin' that," Hardy complained. "The sooner I get these checks paid, the sooner we can get outta here."

"You've been saying that for the past hour," Jason said, nodding toward his snowboard. "We should've been over at the Air Garden by now."

"I know, but I promised my boss I'd stick around 'til these last two tables cashed out. How was I supposed to know they'd wanna sit around all day, getting wasted on creamy coffee drinks? I even switched them over to decaf, but it's not working."

"I can't believe this. Casey Bailey finally breaks down and gives me some time off, it's snowing like crazy, and you decide to pick *today* to become Mountain Village's most responsible waiter."

"Shh!" Hardy cautioned with a sly smile behind his drooping dreadlocks. "Let's not be resorting to words like *responsible*. I've got a reputation to protect here."

Jason grabbed his snowboard and began tapping it loudly on the edge of the bar. Nearby patrons turned toward the source of the noise.

"What are you doing?"

"I'm about to announce," Jason began in a raised voice. "That Hardy Bennett needs everyone's support and encouragement to reach his lifelong goal of becoming the AlpenHaus employee of the month for February."

"Okay, okay," Hardy protested, his face blushing. "I'll meet you out front in three minutes."

Jason noticed a slight commotion to his right. He turned to see Paul Brader, clutching his skis and ski poles, pushing his way through the crowded bar. Leaving disgruntled patrons in his wake, Brader walked right up to Hardy Bennett and dropped his ski equipment on the floor. He reached into the pocket of his ski jacket, found his billfold and shoved a folded bill into Hardy's free hand.

"I've got an emergency. I need to borrow your truck for an hour."

Hardy looked down at the bill and smiled. "For a hundred bucks, you can keep it for a week."

Paul Brader grabbed the tray of drinks. "I'll hold this. Give me the keys."

Hardy fished his keys from the front pocket of his jeans and handed them over. "It's around the side, next to the dumpster."

Impatient and harried, Brader handed the tray to Jason Zuckerman instead of Hardy, picked up his skis and poles and beat a hasty retreat out of the AlpenHaus.

— Chapter 27 —

Even with its four-wheel drive engaged, the Chevy pickup had difficulty climbing the slick, unplowed road. As he gunned Hardy Bennett's truck up the steeply pitched Last Dollar Road, Paul Brader stole frequent glances in the truck's side-view mirror. He had passed the Toyota 4Runner a mere two blocks from the AlpenHaus Restaurant, but was fairly certain that its female driver had not recognized him as he sped through the snowstorm out of Telluride Mountain Village. He had followed Highway 145 west—away from Telluride—and turned right on Last Dollar Road: a backcountry jeep trail that rose through a thick forest of aspens and spruces. He presumed that the single set of fresh tire tracks on the otherwise deserted road has been made by Sam Moultrie's pickup.

After four nerve-racking miles of uphill driving, Brader saw that the tire tracks veered off the road onto a tree-lined drive barely wide enough to accommodate a single vehicle. He bounced along the deeply rutted road, the undercarriage of the pickup scraping against the snow. Although it was three-o'clock in the afternoon, the thick storm clouds had cloaked the forest in a dusk-like shadow.

Sam Moultrie's red pickup was parked next to an abandoned mining cabin. The weathered planks of the one-story building seemed to strain under the weight of its snow-covered roof. As Brader pulled up behind the pickup, Moultrie stepped out from the woods to the right of the cabin, his eyes still trained on the narrow drive.

"Whose truck is that?"

"A friend of mine's," Brader replied as he climbed down from the truck and walked to the open door of the mining cabin. "I didn't want to take any chances that I'd be followed."

"I'm surprised you were bright enough to think of that. I was betting you'd show up with a whole swarm of cops on your ass like last night."

"Very funny, Sam," Brader said as he ducked inside the doorway of the cabin. "Let's be quick about this. Today's my day for cleaning up loose ends. After this, I've gotta get home and figure out what to do about Dr. Philips."

"At least you've got a home to go to. Where the hell am I supposed to go?"

"Not my problem, Sam. I really don't care where you go."

"*What?*" Moultrie replied, eyeing the man curiously. "Don't start playing wise-ass with me, mister money bags. I can still call this whole thing off and cut a deal with Johnny Law."

"Yeah, yeah, yeah," Brader said with a sigh, taking several steps backward into the dark, empty cabin. "You've told me that three times now. But I've gotta tell you; it hasn't exactly left me in a very trusting mood."

"I don't give a rat's ass what kind of mood you're in," the pilot shouted as Brader took several more steps backward. "By the way, where's my money? Fifty grand doesn't exactly fit in somebody's pocket."

"It's in the pickup. I hope you don't mind, but I put it in a backpack instead of one of my briefcases. I figured if anyone saw a loser like you carrying an expensive briefcase, they'd immediately get suspicious."

"I don't know when you grew a set of balls, but I ought to beat your ass, just for good measure."

"That's another thing I've been meaning to talk to you about," Brader added in a mocking tone. "What is your fixation with asses? You can't even say a sentence without using the word. Is that something you picked up in the Army, on those lonely nights in the barracks?"

"That's it!" Moultrie declared, whipping off his down parka, "I'm gonna stomp you silly."

Out of the darkness, Sam Moultrie saw Paul Brader's finger pointing over his shoulder toward the open door of the cabin. The multimillionaire shouted in a shrill voice, "Who the hell's that?"

Moultrie spun around, but saw nothing. As he turned back to face Brader, a loud explosion shattered the silence. Sam Moultrie was still wondering about the source of the noise when he felt himself being propelled backward through the open doorway. It was not until he was sprawled in the snow on his back that he felt the pain spreading through his chest. He looked up at Paul Brader quizzically.

Brader looked down at the Beretta like an amputee inspecting a new prosthesis. Both the earsplitting sound of the pistol's report and the force of its recoil had surprised him. Then, seeing a dark red stain oozing from the front of Sam Moultrie's white sweatshirt, he felt a surge of adrenaline like none he had ever experienced. The man who had once been so threatening was now lying at his feet, trying to comprehend what had just transpired. Suddenly, the gun felt like a vital part of him. A wicked smile spread across his face.

"What's the matter, big boy? Got nothing to say for yourself?"

Moultrie's eyes were wild as he stared up at his assailant, both hands trying to stem the flow of blood from the wound in his chest. He stammered in a weak voice, "You asshole."

"Very fitting," Brader replied, lifting the pistol in an elaborate gesture. He stepped out into the snow and sighted down the barrel at Sam Moultrie's head. "Let's let those be your last words."

— Chapter 28 —

Lyle and Casey had been following the narrow 24-gauge rail tracks into the mine complex for half a mile. The tracks were centered between the ten-foot-wide tunnel walls, giving them four feet of clearance on either side. Casey walked down the left side of the tracks, keeping pace with Lyle on the opposite side of the rails. The slap of their boots against the wet rock floor echoed off the walls of the narrow passageway, and the beam from Casey's flashlight illuminated thousands of tiny particles that seemed to hang in the thick air around them. Moisture clung to the walls and ceiling of the tunnel like a hot sweat, and the sound of dripping water echoed through the subterranean passage. Casey focused her beam on a shallow trough that ran along the base of the rock wall to her left.

"That's a piss ditch," Lyle explained. "It channels water out of the mine."

"Piss ditch?" Casey repeated. "I take it mining is a predominantly male profession."

"Not as much as it used to be. Watch out for those rails."

Casey swung her beam to the ground. A set of rails veered away from a switch on the main tracks and arced to the left, entering a tunnel that had been bored into the rock wall. The tracks bent out of sight as they followed the curve of the feeder tunnel.

"Which way do we go?" she asked.

"We follow the main rail line. There are going to be dozens of off-shoots like that one as we get further into the mine."

Casey stopped and shined her light into the tunnel to her left. "Where does that tunnel go?"

"Technically, that's not a tunnel, it's a drift. A tunnel has two openings called portals with daylight on each side. A drift is an offshoot from a tunnel that follows a particular vein until it peters out. There are hundreds of drifts in here and none of them lead back to the surface. That's why we have to make sure we stay in the main tunnel."

"You weren't kidding when you said this was a maze."

"It would be a lot simpler if it were just a maze. This place is more like a huge hamster trail with both horizontal tubes and vertical tubes. We have to pick the right combination of horizontal and vertical paths to get out of here. This complex has a different horizontal layer every hundred feet or so," Lyle explained. "We're now on the 2930 level, which means we're over twenty-nine hundred feet below the surface of the mine's uppermost workings. To get to the Treasury Tunnel, we have to climb to the 1200 level, which is seventeen hundred feet above us. That means we're gonna have to climb through seventeen different horizontal passageways on our way out of here."

Casey nodded but remained in place.

"We have to pick up the pace," Lyle urged her. "There's no telling when we're gonna run out of oxygen."

Casey trained her flashlight into the drift. The dark subterranean passage curved sharply to the left, making it impossible to see more than twenty feet into the hole. As she walked, she could see farther into the drift. A dull reflection along the far left-hand wall caught her eye.

"Hang on a second," she called to Lyle.

Seeing Casey walking into the feeder tunnel, Lyle called to her. "Please don't go down there!"

"Quit your whining and get in here. I just found our ride," Casey replied from the dark passage.

Thirty feet inside the drift, Casey was standing next to an olive-colored, all-terrain vehicle that had been backed into the passage. Lyle's beam reflected off the headlights on the front of the ATV, below the base of its handlebar steering mechanism. Decals on the six-wheel vehicle identified it as a Polaris Big Boss 500 6X6.

"Pretty good hiding place," Casey teased. "The average schmo would've just walked right past it."

"Apparently so. Is this Brader's ATV?"

"Yep. It's a lot bigger than most others I've seen and it's got that weird looking bin in the back."

The low-slung green Polaris had a gray vinyl half-bucket seat, black motorcycle-style handgrips, six thick-tread knobby tires and a sturdy suspension. Behind the driver's seat, a shallow three-foot-square dump box was welded to the ATV's frame.

"Looks like this thing's used for both hauling and trail riding. It's a big sucker, all right."

Casey pointed below the handlebars. "The key's still in the ignition."

"Looks like Brader isn't worried that anyone's going to stumble across it in here."

Lyle walked past the ATV and into the drift. He swung his flashlight back and forth along the floor of the narrow passage, then bent over to inspect something on the right side of the passage. At first, Casey didn't understand the significance of the two slim opaque plastic cylinders that were lying on the ground. As Lyle shifted the angle of his beam, the light glinted off the sharp needles at the base of the hypodermic devices. Casey's breath caught in her throat.

"My guess is that Brader used these to inject some sort of anesthesia or sedative. The State Police lab should be able to find out what kind of drug he used."

Casey's rage was manifest in a shrill cry that echoed through the dark passage. "That son of a bitch! He's nearly thirty years younger than Dr. Philips! Why'd he need to shoot him up with drugs?"

"This isn't necessarily bad news. I'd much rather find syringes than spent bullet casings. This could mean that Brader wanted to keep Dr. Philips alive."

Lyle pointed to the ATV. "This thing might have fingerprints on it, but I think we're better off putting it to use than just leaving it here. You drive and I'll sit in the dump bin. That way, I can look over your shoulder and we can both see where we're going."

Lyle straddled the frame of the ATV, then lowered his rear end into the ten-inch deep dump box. Facing forward, he lifted his long legs out of the shallow bin so that they were on either side of the bucket seat. Casey slid onto the narrow vinyl seat and handed her flashlight back to Lyle, whose knees were even with the top of her head.

"This isn't going to be pretty," she warned.

Casey turned the key near her right knee to the 'on' position, but nothing happened. She then slid a square gray button forward and the vehicle's headlights suddenly flooded the tunnel walls in harsh white light. She found a green button labeled *Start* that sparked the engine to life. Even as it idled, the Polaris' rapid-fire four-stroke engine was deafening in the mine's narrow confines. Protruding above the right wheel well, she located a black plastic knob with three settings. She pushed on the knob and the Polaris began to slowly creep forward. Blue-tinted exhaust floated around them like a thick fog.

Below the grip on the right handlebar, Casey found a curved plastic thumb lever. She wrapped her fingers around the handgrip and squeezed her thumb against the lever. The Big Boss 500 lurched forward, sending Lyle sprawling to the rear of the dump box.

"Woa!" she shouted as she released her thumb from the throttle. Once Lyle had repositioned himself, Casey applied gentle pressure against the lever and the Polaris eased forward along the wet floor of the drift.

"I think I've got it," she shouted above the din as the ATV moved through a cloud of exhaust fumes. Lyle grasped the sides of the metal bin as the vehicle's rear four tires bounced over the rail tracks. Casey steered to the left, guiding the machine into the main tunnel. The ATV's six-wheel turning radius was smaller than she had expected, and the vehicle veered toward the tunnel wall to her left. She quickly corrected her error, then maneuvered the ATV so that its tires were positioned on either side of the narrow-gauge rail tracks.

The headlights bore into the darkness, illuminating a thirty-foot stretch of the man-made tunnel. Casey gradually accelerated, careful to keep the wheels astride the rail tracks. Lyle leaned forward in the dump box so he could see over her shoulder. When they reached a speed of fifteen miles an hour, the noise from the ATV's engine seemed to be trailing in their wake.

"Atta girl," Lyle called into the driver's left ear. "We're going at a good clip, but keep an eye out for rail switches. If we run over another set of tracks at this speed, I'm going to get bounced out of here."

Casey kept her eyes focused on the tracks in front of her. When she spoke, the air rushing past her face carried her voice back to Lyle.

"The ground seems pretty level. I thought you said we're going to be doing some climbing."

"We *are* climbing," Lyle explained. "This tunnel is angled at a half-percent grade. Every hundred feet, we climb six inches. We're going in the opposite direction that a loaded ore car would travel on its way to the mill."

"How far do we need to go?"

"It's a mile and a half from the mill portal to the first set of hoists, so we should be there in a few minutes."

As Casey maneuvered the oversized ATV through the tunnel, the stale, chill air felt soothing against her face. Mindful of Lyle's warning about the oxygen level in the mine, she used her mouth like a funnel, inhaling as much air as her lungs would allow.

Gradually, Casey grew accustomed to the ATV. No longer transfixed by the twin ribbons of steel train tracks, she scanned the walls and ceiling of the main passageway. She saw that a series of unlit bulbs hung at regular intervals from the tunnel's ceiling, protected by metal baskets. A faded white sign on the wall announced that they were in the Montana-Argentine section of the mine.

As they traveled into the bowels of the mine complex, drift tunnels appeared more frequently. Rail lines diverged from the main track and disappeared like snakes slithering into a subterranean nest. Whenever a decision had to be made as to which tunnel or track to follow, Lyle reached over Casey's shoulder to point the way. A mile into the core of the mountain, the thin air around them seemed to become warmer and thinner.

Searching the far reaches of the headlight's broad swath, Lyle saw a change in the tunnel's contours, and made a motion for Casey to slow down. She brought the ATV to a sputtering crawl as they entered an expansive chamber that had been blasted along the route of the tunnel. The cavern was thirty feet tall and forty feet wide. Two sets of rail lines branched off from the main tracks and swung toward the chamber's right wall.

Chiseled out of the right side of the cavern wall was a vast shaft that contained four separate vertical compartments, each of which was ten feet wide and separated by thick timber walls. The shafts rose through the ceiling of the chamber, disappearing into the darkness above. The two stalls closest to the ATV appeared to be empty. The two far compartments were occupied by blue metal cages that rested on the tunnel floor. Steering the Polaris next to the cages, Casey looked up and saw a series of drums and cables.

Lyle swung his legs over the edge of the dump box and slid off the ATV. He led Casey into one of the vacant chambers and shined his flashlight up into the hole in the ceiling. Thirty feet above, he saw that a large metal grate had been fitted into place where the shaft rose through the ceiling of the tunnel.

"This is the main ore pass. The ore from the mine's inner workings are dumped down this shaft, then loaded into ore cars. That grate is called a grizzly and it keeps oversized rocks from flying down here and killing somebody."

Lyle moved to the second of the four compartments. At first glance the chamber appeared to be empty. He stepped into it and focused his beam against the far wall. A three-foot wide ladder with thin iron rungs and iron handrails had been mounted against the wet rock wall. The ladder climbed through the top of the shaft and disappeared into the black void above.

"How far up does that go?" Casey asked.

"Nine hundred feet. Unless the skip is working, that's the only way to get to the level that we're looking for."

Casey stared up into the black hole. "If a skip is an elevator, I vote for that."

The two remaining shafts each contained hoists capable of holding twenty people. The walls of the blue cage-like elevators were made of thick steel meshwork. The cages were designed with an open front, so Lyle walked into one and inspected its interior. He shook his head.

"Unfortunately, this isn't like a regular elevator. The controls are in a separate room."

He shined his flashlight across the wide cavern. On the far wall, he saw a ten-by-twelve-foot wood-paneled room. The side facing the hoists had a six-foot wide Plexiglas window. Lyle and Casey stepped over the rails and made their way across the cavern. A six-inch diameter hole had been cut into the center of the scratched Plexiglas window. Lyle shined his beam against the window and peeked through the hole.

"This is the hoist room. The power must still be on, otherwise Brader couldn't have driven any further into the mine."

Casey looked to her right and saw that the tunnel they had been following since they entered the mine continued out of the cavern and deeper into the mountain. "Couldn't he have just kept driving that way?"

"Unless I'm mistaken, this tunnel keeps going for three more miles on this level, but it doesn't connect with any passageway that leads up to the Treasury Tunnel."

"And you remember all of this from looking at a schematic drawing?" Casey replied.

Lyle nodded sheepishly. "Some guys are fans of classic cars; I'm a fan of classic mines. This is one of the most famous mine complexes on the western slope."

Lyle opened the door to the hoist room, walked inside and flipped a light switch. Florescent lights illuminated the cramped room. Two metal stools were positioned behind a dull yellow control panel that sloped upward from Lyle's waist to the Plexiglas window. The panel featured an array of levers, buttons, switches and gauges. He scanned the control board carefully while glancing through the window at the hoists at the far end of the cavern.

Casey saw his concern. "Do you know how to work one of these things?"

"It's been a while."

Lyle pushed a red lever forward and the control panel blinked to life with a faint hum. Four red lights on the upper part of the panel flickered, then remained lit. Lyle selected a large black lever on the left side of the panel and eased it forward. On the far side of the tunnel, the hoist in the left shaft rose from the floor. A bell attached to the hoist room wall began to chime. Lyle pulled the lever in the opposite direction and the hoist came back down the shaft, settling once again on the solid rock floor.

"We've got a problem," he announced. "I was hoping there'd be some lag time before the skip started climbing."

Casey stared out at the hoist and nodded. "So there's no way that we can push that lever and run over there in time. It looks like one of us is going to have to operate the lift down here while the other one rides up the elevator with the ATV. So, which one of us has a nine-hundred-foot ladder climb in our future? Wanna flip a coin?"

"We must be missing something. I just can't believe that Brader or Sam Moultrie scaled that ladder twice in one night. That's almost two thousand feet of hand-over-hand climbing. The problem is that Brader had weeks to plan this thing, but we're trying to figure it out on the spot."

Lyle continued to fiddle with the control panel as Casey searched the floor and walls of the hoist room. She looked behind the open door to her left. Hanging on a coat hook on the back of the wooden door was a coil of white clothesline encrusted with dark mud.

"How about this?"

Realizing what Casey had found, Lyle burst into a wide grin. "That's how he did it! Pull the ATV into the skip on the left and I'll be over there in a second."

Casey backed the Polaris into the hoist while Lyle tied one end of the clothesline to the knob-handled lever that operated the skip. He threaded the cord through the round hole in the Plexiglas window and walked out of the hoist room. Careful not to create tension against the lever, he unwound the clothesline and fed it along the floor of the tunnel. When he entered the open front of the hoist, there was fifteen feet of line to spare.

"We would've been out of luck if Brader hadn't left that rope there," Casey noted.

"I was just thinking the same thing. The ATV, the hypodermic needles and the clothesline all would've eventually been found by the mine employees, so it looks like Brader hasn't had time to clean up his mess yet."

Lyle slowly took up the slack in the clothesline, winding the muddy cord around his fist. "Hang on."

He yanked on the clothesline, which snapped taut across the width of the tunnel. As the hoist lurched upward, Casey clawed her fingers through the thick mesh walls of the hoist to keep her balance. Lyle waited until the last second to release his grasp on the line.

Fifty feet above the cavern floor, the hoist settled into a smooth climb. The only illumination in the lift came from the headlights of the ATV, which were facing the front of the hoist car. The beams shone against the dark rock wall of the shaft less than a foot in front of the open cage. Casey saw that there was little clearance between the hoist car and the other walls of the shaft. The sensation of ascending through the solid rock in a narrow chute produced a nauseous feeling in the pit of her stomach. She closed her eyes in an effort to quell the onset of claustrophobia.

"Are you okay? You look a little shaky," Lyle asked over the persistent noise of the cables spooling over metal drums.

"I'll get used to it," she replied, taking a deep gulp of air. "Hey, if the control room's down there, how are we going to stop this thing at the right level?"

"We caught a break this time. We're heading from the twenty-nine-hundred-foot level to the two-thousand-foot level, which is as high as this shaft goes, I think. It should stop automatically once we get to the top level."

As the car eased upward, they saw a large white sign mounted to the stone bulkhead in front of the open cage. The words '2400 Level' were stenciled in large red letters. Fifteen feet above the sign, they passed a large square hole in the shaft wall. The ATV's headlight beams afforded Casey a glimpse of the interior of the 2400 level, which seemed identical to the narrow tunnel they had followed into the mine from the Pandora Mill. Within seconds, the hoist climbed above the opening and the dark, wet shaft wall once again loomed within inches of the moving cage.

"The next stop is ours," Lyle announced. Looking over at Casey, he saw that she was swaying from side to side. "Are you feeling light-headed?"

"Just feeling a little closed in, that's all. I don't think it has anything to do with the oxygen level," she promised.

Lyle took her hand and helped her onto the driver's seat of the Polaris. "You're going to have to drive this thing out, so you might as well get ready."

Sixty seconds later, a sign on the shaft wall identified the next passage as the 2000 level. The hoist slowed its ascent as the bottom of the passageway came into view above their heads. As soon as the front of the car was flush against the edges of the opening in the wall, the car groaned to a halt.

As Casey piloted the six-wheel green Polaris out of the skip, she noted with relief that the chamber they were entering was even more spacious than the cavern at the 2900 level. She pointed the ATV to the right so the vehicle's headlights exposed the interior of the grotto.

"This is one of two main congregation areas in the Mineral King complex," Lyle explained. "Miners who lived on the Telluride side would've taken the same route that we just took, except they would've used a man-trip, which looks like a bus mounted on rail wheels. This area is where they would come to pick up their equipment before heading into the drifts."

Shining his flashlight deeper into the cave's recesses, Lyle estimated that the congregation area was thirty-five feet wide, twenty feet high and seventy feet long. A jumble of rail lines converged in the middle of the subterranean workplace, then spread out like palm fronds into a labyrinth of drift tunnels.

Five separate wooden structures had been built against the side walls of the cavern. Each of the rooms had been constructed with the same dark paneled wood that Lyle and Casey had seen throughout the mine. Each squat building had at least one long panel of Plexiglas that faced the center of the cavern. Lyle aimed his beam toward the two long, narrow rooms on the left side of the tunnel.

"Those are called dog houses. It's where the miners eat their lunch. Once they arrive for work, they don't see the light of day until their shift is over. So when it's time to eat, miners are strictly brown-baggers. You don't see a lot of pizza deliveries being made down here."

Casey shook her head. "Let me get this straight: no fresh air, no sunshine, you work thousands of feet below ground in a cold, smelly, wet tunnel, and to top it off, you have to eat in a place called a dog house. Where do I sign up?"

Lyle then focused his beam on the cavern's right side. He pointed out the three other rooms. "The building closest to us is the powder magazine room where they keep blasting powder. The one in the middle is probably the Chief Geologist's office. The big one at the end of the row is the machine shop."

"I have to admit, this is pretty amazing. It's as if they've blasted an entire little city into the belly of the mountain."

Lyle nodded his agreement. "And this is like seeing a ghost town. If this place were in operation, there'd be locomotives pulling strings of ten-ton ore cars, man-trips filled with miners and the sound of drilling and blasting coming from all directions. It's a helluva sight to see."

"The only sight I'd like to see right now is the other side of this complex. I still don't know exactly where we're going to wind up."

"I want you to see for yourself," Lyle said. "We've got one more hoist ride left."

Casey swallowed hard at the prospect of another ride through the cramped confines of a hoist shaft. She eased the Polaris forward, keeping pace with Lyle as he walked beside the ATV. Crossing over dozens of rail lines, they passed several rooms until they reached the far end of the hollowed-out chamber. As the tunnel began to narrow, they spotted two side-by-side hoist cages to their right. Knowing where to look, Casey located the hoist room against the opposite wall of the cavern. She backed the ATV into the nearest skip as Lyle walked over to the room. Dismounting, she jogged across the tunnel, using the headlights of the Big Boss 500 to guide her.

Casey caught up to Lyle as he opened the hoist room door. "I guess there was no way to hang onto that rope. Hopefully, there's another one in here."

"This one's going to be more complicated," Lyle said as he perused the control panel. "We need to get off at the 1200-foot level, but these hoists won't stop automatically until they reach the top of the shaft, which is at the 1000-foot level."

Casey looked behind the hoist room door. There was no coat hook.

"So even if we had some clothesline, we couldn't pull the same trick because we'll wind up two hundred feet higher than we need to be," Casey mused before suggesting an alternative. "But if we found some rope, we could ride up to the 1000 level and take the ladder down two hundred feet."

"Which one of us is going to carry the ATV down the ladder on our back? We still have over four miles to travel once we get to the 1200 level tunnel."

"Good point."

"Looks like we don't have a choice. You'll have to ride up in the skip while I stay down here at the controls. Once I stop the hoist at the 1200 level, you drive the ATV out and I'll climb up the ladder to meet you."

Casey considered his suggestion. "There's got to be an easier way. Like you said, there's no way Brader would've had the time to climb a thousand-foot ladder."

Lyle closed his eyes, trying to recall details of the schematic drawing he had seen. "The 1200 level is the other main hub of the mine, so there could be another hoist room up there. If so, you'll need to bring me up in the second skip. Wanna give it a shot?"

"As long as you show me how to work the controls."

Once he had given Casey a quick overview of the control panel's operation, she practiced raising and lowering the hoists on the far wall of the chamber.

"I'm ready," Casey declared. "If I get up there and there's a hoist room, I'll give you three quick blasts on the air horn. If not, I'll sound the horn for thirty seconds or so."

"Sounds good. Let's go."

Once Casey was inside the hoist car, Lyle nudged a lever forward on the right side of the control panel and watched the skip rise out of sight. A gauge on the panel indicated that the elevator was climbing toward the 1900 level. He continued to monitor the gauge as it moved between the 1300 level and the 1200 level. On cue, he heard two muffled reports from the air horn: their prearranged signal that Casey had seen the sign for the 1200 level. Lyle eased the lever back and a red light flashed on the control panel, indicating that the hoist had settled into position at the shaft opening. Seconds later, the air horn sounded twice again, signaling that Casey was driving the ATV out of the skip.

Lyle walked out of the hoist room, not relishing the thought of an eight-hundred-foot climb in the dark. He checked the pockets of the yellow slicker for the work gloves. As he drew in a deep breath, he felt a sharp pain on the right side of his chest. He had not sought treatment for the injury he sustained in the Uncompahgre Gorge on Tuesday night and he was now paying the price. Although he had said nothing to Casey, during the past fifteen minutes he found himself having to draw deeper breaths to satiate his lungs. He had also been yawning frequently, which he knew was his body's reflexive attempt to ingest more oxygen. To make matters worse, the sharp sting accompanying each deep breath forced him to exhale before his lungs were full.

Convinced he was exhibiting the early signs of oxygen deprivation, Lyle walked quickly toward the remaining hoist car. When he squatted down next to the hoist to wait for Casey's signal, his legs began to tremble. He was surprised at how quickly his body was succumbing to the declining level of oxygen in his blood. Deciding that he could wait no longer for Casey to find a hoist room that might not exist, he rose unsteadily and walked into the chamber that contained the ladder.

Leaning his six-foot, six-inch frame against the iron ladder, Lyle shoved the flashlight into the pocket of his slicker and pulled on his work gloves. Since it would be impossible to climb the ladder and hold the flashlight at the same time, he knew that he would be climbing blind through the pitch-black shaft. He stepped onto the bottom rung, grabbed the ladder system's sweaty iron handrails and began climbing.

Twenty feet above the tunnel floor, his ears began to ring. He forced himself to yawn, hoping it would clear the high-pitched tone from his head. In the middle of his yawn, he heard a series of noises that were flatter and duller than the incessant ringing he was trying to vanquish. It took him several seconds to realize that the faint sounds he heard were three horn blasts drifting down the hoist shaft from the 1200 level.

"Way to go, Casey!" he bellowed into the blackness that surrounded him.

Lyle shimmied down the handrail until he was ten feet from the ground, then jumped down from the ladder. As he bounded toward the hoist car, his boots felt heavy and slack, and his body began to sway wildly. Stumbling into the skip, he steadied himself against the cage wall, then shouted toward the ceiling of the car.

"Go!"

At the controls in the hoist room, Casey watched the gauge that marked the upward progress of the skip. As the blue car rose into the dark void across the tunnel, she locked the hoist control lever into place. Seeing that the car had come to rest neatly framed against the square opening in the wall, she raised her arms in triumph.

"Yes!"

Casey sprinted out of the small control room, hopped onto the idling ATV and whipped it around so that it was pointed toward the hoist. As the Polaris bounced over five sets of rail lines, its headlights flooded the interior of the cage with light. What Casey saw inside the hoist shocked her. Lyle was crouched in the far-left corner of the car, his head hanging limply from his shoulders and his hands pressed flat against the steel floor.

She brought the ATV to a skidding halt on the smooth, wet tunnel floor and ran into the skip. She grabbed Lyle's elbow and heaved upward. The large man's response was labored, forcing Casey to tug even harder. As soon as Lyle had struggled upright, he listed forward onto Casey's five-foot, three-inch frame. Casey pushed him against the mesh wall and saw that his eyes were unfocused and his expression was muddled.

Lyle blinked his eyes several times, then licked his lips with a lazy tongue. When he spoke, he sounded as if his throat was filled with cotton.

"We're almost there," he assured her in a listless tone. "No matter what happens, just keep driving. I need to get out into the air."

"You said it was going to be a little over a six-and-a-half-mile trip. I don't think we've even gone two miles yet. Wouldn't it be easier to go back out the way we came in?"

Lyle shook his head feebly. "We're on the Ouray side now. No more hoists. It's a straight shot."

Casey pulled him toward the ATV. He sat down heavily on the driver's seat, then with great effort, he reached back and grabbed the sides of the dump box. His arms quivered as he hoisted himself over the back of the seat and into the shallow bin.

He nodded at Casey, who quickly straddled the driver's seat, pushed the gear lever forward and wheeled the ATV away from the hoist. The cavern on the 1200 level was comparable in size to the chamber eight hundred feet below. She drove toward the center of the high-ceilinged congregation area and steered to the right, assuming she should head in the same direction that they had been traveling since they entered the mine complex. At the center of the chamber, the cavern walls began to taper down and in. Two separate passageways led away from the congregation hub. Casey stopped and tried to decide which of the tunnels she should choose.

She looked back at Lyle, who was looking from one passageway to the other. He slowly lifted his hand and pointed to the tunnel on the right. Casey accelerated quickly, which sent Lyle flopping back against the rear of the dump box. She stopped the ATV, then reached back and grabbed hold of his arms. Once she managed to tilt Lyle's torso toward her, she draped his arms over her shoulders so he was leaning against her back.

His voice was a mere whisper. "Sorry about this."

"*I need you*, Lyle," she called over her shoulder. "You keep us pointed in the right direction and I promise I'll get you out of here as fast as I can."

Casey gunned the Polaris into the tunnel, steering the tires bestride the rail lines. She crushed her thumb against the accelerator and watched the speedometer climb to 20 m.p.h. The section they were now traversing was more frequently intersected by drift passages, crosscuts and vertical shafts. In most cases, Casey didn't need Lyle's help to decide which path to follow. Signs were posted intermittently on the tunnel walls identifying the names of drift passages and raises. Casey drove past signs labeled Argentine, Black Bear and Barstow. At the end of a sweeping curve to the right, she saw a long stretch of straight tunnel ahead of her. She took the opportunity to glance back at Lyle, who was struggling to keep his head up and his mouth open, using the forward momentum of the ATV to channel air down his throat as they sped through the tunnel. His eyes were vacant.

After ten minutes of racing headlong through the core of the subterranean complex, they passed a large vertical passageway on their left. A sign next to the yawning hole identified the shaft as Treasury Raise. Casey knew that their rendezvous point with Bill Withers was at a location called Treasury Tunnel. She called back to Lyle.

"Do we have to make any turns to get to this Treasury Tunnel place?"

Lyle shook his head. He mumbled a reply, but Casey couldn't hear it above the roar of the Big Boss' engine.

"We must be getting close," she shouted, trying to keep Lyle's attention. "I've had this thing cranking at twenty-five miles an hour for the last ten minutes."

She felt Lyle's arms slowly sliding back on her shoulders. Fearing he was slipping into unconsciousness, Casey thumbed the throttle all the way open and the Polaris responded with additional torque to all six wheels. Speeding through the narrow tunnel, Casey was worried that she was out-racing her headlights; that she wouldn't have time to react to any sudden change in direction.

After three more minutes of straight-ahead driving, Casey saw a weak reflection from a metal sign posted on the tunnel's left wall. The words *Treasury Tunnel 2300 Feet* were stenciled in white letters on an arrow-shaped sign that pointed in the direction she was driving.

"We're less than a half-mile away. Stay with me, Lyle!"

Casey squeezed the throttle even harder and the Big Boss' engine thundered off the solid rock walls. She had assumed the Treasury Tunnel was an open-air portal that led to the surface but she couldn't see any hint of daylight as she strained to see beyond the range of the ATV's headlights. Then, recalling Lyle's comment about the passageway being pitched at a half-percent grade toward the open end of the mine, she realized that any outside light would first be visible along the tunnel's floor.

Ten seconds later, she was surprised to see two separate pinpoints of light that seemed to be moving from side to side, but independently of one another. Then, between the two beams, she saw a dim reflection from what looked like a row of blue marbles suspended in the air. Suddenly, a thin sliver of daylight began seeping over the black horizon of the tunnel floor. She squeezed the throttle to its maximum tension.

Three hundred feet from the end of the tunnel, the encroaching daylight silhouetted two shapes behind the beams now pointed directly at the ATV. Behind them, Casey could see the large, block-like shape of a vehicle parked in the narrow confines of the tunnel. She realized that the blue reflection was coming from the truck's rack of roof-mounted police lights.

At a distance of one hundred feet, there was a clash of beams. Two high-intensity lights trained on the ATV blinded Casey. She shielded her eyes with her left hand.

A voice boomed from fifty feet away. "Slow down!"

"It's us!" she screamed. "Get that truck out of here!"

Casey squeezed the handbrake and skidded the Polaris to a stop ten feet in front of two men who were pressed against opposite walls of the tunnel. Deputy Perry Yancey was on the right, one hand on his holster. Bill Withers approached from the left, his beam aimed over Casey's right shoulder. They saw Lyle's head slumped against the woman's back, his eyes closed and body inert.

"I've got to get him some air and that truck's blocking the way!" Casey cried.

"This is a crime scene. There's a dead man in that Jeep."

"You're going to have another dead man on your hands if you don't move that damn truck, *now*!"

— Chapter 29 —

Two white Jeep Cherokees with Ouray County Sheriff's Department decals were parked next to a metal Quonset hut in the Mineral King Mining Company's Red Mountain surface plant. It had been built against the side of a cliff wall and was protected by a metal snowshed. The Treasury Tunnel's gaping blackness could be seen through the building's open garage door.

Deputy Mark Turlington's body—stiff from rigor mortis—was sprawled across the back seat of one of the vehicles with two gunshot wounds in the chest. The Jeep had been backed out of the Treasury Tunnel by Bill Withers to clear the way for Lyle Morrison. To ensure that the crime scene was not compromised further, the sheriff had made it plain that the vehicle was not to be approached.

Twenty-five feet away, Lyle Morrison sat in the passenger's seat of Bill Withers's patrol vehicle. With the Jeep's heater turned up, a stream of hot air blew his thick silver hair behind his neck. Casey Bailey stood next to the open passenger door, watching the big man inhale bottled oxygen through a plastic facemask. Perry Yancey sat in the driver's seat, a stethoscope and blood pressure cuff in his lap. After checking Lyle's pulse rate, the mustachioed, slack-jawed deputy released his grasp on the snowplow driver's wrist.

"He's pretty much back to normal," the deputy announced to Casey.

Seeing the skeptical look on her face, he added, "I'm also an EMT. His breathing is shallow on account of his broken ribs, and his blood pressure isn't quite where it should be but his pulse is fine, his lungs are clear and his reflexes are sharp. Just to be sure, he should get checked out back in town, too."

"Oh, I'll make sure of that," she vowed, looking directly at Lyle. "Maybe now he'll realize he's not Mister Indestructible."

Ignoring her jibe, Lyle placed the oxygen canister on the floorboard and climbed out of the Jeep. Looking over the roofs of the surface plant buildings up to Highway 550, he saw the flashing blue and amber strobes of a CDOT Colorado Special parked in the turnout area overlooking the plant.

"That must be Hamp," he reasoned. "He's probably wondering when I'm gonna get my lazy butt back to work."

The snowstorm had not slackened since Lyle and Casey had first entered Pandora Mill's gates ninety minutes ago. In the clear, flat yard of the Red Mountain surface plant, the wind's steady moan was interrupted by the occasional crackling of police radios and the sound of frozen pellets pinging against the hood of the two Jeeps. Through the blowing snow, Lyle could make out Bill Withers striding purposefully down the snow-covered road that swept down from the highway. As Withers approached, his jaw was firmly set and his wide-brimmed uniform hat was pulled down low on his head. The sheriff hollered to the threesome congregated around his Jeep.

"Hamp's gonna plow the turnout up there 'cause this place is going to be swarming with people soon. The State Police are sending their forensics team down and the coroner's on his way. Tim Vanderwall's getting the Hasty Rescue Team mobilized and set up with oxygen. My dispatcher's calling the Mineral King manager at home to see if we can get the whole complex powered up and find out if their ventilation system is still intact. Hopefully, we can get some of those Mineral King boys down here to guide us through that hodgepodge of tunnels."

Yancey spoke up as Withers mopped his brow with his jacket sleeve. "Lyle doesn't seem to think that we're going to find Dr. Philips inside the mine."

Without saying a word, the sheriff unzipped his green uniform jacket and removed a clear plastic bag from an inside pocket. He held up the evidence bag so Lyle and Casey could see that it contained a pair of black-framed eyeglasses.

Casey took a step backward. "Those are Dr. Philips's! Where'd you find them?"

"They were sticking out of the snow near the Quonset hut door. This storm would've buried them completely if they weren't underneath the roof line," Withers replied, his irritation growing. "That's why we decided to head into the tunnel. Then a hundred feet into the mine, we found a Jeep, *one of my Jeeps*, with the dead body of a deputy, *one of my deputies*, stuffed inside it. Now I'm gonna have to call his mother in Utah and tell her that her only son's been killed—on my watch."

The sheriff stormed off toward the Quonset hut's open garage door. "Let's get inside. If we're going to have a debate, I don't want to do it in the middle of a snowstorm."

As she, Lyle and Perry Yancey trailed after the lawman, Casey suspected that Withers's real issue was not with the blowing snow, but with the dead man in the Jeep. For the past twenty minutes, the sheriff had been stalking off in different directions, never staying near the Jeep containing Mark Turlington's corpse for more than a few seconds. She also noticed that neither Lyle Morrison nor Perry Yancey had glanced over at the vehicle or mentioned the deceased deputy by name. Casey admitted to herself that she was also relieved to be moving away from the Jeep. Entering through the Quonset hut door, Casey saw that the curved-roofed building contained the idle surface plant's dry room, carpenter shop and warehousing operations.

Withers was waiting for them just inside the garage door. He picked up where he had left off, directing his comments to Lyle. "I may not have all the forensic equipment the State Police have, but I know how to follow a trail of evidence. We had two missing people on our hands, right? We found one of them in the mine and we found Dr. Philips's glasses fifty feet from the portal. It doesn't take a genius to figure out that all trails lead into this mine complex. With over ninety miles of tunnels, it's the perfect place to stash someone, dead or alive. I know you may not be thinking straight right now, Lyle, but facts are facts. Unless you know something about this case that has escaped me, I'm going to follow the trail of evidence right into that tunnel!"

Before Lyle could respond, Casey spoke up. "If all we're looking for is a body, then you're absolutely right. But Lyle and I just spent an hour in that place and unless Dr. Philips was left with a huge supply of oxygen, there's no way he can survive in there."

"I don't mean to burst your bubble, Casey, but I'm not convinced that Brader gives a damn about whether Jim survives or not," Withers said sharply.

"Then how do you explain those hypodermic needles we found?"

"Until I get in there and get those syringes lab-tested, I don't know what to make of them. For all we know, they could be the murder weapons. Maybe a weasel like Brader prefers needles to a gun when it comes to killing."

Lyle leaned against the doorframe and addressed Yancey. "Did you ever get a chance to talk to Sara Moultrie?"

"Bill and I questioned her this morning down in Silverton," he reported. "She isn't the brightest bulb in the chandelier, and it was easy to catch her in a few quick lies. When we warned her that she could be charged as an accessory to murder, she decided her brother wasn't worth going to jail for. The guy's been living under her roof rent-free for four years now and I gather she's pretty fed up with him."

"What'd she say about Dr. Philips's visit on Tuesday?" Lyle asked.

"She said that it was Sam's idea to arrange the appointment with Jim. He even told her what time to set it for. Sam claimed it was a big ruse to get Dr. Philips away from Ouray so a bunch of Jim's friends could arrange a surprise party for him when he returned. Sara was even proud of the job she did in faking stomach pains. Apparently it fooled Jim enough that he prescribed some medicine for her.

"Sara got suspicious when she got a call from our dispatcher on Wednesday, but she stuck to her story in order to protect her brother. On top of that, she also told us that Sam had been bragging for the last two weeks that he was about to come into some serious money."

"Does she know where Sam was on Tuesday?" Casey inquired.

"That's where it gets interesting. We're still trying to make all the pieces fit," the deputy said, absently scratching his chin.

"Around ten-thirty in the morning, Sam asked her to follow him to the airport in Montrose. He said his truck was having engine trouble and he was afraid he'd get stuck along the way. About halfway to Ouray, he pulled over to the side of the highway and told Sara that his pickup was losing power. Sam pulled the truck behind a mining cabin near the side of the road—so it wouldn't get stolen—and had Sara drive him the rest of the way. She didn't hear from him the rest of the day, but sometime after midnight, he called her and said that he was going to be stuck overnight in Montrose on account of the weather. Wednesday morning, she drove up to the airport and gave him a lift back to his truck."

A female voice sounded from the two-way radio clipped to Bill Withers's belt, echoing off the metal walls of the Quonset hut. The Ouray County Sheriff's Department dispatcher relayed a message from Jill Samsky, who was still over in Telluride.

"The suspect just left his residence in a black Chevy Suburban. He's heading west on Colorado Avenue. Deputy Samsky is requesting permission to detain him."

"Negative," Withers called into the radio. "Tell her to maintain surveillance and keep me posted every five minutes. If he turns back around and heads toward the Pandora Mill, I want to know about it."

"We lost our tail on Brader earlier today," Withers explained, clipping the radio back onto his belt. "He hopped a gondola over to Mountain Village and Jill arrived too late to see him getting off on the other side. She lost sight of him for forty-five minutes but finally spotted him walking out of a place called the AlpenHaus. Brader got back on the gondola, rode back over to Telluride, picked up his truck and drove home."

"Aren't you worried he'll give Jill the slip again?" Casey asked.

"There's nothing to be gained by bringing him in yet," Withers countered. "Our case is strong enough to bring to the District Attorney, but I'm still missing a body. We'll give Brader a little rope and see where he takes us."

"What if he's making a run for it?" Casey asked.

"He won't get far in this weather; all the airports are closed and he doesn't have access to Sam Moultrie's helicopter any more. My guess is that once he's convinced he's not being followed he'll backtrack to Pandora Mill. As soon as he steps foot on the mill property, I'll have Jill arrest him."

"Let's get back to Moultrie for a second," Lyle said. "Did you find out where he took the helicopter on Tuesday?"

"I'm not sure any of this matters now, but we did. The charter outfit that Sam works for has two helicopters. They do some heli-skiing tours and they help out with game counts for the Wildlife Division, but they also ferry corporate muckety-mucks to their vacation homes from the Montrose, Telluride and Durango airports. Sam's boss said that Moultrie had booked a lot of business over in Telluride in the past month. Since most of his customers paid in cash, the charter company can't verify that the people Sam listed in his pilot logs were actually on board his copter. So it didn't surprise us when we checked out his list of cash-paying customers for the past three weeks and found that they're all fictitious.

"Helicopter pilots don't have to file a flight plan, so all we have to go on is what Sam's log says. On Tuesday, Sam took one of the copters over to Telluride for a cash-paying heli-skiing job. His log says he put down at Telluride Airport around two-thirty, picked up his customer, spent two hours in the back bowls, then landed back in Telluride at five-o'clock. Around six o'clock, when the snow started coming down pretty heavy, he checked in with the charter company in Montrose and said he was going to keep the helicopter over at the Telluride Airport for the night."

"That doesn't jibe with what he told his sister," Casey pointed out. "She said he spent Tuesday night in Montrose."

"Sam's boss says he definitely remembers seeing the helicopter back in Montrose when he came to work on Wednesday morning," Withers added. "As far as I'm concerned, Moultrie's pilot logs are useless."

"I figured as much. That's why, when I was over in Telluride this morning, I spoke to the head of flight operations out at the airport," Lyle informed the sheriff. "He says that Sam hung around the airport between two-thirty and three-thirty, then disappeared -- but not in his helicopter. The airport closes a half-hour after sunset and the flight ops guy swears that Moultrie never took the helicopter up again while the airport was open. He did notice, however, that it was gone the next morning. What does Moultrie's log book say about the past couple of days?"

"He had the helicopter booked on Wednesday night and Thursday night. For both flights, his log says he flew a cash-paying customer from Telluride Airport to Durango Airport. We know that Thursday's log is bullshit because we saw him putting down over near Ridgway. Who knows where he really was on Wednesday night?"

The dispatcher's voice came over Withers's radio. "Deputy Samsky reports that the suspect turned left on Highway 145 toward Ophir."

"Ophir?" Withers pushed his hat higher on his forehead. "Ten-four. Tell her to keep the updates coming."

Frustrated at not being involved in what was unfolding in Telluride, Withers kicked his boot against the concrete floor, then turned his attention back to Lyle. "Where are you heading with all this? It sounds as if you have your own ideas about what happened to Jim."

Lyle closed his eyes and spoke in an unhurried tone, "Here's how I see it. Sam Moultrie flies into the Telluride Airport at two-thirty on Tuesday. Around three-thirty, he hires someone to drive him from the airport to Bridal Veil Falls where Brader's been ice climbing. Brader makes it a point to talk to a few other climbers so he can establish an alibi until four o'clock. A little after four, Brader meets Moultrie in the Bridal Veil Falls parking lot and they drive down the road to Pandora Mill. They park the Suburban behind the mill building and head into the mine."

Lyle opened his eyes and addressed Withers. "When you get a chance to talk to the guys over at Pandora Mill, ask them if they know how Brader became so familiar with the layout of the mine. My guess is that he managed to talk someone over there into giving him an unsanctioned tour of the complex."

"That makes sense," Casey agreed. "There's no way he could've made his way through there sight unseen."

"The whole key to Brader's plan was timing. He and Moultrie must've gone through a few dry runs in the past two weeks to get their timing down." Lyle continued. "So anyway, a little after four-o'clock, they head into the mine where the ATV is gassed up and ready to go. With all the practice they've had with the hoists and the ATV, they probably made the trip in around twenty-five minutes.

"Once they come out on this side of the mine, Brader goes up to the highway to keep his five o'clock appointment with Dr. Philips. He and Sam overpower Jim, stuff him in his pickup, and drive it back down here so it can't be seen from the highway. Then they sedate Jim for the trip through the mine so he doesn't put up a fight and slow them down. The trip back to Pandora probably takes a little longer since there are now two people in the ATV's dump bin. Once they get back to the Telluride side, Moultrie stays near the Pandora portal where there's plenty of fresh air. His job is to keep Dr. Philips sedated. By five-thirty, Brader's ready to drive back into town."

Casey shook her head. "Where he goes jewelry shopping and has a leisurely dinner with his wife. Talk about cold-hearted."

"Do you think Brader's wife is in on this too?" Yancey asked.

"I doubt it; he's taken a big enough risk getting Sam Moultrie involved," Lyle said. "So, after dropping his wife off at home, Brader goes to that bar in Telluride, takes time to talk to the bartender, then high-tails it back up to Pandora. He and Moultrie leave Dr. Philips sedated—and probably tied up—then drive the ATV through the mine again. This time, their mission is to ditch Jim's truck."

"Why did they even have to make a second trip?" Yancey asked. "They could've saved themselves a lotta trouble by stashing Jim's truck a mile or two from here on their first trip."

"That would've been too sloppy for Brader. Remember, he's thinking long-term here," Lyle explained to the deputy. "First of all, he wanted to get Jim's truck away from the Treasury Tunnel so no one would start snooping around here and put two and two together."

"Which is probably what Turlington was doing when he met up with one of them down here," Yancey noted.

"Also, Brader was trying to set up a plausible long-term explanation for Jim's disappearance. You've got to give him credit; if he'd been able to send the truck off into the deepest part of the gorge, we probably wouldn't have found it until May or June. By that time, even if we didn't find Jim's body in the wreckage, we probably wouldn't have suspected foul play.

"In order to make his alibi work, he had to make two separate trips in less than ninety minutes apiece; one trip to kidnap Dr. Phillips and one trip to send his truck into the gorge. As it turned out, with eight inches of snow on the road, he needed every bit of that time on his second trip to get the truck to the accident site."

"Now Sara Moultrie's story is starting to make sense," Yancey added. "Once Brader and Moultrie come out of the Treasury Tunnel on the second trip, Sam retrieves his truck from where he left it earlier in the day, which is probably behind that run-down cabin a quarter-mile south of here. Brader drives Dr. Philips's truck up to the highway and the two of them drive up past Riverside slide. Once they get to Mother Cline, they run into problems sending Jim's pickup down into the gorge."

"They've got the truck right where they want it and the highway is deserted, but the icy road and the stick shift are giving them fits," Lyle agreed. "They probably used Sam's truck to try and push it off the road, but his tires keep spinning on the ice. Before long, they see the strobe lights from my snowplow coming through the canyon, so they have to abandon the truck. They drive back past here, hide Sam's pickup behind the old cabin, then probably try to fill in the tire tracks where they pulled off the highway. They hike back down here, cover their tire tracks near the front gate, then take a quick trip back through the mine to the Telluride side. Then, the tire tracks they left on the highway are erased when the CDOT crew from Silverton comes over the pass and plows up to the accident site."

Sheriff Withers shrugged his shoulders. "I have no quarrel with anything you've said so far, but you still haven't told me why you don't think Brader stashed Jim somewhere in the mine."

"I still haven't figured out what Brader's end-game is yet," Lyle admitted. "If he simply wanted Dr. Philips dead, he had the perfect opportunity to make it look like an accident on Tuesday night. But since we didn't find a body when we searched the gorge, we have to assume that he needed to keep Jim alive but out of sight. If that's the case, then Dr. Philips can't be in the mine. Like Casey said, there's no way to survive in there for long."

"So where is he?" Withers challenged him.

"That's where the helicopter comes in," Lyle reasoned. "Why did Brader need access to it on Tuesday, Wednesday and Thursday night? If he's hiding Jim in the mine, all he has to do is take a fifteen-minute drive from his house to Pandora to check on him."

Casey nodded vigorously. "So Sam Moultrie is shuttling Brader around because he's keeping Dr. Philips somewhere they need a helicopter to get to. And the fact that they're going to such trouble to check on him night after night could mean he's still alive!"

"I think we're getting too far ahead of ourselves," Withers cautioned. "On his second trip, Brader barely had enough time to stage the accident and get back to Telluride. There's no way he could to get back to Pandora, grab Jim, drive to the Telluride Airport, make a round-trip in the helicopter and get home before midnight. Besides, it was snowing like a son-of-a-bitch; they couldn't have taken that copter up on Tuesday night."

"I'm having trouble with that one too," Lyle informed the group. "But if I remember correctly, the storm tapered off around two in the morning. And let's not forget that the helicopter must've been flown out of Telluride Airport sometime before dawn on Wednesday. Apparently, Brader's wife is the only person who can verify that he got home around midnight. If we're assuming she's not involved in this, then the only explanation is that Brader managed to sneak out of the house some time after two o'clock in the morning and got back before she woke up."

Casey interrupted. "It wouldn't surprise me if Paul and Sissy sleep in separate beds; maybe even in separate rooms."

"So as soon as the storm starts to slack off," Lyle continued, "Brader drives back up to Pandora where Moultrie's waiting with Dr. Philips. They load Jim into the Suburban, drive to the airport—which would have been deserted—and take off in the helicopter."

"It couldn't have been a long trip," Yancey speculated. "Moultrie had to fly Dr. Philips to some remote place, drop Brader back at Telluride Airport, then fly to the Montrose Airport before the morning crew arrived."

The radio crackled again. "The suspect has passed Ophir and is continuing south toward Lizard Head Pass at twenty-five miles an hour. Deputy Samsky reports the road conditions are not ideal."

Withers wrapped his large hand around the two-way radio and raised it to his mouth as if to take a bite out of it. "Tell her to report back immediately if the suspect turns off the highway. We have reason to believe that he may be headed toward a campground or some other remote location."

"Ten-four," the dispatcher replied. "Tim Vanderwall has the hasty team mobilized, equipped with oxygen and awaiting your direction. Also, Rick Quinn is standing by to assist in the search."

Lyle whispered to Casey, "Rick's the geologist who used to work at Mineral King. He's the one who showed me the schematic."

Withers began pacing back and forth in front of Lyle, Casey and Perry Yancey. "This is the damnedest situation. I've got enough evidence to arrest Brader, but he might be leading us right to Jim. I can't give Jill any backup because she's a hundred miles away from my closest deputy. I've got a search team ready to go into the mine, but according to Lyle here, it's going to be a wild goose chase."

After ten more seconds of pacing, he keyed the radio's transmitter. "Tell Vanderwall to send up the hasty team and to bring Quinn with 'em. Get Deputy Mapes up here too; I'm going to set up a command post here for the time being. Call over to San Miguel County and see if they can roll a deputy in an unmarked car south on Highway 145 to give Jill some backup."

Withers signed off and turned to face Lyle and Casey. "Looks like you two are stuck over here without a ride home."

"I'll wait and head back into the mine with the search team," Lyle offered. "All I need is an oxygen tank and I'll be fine. I can vouch for Casey, too. She held up a lot better than I did in there."

The sheriff shook his head. "Hamp tells me you haven't slept in thirty-six hours. I'm gonna need fresh bodies up here to conduct this search."

"Please don't cut us out of this now," Casey pleaded.

"I have no intention of cutting you out of anything; I need your help back in Ouray," Withers said. "Mapes will be here soon, so you can take my Jeep. Lyle, you get a second search team ready back at the barn then try to catch some sleep until we need you; there's no telling how many people we're going to need to search this place properly.

"Casey, I'm going to have Nancy set you up in my office so you can have some privacy on the telephone. Since Brader's away from home, this is a good time to find out what his wife really knows. This isn't anything official, just a couple of gals talking. No matter what happens tonight, we're going to arrest Paul Brader before he can make it back home, so you don't have to worry about tipping our hand. Tell her you've found out her husband's in trouble and see what she has to say about it.

"Both of you are going to have access to our radio, so you're not gonna miss out on anything. I have a feeling things are going to start moving pretty quickly."

— Chapter 30 —

Darkness had engulfed Red Mountain Pass, and blowing snow had reduced visibility to thirty feet on US Highway 550. Having crested the summit of the pass, the auto parts deliveryman was driving back to Montrose after dropping off a pair of brake rotors to a repair shop in Silverton. Trying to follow the contours of the dark, twisting road in a snowstorm was difficult enough, but now he had to contend with a tailgater.

The headlight beams of the vehicle behind him were shining in his rearview mirror, forcing him to duck down in his seat to avoid the reflected glare. For the past three miles, the vehicle had been following less than ten feet from his rear bumper.

"I'll be damned if I'm gonna drive any faster," the deliveryman muttered, easing off the accelerator. "Just pass me!"

Two miles south of the Riverside snowshed, the driver of the tan Range Rover finally took the hint. In a burst of speed, he swung into the opposite lane and passed the slower car. The deliveryman let out a heavy sigh.

"Good riddance, hotshot."

• • •

Fresh snowflakes fell atop the drift, bonding to one another and settling onto the dense snowpack. Thirty-two-hundred feet above the highway, the snowpack clung to a rocky slope that slanted at a 38-degree angle. Sculpted by constantly shifting winds, the snow mass was cradled in the hollow of a northwest-facing catch basin that served as the starting zone for one of America's most notorious slide paths.

Beneath its surface, the deep drift was a multi-tiered archive of recent snowstorms and temperature cycles. Like the rings of a tree trunk, the snowpack's individual layers could chronicle its history. Each successive layer was the manifestation of a previous storm, characterized by different crystal formations, densities and adhesion strengths. Layers once exposed to sunlight and warmer temperatures were interspersed with those containing colder, lighter, powder-textured snow.

As the storm blew through the San Juan Mountains, the new blanket of snow added fractionally to the weight of the snowpack, increasing the burden that deeper layers were forced to support. The pitch of the slope beneath the snow mass added a constant measure of stress as the force of gravity exerted a subtle, yet unyielding downward tug.

Four feet beneath the drift's surface, the weakest layer finally succumbed to the mounting pressure, its crystals loosening their tenuous grip on the layers immediately above and below. Fracture lines spread horizontally across the crown of the snowpack, rapidly defining the width of the avalanche's initial slab. In an instant, fissure cracks spread down along the slope as the slab began to separate from its deeper layers. A loud *whump* sound signaled that the slab had shivered free of its icy bonds.

Forty-feet wide and seventy-five feet long, the slab slid downward, nudging its way over the bottom lip of the catch basin. As it raced further down the mountainside, the plate crashed against lower sections of snowpack, creating a chain reaction that sent a white plume of powder into the air along the slab's advancing edge. Vast sheets of frozen snow were pulverized as the slab crashed down the face of the slope. Gaining speed and power, the slab fractured into thousands of separate chunks as the initial plate began to disintegrate. Within seconds, the entire northwest slope of the mountain appeared to be crumbling. Following a well-worn path, the avalanche hurtled down an expanse of rocks, crevices and frozen creek beds that had borne the brunt of similar assaults over the centuries. Chunks of the crumbling snowpack catapulted in all directions, triggering secondary slides.

The avalanche gained momentum as the thundering slide tore down the mountain, loosening rocks and snapping trees that had withstood the impact of previous slides. When the volume of the debris overwhelmed the existing contours of the slide path, careening slab chunks were channeled to the sides of the main flow. Jumping the boundaries of the normal slide zone, the avalanche crashed into stands of mature pines, aspens and firs that bordered the white vertical ribbon of the avalanche path. Dozens of trees snapped under the weight of the fast-moving mountain of snow.

By the time the avalanche was visible from US Highway 550, the torrent of snow and debris was moving at close to 100 m.p.h., having fallen more than a half-mile in mere seconds. The hundred-foot-wide avalanche materialized like a nightmare over the cliffs above the sole north-south roadway between Ouray and Silverton. In advance of the slide, a powder burst—as thick as a sandstorm and as strong as a hurricane—bore down on the man-made thoroughfare.

Blasted out of the cliff walls that rose from the Uncompahgre Gorge, the Million Dollar Highway was a mere shelf outcropping along the slide path, destined to bear the full fury of the descending avalanche. When it hit US Highway 550, the slide's impact could be heard for miles as the concussion echoed off the canyon walls. In the center of the slide path, the down-sloping concrete snowshed channeled the rock-laden snow mass over the roadway, depositing it on top of an existing debris pile on the west side of the Million Dollar Highway. On the extreme northern fringe of the slide, the highway acted as a springboard, absorbing the impact of the avalanche, then hurtling the snow an additional two hundred feet into Uncompahgre Gorge on the far side of the road. It was the unprotected stretch of road directly north of the snowshed that served as the avalanche's killing field.

Fueled by a three-thousand-foot vertical drop, the slide slammed against the asphalt highway. Tons of snow that had previously covered acres of mountainous terrain were compressed into a pile as dense as the nearby cliff walls. Thirty-feet tall and fifty feet wide, the avalanche pile entombed the road and anything unlucky enough to be caught in its path.

— Chapter 31 —

The emergency phone under the Riverside snowshed had served its purpose: to provide motorists with immediate access to the Colorado State Police. The auto parts deliveryman had driven toward the snowshed at thirty miles an hour. Unlike the hundreds of previous times he had driven beneath the protective structure, tonight he saw his headlights reflecting back at him. Realizing that the far side of the shed was completely blocked by a wall of snow, he slammed on his brakes ten feet from impact.

Asked by the police dispatcher whether anyone had been trapped in the slide, the deliveryman volunteered to assess the situation. Walking out the open end of the snowshed, he saw two cars approaching from the south. After flagging the drivers to a stop, he jogged fifty yards up the steeply pitched highway so he could see above the snowshed to the massive debris pile to the north. He spotted the headlights of a vehicle that was parked on the far side of the slide pile. Staring through the wind-whipped snow and the fading twilight, he tried to make sense of the shapes protruding from the vast heap of snow blocking the roadway. When he returned to the phone, he told the dispatcher that all he could see sticking out of the pile were half-buried trees and branches. As the dispatcher was cautioning him to remain beneath the snowshed, a terrifying thought occurred to him. *Where was the tan Range Rover?*

The communication between state and local agencies was both rapid and efficient. The broadcast of a major avalanche along the Million Dollar Highway was not uncommon, but the personnel assigned to respond to such an emergency knew their task was never routine.

Cut off from his base of operations in Ouray, Bill Withers used his two-way radio to communicate with his dispatcher from the Mineral King surface plant. The antenna-assisted radio relay system known as the Red Mountain Repeater allowed him to coordinate his department's response.

A deputy was immediately dispatched to the switchbacks above Ouray. Blocking access to the Million Dollar Highway with a patrol vehicle, he rerouted southbound motorists. Two northbound drivers who were easing their vehicles down the slippery switchbacks were stopped and interviewed. After being told that they had escaped being struck by an avalanche by a matter of minutes, the drivers were asked if they could recall passing any southbound vehicles heading toward the Riverside snowshed. Both drivers reported passing a white extended-cab pickup with four rear wheels. The information was relayed to the Ouray County Sheriff's Office, where it was broadcast into Red Mountain Pass. The deputy also reported that the tan Range Rover had not passed through the checkpoint. Satisfied that the last vehicle had emerged from the pass, the deputy placed wooden barricades across the highway and headed south through Uncompahgre Gorge toward the debris pile.

Up at the Mineral King surface plant, Withers ordered Deputy Mapes to drive to the summit of Red Mountain Pass and turn back all northbound traffic. Mapes was also instructed to keep a log of all vehicles driving south from the Riverside Slide area and to interview motorists about any vehicles they had passed. The purpose of the double-checkpoint strategy was to identify all recent traffic activity through Uncompahgre Gorge and, by process of elimination, determine whether any vehicle might be trapped in the slide.

Meanwhile, Withers's sole remaining deputy in Ouray was charged with transporting avalanche poles and specially trained dogs to the Riverside area. The hasty rescue team, headed by Tim Vanderwall, had passed beneath the Riverside Slide just eight minutes before the avalanche hit. They heard the emergency transmission over their radio as they were entering the Mineral King surface plant. Still without a vehicle, Sheriff Withers piled into the Ouray Mountain Rescue truck along with four members of the hasty rescue team and Rick Quinn and headed north to the avalanche site. They were followed by a state patrolman who had arrived to help with the investigation of Mark Turlington's death.

The fourteen Ouray Mountain Rescue Team members who had reported to their headquarters in anticipation of a full-scale search of the Mineral King mine complex were told to await instructions regarding a possible avalanche search and rescue operation. To avoid creating a bottleneck in the avalanche-prone pass, the team remained at the rescue barn until the hasty rescue team could assess the situation. Upon hearing the emergency broadcast about the avalanche, their team captain bolted out of the headquarters on Sixth Avenue and ran to the CDOT barn.

By the time Lyle Morrison had sprinted the half-mile distance, Patrol 14 was already responding to the crisis. Driving one of the patrol's two Colorado Specials, Hamp had been plowing just south of the Riverside Slide when the call came over his radio. As the first emergency worker on the scene, his first concern was the safety of motorists stranded on the south side of the snowshed. Hamp instructed the drivers to move their vehicles up to the Riverside turnout area five hundred yards to the south, explaining that the initial avalanche had undoubtedly destabilized the remaining snowpack above US Highway 550.

Each member of CDOT Patrol 14 had a specific assignment. Phil Treacher was the first to leave the barn, driving the patrol's other Colorado Special through the Uncompahgre Gorge toward the avalanche site. Arnie Watson followed in the slow-moving bull plow tractor, trailed by Rick Merritt in the rotary blower. At the CDOT barn, Jasper Peytko loaded sand into the bed of the smaller snowplow and awaited Lyle Morrison's arrival. As the rescue team captain and a CDOT employee, Lyle pulled double-duty when an avalanche buried the highway. Hamp had reserved the patrol's remaining snowplow for Lyle so he could have access to the avalanche site.

•••

Casey Bailey had left the Ouray County Sheriff's Office ten minutes before the call came in from the State Police. Her repeated calls to the Brader home in Telluride had gone unanswered. Unable to contact Sissy Brader, Casey had paced back and forth in Bill Withers's cramped office, listening intently to the Sheriff's Department radio broadcasts. Paul Brader's Chevrolet Suburban was continuing south on Highway 145 toward the town of Rico. A San Miguel deputy had joined Jill Samsky in the slow-speed surveillance, but their quarry had yet to venture off the main road.

Nancy Alvarez, the on-duty dispatcher, had suggested that Casey take advantage of the lull by grabbing a quick meal, shower, and a fresh change of clothes. Confused by the woman's comment, Casey had inspected her reflection in the office window. Her face was smudged with dirt and her yellow slicker streaked with dark sludge. Splattered by the ATV's tires, the legs of her faded jeans were caked with dry mud.

Since her Jeep Wrangler was parked sixty miles away at the gates of Pandora Mill, Casey decided to make the nine-block journey home on foot. Walking south on Second Street, Casey trudged through ankle-deep snow covering the dirt road. Turning right on Third Avenue, she proceeded toward the southwest corner of town. Thick sheets of snow slanted through the yellowish glow cast by an overhead streetlight.

At the intersection of Third Avenue and Oak Street, a concrete bridge spanned the Uncompahgre River at the confluence of Canyon Creek. When she was halfway across the bridge, Casey heard the high-pitched wail of the town's emergency siren. Seeing headlights approaching from the far side of the bridge, she stepped up onto the sidewalk. A red Ford Explorer slowed down as it crossed the narrow bridge, affording Casey a clear view of the vehicle's interior through the passenger-side window.

When she saw who was driving, Casey's heart leapt in her chest. Six feet and a glass window separated her from Paul Brader, whose wide-eyed expression mirrored her own. When the SUV skidded to a stop on the east side of the bridge, Casey saw that Brader was towing a shallow trailer that carried a black snowmobile. Frozen in place on the sidewalk, Casey couldn't make sense of what she was witnessing. But when the driver's side door of the Explorer swung open, her survival instincts kicked in. Without hesitating, she wrapped her gloves around the bridge's waist-high metal railing and mounted it like a pommel horse. In one smooth motion, she swung her legs over the railing and flung herself toward the gurgling river below. The fifteen-foot drop seemed like an eternity as Casey fought to straighten her legs before entering the Uncompahgre River.

Her left boot landed in the center of the knee-deep river, a thick layer of silt cushioning the impact. Her right boot slid across the crown of a tall rock, buckling her knees and pitching her face-first toward the icy water. Thrusting her arms in front of her, Casey's gloves sunk into the pebbly sediment at the bottom of the riverbed. She locked her arms and managed to keep her head from plunging below the surface of the frigid, swift-moving water. She scrambled to find secure footing on the river bottom, then stood up, a flood of skin-numbing river water pouring out of the sleeves of her slicker. Her baseball cap dangled backward from her short ponytail, which was still threaded through the back of the headband. Unsure where to run, Casey twisted around so she could see the road above her. Behind a thick clump of pine trees flanking the side of the riverbank, she saw the Explorer's red taillights disappearing from view.

Convinced that Brader was fleeing the scene, Casey trudged through the river and scaled its steep, snow-covered bank. By the time she climbed up to the road, there was no sign of the Explorer. With ice-cold water sloshing inside her hiking boots, Casey followed the path of Brader's tire tracks. It suddenly occurred to her that the emergency siren near Town Hall was no longer blaring. She wondered if there was a connection between the siren and Brader's unexpected appearance in Ouray. Casey was still puzzling the matter when she saw that the fresh set of tire tracks veered off the road to the right. The tracks led up a steep access road toward the Box Canyon Falls parking lot. Brader was driving the wrong way on the exit road that swept down from the popular tourist site.

Casey quickly considered her options. It would take her five minutes to run back through town on slick, slush-covered roads to the Sheriff's Office. If, however, she followed Brader's tracks through the Box Canyon Falls parking lot, she would emerge on County Road 361 directly across from the CDOT barn. She took off up the access road on a dead run.

— Chapter 32 —

Lyle Morrison was steering the mid-sized snowplow out of the CDOT yard when he saw Casey Bailey sprinting up the hill from the Box Canyon Falls parking lot. He wouldn't have seen the lone figure emerging from the darkness if he hadn't spotted the bright yellow slicker through the falling snow. He engaged the parking brake and jumped down from the driver's seat as Casey ran frantically toward the truck. As she waved her arms above her head, water sprayed in arcs from her sodden gloves. Her jeans were drenched to her thighs. She was running with such abandon that Lyle had to grab her shoulders to keep her from sliding into him.

"What's going on?"

"Brader! I just saw him. He's towing a snowmobile and he's headed that way," she screamed, pointing up the steep incline of County Road 361.

"Are you sure?"

"He's driving his wife's Explorer," she explained breathlessly. "I can't believe you didn't see him drive by here."

"I just got out of the garage two minutes ago," Lyle replied. "You mean he drove right through the middle of town?"

"He took the back way through River Road and Oak Street. We need to call the Sheriff's Office and get some help!"

"There's not much they can do for us right now. They're all up at the Riverside Slide and half the department's stranded on the wrong side of the avalanche."

"Avalanche? When did that happen?"

"We got the call around fifteen minutes ago. They say there might be a Range Rover under the debris pile. That's where I was headed."

"You can't go," Casey pleaded. "I know you're Mister search and rescue, but they don't need you as much as I do."

After a moment's hesitation, Lyle grabbed the door handle, hoisted himself into the driver's seat and slapped the gearshift into reverse. "Meet me in front of the barn."

The sound of the snowplow backing up at a high rate of speed brought Jasper Peytko out of the CDOT garage. The truck had barely stopped moving when he saw Lyle leaping to the ground. The look of intensity in the huge man's eyes startled the twenty-three-year-old part-timer.

Lyle tossed the snowplow keys to the tow-headed young man. "I need your pickup."

Peytko reached into his pants pocket and handed over a bulky set of keys. "Something wrong with the truck?"

"Nope, it's running fine. Hamp's going to need everything we've got up at Riverside, so get that truck up there on the double."

Peytko saw Casey Bailey rounding the back corner of the truck. He looked up at Lyle. "What's going on?"

"You'll hear it over the radio. Get moving!"

As Peytko drove off in the snowplow, Lyle led Casey through the empty CDOT garage and into a narrow L-shaped office at the rear of the building. A black two-way radio sat atop a scarred wooden desk. Lyle snatched up the microphone.

"Ten Mary 14, this is Ten Mary 14-5."

Casey shook her head. "We don't have time for this. Brader's already got a five-minute head start."

Through the small receiver, Hamp's voice sounded thin and distant.

"Ten Mary 14 here. Go five."

"I need to get a message to the sheriff. Is he with you?"

"Ten-four. What's the message?"

Lyle decided that there was no time for diplomacy. "Tell him that the suspect is not driving the vehicle that Deputy Samsky is following. Casey Bailey just spotted the suspect in a red Explorer towing a snowmobile up the Camp Bird Mine Road. We are in pursuit. Over."

Without waiting for a reply, Lyle dropped the microphone, grabbed Casey's elbow, and ran out of the garage. Peytko's white Ford F-150 pick-up was parked along the chain-link fence on the yard's far side. Casey opened the passenger door and swept an open box of donuts onto the floor. Lyle turned the key in the ignition and shifted the truck's transmission into four-wheel drive. As he stomped on the gas pedal, all four tires dug into tightly packed gravel beneath the snow. Racing through the gates that bordered County Road 361, Lyle cut the wheel to the left, sending the truck's rear end fishtailing across the road. The compound gearing quickly corrected the skid and the Ford lurched forward. Passing the entrance to the Box Canyon Falls parking lot, Casey pointed to a set of recent tire tracks.

"Looks like Brader's the only one who's been back here lately. He should be easy to follow."

"As long as he stays in his truck. It's the snowmobile that's got me worried."

"You're right. No matter what kind of truck he's driving, he's not gonna get very far on this road. He's gonna need that snowmobile if he hopes to go beyond Camp Bird."

"Waddaya think he's up to?"

"He wouldn't have used his Suburban as a decoy unless he knew he was being watched in Telluride. And even though Withers has been all over him, he still risked driving right through Ouray. For such a cool customer, what he's doing sure smacks of desperation."

A sudden thought occurred to Casey. Instinctively, she grabbed Lyle's forearm. "He's headed right to your house! Do you think he's trying to settle a score with you?"

Lyle shook his head. "In the grand scheme of things, Brader just sees me as a nuisance. The only reason I can think of for this kind of a gamble is, for some reason, he desperately needs to get to Dr. Philips tonight."

Casey's head snapped to the left. "It's not just me, then! You think he's alive and Brader's leading us right to him, don't you?"

"I didn't say that," Lyle cautioned her. "But I can guarantee you that this isn't a mission of mercy. We need to catch him before he can get his hands on Jim again."

Through the snow-splattered windshield, County Road 361 was a narrow white runway that sliced through a thick forest of aspens, pines and spruce. Having traveled the road daily for the past five years, Lyle was able to push the truck to its limits. The frozen rutted road jostled the truck up and down and side to side, bouncing the headlight beams into the low-hanging boughs jutting out from the fringes of the roadway. Casey pushed the heels of her waterlogged boots against the dashboard, pinning her shoulders against the pickup's bench seat.

"We don't want to run up on him too soon," she warned through chattering teeth. "He might see us behind him and call the whole thing off."

"I know, but we're going to lose some ground when we make this stop."

"What stop?"

"Hold on tight!"

Lyle eased off the accelerator and cut the wheel to the left. The pickup's front wheels hit a drainage ditch on the left side of the road, bouncing Casey off the seat. When she hit the seat again, she saw they were heading up a steep tree-lined incline. It took her a moment to realize that they had turned in to Lyle's driveway.

"Good idea," she shouted over the whine of the engine. "Do you have an extra gun for me?"

"I don't own a gun."

"You're kidding! I thought all you people owned guns," she said as the truck crested the hill. "Then what are we stopping for?"

Lyle swung the truck in a wide arc, then backed the pickup against his garage door. "I'm going to ignore the 'all you people' comment. Come on, I need a hand."

Jumping down from the pickup, Casey immediately felt something bump against the back of her legs. She whirled around, thrusting her hands forward defensively. Lyle's cream-colored Labrador leaped up and licked her face.

"Sandy! You scared the snot out of me." She turned to Lyle with an accusing stare. "You left her outside all day in this snowstorm?"

Lyle leaned over and pushed against one of the bottom panels in the garage door. The wooden panel swung open at the bottom, revealing a set of hinges at the top of the panel. "She comes and goes as she pleases."

Lyle yanked the garage door open and flipped on a light switch. He pointed to the corner of the cluttered two-car garage.

"There are some snowshoes hanging on the wall. Grab two pairs: the biggest one and the smallest one."

Trailed by Sandy, Casey picked her way between stacks of lumber and a hodgepodge of hard-rock mining tools. In the corner of the garage, she found six snowshoes hanging from a long j-hook on the cinderblock wall. As she grabbed two pairs off the hook, she heard a loud scraping noise behind her. Cradling the metal-framed snowshoes against her chest, Casey sidled to the front of the cluttered garage.

"We'd better keep these in the cab with us," she called to Lyle. "If we put them in the back, they'll bounce right out of the bed."

"I hope this thing doesn't bounce out."

A blue tarpaulin wadded at his feet, Lyle was pouring gasoline into the tank of a low-slung red snowmobile that was scarred by dents and scratches along the right side of its frame.

"Does that thing work? It looks like it came out of a salvage yard."

Lyle capped the gas tank. "It runs fine; I had it out last week. It's just been flipped a few times, that's all."

Lyle started pushing the snowmobile along the garage floor until its front end faced the rear of the pickup truck.

"Flip that hatch down for me, would you?"

As Casey lowered the pickup's rear hatch, Lyle walked to the front of the sled, then grabbed the front tips of the snowmobile's skis, bracing them against his forearms. When he stood up, the nose of the five-hundred-pound snowmobile rose off the ground.

"You can't lift that thing into the truck!" Casey warned him. "You're gonna bust a gut."

"I don't have a choice; my trailer's down at the cee-dot barn."

With the weight of the front end of the snowmobile pressing against his arms, Lyle walked backward, pulling the snowmobile closer to the pickup. The snowmobile's drive belt scuffed along the concrete floor. Once he had backed himself against the bed of the pickup, Lyle lifted the skis until they leaned against the hatch. He moved to the rear of the snowmobile, placed his hands under the vehicle's frame and squatted down.

Casey shook her head. "At least let me give you a hand; I'm not the one with broken ribs."

In a powerful burst, Lyle used his legs as pistons to jerk the snowmobile off the ground. The fifty-one-year-old man let out a loud grunt as he raised the back end of the snowmobile from his waist to his shoulders. Casey could see the veins in his neck bulge as he braced the full weight of the snowmobile on his left shoulder. Pausing for a moment to adjust the load, he lurched forward, thrusting the snowmobile into the bed of the pickup.

As Lyle caught his breath, Casey closed the pickup's rear hatch and carried the snowshoes to the passenger-side door.

"You're one stubborn old man," she chided Lyle, dropping the shoes onto the truck's floorboard through the open door.

"Old is the operative word," Lyle wheezed, grinning between mouthfuls of cold air. "I'll be right back."

Lyle marched through the garage and into his house. When he emerged, he was wearing his red Ouray Mountain Rescue jacket and carrying an armful of clothes. Over the side of the pickup, he draped a thick gray sweatshirt, a pair of thermal socks, another red rescue team jacket, a pair of insulated nylon gloves and an orange wool cap.

"Sorry, but I don't have any boots or pants that'll fit you."

Casey began peeling off layers of wet clothing. She tossed her gloves onto the garage floor, where they landed with a soggy slap. She whipped off the miner's slicker and the jacket beneath, its sleeves still dripping water from the Uncompahgre River. When she started pulling her sweater over her head, Lyle turned to close the garage door. Her upper body clad only in white brassiere, Casey felt the cold sting of wind-driven snow against her bare shoulders and back. She quickly slipped into the oversized sweatshirt and bulky jacket, tugged on the orange watch cap and tossed her wet clothes into the bed of the truck.

When they climbed into the cab, Casey saw that Sandy had leapt into the back of the truck.

"She'll be okay," Lyle assured her. "I haven't bounced her out of a truck yet."

Lyle gunned the truck down the icy driveway and turned left on County Road 361 toward Camp Bird Mine. Brader's tire tracks, though fainter than before, were plainly visible.

As they drove deeper into the San Juan National Forest, the pickup's headlight beams bore through the storm like fish swimming through a silt-choked stream. Two miles south of Lyle's driveway, they passed the Weehawken campground. Knowing that the stretch of road that followed would be treacherous, Lyle eased off the gas pedal and shifted into low gear. As the road began to incline, he saw that the pickup's tires were churning through ever deeper snow.

"Things are going to start getting interesting," Lyle said. "With so little mining in the back basins these days, the county doesn't plow this road as often as they used to."

"Can't say I blame them. The last house we passed was yours and that was a couple miles back."

"I should've grabbed Jasper's tire chains back at the barn but it looks like Brader didn't bring his along either. Let's see how he handled the switchbacks."

As if on cue, the road swept up and sharply to the right. Lyle used the full width of the roadway to steer through the elbow of the turn. In the middle of the curve, he floored the gas pedal to build momentum for the uphill climb. The pickup's engine roared as its tires hopped, spun, and skipped up the icy incline. Lyle could see the swerving, slushy grooves that Brader's tires had cut into the snow only minutes before. Casey looked through the cab's rear window to see Sandy sprawled on the pickup's bed, keeping a wary eye on the shifting snowmobile.

The road leveled out momentarily before making an impossibly steep hairpin turn to the left. Lyle kept the gas pedal flush against the floorboard and cut the wheel to the left. Loose gravel spun into the pickup's wheel wells as all four tires ripped through the deep snow and dug into surface of the dirt road. Halfway up the hill, the truck began to lose momentum as its tires spun onto a wide patch of ice beneath the snow. The high-pitched noise of furiously spinning tires and the smell of burning rubber filled the cab.

"Get ready to bail out!" Lyle shouted to Casey. "I'll stay with the truck."

Casey pulled on the door handle, ready to jump out if the pickup begin to slide backward. Suddenly, the truck lurched forward, slamming Casey against the back of the seat. The pickup's front tires had finally found purchase in a bare, wind-blown stretch of tightly packed gravel above the ice patch. Lyle pounded his fist against the steering wheel.

"Go, baby! You've got it licked."

Cresting the top of the hill, Lyle lifted his boot off the accelerator and let out a loud sigh of relief. When he checked on Casey, he saw that she was staring through the windshield with a look of dread.

"You okay?"

Casey shook her head. "I hate it up here. In the summer, the jeep tours stop here so tourists can take pictures, but it gives me the willies."

The climb through the switchbacks had deposited them on a narrow corniche that had been carved out of the sheer cliff wall to their right. On the left shoulder, there were no barriers to protect against a plumb drop into Canyon Creek, which ran north along the canyon floor, hundreds of feet below. Originally designed as a means of hauling ore, mail and supplies to and from the remote mining camps, the rutted, twisting road had seen little improvement over the past century.

As they drove along the ledge, the truck's windshield was buffeted by slanting curtains of wind-whipped ice pellets. In the dark void to her left, Casey could hear the wind howling angrily through the gorge as the snowstorm was channeled through the narrow walls of the canyon. Lyle kept the pickup on the right side of the road, using the overhanging cliffs to shield the truck from the gusting winds. Massive ice formations clung to the cliff walls and shimmered in the truck's headlights.

A half-mile beyond the switchbacks, Lyle saw a long trail of skid trails on the road ahead. Pumping the brakes, he slowed the pickup to a crawl as the road began to bend to the right. It was obvious that Brader had lost control of his SUV on the icy downhill stretch leading into the curve. Around the bend, the skid marks continued onto the left shoulder, then veered back toward the center of the road.

"Look how close he came to skidding into the gorge," Casey exclaimed. "No wonder this place spooks me!"

Lyle coaxed the brake pedal as the road pitched downward toward the canyon floor. The walls on the far side of the canyon pinched closer to the middle of the gorge, making Casey feel as if they were approaching the bottom of a deep pit. As the storm system squeezed through this narrow section of the canyon, the winds intensified. The bulky truck began to rock as it was struck headlong by the furious gale.

Now fifty feet above the canyon floor, the road leveled out and the pickup's headlights illuminated a long stretch of road. Lyle and Casey saw the reflection of the Ford Explorer's taillights at the same time. As they drove closer, the dark shape of the sports utility vehicle came into focus through the storm.

"The trailer's empty," Casey said. "I'll bet that skid scared him into switching over to his snowmobile."

"Nope, looks like he ran smack into the Waterhole Slide."

Brader's truck was parked along the left side of the road. Directly in front of it was a towering mass of snow that blocked the entire width of the roadway. The debris pile was over fifteen feet tall on the left side of the road, tapering to a height of six feet where the snow mass met the cliff walls on the right.

"My God!" Casey exclaimed. "Where'd that come from?"

Lyle climbed down to the snow-covered roadway with Sandy at his heels and checked the doors of the Explorer. They were locked. Casey walked over to the shoulder to try and locate the source of the towering debris pile. Even in darkness, the Waterhole Slide's vertical white path was easy to distinguish. It began near the top of a peak on the far side of the canyon and cut an ever-widening swath through a forest of pines before entering the narrow canyon below her. A narrow section of the thirty-foot-deep canyon floor was buried in a fifty-foot-wide pile of densely packed snow that extended fifteen feet above the road.

"This is one of the most active slides around," Lyle explained as he inspected the footprints and snowmobile tracks behind the open trailer. "Once the canyon fills in, the slide path channels everything up here to the road. It takes weeks to open this road come springtime."

"What's the plan?" Casey asked.

Lyle pointed to the debris pile. "I need you to climb up there and find Brader's snowmobile tracks. You're going to have to drive the snowmobile over the top of that thing too, so you might as well follow his path."

Lyle unlatched the pickup's tailgate and pulled the snowmobile along the bed-liner until it was resting on the edge of the open hatch. He got into the cab of the pickup, dropped the gearshift into reverse and stomped on the accelerator. When the truck picked up speed, Lyle slammed on the brakes. The sudden deceleration sent the snowmobile sliding backward until it tipped over the tailgate, crashed onto the road and flipped onto its side.

Casey dug her boots into the right side of the debris pile and began climbing. The base of the pile inclined steeply from the road until it reached a six-foot plateau. Near the cliff wall, Casey saw the twin ski tracks and deep center groove of the snowmobile's center drive belt. As she had expected, Brader had chosen to drive up the right side of the snow heap. Reaching the top of the pile, Casey saw that the snow mass was relatively flat for twenty feet, then sloped back down to the road at a precipitous angle.

"It should be a piece of cake," she called to Lyle, who was warming up the snowmobile's sputtering engine.

"Good. It looks like the storm's letting up, too. You've driven these things before, so come on down and drive this sucker over the top."

Casey slid down the pile on the soles of her boots and jogged to the snowmobile. Lyle held the machine in place as she straddled the narrow black seat and wrapped her gloves around the handgrips.

"I only had one helmet back at the house—and it's too big for you—so I figured we'd both have to make do without one."

"No problem," Casey said as she scanned the controls. "Are you going to meet me on the other side of the pile?"

"I'll be over in just a minute. First, I'm gonna rearrange the parking scheme around here."

Casey steered the battered snowmobile toward the right side of the debris pile, opened the throttle all the way, then raised herself off the seat. She leaned forward as the front skis hit the base of the slope. The ribbed drive belt dug into the densely packed snow and propelled the machine up the steep incline. At the crest of the slope, the front skis continued upward, losing contact with the snow. The snowmobile then pitched forward and the skis crashed down onto the surface of the pile. Bouncing onto the seat, Casey eased off the throttle and steered into the path Brader had blazed. She maneuvered over the bumpy crown of the frozen heap then squeezed the handbrakes as she neared the drop-off at the far end. She leaned back and let gravity guide the five-hundred-pound machine down the slope.

Pointing to the avalanche pile, Lyle called to Sandy. "Go get her, girl!"

The Labrador bolted, scrambling up the path Casey had just taken. As soon as the dog was safely atop the snow mass, Lyle climbed back into Jasper Peytko's pickup truck. He slid behind the wheel and buckled the safety belt around his shoulder and waist.

"Sorry, Jasper," he muttered to himself. "I owe you one."

Brader's red Ford Explorer was thirty feet in front of the pickup, parked along the left shoulder of the road. Lyle shifted into low gear and let the pickup roll forward. Accelerating gradually, he drove the truck along the right side of the road, hugging the sheer cliff wall. Fifteen feet from the avalanche pile, he pressed the gas pedal to the floor and spun the wheel to the left. As the pickup gained speed, Lyle clenched his teeth and braced for the collision.

The Ford F-150's front bumper slammed broadside between the Explorer's passenger-side doors. The sound of buckling metal and breaking glass filled the canyon as the Explorer was jolted sideways by the impact. The sport utility vehicle's left-side tires slid off the shoulder of the road, tipping the Explorer's roof toward the canyon floor. As the vehicle and its trailer began to flip, the Explorer's undercarriage filled Lyle's windshield. He watched the truck topple into the darkness, then listened as the careening hunk of metal scraped against the canyon walls.

Climbing out of the pickup and pocketing the keys, Lyle announced with satisfaction, "Now that's how you send a truck off the road."

— Chapter 33 —

Although the two deputies had never met before, they executed the maneuver with textbook precision. Ordered by Sheriff Withers to stop the Suburban at all costs, Jill Samsky radioed her strategy to the San Miguel deputy following two car lengths behind her.

In a matter of seconds, Samsky closed the gap between her vehicle and the large Chevy traveling at a deliberate pace along Highway 145. Placing a blue strobe light on her dashboard, Samsky pulled into the northbound lane and passed the Suburban. When she cleared its front bumper, she swerved in front of the boxy black truck and eased off the accelerator. The irritated driver responded by leaning on the horn and flashing the vehicle's high beams. Careful to avoid a collision on the snow-covered highway, Samsky waited for the driver of the Suburban to slow down before applying her brakes.

As Samsky ran interference, the San Miguel deputy maneuvered his truck alongside the Chevy, boxing it against the right edge of the highway. In close-quarters formation, the three vehicles slowed to a crawl in the southbound lane. Once the Suburban was forced to stop, the San Miguel deputy steered to the right, pinning the driver's side door shut.

Exiting in tandem, both deputies took cover behind their trucks and drew their weapons. Samsky shined her flashlight through the windshield of the Suburban.

"Hands up!" she shouted. "I wanna see hands!"

As the San Miguel deputy aimed his pistol at the dark figure inside the truck, Samsky eased around the Suburban's right front bumper, her flashlight trained on the driver. Through the windshield, she saw two thin arms waving frantically. The driver reached up and pulled off a dark knit cap, releasing a thick wad of dark hair that spilled onto her shoulders.

"It's the suspect's wife!" Jill called to the other deputy. "I'm going to open the passenger door."

Holstering her weapon, the tall blonde-haired deputy pulled open the door. Sissy Brader's shrieks spilled into the cold night air. She pleaded in a hysterical voice.

"Don't shoot me! It's not my fault. He's gone crazy!"

"Calm down, Mrs. Brader. We're not going to hurt you. Slide over here and I'll help you climb down."

Sissy Brader unlatched her seat belt and complied with the deputy's order, spewing a string of apologies and excuses.

"I've never seen him like this before. This Saratoga stuff is making him schitzo. He told me if I didn't do this, we were gonna wind up broke! He said the Sheriff over in Ouray is in cahoots with Jim Philips and they're both trying to screw us outta our money. He made me promise that I'd drive all the way down to Durango and back, real slow. Can you imagine a husband asking his wife to do such a thing on a night like this? I'm telling you, he's gone loco."

"Did he tell you that you were going to be followed?" Samsky asked.

"Yeah. He turned out the lights in our living room and pointed out your truck. He said I should let you follow me, but not let you get close enough to see my face."

"Did he say where he was planning to go while you were creating this diversion?"

"He just said he needed to clean up some loose ends, whatever that means."

Sissy Brader then looked up at Deputy Samsky with a puzzled expression. "You don't think he's in any kinda trouble, do you?"

— Chapter 34 —

"Is Sandy still with us?" Casey shouted over the whine of the snowmobile's twin-cylinder engine.

Pressed against the back of the vinyl seat designed for only one rider, Lyle looked behind him and saw his dog bounding along the path of snowmobile tracks, trying to keep pace.

"Once we're out of sight, she'll head back to the pickup," he assured her. "Don't worry, she's got enough sense not to follow us for too long."

The snowmobile's low windscreen provided only a modicum of protection for Casey, who was sitting far forward on the machine's saddle. Without the aid of a helmet and face shield, she ducked down behind the windscreen to protect her eyes from the onrush of blowing snow. Although the headlights afforded her a thirty-foot path of illumination, she kept her head titled downward and her eyes focused directly in front of the snowmobile. She no longer felt the sting of individual pellets of snow and ice as they continued to pelt her cheeks, chin and throat. Instead, she felt a gradual tightening of the frozen skin around her lips and jawline.

Seated behind her, Lyle struggled to balance his weight on the back of the long narrow seat. As he scanned the road, his thighs were pressed against the outside of Casey's legs. With his left arm clutched around the driver's waist, Lyle used the snowshoes strapped around his right arm to shield his face from the snow.

"The road forks up ahead," Lyle said, leaning forward. "Let's see where Brader's tracks lead."

Casey surveyed the road ahead. As they crested a small hill, the road diverged around a thick stand of evergreens. From her numerous summertime trips into the alpine basins, Casey recognized the fork as the Camp Bird Mine junction. The path to the left led down into the Camp Bird Mine surface plant, its "Private Property" signposts generally respected by tour guides and visitors alike. To the right, the main road climbed to a corniche overlooking the Camp Bird complex, then followed the path of Sneffels Creek toward the Yankee Boy, Governor, and Imogene basins. Casey steered the snowmobile to the right and girded herself for yet another precarious trek along an elevated shelf road.

"Left! Left!"

Assuming that Brader would follow the jeep road into the back basins, Casey was surprised by Lyle's directive. She jerked the steering mechanism to the left and leaned into the turn. The snowmobile responded immediately, swerving toward the entrance of the Camp Bird Mine complex. As the machine's headlights swung to the left, Casey saw a pile of hardened snow stretched across the access road ten feet in front of them.

"Bust on through it!" Lyle shouted.

Spotting a small breach in the five-foot-tall bank of plowed snow, Casey pointed the front skis toward the opening and leaned back against Lyle's chest. As they crashed through the narrow, jagged hole that Brader's snowmobile had punched through the wall, chunks of dislodged ice struck them in the face and shoulders. The impact lifted the snowmobile off the ground, catapulting the machine down the steep access road, which was buried under a three-foot-deep blanket of fine powder. A thick spray of snow completely frosted the windscreen, obscuring Casey's vision as the snowmobile careened down the dark access road.

"Which way?"

"Just let it slide and hang on," Lyle replied, his voice muffled.

Unable to stop the machine's forward momentum, Casey fought to keep the handlebars straight. Rising off the seat to see above the snow-crusted windscreen, she saw that they had reached the bottom of the sloping access road. She squeezed the handbrakes until the snowmobile slid to a sputtering stop. Her entire body shaking, Casey looked back at Lyle.

The tall man's upper body was covered in a thin layer of snow from the spray of loose powder that had washed above the windscreen. He had managed to brush the powder away from his eyes, but his hair, cheeks and shoulders were caked in a frozen white shroud.

"Sorry about that. This place must not get plowed in the winter."

After checking that he hadn't dropped any of the snowshoes that dangled from the right sleeve of his jacket, Lyle continued brushing the snow from his face.

"Things aren't going to get any better up ahead of us. Let's keep moving. We need to make up some time."

Casey used her gloves to wipe the coating of snow from the idling snowmobile's windscreen, then continued following Brader's tracks through the undulating snowdrifts along the deserted access road. To her left, Casey saw the dark outline of several tin-skinned structures that surrounded a frozen tailings pond. Up ahead, a long elevated trestle that was covered by a peak-roofed metal snowshed snaked through the surface plant. On the right side of the road, two large white Victorian houses stood vigil over the idle mine complex.

"I don't get it," she called back to Lyle. "The only way I know how to get to the back basins is by taking a right back at that fork. Where do you think he's headed?"

"By taking this shortcut, he just told us where he's headed."

"What do you mean?"

"The quickest way to get to Yankee Boy Basin and Governor Basin is to follow the jeep road but if you cut through here, you shave two miles off the trip to Imogene Basin."

Lyle's remark hung in the air like a foul odor; its presence palpable and unwelcome. Casey felt a flood of panic. Until this moment, she had surmised that Brader had sequestered her landlord in one of the dilapidated mining shacks scattered beside the remote jeep road leading through the Yankee Boy and Governor basins. Not once had she considered that Brader might attempt the murderous climb up to Imogene Basin or, even more staggeringly, that he would be foolhardy enough to risk an assault on the 13,114-foot summit of Imogene Pass.

"He's a madman!" Casey shouted. "There's no way he's gonna make it. He'll get us all killed in the process."

Lyle felt Casey's body begin to shiver.

"He might not be heading all the way into Imogene Basin; there's a mining cabin on the way that's isolated enough to suit Brader. But either way, there's no shame in turning back. I can take it from here. By the time you hike back to the truck, Withers might be there. In fact, by letting Bill know what's going on, we'll be able to get some reinforcements sent in from the Telluride side of Imogene Pass."

Casey didn't respond to Lyle's suggestion. She saw it as a well-intentioned but transparent attempt to provide her with a face-saving excuse to bail out of the trek into the desolate alpine basin. Casey lowered her head and powered the snowmobile forward through the deep snowdrifts along the access road, sending twin waves of snow curling away from the machine and raising a plume of powder that spiraled into the air behind them.

She yelled over her shoulder, "Like you said back in the mine: if Brader can do this, so can we. I may not be able to drive this thing as far as the summit, but I guarantee you I can make it as far as he can."

Reaching the far end of the surface plant, they passed directly in front of the now-vacant Victorian mansions that once served as opulent private residences for Camp Bird Mine's owners and managers. The road then bent to the left, leading past a jumble of mill buildings, storage sheds, railroad trestles and ore chutes.

"Uphill right hand curve ahead," Lyle announced. "Start getting your speed up."

Casey leaned forward and opened the throttle. The snowmobile's drive belt churned through the deep unplowed snow, spinning faster with each revolution. The road dove down between two thick stands of firs, then veered sharply to the right. Casey twisted the steering mechanism to the right, keeping the accelerator at its maximum setting as the machine skidded through the turn.

Coming out of the hairpin turn, Casey over-corrected her steering, propelling the snowmobile toward the tree-lined left shoulder. When she yanked the handlebars to the right, the machine snowplowed across Brader's tracks in the center of the road. With each successive correction, the back end of the snowmobile swung like a tadpole's tail.

Lyle felt the snowmobile beginning to bog down along the steep incline. "Steer back into Brader's groove; let him do the work for us."

Casey obliged, and as the front skis settled into the deep tracks left by Brader's machine, the vehicle began to pick up speed. No longer having to churn through three-foot-deep drifts of virgin powder, the steel-reinforced drive belt worked efficiently against the packed snow Brader had left in his wake.

The jeep road that led out of the south end of the surface plant climbed through a multi-tiered forest of snow-frosted evergreens, flanked on the left by striated layers of overhanging cliffs. Casey noticed that the wind's intensity had decreased, no longer forcing her to shield her eyes from the driven snow and swirling spindrift. The snowmobile's headlight beams reflected far fewer flakes, providing Casey with an expanded line of sight up the deeply rutted private road.

Now nearly 500 feet above the Camp Bird Mine complex, the road arced to the left, continuing its ascent from the canyon floor. She felt her eardrums pop, reminding her that they were still more than four thousand feet below the summit of Imogene Pass. Navigating up the snow-choked lane that sliced through the dark, quiet forest, she tried to ignore the enormity and absurdity of the journey ahead.

"This road's going to dead end in another quarter-mile," Lyle warned. "It runs into the jeep road coming up from Sneffels Creek. Unless Brader's getting cute with us, his tracks should go to the left."

"There was nothing cute about the look on his face down in Ouray," Casey said. "Have you ever been up to Imogene in the winter?"

"Three years ago I had to go up there with the hasty team. We got as far as the U.S. Mill on snowmobile, then we had to snowshoe it up to the bowl from there," Lyle replied.

"What happened?"

"A thirty-five-year-old guy on a cross-country skiing vacation thought it would be really cool to ski from Ouray to Telluride over Imogene Pass," Lyle shouted over the noise of the engine. "When he didn't show up in Telluride that afternoon, we got the call to go up and find him. We tracked him into Imogene basin, but a half-mile into the bowl, his tracks ended at the top of a fresh slide. It took us two hours to find his body and another four hours to haul him back to Ouray. The cause of death was listed as a massive heart attack, but the coroner couldn't say for sure whether he keeled over from exertion and started the avalanche or he got caught in a slide and died trying to fight his way out of the debris pile."

"That's a very reassuring story, Lyle. Sorry I asked."

Lyle turned and looked at the trail behind them.

"Looks like we've lost Sandy. She's probably already on her way back to the truck."

As Lyle had predicted, Brader's parallel ski prints turned sharply left when they crested the hill at the end of the Camp Bird Mine access road. On the far side of the intersection, there was a vast gap in the alpine forest. Unable to penetrate the depths of the frozen night air, the snowmobile's headlight beams seemed to be devoured by the pitch-black void. Casey swerved left onto the corniche that would lead them up to Imogene Basin.

"Keep the throttle back a notch through here," Lyle instructed. "We're up on a shelf road and there's no room for error on your right. Also, United States Mountain is directly above us and it's got a couple of active slide paths that run through here."

Inside her gloves, Casey felt her palms go clammy. "Let me know when you have any good news to report."

"Okay," Lyle replied. "Remember that mining cabin I told you about? It's left over from the old Yellow Rose Mine, and it's about a mile up the road. It's the only place I can think of between here and the top of Imogene Pass where Brader could've stashed Dr. Philips."

Casey kept her eyes focused on the uneven surface of the snow-covered jeep road. In spots, the wind had scoured the exposed shelf, leaving only a thin glaze of ice between the snowmobile's drive track and the frozen dirt below. In other sections, Casey had to follow Brader's path over, around and through steep-faced snowdrifts that were taller than the snowmobile.

"We must be gaining on him," Lyle said. "He's having to do all of the trail-breaking through these drifts."

As they continued to climb the shelf road, thick wisps of gray mist floated in from the canyon to their right. Now at 10,000 feet, Lyle saw that the tail end of the storm system had finally arrived. The dense, multi-layered tempest had been fractured into a jumble of trailing clouds. Intermittent pinpoints of weak moonlight bathed the snowcapped slopes, then disappeared behind broken cloud cover. With the storm unraveling, Lyle saw that there were fewer evergreen trees clinging to the steep mountain walls. They were getting closer to the timberline.

As they ascended out of the canyon, Lyle saw that Casey was looking to the right. Fifty yards from the ragged edge of the road, a pale ray of moonlight fell upon a solitary structure perched along the face of a steep slope. In the doughy light, the crumbling remains of the United States Mill building seemed to glow from within. Flanked by bulbous tailing piles that tumbled down the slope into the canyon below, the dilapidated building looked like five long rows of wooden matchsticks stacked on top of one another. Teetering, but stubbornly refusing to buckle, the structure's skeletal core had withstood the ravages of time and weather for nearly a century.

"Does Divining Rod Enterprises own that, too?" she called over her shoulder.

"Yes."

"So in the end, that's what this is all about, right? It's just a pissing contest over who owns a few holes in the ground and a couple of condemned buildings."

Lyle knew that Casey's contempt was partially aimed at him for his role in helping Dr. Philips amass his portfolio of claims. His first inclination was to point out that millions of dollars' worth of minerals lay undiscovered in the *holes in the ground* that Casey referred to. He could also argue that they were not merely on a rescue mission; they were helping to protect the future of the San Juan Mountain backcountry from profiteers and land rapists. But having spent the better part of the last two days with her, Lyle knew that Casey would consider both arguments to be self-serving and irrelevant; her sole motivation was to locate her landlord and friend. He kept his mouth shut.

"Creek coming up," Casey announced.

The grooves from Brader's snowmobile veered to the right, bypassing a narrow snow-covered bridge over Imogene Creek. Casey followed the kidnapper's trail down a short embankment and into the rock-strewn, partially frozen stream. As the front skis splashed into the middle of the creek, Casey kept the throttle wide open, steering onto a thick tongue of ice jutting from the base of the far embankment. The wet drive track spun along the slick surface until the snowmobile slid into a thick ice-covered snowdrift piled against the far embankment. The machine pitched upward and lumbered out of the creek as Casey pointed the ski tips to the left and steered back onto the jeep road.

"Good job!" Lyle shouted. "The mining cabin is just ahead on the right."

The road crested, then leveled out at the fringe of a broad alpine meadow to their right. The cloud cover had thinned even more and a three-quarter moon bathed the meadow in an eggshell glow. Casey was shocked to see how much snow had been heaped onto the meadow over the course of the winter. Head-high alpine shrubs and brushwood that sprang from the meadow during summer were completely covered, no trace of their existence evident on the smooth surface. Along the borders of the expansive clearing, the trunks of mature fir trees were encased in ten-foot drifts, as if the trees had sunk into the earth up to their lower boughs.

"I remember this meadow, but where's the cabin?" she asked.

Lyle pointed to a ridge-like shelf in the snow thirty feet to the right.

In the glare of the headlight beams, the only sign of the twelve-foot tall structure was a triangular bulge that rose to a blunt peak two feet above the wintry surface. A slender black stovepipe protruded from the roofline like a periscope peeking up through the snow. A small square hole just below the roof's overhang was the only visible entrance to the buried structure.

Lyle patted Casey's shoulder. "I know this isn't what you want to hear, but it looks like we're headed up into the basin. Brader's tracks don't go anywhere near that cabin. Are you sure you still want to go through with this? Once we climb above the timberline, there's no place to take shelter, so now's the time to tell me if you're having any second thoughts."

After a final glance at the Yellow Rose mining cabin, Casey pointed the snowmobile up the road and revved the engine.

Crosscut frequently by Imogene Creek's serpentine path, the back-country jeep road tilted at a sharp rake as it climbed out of the meadow. Wherever the creek bisected the road, the thick snowpack was furrowed by deep sluices, forcing Casey to plunge the snowmobile into the narrow runnels with enough thrust to propel it up the steep icy embankments on the other side.

Having climbed above 11,000 feet, Casey could feel the temperature dropping. The exposed skin on her face and neck grew tighter and her nose felt waxy and numb. Although the rescue team jacket's neoprene shell protected her torso from the cold, her legs were shaking uncontrollably. Still wet from the plunge into Uncompahgre River, the legs of her jeans had frozen stiff. She flexed her knees, trying to keep her skin from freezing onto the icy denim fabric.

As they continued their ascent toward Imogene Basin, the corniche became more treacherous. A mile beyond the meadow, the snowmobile started sinking deeper into the sea of dense snowdrifts. The drive track no longer skimmed along the surface of the mounds, but cut a deep channel into the fine powder of the snowpack. Brader's tracks revealed that his snowmobile had fishtailed over this stretch of road, often sending him precariously close to the steep drop-off along the right edge of the corniche.

The task of controlling the snowmobile on the uneven, slender shelf road was an exercise in patience and finesse. Maneuvering the machine through an obstacle course of slanting moguls and unstable drift piles demanded deft steering and a light touch on the throttle. At the same time, the snowmobile required enough torque to churn through the loosely packed powder and propel them up the steep grade.

"We're passing through what used to be the Upper Camp Bird Mine, so we're getting close to the northern rim of the basin."

While Casey urged the snowmobile up the left shoulder of the shelf, Lyle looked across the canyon to his right. The summit of Chicago Peak, two thousand feet above the road, was back-lit by a low gibbous moon, casting a broad shadow into the canyon and onto the roadway. Despite the darkness, Lyle could see a discernable change in the alpine landscape. The thick forest of spruce, pine and firs that had bordered the road throughout their trek now thinned to a scattering of squat green clumps. After an hour of nerve-racking driving, they had reached the timberline.

As they neared the rim of Imogene Basin, the road pitched sharply. Lyle fought to keep himself from sliding off the back of the snowmobile as Casey powered the machine through a vast drift of granular snow. Tilted at a severe angle, neither driver nor passenger could see the road in front of them. The snowmobile's headlights melted helplessly into the vast night sky. Hurtling toward the star-dappled void with the force of gravity pressing her back against Lyle, Casey felt as if she were being launched into orbit.

She cocked her head to the side and heard a sudden change in the timbre of the snowmobile's engine. She knew immediately that the drive belt had lost contact with the snow. Through the powder-splattered windscreen, Casey saw the tips of the snowmobile's skis rising into the air.

"Don't flip on me!" she screamed.

Helpless to exert any control over the snowmobile, she found herself counting the seconds that they were airborne.

"One, two, threeee!"

The drive track came crashing down on the snowpack, followed immediately by the front skis. Casey's head snapped forward. She felt

Lyle's bulk, pressed hard against her back, now shoving her forward. She stood up and squeezed the handbrakes, desperately trying to arrest the vehicle's forward thrust.

The snowmobile had vaulted over a saddle-like ridgeline and onto a flat shelf along the northern rim of Imogene Basin. To her horror, Casey saw that the jeep road bent to the left, but the snowmobile was sliding straight ahead along a rock spur that extended fifty feet into the mouth of the deep bowl. As the snowmobile careened toward the brink of the snow-covered shelf, she clamped her fists desperately around the hand-brakes. Lyle thrust his boots into the snowpack, using them like twin anchors. Finally, the machine came to a side-sliding halt five feet from the jagged edge of the basin's upper rim.

Her legs trembling, Casey sat down heavily on the narrow seat and collapsed backward against Lyle's chest. The big man responded by hooking his left arm around Casey's shoulders.

"I've never been so scared in my life," Casey exclaimed, exhaling deeply.

Although he felt himself inexplicably comforted by the gentle pres-sure of the petite woman's body against his, Lyle knew that they had to act quickly. He unstrapped the snowshoes from around his right arm and slid off the back of the snowmobile.

"Turn off the headlights. I don't want to tip off Brader that we're on his tail."

Casey flicked the switch, dismounted the machine, and stared into the immense cavity beneath the wind-scoured ledge. Her first exposure to Imogene Basin in the winter was both unsettling and awe-inspiring. Beneath a star-choked sky, a nearly unbroken expanse of white stretched before her. Except for the steep gray cliffs that ringed the bowl, the entire basin was devoid of color. To Casey, the remote mountain basin had al-ways been an oasis brimming with vibrant colors and exquisite fragranc-es. But now, gawking into the lifeless crater, she concluded that the only term that could adequately describe the scene before her was "nuclear winter."

A constant howl arose from the bowels of Imogene Basin. The swirling wind created tall funnels of spindrift that skittered across the basin floor. Looking down into the moonlit bowl, Casey saw that the deep hollows and slit crevices that were evident during the summer had been filled in and smoothed over by five months of drifting snow. Only the most prominent rock outcroppings and the tallest ridgelines were able to penetrate the snowpack's surface. At the far end of the up-titled bowl, the summit of Imogene Pass appeared as a faint shadow that seemed to pulse in and out of view behind constantly shifting curtains of blowing snow.

Lyle was lying on his stomach, his head only inches from the edge of the shelf. He cupped his hands around his eyes and stared into the basin as if sighting a pair of binoculars.

"If you're trying to find the jeep road down there, you're not going to have much luck," Casey said. "It wasn't much of a road to begin with and now it's completely buried."

"I'm not trying to find the road; I'm trying to find Brader."

Believing they had gained considerable ground on their quarry, Lyle searched the basin floor directly below the rim. Seeing nothing but rolling white mounds beneath him, he shifted focus further into the sloping bowl. His eyes were drawn to a small dark shape that seemed to be sticking out of the snow four hundred yards to the south.

"Is that thing moving?" he asked Casey.

Looking where Lyle was pointing, she saw a figure in the distance silhouetted against the pure white carpet of snow. Using the top of an exposed ridgeline in the foreground for reference, she could tell that the black shape was moving up the slope at a slow, deliberate pace.

"He's on foot!" she exclaimed. "He must've ditched his snowmobile."

Lyle sprang to his feet. The dark figure was tantalizingly close, yet maddeningly distant. In an open field, Lyle knew it would take him little more than a minute to sprint the quarter-mile distance separating him from Paul Brader. But given the circumstances, he wondered whether Brader's lead was insurmountable.

"We've got to cut him off before he scales the summit."

Surveying the hollow, wind-blown basin, she gave voice to her worst fears.

"Dr. Philips is in that old power shack on the top of the pass, isn't he?"

"Either that or the pump house at Ptarmigan Lake," Lyle confirmed, handing the snowshoes to Casey. "I'll drive from here on in. It's going to be a bumpy ride down into the bowl, so hang onto these tight. It looks like we're going to need 'em."

Lyle slid far forward on the seat so Casey could squeeze in behind him. The awkward position forced him to wrap his arms around his knees in order to operate the controls. Casey trapped the snowshoes between her chest and Lyle's back by reaching around the man's thick chest and grasping her wrists. Without turning on the headlights, Lyle swung the snowmobile to the left, following the jeep road along the northern rim of the basin.

Brader's snowmobile tracks followed the contours of the overhanging spur for fifty yards before making an abrupt right turn and diving into the basin. Before descending the steep slope, Lyle paused at the edge of the rim. The jeep road was indistinguishable as it swooped down into the bowl. Lyle knew that the smooth surface of the slope was deceiving. The wind-sculpted snowdrifts concealed huge boulders, broad hollows and deep crevices. To make matters worse, the steep ridgelines that crosscut the entire bowl created a gauntlet of avalanche-prone slopes that could be triggered by the slightest shift in the buried layers of the unstable snowpack.

"We're going to be flying blind," Lyle called back to Casey. "Our best bet is to stick to Brader's line. He lost his ride somewhere down there, but he's still alive and that's about as good as we can hope for."

"Sounds like a plan. Let 'er rip."

When Lyle eased the snowmobile over the rim and onto the face of the near-vertical slope, the machine immediately picked up speed. Each time he squeezed the handbrakes, the snowmobile continued its unabated slide down the steep gradient. Although the skis were plowing through a thick surface layer of loose powder, he could tell that the drive track was gliding on top of a sheet of ice some eight inches below the surface. Prior to the recent snowstorm, two days of sunshine had glazed the snowpack with a solid crust of ice.

As the snowmobile hurtled down the slope, the skis bounced along the rippled surface, jostling both riders up and down on the single seat. Lyle saw that Brader had elected to blaze a straight-line path down the slope, ignoring the fact that the obliterated jeep road descended via a series of looping switchbacks.

Halfway down the incline, a dense vortex of wind-whipped ice pellets raced across the face of the slope, engulfing the snowmobile in a virtual whiteout. Lyle felt the prow of the machine rise up, then tip back down at a sharp angle. When his vision cleared, he saw that the snowmobile was barreling toward a steep snow-capped ridge that ran laterally across his path. Unable to see what lay over the top of the ridge, Lyle braced for a free-fall.

"We're going up and over. Hold on!"

The snowmobile shot over the top of the ridge into the air. With his stomach in his throat, Lyle looked between the ski tips to see where the craft would land. The vast white background was disorienting, yielding no hint of depth or distance. After what seemed like an eternity, the snowmobile bounced once on its drive track, then thudded against the powder-packed slope.

Lyle's relief regarding their soft touchdown was short-lived. Looking over the windscreen, he saw that their downhill slide was about to come to an abrupt end. His first impression was that they were about to plummet into the throat of a dark well. Thirty yards below, he saw an oval of black at the bottom of a wide pit. Tall snowdrifts flared up from the depths of the hollow, forming a curved white tunnel around the entrance to the pit. Lyle couldn't tell whether the black object they were hurtling toward was an exposed rock, a deep crevice, or Brader's abandoned snowmobile. All he knew for sure was that it would be impossible to steer the out-of-control snowmobile around the mouth of the pit.

"Bail out!"

Her view blocked by Lyle's body, Casey was startled when Lyle grabbed hold of her forearms and sprang up from the seat. Casey's grasp around Lyle's waist was broken as they tumbled off the back of the vehicle. Casey's head struck the slope with a thud at the same time that Lyle landed on her chest, knocking the wind out of her. Fighting to draw a breath amid a thick spray of up-churned snow, Casey was vaguely aware that Lyle had slid off of her and was hurtling feet-first down the slope faster than she was.

Lyle saw that his five-hundred pound snowmobile was sliding ahead of him toward the bottom of the pit. He rolled onto his stomach and tried to arrest his slide by flailing his limbs against the face of the slope. The 235-pound man pounded his boots into the snow and wielded his fists like a pair of ice axes in a desperate attempt to gain purchase. Sliding into a narrow chute at the mouth of the deep cave-like formation, Lyle dug his elbows into the snowpack and pressed his weight against them.

Just as he was beginning to gain traction, Lyle heard his snowmobile crashing into the bottom of the pit. The sound of a sharp collision reverberated through the hollow. Seconds later, the soles of his boots slid into something solid. Cushioning the impact by flexing his knees, Lyle came to an abrupt halt with his chest pressed against the steep incline. He was perched atop the frame of Paul Brader's black snowmobile, which lay on its side at the bottom of the hollow. His own vehicle had flipped over after colliding with the kidnapper's snowmobile, leaving its underbelly exposed like an overturned beetle.

Looking up, Lyle saw a flash of red fabric and a tangle of arms and legs bouncing, rolling, and sliding toward the hollow. As he strained to keep his eyes locked on Casey Bailey through a shower of down-sliding snow, the aluminum frame of a falling snowshoe struck him on the bridge of his nose, momentarily blinding him. With a searing white light flashing behind his eyelids, Lyle raised his arms, hoping to catch Casey before she slammed into the heap of splintered snowmobile frames.

When Casey came sliding into him, Lyle managed to hook his arms around the woman's shoulders, but the impact sent them tumbling onto Brader's wrecked snowmobile. The three other snowshoes rained down on them in rapid succession, followed by a thick shower of loosened snow.

"Are you okay?" an out-of-breath Casey asked Lyle, who was sandwiched between her and the snowmobile.

"I will be once you get off of me," Lyle answered calmly.

As Casey struggled to her feet, Lyle heard a series of high-pitched yelps coming from above.

"It's Sandy!" he shouted. "See if you can break her fall."

Casey saw a boulder-sized object sliding down the slope. The dog was sliding tail-first down the incline on her belly. Casey reached up and caught the animal. Still in a panic, Sandy tried to twist out of Casey's grasp. Lyle reached around Casey, grabbed the dog by its collar and wrapped his arms around her. Shuddering against her owner's chest, Sandy panted loudly as she licked Lyle's face with a dry, bristly tongue.

"I can't believe she followed us all the way into the basin." Casey said.

"Not bad for a rescue team drop-out. That's the best trick she's ever performed and I don't even have a treat to give her. Now, let's figure out how to get out of here."

The only solid wall of the deep cave was the one they had slid down. Towering snowdrifts had formed around the rim of the hollow, bending toward the center of the pit like a hurricane vase.

"Looks like the only way out is the way we came in," Lyle concluded. "You climb out first. Grab two of the snowshoes and strap them to your arms so you can keep your hands free. I'll carry the other pair up along with Sandy."

Casey found a pair of yellow snowshoes at the bottom of the pit. She slid her arms through the loose straps, then slipped her gloves through a hole in the nylon decking of each shoe. She pulled them up the sleeves of her jacket until they fit snugly around her upper arms.

Casey used the toes of her boots to kick footholds into the slope while simultaneously punching handholds with her gloves. Hand-over-hand, and boot-over-boot, Casey climbed out of the hollow and above the snowdrifts ringing the mouth of the pit. Pausing only to shake the fatigue out of her arms, she continued up the slope until she reached the flat peak of a horizontal ridgeline. Looking up the slope, she could see a succession of impact craters that the out-of-control snowmobiles and tumbling bodies had made along the otherwise undisturbed snowpack. To her right, a trail of boot prints led along the top of the narrow ridge.

The prints led to a patch of trampled snow twenty feet to her right. She called down to Lyle, who was scaling the slope ten feet below her.

"I can see where Brader put on his snowshoes."

"Good. I'll be right there."

Lyle was following the trail of handholds and footholds Casey had just made. Two orange-colored snowshoes dangled from his left arm and Sandy was draped over his right shoulder. His right arm clutching the dog against his body, Lyle was climbing one-handed, struggling awkwardly up the steep grade.

"Start strapping on your snowshoes," he called through ragged breaths. "We've lost a lot of time and Brader's got a helluva head start."

Casey followed Brader's boot prints until she reached the trampled-down section of snow. Having never worn a pair of snowshoes before, she tried to determine how to strap them to her boots. A yellow oval-shaped piece of mesh nylon fabric was stretched along an aluminum alloy frame, secured by a series of decking clips. The oblong frame was rounded at the toe and tapered to a point at the heel. Two crampons were mounted on the shoe's underside. Casey slipped her boots into the snowshoes' bindings, locked the toe and instep in place with flip hooks. She adjusted the nylon straps around her boots and yanked them tight.

As she stood up, she felt Lyle's hand under her arm, steadying her from behind as she took her first tentative steps in the oversized shoes. She tried to step around Sandy, who was running in circles, obviously euphoric about being reunited with them.

"I don't know how much help I'm gonna be, but I'll give it my best shot."

"It would be easier if we had ski poles, but we never would've been able to lug them up here in the snowmobile anyway."

Casey turned in a wide semicircle, taking small shuffling steps in an effort to face Lyle, who was strapping on a pair of snowshoes.

"Those are a lot bigger than mine," she commented.

"The more you weigh, the bigger your shoes need to be. These help spread my weight over a bigger surface so I can stay on top of the snow rather than sinking into it."

Getting to his feet, Lyle looked south along the ridgeline, orienting his vision along the vast moonlit surface of the upward tilting bowl floor. Once again, he spied the dark speck framed against the white snowfield. He estimated that Brader was now halfway through the basin, about to begin the long uphill climb toward the summit.

"I'll go first. Brader's already broken the trail and I'll be packing it down even more, so try to step in my tracks. Keep a steady pace, but listen to your body; the air is dangerously thin up here."

"Don't wait for me; you've got too much ground to make up. I'll be fine."

Striding out along the ridgeline with Casey trailing behind, Lyle called over his shoulder, "Keep Sandy with you. If you keep talking to her, she'll stay by your side. If you can't go on, just hunker down with her and turn your back to the wind. I'll be back for you later."

"Don't worry about us. Just go!"

— Chapter 35 —

Sheriff Withers was fuming. When the report came in that Brader was apparently fleeing his home in Telluride, Withers had been at the Mineral King surface plant, sixty miles from the action. When the avalanche hit, he was trapped on the far side of the slide, cut off from his headquarters. When Lyle Morrison radioed that Brader had brazenly driven through Ouray en route to the back basins, Withers was helpless to give chase. Now, standing on an exposed shelf road a half-mile from Camp Bird Mine, his progress was blocked by the Waterhole Slide.

When Lyle's message came through at 7:15 p.m., two of his deputies were with him on the wrong side of the avalanche. One was bringing rescue gear and dogs over the debris pile, one was pursuing an unknown driver near Rico and one was lying dead up at the Mineral King surface plant. With only one deputy on the slide's north side, he immediately radioed across the avalanche pile and instructed Deputy Ed Read to drive back to Ouray and join the chase on County Road 361. It had taken Read thirty minutes to reach the Waterhole Slide, where he reported the road was impassable and that snowmobiles would be needed to continue the pursuit. At the same time, an alert Montrose police officer had pulled over a tan Range Rover and confirmed that the driver had recently traveled through Red Mountain Pass. By the time the checkpoint had been set up in Ouray, the Range Rover was already halfway between Ouray and Ridgway. With the only missing vehicle now accounted for, the rescue mission became a CDOT clean-up mission.

The sheriff had spent fifteen nerve-racking minutes picking his way across the top of the unstable avalanche pile with Perry Yancey and Tim Vanderwall at his side. Commandeering the patrol vehicle that had transported the dogs up to the Riverside Slide, they drove down into Ouray. The process of loading two snowmobiles onto two separate trailers and hauling them up the shelf road toward the back basins had taken another forty minutes. Now, ninety minutes after Lyle Morrison's radio message from the CDOT barn, they were finally ready to join the chase.

While rescue squad member Vanderwall and Deputy Read unloaded the snowmobiles from the trailers, Yancey approached Sheriff Withers, who was standing at the edge of the road, shining his flashlight down at the wrecked Ford Explorer on the canyon floor.

"I think Vanderwall and I should be the ones to ride over that avalanche pile," Yancey said to the sheriff's back. "No offense to you or Ed, but Tim and I have more experience with snowmobiles."

Withers spun on his heels.

"Let me get this straight," he barked. "A felony suspect is on the loose because he gave one of my best deputies the slip. So now, instead of having the law on his heels, he's being chased by a damn snowplow driver and a florist. And if that's not bad enough, you want me to send an ice-climber after him while I sit here cooling my heels?"

"You won't be cooling your heels," Yancey explained patiently. "I'll be in contact for as long as the radio signal holds up. As soon as Tim and I can figure out which way Brader's headed, I'll let you know so you can figure out our next move. Don't take this the wrong way, but you're a lot better at managing a crisis than you are at driving a snowmobile."

Somewhat mollified by the deputy's reasoning, Withers nodded slowly. Given the rugged terrain and extreme weather conditions in his jurisdiction, the Sheriff's Department relied frequently on trained experts such as those in Ouray Mountain Rescue. Withers also knew his crack about Lyle was misplaced. As a young man, Withers had fought in the jungles of Southeast Asia with Lyle at his side. Thirty years later, if he had to pick one person to go into battle with, it would still be Lyle Morrison.

"I've got the state police standing by with air support in Montrose," Withers said. "Those fly boys are good, but the wind currents through these mountains are murder. Before I get them airborne, I'm going to need a better fix on where this chase is headed. Otherwise, they'll be looking for a needle in a haystack."

"Like I said, we'll radio you as soon as we have something to report. I gave Tim my extra piece, so we'll both be armed."

"Good," Withers replied. "I know for a fact that Brader owns a gun and Lyle doesn't. I want this thing ended peacefully, but I don't expect you to hold your fire if you're being shot at. And if you do have to use your weapon, make sure you put two holes in that son-of-a-bitch: one for me and one for Mark Turlington."

"You got it."

As Yancey and Vanderwall mounted the snowmobiles, Withers strode over to the white Jeep Cherokee. Seeing the Ouray County Sheriff Department decal on the driver's door, he punched it with his fist.

"To protect and serve," he muttered disgustedly. "We're not doing a whole lot of either tonight."

— Chapter 36 —

T rudging into the teeth of the wind gusting down from the summit of Imogene Pass, Lyle Morrison's face was a frozen mask. Ice pellets from swirling spindrift clung to his eyebrows and the stubble on his chin. His nostrils were frozen shut; his only option was to breathe through his mouth. Several times during the past ninety minutes, he had caught the toe of his snowshoes on the frozen crown of an icy mogul and fallen face-first into the snowpack. Rather than spending valuable time wiping the powder from his face, Lyle had allowed it to freeze to his sweat-drizzled forehead and cheeks.

In spite of the steady gale that swept along the basin floor, Lyle could feel the air becoming thinner all the time. As he trekked up the pitched bowl, it took larger gulps of the frozen San Juan Mountain air to sate his body's growing appetite for oxygen. Each time he inhaled, his fractured ribs caused him to wince in pain. His hamstrings and calf muscles burned with every step toward the summit. Without the aid of ski poles, he had nothing to lean against for either leverage or balance. Traversing a constant succession of steep mounds, Lyle had to crab-walk up the steepest inclines, using his gloved hands to stabilize himself before lifting his bulky snowshoes.

The debilitating effects of pain, exhaustion, and freezing cold were offset, however, by the rising tide of adrenaline coursing through him since he first realized he was gaining ground on Paul Brader. At first, the signs were circumstantial. Barely a quarter mile from the abandoned snowmobiles, Lyle saw that Brader was having trouble keeping his balance. Rather than maintaining a wide stance and lifting his snowshoes off the frozen ground, Brader was keeping his feet close together, sliding them along the snow like a cross-country skier; his tracks evinced that the younger man had been toppling into the snow frequently.

Lyle's hopes were buoyed also by the circuitous path Brader was taking to the summit. Clearly, he was taking pains to avoid scaling the dozens of steep mounds that rose from the basin floor. By circling the base of the sizable knolls, Brader was adding hundreds of steps to his journey. To Lyle, Brader's peregrinating snowshoe prints spoke volumes about the man's character.

"There's no easy way out of this one," he had commented aloud. "You gotta pay your dues."

After tracing the kidnapper's trail for a half-mile, Lyle opted to break a fresh trail along the basin floor, deciding that blazing a direct path over the mounds outweighed the benefit of continuing to walk in Brader's packed prints.

Throughout the tortuous slow-motion foot chase, Lyle divided his attention between Brader in front of him and Casey behind him. He had hoped to narrow the gap on Brader while keeping Casey in sight. Whenever he crested a ridgeline or mound, he made a quick estimate of the distance separating the three climbers. Ninety minutes ago, Brader was visible only as a faint speck on the chalky landscape. Now, at an altitude of 12,700 feet, roughly 400 vertical feet from the summit, Lyle was blazing a trail he hoped would bring him face-to-face with the criminal in a matter of minutes.

Even more amazing than the amount of ground he had gained on Brader was the astonishing pace that Casey had maintained throughout the two-and-a-half-mile ordeal. The first time he looked over his shoul-

der, she was struggling to keep her balance. But in spite of her inexperi-
ence with snowshoes, Lyle saw that Casey had chosen to follow the trail
he had broken rather than continue along Brader's less strenuous route.
Over the course of the past hour and a half, she had not only mastered
the art of climbing up vertical mounds in snowshoes, she had actually gained ground on Lyle. Each time he glanced behind him to see the
diminutive woman bent forward, her eyes focused on the trail in front of
her and Sandy following close behind, Lyle felt a sharp tug in his chest
—unrelated to his broken ribs. With a shorter stride and less muscular
frame, Casey was operating on sheer pluck and willpower, exhibiting
a measure of fortitude that put both Lyle Morrison and Paul Brader to
shame.

Lyle hoped that Brader's latest technical error would prove his undo-
ing. Two-thirds of a mile from the summit, Brader had veered left, plot-
ting a course toward the bowl's eastern rim. Through a thick squall of
swirling spindrift, he saw that Brader had located and was climbing up
the jeep road along the basin's far-left side: the path of least resistance to
the 13,114-foot summit. Lyle knew that the road climbed through a series
of steep switchbacks up to the southeast rim before making a sweeping
right turn across the bowl's southern face. By choosing to follow a familiar route rather than a direct route, Brader was not only wasting time,
he was allowing Lyle to climb undetected between the steep mounds,
ridgelines, and rock outcroppings in the basin's center.

Having made a beeline through the throat of the basin, Lyle was now
closer to the summit in terms of linear distance than Brader was. In Imogene Basin, however, linear distance was a poor standard by which to
measure travel time to the summit. The trail Lyle blazed had deposited
him at the foot of a sheer incline at the southernmost edge of the basin
floor. Scanning the rim of the basin directly above the steep slope, he was
able to trace the faint outline of the jeep road running horizontally from
left to right. He knew that if he scaled the slope quickly, he would be able
to intercept Brader 200 vertical feet from where he was now standing.
Lyle stepped forward and mounted the wall of snow.

As he began his ascent, Lyle quickly realized his snowshoes were ill suited for the severely pitched slope. The bulky, blunt-toed shoes made it difficult to kick footholds deep enough to support his weight, so he unfastened the snowshoes and let them slide down to the base of the slope. When he stomped his unencumbered boot into the face of the incline, his entire leg sank into the snow. He realized that he was actually scaling a deep snowdrift stacked vertically against the entire face of the slope. With his boots breaking through the frozen shell of ice that coated the drift, each ensuing step caused him to sink knee-deep into the 200-foot tall pile that had formed against the contours of the cliff wall.

By the time he had climbed 100 feet above the basin's floor, Lyle's pant legs were caked in snow. His arms were fatigued from constantly having to pull himself out of the craters his boots were punching along the pitched surface of the drift. Every few minutes, he had to stop to satisfy his lungs' ravenous thirst for oxygen. During one such break he heard a faint whistle from below, followed by a succession of barks. Looking down the slope, he saw that Casey and Sandy had arrived at the base of the drift. Lyle waved his hands in front of his chest, urging Casey not to attempt the climb. The rescue squad leader knew he was tempting fate with each hole he pierced into the unanchored snowpack.

Lyle continued his ascent, acutely aware of the pain in his ribcage and the effect it was having on his breathing. The climb was taking much longer than he had anticipated. Given the altitude, he was driving himself at a dangerous pace; he could hear the rapid thumping of his heart echoing in his ears. Convinced he could not afford to stop and catch his breath, he battled the torpor now spreading through his body like intravenous anesthesia. His climbing technique became hurried and slipshod. Instead of carefully anchoring one leg into the snowpack before lifting the other, Lyle scrambled through the drift, using all four limbs to propel himself up the slope.

After climbing 185 vertical feet, he was able to see the near edge of the jeep road, 15 feet above. He planted his legs firmly in the snowpack and slowly raised himself from his stooped climbing posture. From his vantage point beneath the shoulder of the road, he had a clear view of the jeep road as it cut a downward-arcing horizontal path from east to west.

Based on Brader's previous pace, Lyle had expected to see him emerging atop the switchbacks to his left and snowshoeing toward him along the narrow road. Seeing no sign of Brader either to the left or to the right, Lyle began to doubt his assumptions. Only two possible explanations came to mind: either Brader had elected to take an alternate route to the summit or Lyle had failed to reach the road in time to intercept him.

The matter was settled when he heard a voice call to him from above.

"That hill must've been a bitch to climb. Need a second to catch your breath, old man?"

Looking straight up, Lyle saw Paul Brader standing on the edge of the road. He had been lying in wait, hiding directly above him at the far shoulder of the jeep road: the only part of the road that Lyle couldn't see from where he was standing. Brader lowered the hood of his black ski jacket and the sheen of his slick black hair reflected the moonlight. But Lyle's attention was focused on the shiny silver pistol in his bare right hand. At a range of only fifteen feet, Lyle knew that Brader wouldn't have to be a skilled marksman to hit him. Buried up to his knees in the sloping snowdrift, Lyle's options were few. His only chance for survival was to dive back down the slope and hope for the best, but that would dash any hope of reaching Dr. Philips before Brader. The fact that Brader was attempting to mount the summit of Imogene Pass had confirmed Lyle's suspicion the doctor was being held captive in the dilapidated power hut atop the southern rim of the bowl, 250 vertical feet above him. Lyle saw no alternative but to stand his ground and hope that he could goad the gun-wielding kidnapper into making a tactical error.

"I'd say you're the one who needs to catch his breath. You had a half-mile head start on me."

Brader laughed. "I didn't know that I was being followed until I saw someone climbing that hill. And imagine how thrilled I am to see that it's my new buddy: the snowplow-driving vigilante. For a second there, I thought I might have to shoot a sheriff or a deputy; you know, someone of consequence."

Lyle had to shout above the howling wind to be heard. "So, how many people are you prepared to kill tonight? In case you haven't noticed, the game's over. I'm the first person to reach you, but there's plenty more on the way."

"No doubt. As soon as I ran into Casey Bailey down in Ouray, I knew I was in deep shit. I expect this place will be chock full of cops in an hour or two, but that's all the time I need."

"It's a little late to start covering your tracks. If Dr. Philips isn't already dead, it won't do you a bit of good to kill him now. And you're not going to be able to hide his body up here, either. Every move you make will be imprinted in the snow."

"I fully expect to be sitting in a jail before the night's over," Brader snarled. "These could be my last few hours as a free man for a long time, so I'm going to do everything I can to make things tougher for whoever's going to prosecute me. You'd be amazed what a good defense lawyer can do if you give them a crack or two to work with."

"You're just digging a deeper hole for yourself," Lyle said. "You kill me and now you've got two bodies to dispose of."

Brader waved his gun over Lyle's head, pointing further down the slope.

"Actually, three."

Lyle turned to look in the direction of Brader's gesture. Casey was standing at the foot of the drift watching helplessly as a crisis was unfolding 200 feet above her.

"I'm not stupid enough to leave an eyewitness behind who could nail me in court. Wave her on up here."

"I'm not waving her anywhere," Lyle replied defiantly.

"Let me make myself clear," Brader shouted in a deliberate tone. "If you don't convince Casey to climb up here, I will shoot you in the head."

"Let me make *myself* clear. You'd better be a damn good shot with that pistol, because this is as close as you're ever going to get to her."

Infuriated by Lyle's intransigence, Brader made his move. He shifted his weight forward and widened his stance, stabilizing his snowshoes in anticipation of the gun's recoil. He aimed the barrel of the handgun at Lyle's chest.

The Vietnam veteran's reaction was instinctive and instantaneous.

As Brader fingered the trigger, Lyle dove to his left, hurling himself into the snowdrift. He heard a loud explosion of gunpowder just as his body broke the crust of the deep snowpack. As he sank into three feet of packed powder, Lyle heard the muffled report of a second gunshot. Knowing that the thin blanket of snow afforded him no protection from an accurately fired round, Lyle twisted his body beneath the snow in an attempt to roll down the slope, away from Brader.

Suddenly, Lyle felt himself falling instead of rolling. The ground beneath him sprung open like a trap door. He felt a sickening sensation as the earth below seemed to give way. In a rush of clarity, Lyle realized he was trapped inside the starting zone of an avalanche. Oddly, he found himself wondering whether the slide had been triggered by his 235-pound body crashing into the snowpack or by the sharp concussion of Brader's pistol. Regardless, Lyle knew that he was now at the slide's mercy.

Jumbled fragments of avalanche-related information raced through Lyle's mind as he was pulled, spun and thrust inexorably down the slope. Although he had witnessed dozens of avalanches in Red Mountain Pass and pulled both corpses and survivors from the steely death grip of debris piles, Lyle had never been trapped inside the turbulent core of a runaway slide. Flashing back to training manuals he had studied, Lyle now knew with frightening certainty that the documented accounts of how it felt to be ensnared by the grip of an avalanche were neither embellishment nor hyperbole.

Engulfed in the rapidly crumbling wall of snow, Lyle sensed he was part of the avalanche, his body now a minor component of the slide's overall physics. The flow of avalanche material encasing his body seemed more like water than snow. The sensation was comparable to plunging headlong through a long stretch of river rapids. Lyle's head bobbed to the surface but was sucked back into the surging flow before he could draw a breath. Unable to open his eyes beneath the surface, he used his limbs like antennae to determine his body's position, direction and velocity. When he could no longer discern whether he was sliding on his back or stomach, Lyle's disorientation was complete. Although the entire event transpired in a matter of seconds, Lyle felt as if his tumbling, jerking, pounding ride would never cease. When it did, he knew immediately that he was in dire trouble.

The avalanche ended as abruptly as it had begun. Snow that had been flowing like water congealed instantly into a solid mass, trapping Lyle in its frozen grip. Ratcheted tightly into the core of the debris pile, Lyle felt pressure against every part of his body -- especially his face. In the darkness, he could not tell if his eyelids were open or if the surrounding snow had plastered them shut. He tried to spit out a mouthful of snow he had inhaled, but the snowpack was flush against his lips.

Lyle knew he had to act quickly. Unless he managed to free himself, he would suffocate in less than thirty minutes. From his rescue squad training, he was aware that only a small percentage of avalanche victims survive long enough to die from hypothermia; the vast majority run out of air trying to escape from their icy tomb. He tried wiggling his limbs, hoping to discover that part of his body was sticking out of the debris pile. His right arm was pinned against his chest, his hand clenched in a fist just beneath his chin. His left arm was splayed out away from his body, firmly encased in the snowpack. Both of his legs were fully extended. When he tried to move his feet, he found they too were locked in place by the dense crush of snow. Even though the slide path had been only 200 feet long, the resulting debris pile was deep enough to engulf and paralyze his entire body.

Lyle decided that his best course of action would be to free his hands and try to move them toward his face in order to carve out a pocket of air. As he dug his fingernails into the ice and flexed his hands, he tried to assemble clues as to his orientation in the pile. But in the icy blackness, he couldn't tell if he was buried headfirst, feet-first, faceup or facedown. Lyle knew he was facing every avalanche victim's worst nightmare: buried alive without a clue as to which way to dig.

•••

From the base of the slope, Casey tried to make sense of what she had just witnessed. At first, the two silhouetted shapes appeared to be talking. Their voices were swept into the night air, making it impossible for her to tell if they were talking or shouting. Without warning, two loud pops accompanied a pair of bright flashes from above. She watched in horror as Lyle tumbled to one side. At the sound of gunfire, Sandy began howling uncontrollably, as if she knew her owner was in grave danger. Suspecting she had just watched Lyle being murdered in cold blood, Casey frantically stormed the frozen hillside.

Barely five feet into her ascent, Casey's snowshoes lost their grip on the snowpack and she slid back down to the foot of the slope. A deep rumbling noise drew her attention to the top of the incline. She had seen enough footage of avalanches on television to recognize a snow-slide in progress. By the time she realized she was standing in the avalanche's killing zone, the slide was already rippling down the cliff wall.

Casey spun around and desperately searched for an avenue of escape. Pushing off with her right foot, she pointed her snowshoes toward a craggy rock outcropping thirty feet from the base of the crumbling snow-drift. She reached down and grabbed Sandy's collar, lifting the Labrador off its feet. After four more strong kicks with her right leg, Casey had generated enough speed to use her snowshoes like skis, plowing through the surface layer of snow. Bringing her feet together, she leaned forward with Sandy in her arms, hoping to gain even more momentum down the moderately sloping grade.

The jagged rock formation she was sliding toward jutted out from the basin floor at a sharp angle, its triangular-shaped tip pointing toward the northern rim of the bowl. Sticking eight feet out of the surrounding snowpack, the six-foot-wide outcropping was the only source of shelter in sight. The high-pitched sound of Sandy's barking was eclipsed by the furious roar of the collapsing snow. Feeling the ground beneath her beginning to vibrate, Casey used her right snowshoe like a canoe paddle, frantically digging it into the snow to propel her forward. Without looking back, Casey could tell she was in a desperate race against the flow of advancing snow being pushed ahead of the avalanche's main body.

Ten feet from the left flank of the outcropping, the spearhead of the avalanche flow struck the back of her legs. As she fell forward, Casey tossed Sandy toward the front of the forward-leaning rock formation. Scrambling on all fours, Casey felt the ground swelling beneath her as the snow's forward-most wave washed along the basin floor. She rounded the left edge of the slanting slab, then dove to her right, joining Sandy behind the up-heaved column of the Earth's crust. Casey huddled with Sandy in anticipation of the avalanche's violent impact against the rock. She was sure this was not the first time the precariously titled crag had borne the brunt of an avalanche's fury and she prayed it would be able to withstand another blast.

The ground shook as the core of the slide thundered down into the basin. As Casey clutched Sandy to her chest, a thick tide of snow rumbled past the outcropping. The avalanche flowed around the rock formation like a stream, depositing vast piles of snow around the shelter. As the vibrations from the initial avalanche rippled through the snowpack, Casey could hear secondary slides being triggered in lower sections of the bowl.

When the ground stopped moving, three feet of new snow had piled up around the shelter's perimeter, creating a thick ringed wall that mirrored the outline of the overhanging rock. Casey got to her feet and hoisted Sandy off the ground, depositing her on top of the elevated snowpack surrounding the crag. Boosting herself over the newly formed wall, Casey looked to her left. Five minutes ago, a smooth shell of pure white snow covered the slope Lyle had ascended. The entire incline was now laid bare, revealing the dusty gray expanse of the basin's formidable southern wall. The towering snowdrift that once angled up toward the jeep road had completely crumbled. Having shed its frozen rind, the deeply creviced cliff wall loomed before her like a rampart. The drift, sculpted over a period of five months by snow and wind, had been reduced to a pile of rubble within a matter of seconds.

Trying to catch her breath and calm herself, Casey walked toward the base of the cliffs. She saw that the intervening snowpack was now pitched at a much more severe angle. During her hasty retreat to the rock outcropping, the downward grade had been maddeningly moderate. Tracing her route in the opposite direction, however, Casey had to dig her snowshoes' crampons into the steep snowpack to keep from sliding backward.

Failing to see any sign of Lyle, Casey felt her throat begin to tighten and her pulse race. Walking in a daze up the twenty-foot-tall pile of densely packed snow, she heard whimpering noises behind her. Sandy was staring at the base of the cliff and making a pitiful whining sound. Recalling Lyle's comment about the Labrador's aborted rescue training, Casey shouted a command to the dog.

"Find him!"

Sandy barked, but didn't move.

Casey bent down and placed her gloved hands over the animal's nose, hoping that Sandy could pick up Lyle's scent on the gloves he had lent her.

"Find him! Find Lyle!"

Sandy ran in circles around Casey, but made no attempt to search for her master.

Casey grabbed the dog once again, unzipped her borrowed jacket and rubbed Sandy's nose over the inner lining. She pointed toward the base of the cliff wall and hollered a litany of commands.

"Find him! Find Lyle! Get him! Search him out! Go!"

Sandy suddenly darted off, sniffing the ground in the direction that Casey was pointing. As Casey gave chase, the dog continued smelling the top of the snowpack, crisscrossing the upward sloping debris pile in a seemingly random manner. Casey continued to shout encouragement.

"That's it! Get him. Find Lyle."

Sandy trotted to the left, then switched directions and ran to the base of the cliffs, all the while keeping her nose to the ground. Turning away from the cliff walls, she made a beeline across the debris pile toward Casey, barking and wagging her tail excitedly. Assuming that the dog had confused her scent with Lyle's, Casey shouted in frustration.

"Not me! Find Lyle."

Ten feet in front of Casey, the cream-colored lab stopped abruptly and began pawing at the ground. Sandy's barking grew louder as she tried to dig deeper into the snowpack. Casey quickly unlatched her boots from the snowshoes' bindings and ran to the spot Sandy was frantically clawing. Dropping to her knees, Casey pushed Sandy aside and started digging with one of her snowshoes, using the curved metal frame of the snowshoe's toe as a shovel.

— Chapter 37 —

I t took Brader twenty minutes to reach the short but steep incline that led to summit of Imogene Pass. The barely perceptible jeep road was crosscut by a series of towering drifts, each of which had to be surmounted with extreme caution. Because the road crossed several talus piles, Brader knew the snowpack was resting atop an unstable base. Along the bowl's southern rim, the penalty for any misstep was death—a plunge down sheer cliffs to the basin floor.

During his ascent to the dark hut on the Ouray side of the summit, Brader found himself reliving his confrontation with Lyle Morrison. He replayed the scene over and over in his mind, each time milking a fresh surge of elation from the decisive victory over his brawny foe. The simple act of squeezing the pistol's trigger while pointing the barrel at Morrison's chest had given him the same rush of raw power that he felt earlier in the day as he stood over Sam Moultrie's prostrate body. He found delight in recalling the feeling of the gun's forceful recoil against his hand, the sulfuric smell of gunpowder in his nostrils, and the look of dread on the snowplow driver's face. Even though he wasn't certain that his bullets had found their mark, Brader reveled in the knowledge he had made amends for his pathetic showing in his initial encounter with Morrison. His only regret was that the avalanche had swept the man away before he could jump down from the road to administer the coup de grace to his skull.

While the slide had robbed him of his ultimate gratification, Brader saw the avalanche as a sign that his luck was beginning to change. As the hillside disintegrated below him, Brader saw Casey Bailey trapped at the base of the slide path. The thick plume of snow the avalanche had sprayed into the air had obscured his view, but when it finally cleared there was no sign of either Lyle or Casey: the only eyewitnesses who could place him in Imogene Basin.

Reaching the corrugated metal-skinned shack, Brader made a quick inspection of the decrepit structure. The section of the hut wall that Dr. Philips had pried open had been bent back to its original position and there were no fresh footprints anywhere to be found. Although the steady gale blowing over the summit could obliterate prints in minutes, Brader was confident the doctor had not ventured out of the shack since the onset of the storm.

Removing his snowshoes and walking to his left, Brader saw that the old mailbox was now only three feet above the snow's surface. He cleared the drifting snow away from the steel pole and located the padlocks securing the two lengths of chain. The pole bore the telltale scratches of Dr. Philips's frantic attempts to free himself, but the ice-covered padlocks and thick truck chains had not been defeated. They were buried under eight inches of new snow: another sign that Jim Philips hadn't been out of the power hut in several hours. Tracing the path of the chains to the hut, Brader crouched at the opening in the shack's east wall. He pulled slowly on the chain that was threaded beneath the planks, taking up the slack between the wall and Dr. Philips's body. He gave a powerful tug and listened for a response from inside the hut. The only sound to be heard was the plinking of wind-whipped spindrift against the metal skin of the engineer's shack.

He shouted urgently, "Jim. Are you there? Talk to me!"

There was no reply from the other side of the wall.

Convinced that Jim Philips was either dead or near-dead, Brader circled the twelve-by-eight-foot hut, trudging through knee-high snowdrifts until he reached the southwest corner of the shack. From the top of a tall snowdrift piled against the building, he could see through the three-foot-square hole in the rickety structure's slanted roof. Aided by a shaft of thin moonlight, Brader could make out the dark outline of Dr. Philips's body. His head and shoulders were leaning against the far wall, the dark blue blanket draped around his face and upper body like a shawl. His legs were stretched out on the ground, unprotected by the blanket. The hole in the roof had allowed the storm to funnel six inches of snow on the cabin floor. Brader saw that the doctor's feet were nearly buried in snow, the toes of his woolen socks sticking out of a drift that had piled around his legs.

The sight of Dr. Philips's lifeless body brought a smile to Brader's lips. Freezing to death, Philips had spared Brader from having to shoot him or strangle him with a length of chain. While not opposed to using either tactic, Brader preferred that any future autopsy would assign the cause of death to acute hypothermia. And by tossing his body into the deep canyon on the Telluride side of the summit, Brader hoped the corpse would begin to decompose before it was discovered. By that time, the handcuff marks on Jim Philips's wrists might no longer be obvious.

Brader continued his clockwise circuit to the shack's north side, which faced the deep bowl of Imogene Basin. A wooden door was centered in the twelve-foot-wide wall at the front of the structure. Although Dr. Philips's tether kept him from reaching the door, Brader and Sam Moultrie had opted to fasten the door shut from the outside with a metal hasp and padlock. Selecting a key from his key ring, Brader unlocked the padlock, shoved it into his pocket and pulled on the rickety door. It wouldn't budge. Two feet of snow and ice had piled against the bottom of the door since he sealed it shut three nights ago.

Brader dropped to his knees and started scooping snow away from the door with his gloves. It took him five minutes to dig and pound his way through the nearly frozen drift. When he was finally able to swing the door open, its rusty hinges squealed in protest. Before entering the shack, Brader paused in the doorway to catch his breath. At an altitude of over 13,000 feet, the simple chore of clearing away the snowdrift had left him gasping for air.

Although weak moonlight slanted into the shack from the hole in the roof to his right, the shack's left side was still dark. Dr. Philips's body hadn't moved since he had peeked through the roof. Taking two steps to his left, Brader stopped short of the doctor's outstretched legs and, with a swing of his boot, kicked hard against the soles of the physician's socks. Jim Philips's torso slid to the left along the wall in response to the kick, leaving him slumped against the northeast corner of the hut. Seeing no further movement under the blanket, Brader assumed the force of the blow had shifted the dead man's body.

He kneeled next to the doctor and lifted his right leg out of the snow-drift, exposing the chain that was looped around his ankle. Since the pad-lock securing the chain around Dr. Philips's leg was encrusted with snow, he had to work the key back and forth before the steel loop finally sprang from the body of the lock. He unwound the chain from his prisoner's ankle and pocketed the padlock. He intended to dispose of the hardware he had brought to the summit on Tuesday night, eliminating as much evidence from the crime scene as possible.

Straddling Dr. Philips's legs, Brader looked down at the blanket wrapped around his head, shoulders and chest, relieved that he didn't have to see the man's face. Knowing he would have to lift the body onto his shoulders and carry it to the top of the steep canyon wall, Brader steeled himself by taking a deep breath before touching the man again.

Grabbing the tightly wound blanket and pulling it to the right, Brader managed to return Dr. Philips's body to a sitting position. The man's arms swung down from beneath the blanket and settled limply in his lap. Below the sleeves of the doctor's brown tweed jacket, two pairs of handcuffs shackled his bare wrists. As Brader inserted a key into the pad-lock that connected the center of the handcuffs to the eight-foot chain, he noticed a slight trembling in Dr. Philips's right index finger.

Suspecting that he was merely witnessing the onset of rigor mortis, Brader nonetheless decided to proceed cautiously. He held the center of the handcuffs in his right hand and removed his left glove. Brader lowered the doctor's right hand until the tips of the man's fingers were touching the palm of his bare hand. He pushed his palm up against the physician's fingers, expecting the joints and muscles to be locked due to post-mortem rigidity. Instead, each of the man's ice-cold fingers bent easily at the knuckles. Suddenly, Dr. Philips's fingers spread wide and his frozen digits curled around Brader's hand.

The sight of a presumed dead man grabbing his hand sent Brader into a frenzy. He let out a startled yelp, jerked his hand away and leapt to his feet. Pulling his revolver from his waistband, he trained the gun on the still-shrouded figure.

"Don't move an inch!" he sputtered breathlessly. "I'm going to take that blanket off, but if you even twitch, I swear I'll kill you."

He inched closer to the doctor, found an exposed corner of the fabric and unwound the blanket roughly. After two circuits of the man's head and shoulders, he yanked the rest of the blanket away in a single violent tug. Dr. Philips's body jerked forward, bent at the waist with his face down near his knees. Brader watched in astonishment as the elderly man slowly lifted his head, then raised his shoulders until his back rested against the wooden planks of the shack's wall.

Dr. Philips's thinning gray hair was plastered against his icy scalp. His mouth was open, frozen in a permanent expression of surprise. Brader could see his tongue lolling behind frozen lips, as if he was trying to speak. The doctor's dark eyes rolled lazily before fixing on Brader. He attempted to lift his shackled wrists, but was unable to raise them more than a few inches off his lap. Brader saw that he made no attempt to move his legs or pull his feet out of the snowdrift.

"The worst is almost over," Brader told him. "I'm going to unlock that chain from your handcuffs and carry you outside. If you cooperate, things will go a lot smoother. You got me?"

Jim Philips made no attempt to respond. Even his tongue had stopped moving. He continued to stare at the kidnapper with mouth agape. Brader returned his gun to the back of his waistband. Moving quickly, he opened the padlock then patted Dr. Philips's jacket and pants pockets, searching unsuccessfully for the physician's pager. He draped the blanket over his shoulders and pulled on the handcuffs, raising Dr. Philips's hindquarters off the ground. His prisoner made no attempt to cooperate; his legs were locked in their stiff, outstretched position. Brader bent down on one knee and folded Jim Philips over his shoulder, bending him at the waist. Standing up with his captive draped over his frame, Brader searched the hut floor for anything he might have overlooked. The only incriminating evidence he saw were the two lengths of chain that snaked under the wall.

He adjusted Dr. Philips's body to center the burden over his right shoulder, then ran his hands over the doctor's back pockets but didn't find either a pager or a wallet. Exiting the power hut, Brader kicked the door shut with his boot. Breathing heavily, Brader carried the doctor through knee-deep snowdrifts to the southeast corner of the building. Five feet from the mailbox, he felt Dr. Philips's hands patting the back of his jacket. Startled, he suddenly realized that his business partner was groping for his gun. Despite his enfeebled condition, the doctor was obviously lucid enough to take note of where Brader had placed his weapon. Feeling his jacket being lifted and the pistol inching out of his waistband, Brader hurled Philips to the ground near the base of the mailbox. As his back collided against the frozen ground, Philips's head snapped backward, striking the steel mailbox post with a sharp crack. The impact jarred the pistol from his frostbitten fingers, and Brader quickly leaped over the doctor's body and retrieved it from the snow.

Wheeling around to face the doctor, he saw that the elderly man was lying faceup, barely able to move. The back of his head buried in the snow, Philips stared toward the heavens, blinking his eyes continuously as if signaling a message to the constellations in the clear night sky.

Brader shoved the heel of his boot on Jim Philips's forehead, pinning his skull against the snow.

"That was not a smart move, Jimmy boy," Brader taunted. "I'm your only hope of getting out of here alive and you try to shoot me with my own gun. Talk about looking a gift horse in the mouth."

Dr. Philips tried to speak, but his tongue and cracked lips did not cooperate.

Holding the pistol in his right hand, Brader grabbed the center of the handcuffs with his left hand and pulled on the shackles so Dr. Philips's arms were extended over his head. He then dragged his prisoner through the snow as if pulling a sled. He slid Jim Philips onto a bank of untrammeled snow ten feet to the left of the mailbox. The doctor's body sunk into the soft powder.

"Not one move," Brader admonished sternly. "Lie right there; this'll only take a second."

Brader walked over to the shack's east wall, yanked the two chains from under the base of the wall and coiled them into a loop as he walked toward the mailbox, all the while keeping a close eye on Dr. Philips. Satisfied he did not pose a threat, Brader knelt at the base of the mailbox. He set his pistol atop the coiled chains, fished the key ring out of his jacket pocket, and tried to unfasten the padlocks securing the chains to the steel post.

A thick layer of ice had formed around both padlocks, making it impossible for Brader to insert the key. He banged the locks against the post to try and shatter the icy coating. The sound of metal striking metal rang out above the constant wailing of the wind currents that blew over the apex of the summit. After knocking off the bulk of the ice, Brader tried to force his key into one of the padlocks. Tiny granules of ice were still lodged in the keyhole, preventing the key from sliding into the locking mechanism. Knowing that the chains and padlocks might be traced to a recent purchase he had made at a hardware store in Telluride, Brader didn't want to leave them behind. His frustration mounting, the kidnapper continued slamming the frozen lock against the post.

"Open, you son-of-a-bitch!"

• • •

Lyle's lungs were burning with each unsteady stride as he stumbled up the slope to the power hut with Casey only steps behind. Twenty minutes earlier, he had been desperately clawing his way up out of the debris pile while Casey dug down toward him. When their bare hands finally met eighteen inches below the surface, Lyle was never so grateful for the touch of another human. It took Casey another three minutes to dig, pull and lift him out of the icy tomb.

Wheezing for air, shivering, and covered in snow, Lyle had followed Casey to the foot of the exposed slope that led up to the jeep road. Without the thick, towering snowdrift to conceal its contours and crevices, it was easier to scale than it had been on Lyle's first attempt. Still, the slippery hand-over-hand ascent was torturous. Lyle felt himself becoming clumsier and more light-headed with every step. It was only Casey's urgent pleas and shouts of encouragement that had kept him going.

• • •

With his back to the basin and his attention riveted on the recalcitrant lock, Brader didn't hear the faint pattern of crunching sounds over the sharp sound of the padlock striking the steel post. It wasn't until he tried to insert the key for a third time that he first heard the rapid footfalls behind him. Still kneeling, Brader pivoted in time to see an immense shape charging at him. Momentarily frozen in panic, Brader could see that Lyle's long hair was caked in snow and his large white teeth were clenched in a wicked smile. He watched in horror as his attacker's eyes grew wider and a guttural scream erupted deep from within his chest.

By the time Brader reacted, Lyle was fifteen feet away and closing fast. With the snowplow driver's war whoop ringing in his ears, Brader spun around to grab his pistol. In a single fluid motion, he grabbed the weapon and half-dove, half-twisted onto his back to face his assailant.

As Brader brought his right arm up, Lyle left his feet, hurtling through the air with his arms outstretched. He managed to grab Brader's right wrist with both hands as his right shoulder collided with the kidnapper's chest. When Brader squeezed the trigger, his arm was pointed to the right, having been jerked sideways by two strong hands. The gunshot sailed harmlessly over the eastern rim of the basin. Using his left hand to pin Brader's arm against the snow, Lyle swung his right forearm, delivering a savage uppercut to Brader's chin. Blood spurted from Brader's mouth the instant Lyle's forearm sandwiched his tongue between his teeth.

With Brader still reeling from the blow, Lyle grabbed the gun from his hand and tossed it over his shoulder.

"I'll get it!"

Having just reached the top of the slope, Casey Bailey snatched the weapon from the ground. She grabbed the handle of the gun with both hands and aimed it tentatively at the two combatants.

"Get off me!" Brader pleaded, spitting dark red blood onto the glistening white snow. "I'll give you guys anything you want! We can split things three ways. Forget about him. He's already lived his life. It's time to start thinking about yourselves."

Lyle squatted over the kidnapper and pressed his hands against either side of Brader's head with his thumbs locked under the man's chin. As he began lifting the man off the ground, Brader pawed against the snow in search of something to grab hold of. The only solid object he could find was a coil of chain. As his backside was lifted off the ground, the coil began to unwind between his hands. The pressure of Lyle's viselike grip against the younger man's skull increased as he lifted Brader to his feet.

The instant he was able to gain solid footing, Brader drove his right knee into Lyle's groin with a loud grunt. Instead of buckling over in pain, Lyle grimaced slightly, then broke into a wide grin as he lifted Brader's face so that it was level with his own. Brader's boots were now swinging above the snow and the weight of his entire body was supported by Lyle's hands, which were clasped against his jaw.

"I made you a promise earlier today," Lyle stated matter-of-factly as he stared into the struggling man's eyes. "You've abused and tortured a good man and I'm gonna kill you for it."

Realizing he was still holding the end of the eight-foot chain in his hands, Brader reached between Lyle's arms and looped the chain around the back of the big man's neck. He grabbed the chain on either side of Lyle's neck and crossed his hands around the snowplow driver's throat. Using all of his strength, he pulled on both sides of the chain, trying to crush the man's windpipe.

As the metal links dug into his neck, Lyle's face turned dark crimson. His eyes seemed ready to burst out of their sockets. He tried to loosen the man's grip on the chain by butting his head into Brader's face, but Brader only twisted harder. What started as a low rumble in Lyle's throat grew into a deep growl that Brader could feel against his face.

Seeing that the two furious combatants were at a stalemate, Casey grabbed the pistol by the barrel, stepped forward and in a lightning-quick move, hammered the handle of the Beretta up into Brader's face, driving the kidnapper's nasal bone back into his skull at a deadly angle. Brader jerked, convulsed, and then went limp.

With Brader's boasts about the skill and cunning of his attorneys still fresh in his mind, Lyle carried the insensate body closer to the mailbox. He adjusted his grip on Brader's frame, wrapping his left arm around the man's head and his right arm around his shoulders, leaving his legs dangling to the ground. Lyle stretched Brader's neck until it was taut, then bent over and charged the mailbox post as if it was a tackling dummy. As he drove Brader's neck against the steel post with all of the force he could muster, Lyle could hear the loud *crack* of Brader's vertebrae.

"Give me his jacket, and yours too," Casey called as she peeled off her red rescue squad jacket and tucked it around Dr. Philips's body.

Philips stared up at Casey, a glimmer of recognition flashing in his eyes. He lifted his hands to her face and moved his tongue across his mouth to spread moisture over his cracked, frozen lips.

"Don't try to talk," Casey said, her eyes beginning to water. "We're gonna take good care of you, and we'll get you out of here as soon as we can."

Seeing the purplish color of his exposed hands, Casey took off her gloves and started rubbing his fingers in her hands.

"Slip your gloves on his hands," Lyle advised, placing Brader's jacket beneath the physician's head and wrapping his own around Philips's legs. "Rubbing his skin will do more damage than good."

Suddenly, the sound of the wind blowing over the summit of Imogene Pass was drowned out by a rhythmic beating noise. Lyle and Casey looked up into the sky just as a bright beam of light swept over them.

As Lyle used hand signals to guide the helicopter's descent to a flat section of the summit, Casey lay on top of Dr. Philips to protect him from the fury of the rotor blade-induced snow squall. Her face against his frozen cheeks, she whispered assurances in his ear.

"See? Help is already here. You just hang in there and stay with us."

When the helicopter touched down, Lyle yanked open the pilot's door and screamed at the state police pilot, "We need Life Flight *now*!"

— Chapter 38 —

The Life Flight helicopter lifted off into the thin air, its rotating blades creating a virtual whiteout on the summit of Imogene Pass. Inside the helicopter, a black plastic body bag containing Paul Brader's corpse lay horizontally on the floor of its passenger compartment.

With her feet wedged between the body bag and the base of her seat, a Life Flight paramedic used a variety of instruments to monitor Dr. Philips's vital signs. As she had suspected, her conventional thermometer was useless in gauging the man's core body temperature since it was well below the range of a non-hypothermic thermometer. She also saw that Jim Philips's pulse was thin and his blood pressure was alarmingly low. His pupillary reaction was slow and he appeared both confused and lethargic.

Fifty feet above the summit, the snout of the copter dipped toward the Red Mountains, flew over the basin's eastern rim, then banked to the left, setting a direct course for Montrose.

As soon as the Life Flight helicopter cleared the summit, the police helicopter lifted off from the floor of Imogene Basin. With only enough room for one helicopter at the summit, the police helicopter had retreated to the basin floor when the Life Flight helicopter arrived on its mission of mercy.

Alerted by Lyle that his dog was stranded at the base of the cliffs, the helicopter pilot had not been surprised when Sandy came bounding toward the helicopter, braving the downdraft from the craft's rotor blades.

As the helicopter climbed vertically alongside the basin cliffs, Lyle and Casey slumped against the outside wall of the power hut. Too exhausted to speak, Casey took a long look at her surroundings. She knew that Imogene Pass wouldn't be accessible again until July, when the snowpack melted enough to allow four-wheel travel through the basin. The tale of Dr. Philips's kidnapping would undoubtedly be broadcast throughout Southwest Colorado, making the crumbling power hut a tempting destination for curious residents and enterprising jeep tour operators alike.

Casey walked away from the east-facing wall until she was ten feet from the shack, then turned around. Staring at the lonely structure near the crest of the windblown summit, she was amazed that the shack had survived a century of brutal winters and decades of scavenging artifact hunters. She walked slowly toward the mailbox, her legs stiff and aching from the arduous trek through the bowl and the climb up the icy cliff wall.

As Lyle looked on, Casey unlatched the mailbox door and reached inside. She scooped the contents of the box into her left hand. As the fixed landing light from the descending police helicopter bathed Casey in bright light, she held her hands aloft so Lyle could see. Between her fingers, Casey was clutching Dr. Philips's black pager, his wallet, a ballpoint pen and what looked like a business card. Casey flipped the card over, looked at it for several seconds and then tucked it into the vest pocket of her jacket.

• • •

From the Waterhole Slide, Bill Withers had been tracking the progress of the state police and Life Flight crews on the summit. He radioed to Perry Yancey and Tim Vanderwall, who were bivouacked on the northern rim of the Imogene Basin.

"Okay, men, you can head on back now," he said. "Looks like things are under control. Take it easy on the way down; we don't want to lose anybody at this stage of the game."

"Sorry again, Sheriff," Yancey replied. "I should've had you call in the state police as soon as we saw the tracks were heading to Imogene, but I never thought they had a chance of making it to the basin. You wouldn't believe how bad this road is. I kept expecting to see their tracks disappearing into the canyon."

"It's amazing what desperation can make you do," Withers said, then added, "Deputy Read will be waiting on you. I'm taking one of the trucks up to the Montrose Hospital. I've got an old friend I need to catch up with."

— Chapter 39 —

M ontrose Municipal Hospital's main lobby was filled throughout the day. Dr. Philips's friends, neighbors, and patients had shared cramped waiting areas and cafeteria tables with news reporters and investigators from various law enforcement agencies. The bizarre tale of the elderly physician's abduction, confinement and rescue had been told, retold and mistold since the early morning hours.

Although Jim Philips's physical condition kept him from receiving visitors, the throng of well-wishers and curiosity-seekers continued to wait for word of a prognosis or change in status. Philips was listed officially as in critical condition. When visiting hours ended at 7:00 p.m., clusters of Dr. Philips's acquaintances from Ouray, Ridgway, Montrose and Silverton began their separate journeys home, knowing little more about his long-term prognosis than when they had arrived.

Once the Intensive Care lounge had been cleared, Casey, Lyle, and Sheriff Withers moved to the sparsely appointed waiting room to continue their vigil. They hadn't slept since arriving at the hospital the previous night, and had spent the day shuttling between Dr. Philips's bedside and the Intensive Care Unit's staff break room. Slumped in a large pea-green vinyl chair, Casey let out a deep sigh.

In the absence of blood relatives, it had been determined that Sheriff Withers and Casey Bailey would be the hospital's primary contacts regarding Dr. Philips's status and treatment. On admission, Dr. Philips's core temperature was an alarming 81°F. The staff had instituted a re-warming procedure that included the use of heated blankets, warm humidified oxygen, heat packs, and warmed intravenous fluids. Throughout the process, the patient was monitored closely for changes in heart rhythm, blood pressure and respiration. A close watch was also kept on Dr. Philips's metabolic acidosis, a key indicator of how his vital organs had been affected by prolonged exposure to sub-zero temperatures.

The warming process had taken its toll on the elderly man. On three separate occasions during the night, Dr. Philips's heart monitor had detected an abnormal cardiac rhythm requiring immediate intervention by hospital staff. Bouts of arrhythmia were a common by-product of the onset and treatment of severe hypothermia and, as such, the attending nurses and doctors anticipated the reaction. Fortunately, the irregular heartbeats had not escalated to cardiac arrest.

As Dr. Philips's temperature rose above 90 degrees, his body was finally able to assist in the process of thermo-regulation. To aid the internal warming, his brain sent out signals resulting in involuntary muscular activity: he began to shiver uncontrollably. Skin and muscle tissues, once stiff and numb, suddenly became tender and painful, as if lighter fluid had been splashed over his body, then ignited. What began as an irritating dry hack in his throat blossomed into a deep, fluid-choked cough that settled in his chest.

Laboratory tests were fast-tracked to give the attending physicians a snapshot of the damage that their colleague's organs had sustained. The preliminary results were not promising: In addition to cardiac damage, the tests revealed telltale warning signs of pneumonia, renal malfunctioning and pancreatitis. The doctors had explained to Casey and Sheriff Withers that their friend's body was like a war zone with individual battles raging on several fronts. In cases of severe hypothermia among the elderly, they cautioned, secondary complications were often more dangerous that the underlying trauma itself.

Concurrent with their re-warming efforts, the Intensive Care staff had been treating the patient's specific cold-related injuries. Throughout the ordeal, Dr. Philips's body had reacted predictably to the onset of hypothermia. In an effort to protect his vital organs, blood flow was shunted from his extremities and redirected to his body core. As a result, the longer his isolation continued, the more susceptible his hands, feet, ears and nose became to the ravages of freezing temperatures and unrelenting winds.

By covering his head with the blanket and constantly warming his ears and nose with his hands, Dr. Philips had protected himself from extensive deep tissue freezing in the facial area. Although they were clearly frostbitten, the doctor's ears and nose had responded well to the warming treatments. Jim Philips's face had turned bright red -- in stark contrast to the white sheets and pillowcases beneath his head.

His fingers exhibited more extensive frostbite damage. Without warm gloves, Philips had been forced to employ a variety of tactics to ward off the bitter cold. Before succumbing to the insidious grip of lethargy, the doctor had continually flexed his fingers and clapped his hands to keep blood flowing. When the muscles in his fingers became stiff and unresponsive, he had alternated between wrapping his hands in the blanket and placing them against the comparatively warmer skin of his abdomen and groin area. Unfortunately, the metal handcuffs constricted the already limited blood flow to his hands, and also acted as a conductor, providing a contact point between the sub-zero temperatures and his wrists. Despite repeated treatments in warm moving water, four of his fingers had turned a purplish blue color, indicating deep tissue freezing.

When Casey first saw Dr. Philips's exposed feet after a warming treatment, she had to turn her head away to keep from breaking down. Both feet were a sickeningly dark shade of purple with raised blisters erupting from the damaged skin. To Casey, the damaged tissue on his ankles and feet looked like the half-shed skin of a molting black snake. His toes were black as death.

Seeing Casey's obvious shock, Philips had explained that the doctors had not arrived at a final prognosis about the extent of the deep tissue damage to his feet. From his experience, however, he knew that his injuries were severe and might become gangrenous. Dr. Philips told her in a weak, but calm tone that when the deep tissue freezes, ice crystals form in the cells of the tissue, permanently damaging them. The treatment for such injuries, he said, would likely include the amputation of his toes and possibly his feet. At the time, Casey had marveled at his ability to discuss the matter in such a detached, clinical manner.

Due to the extensive level of treatment required, Casey, Lyle and Sheriff Withers had been allowed only three visits to Dr. Philips's bedside. Despite the doctor's obvious pain and discomfort, he had been surprisingly calm and lucid. Between coughing fits, he was particularly interested in learning what had transpired since his abduction and about the chain of events that had driven Lyle and Casey to the summit. Casey noticed that Dr. Philips's eyes were constantly shifting between her and the snowplow driver, as if he was trying to discern what type of relationship had been formed between the two previous strangers. Whenever Lyle tried to retreat into the periphery of the discussion, Jim Philips would strain his damaged throat to draw the hulking man back into the conversation.

Rather than conduct a formal interview, Sheriff Withers decided to take a low-key approach in gathering information from Dr. Philips about the crime. In short order, Withers was able to tie up several loose ends regarding the initial abduction by Brader as well as Sam Moultrie's involvement. Twirling his uniform hat, Withers informed the doctor that the helicopter pilot's body had been discovered by a San Miguel County Deputy in his pickup truck near a cabin on Last Dollar Road. Moultrie's hand clutched an unregistered pistol, giving the impression that it was a suicide, but Withers expected that ballistics tests would reveal that Paul Brader's gun had been the murder weapon. He also announced that Paul Brader's New York attorney was being questioned about his knowledge of the kidnapping. Withers noticed that Jim Philips seemed to have little interest in such developments, preferring instead to learn about Lyle's and Casey's journey through the Mineral King Mine complex and their ascent to the summit of Imogene Pass.

When she left him three hours ago, Casey noted that her landlord looked deeply fatigued, yet remarkably calm. Despite bouts of chest-rattling coughs, extreme pain, a failing body and the seeming inevitable amputation of his feet, Dr. Philips conducted himself with dignity and composure. Still, Casey sensed a deep sadness in his eyes, as if something fragile and precious had been broken and could not be repaired. Casey had seen the same faraway look in Jim Philips's eyes before, when cancer had ushered Mimi from his side. For a fleeting moment, Casey couldn't help but wonder if she and Lyle had cheated him out of a reunion with his lifetime companion.

Dismissing this disturbing thought with a shake of her head, Casey glanced over at Lyle, who was sitting nearby. He was perched on the front edge of a sofa, slowly massaging his temples with his fingers, his long gray hair hanging down the side of his face. Casey noticed that he'd been especially quiet and withdrawn over the past several hours. With Sheriff Withers by their side throughout the day, Casey and Lyle hadn't been able to have a private conversation since they had been flown off the summit.

"Jim's lawyer has been in there for half an hour now. I wonder what that's all about," Sheriff Withers said as he looked at his watch. "I'm gonna grab another cup of coffee from the break room. Anybody wanna join me?"

Both Casey and Lyle shook their heads. As the lawman's boots echoed down the hallway, Casey got out of her chair and walked to the couch, taking a seat next to Lyle.

"You okay?"

Lyle sat back and shifted his weight so that he was facing Casey.

"Yeah," he replied with a slow nod. "Doing fine."

"I thought we had an agreement. Straight questions deserve honest answers. Let's try again. You okay?"

"I wish you didn't have to see what I did to Brader up on the summit."

"That was the most vicious, sickening scene I've ever witnessed and I'm sure that image will stay with me for the rest of my rest of my life," she said, adding, "I only wish I'd done it myself."

As Lyle nodded, Casey could see the line of red welts the chain had left around his neck.

Casey tapped her boot against Lyle's knee to get his attention once again. "Anything else on your mind?"

There was a great deal on his mind. Along with his concern about Dr. Philips's fragile condition, Lyle was trying to unravel a tangle of conflicting emotions. He exhaled deeply before responding.

"Straight questions may deserve honest answers, but sometimes it's best to hold your tongue."

"From what I gather, you've made a lifestyle out of holding your tongue. But being a man of few words could be interpreted as a sign of either arrogance or insecurity," Casey said.

Lyle swiveled to the right so he was facing Casey head-on. His face was impassive, but Casey knew she had gotten his attention.

"On one hand, it's arrogant to think that other people aren't worthy of your thoughts and opinions," she continued. "But it's a sign of insecurity to think that your thoughts and opinions aren't worthy of other people's attention. So, which one is it?"

Casey noticed a slight creasing of the skin around Lyle's eyes, but she couldn't tell if he was amused or offended.

"What's on your mind, Lyle?"

Speaking in a soft, unwavering tone, Lyle's eyes bore in on Casey's.

"I have a thirty-year-old daughter," he began. "I know what she looked like the last time I saw her, twenty-five years ago. I have pictures to remind me, but I don't really need them. I can still see her plain as day. Her hair has the color and feel of the close-in layer of a cornhusk. Her eyes change colors with her moods and the way the sun hits them. Her cheeks are as smooth as a new marble. She has a tiny gap between her two front teeth that she can poke the tip of her tongue through. Her second toe is longer than her big toe and her little toe curls over the one next to it. She has seven tiny freckles on her left arm and five on her right.

When a rainstorm wakes her up at night, she throws open the window so she can hear the thunder and feel the rain blowing through the screen. When it snows, she's always the first person out the door so she can make the first footprints in the yard. She can hit the daylights out of a whiffle ball and she loves to jump into puddles with both feet."

Lyle looked down to compose his thoughts. When he looked back up, he seemed more tentative, his expression pained.

"For the past twenty-five years, I tried to picture Emily growing into a teenager, then a young lady. Each year, it's gotten a little harder to imagine what she would look like if she showed up at my front door." A sad smile crossed his face. "All I can see is my five-year-old's face on a thirty-year-old body. It makes for an interesting picture."

Casey reached for Lyle's hand, but he did not offer it. It was clear he wasn't looking to be consoled or pitied.

"I don't want to burden you with this; I just feel it's unfair not to tell you," he continued. "The last few days, I've been getting some wires crossed in my head. When I try to picture Emily Morrison, all I can see is Casey Bailey. Maybe it's because you're both around the same age. Maybe it's because you both have blonde hair. But maybe it's because you're the type of person that I've always hoped she'd become; someone who's fearless, independent and true to herself."

"I don't know about that last part," Casey replied with an awkward grin.

"I may not be able to picture what my daughter looks like anymore, but I can tell you this: Emily Morrison would've climbed down into the Uncompahgre Gorge to help find a friend. Emily Morrison would've lugged a man twice her size out of the Mineral King Mine and Emily Morrison would've trudged in snowshoes to the summit of Imogene Pass. Emily Morrison's tough enough to grow up without a father to look after her, and stubborn enough to resent him for not being there when she needs him. I may go to my grave without ever laying eyes on Emily Morrison again, but you've made me proud of her. I want to thank you for that."

Casey pushed herself off the couch. She stood in front of Lyle and wrapped her arms around his shoulders. As she was about to speak, she heard footsteps in the hallway. She stepped away from the couch just as

Sheriff Withers and Douglas Shultz appeared in the doorway.

"Doc wants to see the two of you for a minute," Withers announced. "Then he wants us all to leave him be for the night."

Jim Philips's attorney set a scarred leather briefcase on the floor and started putting on his trench coat. He appeared to be lost in thought.

"You were in there for quite a while," Casey commented. "Is everything okay?"

The lawyer shook his head as he buttoned the overcoat. "Jim sent word that I should stop by tonight to go over a few documents. I asked if it was something that could wait until he was feeling better, but he was adamant about seeing me tonight. With all the treatments he's getting, it was hard to get anything accomplished. What he really needs is some rest, but he's not letting the nursing staff give him any sedatives."

"He's not in any condition to be making decisions right now, is he?" the sheriff queried, adding, "Exactly what kind of documents are we talking about?"

"I'm afraid I can't get into that. All I can tell you is that he was alert and lucid, so I have no basis for questioning his state of mind or challenging his judgment. Casey, after you and Lyle finish up with Jim, I think it's a good idea that he be left alone for the night. He looks like he could really use some sleep."

"I'll walk Douglas out to his car and wait in the parking lot," Withers said. "We'll worry about getting your vehicles back from Telluride tomorrow."

Lyle and Casey opened the double doors and walked into the dimly lit Intensive Care Unit. Light green curtains partitioned the large room into six separate patient's quarters. Only two of the six beds were occupied. Philips was in the center stall along the room's right side. The two side curtains were fully extended, leaving a narrow passageway on either side of his bed. An array of electronic monitoring equipment was stacked atop a platform that swung out from the wall behind him. As they approached the foot of Dr. Philips's bed, a portly dark-haired nurse was removing a beeping thermometer from his mouth. After making a notation on Dr. Philips's chart, she addressed her patient.

"We're getting there. Almost warm enough to melt butter in your mouth."

Dr. Philips nodded slowly and joked in a cracked voice. "In that case, I'll have an order of French toast."

As the nurse returned the chart to a Plexiglas pocket at the foot of the bed, she whispered to Casey, "Please be brief. He's in a great deal of pain, but he won't let us medicate him until he finishes up with you."

Casey couldn't help noticing that the thick white bandages wrapped around Dr. Philips's feet and hands made his limbs look like the business end of an oversized Q-tip. She saw that his hair had been combed over the wide bald patch that ringed his scalp. An electric blanket covered him from his ankles to his chest, hiding a network of wires and tubes that led to various monitors, intravenous fluid stands and a catheter bag. The arms protruding from his blue and white striped hospital gown seemed spindly and bony. His eyes appeared sunken and tired.

Despite Jim Philips's age, Casey had never considered him an old man. Tonight, though, he looked frail, pained and weathered. She realized his body had been ravaged by his four-day ordeal, but Casey doubted whether all of the changes she noticed could be attributed to hypothermia and starvation.

Dr. Philips smiled broadly as Casey and Lyle approached. Casey sat down gingerly on the edge of his bed, careful not to jostle him or any of the tubes connected to his body. Lyle stood next to Casey, his hands folded in front of him.

Although sounding as brittle as old hay, Jim Philips's voice still bore the lilting, refined accent of his North Carolina roots.

"I'm glad you two could stick around until I finished up with Douglas," he remarked before succumbing to a sudden coughing spell. When he finally managed to clear the phlegmy rattle in his chest, he continued as if nothing unusual had transpired. "Y'all have to promise me, now, that as soon as we're done here, you'll head on back to Ouray. Is that clear?"

Both Casey and Lyle nodded agreement.

"The reason I wanted to talk to you is because I'm going to be asking each of you for a favor. If you have any problems with what I'm about to ask, just let me know so I can make other arrangements."

"Don't worry about making other arrangements," Casey spoke up. "What can we do for you?"

Jim Philips looked up at Lyle. "You and I have talked about my plans for building a hospice out by Dallas Divide. The groundbreaking is scheduled for May."

"Yes sir."

"I know you hire on as a carpenter once you're finished with cee-dot for the winter, but I'd like you to oversee the construction of the Mimi Philips Hospice Center. The plans are all drawn up and I want you to look at them sometime next week over at Douglas Shultz's office. You can alter the plans as you see fit, but I'd like the hospice center designed as if it were Mimi Philips's home; I want every patient who stays there to feel like one of her guests. She'd want views of the mountains from every bedroom window and enough room for guests to wander the grounds and commune with their maker."

With each intake of air, Dr. Philips's chest hummed like a clogged vacuum cleaner. He was about to continue when Lyle interrupted.

"I'd consider it an honor," he said. "If you want, I'll bring the blueprints back here early next week so we can talk things over."

"Let's not worry about the details," Dr. Philips answered with a wave of his bandaged hand. "All I need to know now is that you're committed to taking on the project."

"Like I said, it would be an honor. Of course, I'm going to need your input on a regular basis between now and the groundbreaking. Can I count on that?"

Casey saw that Dr. Philips was staring up at Lyle. Confused by the lapse in the conversation, she turned to find Lyle returning the man's intense gaze. They appeared to be engaged in a test of wills.

"Am I missing something? What's going on here?"

Without taking his eyes off the elderly man, Lyle asked again. "Can I count on your being around to see this project through?"

"Don't do this to me, Lyle," the doctor pleaded in a pitiful voice.

"They're going to cut off both my feet and some of my fingers. I'm too old to learn how to get by without them. My heart and lungs are never going to be the same again. I'll have circulation problems so bad it'll make May feel like December. Besides, I'm just plain tired."

Casey gripped Jim Philips's arm tightly. "Don't you even *think* about giving up on us! Is that what this is all about? Is that why you met with your lawyer? I'm not going to hear of this! You can fight through this! Please!"

Alerted by Casey's loud pleadings, the duty nurse appeared at the foot of the bed, but Dr. Philips waved her away.

"Calm down. Both of you are overreacting. The whole point of this discussion is to work out a backup plan in case anything should happen to me," Dr. Philips said softly. "Casey, I need a favor from you, too. I've instructed Douglas to transfer ownership of my house to you in the event I don't come home from the hospital."

"Can we talk about this some other time?" Casey implored. "I'm just not ready for this. *You're* not ready for this."

Dr. Philips continued as if he hadn't been interrupted. "Mimi and I built that house together, and I know she'd want you to live in it as long as you'd care to. I don't want you to feel like a boarder anymore. I want you to make it your home. Some day, I want you to share it with a good man, raising a litter of strong-willed hooligans."

Casey laughed in spite of herself. "I am not going to raise a bunch of hooligans. And if I ever do have children, I want you there so they can have a grandpa-type to look up to."

"Oh, my guess is that there are other grandpa-types around who can fill that bill."

To Casey's surprise, Dr. Philips shot a glance at Lyle. This time, the coughing fit continued for two minutes. Casey could see the waveforms on the heart monitor cresting at a rapid pace. Dr. Philips's whole body shook with each cough and his face was etched in pain. She was about to call for the nurse when the spasms subsided.

Lyle continued to press his friend. "Jim, can we put this discussion off for another time? Let's just see what happens in the next day or two. You might have a whole new outlook in the morning."

"Maybe I will," he responded in an upbeat tone that Lyle didn't believe. "All I'm asking is that you agree to what we've talked about tonight, just in case. It'll help me sleep better. Douglas will handle all the details on these two issues, as well as a couple of other things that pertain to both of you. Now, can I have your promises?"

"Only if you promise to try and fight through this," Casey countered.

Jim Philips nodded slowly and looked up at Casey. "I'll do what I can. Now, you two should be heading on home. I understand that Bill is waiting around to give you a lift. It's best not to dawdle when you've got someone waiting on you."

Lyle shook his head, but did not reply. Casey leaned forward and kissed Jim Philips on the forehead. "I'll see you tomorrow."

"Good night, Casey," he said as he gently patted the side of her face with a gauze-wrapped hand. "Can I speak with you privately for a second, Lyle?"

Casey looked back and forth between Lyle and Dr. Philips before excusing herself. "I'll meet you in the hallway, Lyle."

When he heard the ward door swing shut, Dr. Philips beckoned Lyle closer to him. Lyle bent over and placed a hand on the man's shoulder.

"As you know, I think the world of Casey," Jim Philips began. "She came out here all by herself without a soul to rely on, and look what she's done for herself. She's kept this old man company and never accepted a thing in return: not a reduction in rent, a new pair of snow tires or even a buffalo nickel for a soda pop."

He winced in pain, then tried unsuccessfully to clear his throat. When he resumed speaking, his voice was accompanied by high-pitched wheezing.

"Casey may not think she needs help from anybody to get along, but she does. We all do," he remarked through the pain. "Even though you may not realize it, it seems to me that each of you has something that the other one needs."

Lyle nodded in agreement. "I believe you're right."

"Casey doesn't need a support system, a mentor or even a guiding hand. If you ask me, all she needs is the assurance that there's some-one nearby who cares about her, respects her and appreciates her. Now, I don't know what lies ahead for the two of you, but I want you to promise me you'll look after her."

"Like she was my very own."

• • •

Walking down the well-lit corridor that led to the hospital's main bank of elevators, Lyle saw that Casey was pacing nervously along the left side of the hallway. To the right, a cluster of orderlies and nurses waited for an elevator to arrive, shooting occasional glances at the troubled young lady. When Lyle drew near, Casey grabbed the sleeve of his jacket and steered him down the hallway, out of earshot of the staff.

"*What was that all about?* It was like he was saying goodbye to us. Should we say something to his doctors?"

Lyle sighed heavily and looked squarely at Casey. "I'm not worried about him taking his own life. Whether he's given up the will to live is a different story altogether."

"The will to live?" she asked, incredulous. "You mean he's just going to let himself expire in the night? That's impossible. People can't just decide when and where they're going to die."

"No, but they can stop fighting to live. I've seen it dozens of times on the rescue squad. Some people manage to survive through sheer force of will when, by rights, they should've passed away long before we get to them. On the other hand, people who give up hope of being rescued often wind up dying a helluva lot quicker that they should. The way Dr. Philips is acting, I wonder if he might've turned that corner long before we reached him at the summit."

"But he's in a hospital now. It's not like he's still chained up in that freezing shack. He can't just let himself go."

"All I'm saying is that he may have already made his peace and he's ready to move on. I've seen that same far-off, peaceful look in the eyes of gut-shot soldiers. I don't know what's going to happen here tonight, but there's nothing that we can do about it."

With the corridor now empty, Lyle guided Casey to the elevator bank and pushed the button to summon a car. As the elevator doors opened, Casey took a long look down the hallway toward Intensive Care. Lyle led her by the elbow into the car and pressed the button for the lobby. Seeing Casey staring at the elevator buttons, Lyle assumed that she was considering a return trip to Dr. Philips's bedside. He decided that a change of subject might divert her attention.

"Doesn't it seem strange that Dr. Philips hasn't said a word about his mining claims?" Lyle asked. "After all, that's what this whole mess was about."

"That's probably one of the other reasons he met with his lawyer tonight," Casey replied in a flat tone of voice. "He doesn't want anything more to do with them."

"What makes you say that?"

As the elevator doors opened on the lobby level, Casey fished a business card out of the vest pocket of the Ouray Mountain Rescue jacket. She handed it to Lyle as they walked through the doors to the parking lot.

Pausing beneath an overhead light, Lyle looked at the rectangular card that bore Dr. Philips's home and answering service phone numbers. Flipping the card over, Lyle saw that a message had been scribbled in pen in small block letters, followed by Dr. Philips's signature.

"He left it in the mailbox, hoping that someone might find it," Casey explained. "He must've written it just before his fingers froze."

Lyle read the four-line message:

PAUL BRADER DID THIS TO ME.
I HEREBY BEQUEATH ALL OF MY MINING PATENTS AND CLAIMS
TO THE GOOD CITIZENS OF OURAY.
THE ONLY GOLD I'VE EVER NEEDED IS MIMI.

Acknowledgements

My research was enhanced considerably by residents of Southwestern Colorado who were generous and patient in answering all manner of questions from a stranger with a notepad. Don Castle, of Colorado Department of Transportation's Red Mountain Division, provided a wealth of hard-won knowledge about snow removal on Red Mountain Pass, the various avalanche paths that cross Highway 550, and the operation of snowplows. Barbara Muntyan, Director of the Ouray County Museum, described the historic origins of the "Million Dollar Highway." She also provided a detailed recitation of the history of mining in the Ouray, Colorado area, including the Camp Bird Mine and the area around Imogene Pass. Nancy with the Ouray County Sheriff's Department answered questions about local law enforcement and county Search and Rescue operations. Mike Friedman of Telluride Helitrax described winter flying conditions and helicopter accessibility to mountain terrain in the San Juan Range. John Trujillo gave a wonderfully detailed account of the interior of the Treasury Tunnel connecting Telluride to Highway 550 as well as a nuts and bolts description of an active hard-rock mining operation. The proprietors of China Rose Florist & Greenhouse in Telluride explained the business operations of a retail florist enterprise in Southwestern Colorado. Four books written or co-written by P. David Smith were particularly helpful in my research for this story: *Ouray: a Quick History*, *Mountains of Silver*, *The Million Dollar Highway*, and *Mountain Mysteries: The Ouray Odyssey*. My brother Dennis Cunningham helped me understand stock options, futures, puts and calls, and other investment strategies, and my brother Patrick Cunningham provided details on various helicopter models and the challenges of flying a helicopter.

I am grateful for the assistance of several professionals in the publishing field who helped shape the Red Mountain Pass story. Reg Lansberry edited the initial manuscript and helped add tension and urgency to the narrative. Claudia Cross of the William Morris Agency provided helpful advice on how to improve an early draft of the manuscript. Kevin Mulroy used a deft editing touch to help me develop Red Mountain Pass into its final form. Kevin shared the manuscript with a colleague at a publishing house and came tantalizingly close to getting a publishing deal. Literary agent Jeff Gerecke – then of JCA, now of the G Agency – also advocated for the manuscript to the major publishers specializing in the action/thriller genre. Kathy Florence designed the book's cover and interior design, and she formatted the manuscript for publishing. I couldn't have asked for a better team.

My wife Laura introduced me to the Mountain West early in our dating relationship, and suggested that we visit the San Juan Mountain area, which inspired this story. She encouraged me every step of the way, even though it ate into time for our business and our marriage. Laura read every version of the manuscript and was my companion on the roller coaster ride that was/is Red Mountain Pass.

My siblings—Patrick Cunningham, Dennis Cunningham, Sean Cunningham, Grace Krieske—and my mother, Libbie Cunningham, also read the manuscript and provided unflagging encouragement. Brad Catherman and Pattie Baker, former co-workers at Turner Broadcasting and published authors in their own right, were always willing to share in my frustrations and joys with the manuscript. My father, Christopher Cunningham, died when I was 18, but I've been trying to make him proud my entire adult life. I hope he is.

Made in the USA
Monee, IL
10 January 2021